A High Country Tale

By Zachariah Jack

A High CountryTale...

Luke Cevennes, M.D. He liked the way it sounded even after a decade and a half of wearing the mantle. Jeremy Kell, Ph.D. That rolled over Luke's tongue with more flavor than any name in his world. The sexy Jamaican immigrant literally swept him off his feet nearly two decades before. The two fit each other. Luke's and Jeremy's best friends, Jake and Calumet, likewise professional and accomplished, lagged in years by a decade but the bond between the four: as deep as the Marianas Trench. Traversing the 21st century as a new age American family, the two interracial couples complemented each other in ways the majority of people could only look upon in wishing. Hijinks, ribaldry, a touch of activism plus candor and humor, all souffled with a smattering of profundity, gel into a roving epic. From America to Europe to the Caribbean, on the shores of WWII Normandy, to Blue Mountain in Jamaica, up the wuthering heights of the Rockies and down the alluvial plains of the American deep south. These self-deprecating, refined yet lusty menfolk wend their way, together, luring the flotsam, jetsam and A-listers of Humanity along, on the sojourn that is their Tree of Life.

Table of Contents

Chapter 1
Columbine and Bells

"Ma'am, if looks were licks, I'd be an ice cream cone... could you please stop the video?" Jeremy did not like to be streamed live without his consent. It happened more than he or I wished for, what with the current state of technology. My man was verifiably photogenic. And nothing if not outspoken.

We were cooling down at the water fountain by Barton Springs after our morning run and the woman had caught sight of us from somewhere. The dogs lapped greedily from the water bowls at our feet, humid weather taking its toll on the two rescues we lived with. Our running attire consisted of running shorts, sweat socks and Asics in this weather. Jeremy's resultant exposure highlighted the superb anatomy he honed.

Sweating profusely, our shorts must be just about soaked to see-through. Apparently deciding that we desired social media exposure, the lady brazenly approached us, android raised and rolling.

Not. Neither desired, nor happening.

The ill-mannered woman didn't seem to hear, or chose to ignore the polite request. Likewise, the second request. So, JFK's plan B went into action.

"Luke, got your phone?" he palmed his hand my direction. Understanding his intent, without comment I retrieved my iphone from the plastic baggie in my sweat sock, handing it over.

Jeremy raised the device, centered his face in selfie mode, set the video function to record and approached her. Phone in one hand, other hand lewdly cupping his prodigious package.

Head-on, he closed the gap between them, beginning his practiced response to such intrusions, "This be Brother J-Man, coming from Zilker Park in Austin. My man and I are finishing our morning workout here, folks, and are experiencing an uninvited and unacceptable encroachment by an elderly she-male—at least it appears to be-- in search of cheap-ass thrills."

The pear-shaped woman didn't lower her phone, continuing her recording of the minimally-clothed black stud before her. How Ugly-American is this woman, I thought? Go, J-Boy.

Jeremy continued his play-by-play, now flipping from selfie to projection of the video streamer herself, "May I introduce… Cruella De'Ville…recording us without our consent, from a public space here in the heart of Austin, Texas. Capitol city of the state where the Texas Recording Statute 16.02 of the Texas Penal Code --- a law prohibiting single consent recording --- is the law. Please say hello, Ms. Elderella, and could you tell everyone here on YouTube what your real name is so we may make proper attribution? Of course, we can just enter this video into the FBI data bank for auto-match, if you prefer."

The middle age woman finally registered the scenario unfolding, wisely choosing to cease her rudeness. But, only under this flip back duress. She lowered her device, glowered toward the handsome man daring to stream right back at her streaming video, turned on her heel in retreat mode and vacated our vicinity. Epithets leaked loudly from her mouth in diarrheic nastiness, sealing her rep.

Awkwardly tripping over a brick in the paved walkway, she nearly capsized into the adjacent flower bed. "Stand up, Pearl, that is definitely NOT your best angle," Jeremy snickered at the double-wide moonshot, "and if I find my sweaty butt on display by your recording upload, know that not just your extra-wide is gonna be next to it…your subpoena will be posted, too. Have a nice day, sweetie."

I was stifling my own reaction to this hilarity. Both Jeremy and I were well aware that no such law existed in this casino-capitalistic realm. Austin existed as supremely weird, progressive and populated by the most professional populace in the big state. It was, nevertheless, under the quaintly regressive control of red-state ignorance, politically. No-holds-barred laissez faire conservatism, as oxy-moronic as that sounded, thrived here in the home of the Lone Star. Just like in Old West times, 'Anything Goes" remained the state motto. As long as it pushed the far right agenda.

We routinely viewed Wyatt Earp and Dale Evans strutting the streets and by-ways of our city, leg irons strapped proudly on. Much to our chagrin. Dame Ann Richards must be turning over in her grave and Barbara Jordan's sainted ghost was channeling Casper in blanched embarrassment, too, at the ass-backwardness holding sway here… disapproval duly noted.

Though not too common in an area full of self-absorbed college kids, there remained a small portion of the citizenry bent on vicarious involvement in others' doings. The vaunted Ugly American Syndrome. Did we really wonder why the rest of the world viewed us the way they did? The myopic perception held by the Ms. De'Ville types lent itself to the firm belief that Texas was truly 'God's Country'… They really should travel more.

We forgot the gauche event quickly and brushed off the people rooting Jeremy's actions. He and I ran one of our daily loops this way every few days, enjoying the verdant lushness of the area. Many amply-endowed bodies exercised here and attention to individuals approached mundanity at this point.

Jeremy and my jungle fever union had been a presence for years now, and we enjoyed relative anonymity, most times. Episodes such as this were less and less common in the 21st century, in contrast to our early days in the 1990's. The novelty had worn off for the most part.

Discussing the upcoming trip as we headed back toward our home overlooking the old rock bedded, spring-fed public swimming hole, the two of us bantered easily about our hidden eyrie in the highlands.

While we loved the student-frequented park just south of Town Lake in downtown Austin and attended many of the great music offerings commonly hosted just out our front door, loyalties had markedly split upon discovery of Telluride, Colorado, several years before.

Property investment had overtaken us, far up the mountain, in a secluded glen. The rustic log home residing there captured us at first sight. Upon viewing the for-lease sign lying on the floor inside while window-peeking, we had gone all-in by our efforts to secure title to the place.

Months after that we had traveled there, papers in hand, reveling in the knowledge that we were proud owners of high country real estate. Having remodeled and updated the solid log edifice to our standards and style, we took off for it every chance we got. At some point, we would base ourselves there for good.

For the present, we furthered our careers here in the city, Dr. Jeremy Kell, Doctor of Philosophy, University of Texas flagship campus. Myself, Dr. Luke Cevennes, of UMC-Brackenridge Hospital ER. Colloquially known as Brack. We both seamed into our respective professions with satisfaction. The niches were comfortably fitted to our personalities and our college-town lives were exactly what was desired.

Until exposure to Telluride, that is.

* * *

"Honey, have you noticed the revving up of the religious right over the past two weeks?" I sat in our breakfast nook window alcove, cradling my coffee cup as I gathered knees to chest. A cool shower following the 10K fartlek just finished had rejuvenated the two of us, wiping away the effects of the stifling June hot spell currently holding the city in thrall. We now basked in the luxury of three days to ourselves after the spring semester culmination. "They are verging on apoplexy by the Faux-News pundits pontificating the End times, you know."

Jeremy lazed on the granite countertop, bare back propped against the wall, with the newspaper and his own coffee mug. He was nude, per usual, and in position to visually purview the park out the picture window beyond my seat. From this vantage, he could keep an eye on the distant goings-on below us.

Our home balanced on a rock cliff, fifty feet above the meadow below, the grassy stretch itself ending in a rock declivity which overlooked the crystal-clear springs. We enjoyed the three-dimensionality. With the regular gatherings for music and sports events, our seats were first rate.

The Nubian prince lounging across from me liked the coolness of the stone against his cute butt and rangy legs. I wasn't arguing. My view either way was great. Panorama or soft porn...nice choices. "Well, Lukester," he replied, "we're only a few weeks out from a SCOTUS ruling and the bigots are quaking in their sack cloth and thorns. Y'know they're worried they could lose superiority over us dregs of society." He continued perusal of the sports section, soaking up the latest UT baseball stats.

We had worn out the subject over the previous year, playing old King Nebuchadnezzar's role with his 'writing-on-the-wall' storyline as one after another lower court ruling had upheld SSM right-to-misery, just like straight world couples... at least such was the description of nuptial nirvana as boasted by thumpers. One fringe argument had been to ask why the gay community would want access to such a miserable state of existence, anyway...? How odd.

Religious fundamentalists were still intent on reserving that right to themselves, convinced of the decline and fall of the empire should sexual perversion become codified constitutionally.

The conundrums of the contrasting factors were flagrant in our eyes. We hoped for a resounding decision in order to remove the inevitable asterisk the right would no doubt insist upon assigning to anything short of a Dred Scott-esque decision.

The bottom line, we felt, lay with the dichotomy in Christianity's tenet of an all-knowing, all-loving God-figure who so lovingly insisted on a death sentence by stoning or cliff-throwing should His omniscient omnipotence be questioned. What cockamamie bullshit.

Like the institution had remained immutably transfixed through history, anyway. From chattel-status of women and their 'issue' (children), to political marriages, to economic-based marriages, to love-based man-on-woman arrangements, to interracial straight unions, yup, hard to imagine allowing any changes to such an unchanging tradition...

And the straight world had done such a bang-up job with its stewardship over long-lasting, stolidly trust-laden, God-condoned unions. Who the Hell were we low-life faggots (because they told us we were) to dream of living in the security of life-long, loving relationships without discriminatory statutes to keep us in our sorry-ass place?

Most amazing was the gathering steam of the evangelists' twisted logic that the challenge to their marriage monopoly inferred victimization of the downtrodden, woebegone Christian community. Had not this fallback strategy been the same one employed since Saint Peter had requested upside-down crucifixion? He just couldn't stomach being tortured in the same manner as his Savior had been. That would have constituted blasphemy.

That saintly bequest to humanity had set in motion allegorical proof of victimhood for two thousand years, the Basilica the steadfast beacon of that proof. Even though the literalist faction denied allegorical interpretation of their Good Book in dripping ironic contrast. After all, God had written every single word Himself and translations through the River of Time had had no effect on the original intent. The Word bespoke exactly what was written by Him... except when it didn't.

They knew all this, of course, because of their holy conduit to Him by ersatz communication: aka prayer. Which no one but they were privy to. And if we didn't believe it, just ask them... oh, and the deal came with a lifetime 'get-out-of-jail-free' card as a hedge. Just pray to be forgiven. Anything. Quite convenient.

"JK, you could be called a whole lot of things, but a dreg is not one of them, my man," I replied aloud, "especially lookin' like all o' that." He lifted one sinewy leg up and away from the other, allowing his junk to flop downward between them in response, giving me a better view of the little man. Confident in the effect such moves had on me, he employed similar tactics regularly. The paper never wavered from before his face but I could feel the grin behind the newsprint.

After a few more minutes of communal reading, he concluded his thought on the subject, "I guess we'll hear something in the next couple weeks, at least if the media has it right. Did I tell you that I heard back from San Miguel County last week? They are re-configuring the online forms in case of a favorable ruling and we should be able to download the new gender-neutral license apps the day after, if it happens." Satisfaction suffused his voice.

"Oh, then I'd better get back ahold of Jake and Cal to confirm the dates, honey," I knew this would advance our planned ceremony to more a probability than the possibility heretofore hoped. Indeed, our closest friends would be likewise solidifying plans for their own consummation and the thought warmed me.

An ER colleague, Jake Marshall was half of the partners-in-crime duo we had come to count on over the years as we traversed interracial existence along with them. Jake's partner, Cal Broadhearst, was a UT alum, and eight years out now. His entrepreneurial acumen had propelled him into the world of software stardom, now overseeing a network of five offices from his headquarters in the Frost Tower.

The couple had imprinted on our lives since Jake and my meeting on the red-eye shift together during his residency. We had been surprised to discover the similarity in our situations when we met up at a local eatery for an introductory dinner back then.

Choosing to rendezvous at Truluck's Seafood Grill, Jake and I arrived together and sat nursing glasses of wine in awaiting our guys. Both of them had shown up simultaneously and we watched them enter together, startling both us and the clientele by their twin-like images. Cal, or Calumet, was six-foot-six, leanly athletic, ebony-complexioned, shaved head and ripped in his conditioning. By comparison, my Jeremy measured in at only six-foot-three, alike in the ripped physique, swarthy skin and shaved pate departments. We had all four bonded immediately.

Amazed that both of us had spent years in Austin without encountering each other, the fact of their residence being located far in the northwest quadrant of the city, out on Lake Travis, proved the reason. Jeremy and I preferred urban life; our friends were rurally set.

Making up for lost time, we two duos had intermingled easily and now were ready to take the matrimonial plunge in corresponding fashion. A game-changing high court decision would allow fruition. On the other hand, rationalization had led the four of us to the decision in favor of out-sourced formalities, what with the current ascendance of home state social and political animus.

Cal and Jake kept a suite at the Hotel Jerome in Aspen, Colorado, as opposed to our hideaway in up-mountain Telluride, to their southwest. Frequent hookups between the venues allowed for camaraderie and commonality of purpose. Mutual intent was bent on witnessing for each other when and if the big day arrived. Carly Simon must have written her catsup ad song for us as our anticipation for legitimacy grew. Evangelism be damned...

* * *

Three days of solitude and togetherness mixed with a cookout at the Marshall-Broadhearst place overlooking the lake left us rested. We were ready for a home-stretch ten day run as our workloads diminished and plans for retreat to the mountains loomed.

Jeremy would be tying knots in loose-ends on campus while I was preparing the way for an extended leave-of-absence from Brack. Closing down the Zilker Park house was not a challenge. We had arranged for a trusted teacher's assistant of JK's to house-sit while we were away.

The grad-student was a bit of a loner, basking in quietude with books and the cyber world more than living the fast lane, so we were content in the sanctity of the premises. We knew the likelihood of keg parties and pole-dancing were next to nil and his penchant for the occasional joint sat fine with us, occasionally partaking of the evil weed ourselves.

While never dull during duty hours at Brack, the onset of summer and the desertion of campus by the huge student body, as was happening now, played out in relative calm. Jake and I sat in the physicians' break room under less stress from pressing caseloads than normal. Lopping items from our to-do lists in planning for the trek north was proving gratifying.

"So, you really think Cal is gonna do it?" I thought the idea of a hot air balloon setting for their ceremony was romantic, if a bit crowded, considering the four of us and a pilot would be on board. But, cool, no less.

"He has mentioned ballooning three times in the past week, Luke, and you know how that man is. His sense of adventure way outstrips my introverted ass, boi." His reasoning was sound. I had seen some wild occurrences in my years associating with Cal B. Not much would surprise me. Jeremy joked that we would be forced up Kilimanjaro at some point. And he was OK with it, he had assured me, as long as we had a hand in picking the accompanying escort team…translation: hung studs with minimal wardrobes. The picture seemed fine by me…

"Have you guys thought any more about the place on Ajax, Jake?" I was curious about the couple's interest over the stand-alone home in Aspen. Their suite in The Jerome was superb, boasting two bedrooms and a master suite, fireplaces in every room, a full kitchen and even a library/study. The upkeep was taken care of by the hotel, chef and butler included. The fact that they could rent out the place under an independent management firm when the two were not in residence had them sitting pretty. It paid for itself.

Their balcony looking out on Aspen town and the mountain was spacious and well-equipped, too. We had shared time with them there on multiple occasions. So they had it good, but I had noticed Jake's wistful look over dinner the past week as he contemplated the possibility of taking over the all-glass chalet high up the mountain.

Built by Leon Uris, the late author, the place had kept his secret sancha housed in style for the long-term back in the 1970's and '80's. Almost the entire time he was married to his third wife, Jill. Conchita had been bosom buddies with Louise Lasser of 'Mary Hartman, Mary Hartman' fame, and Claudine Longet, Andy Williams ex-wife and Olympic Skier Spider Sabich's lover. The idea of living in the architectural glass marvel amidst the spirits of such vixens had him near drooling-state, I could tell.

"Could you just imagine, living in the place where so much history played out, Luke?" He posed the question as he mentally signed on the dotted line. "Claudine hid there after she shot Spider, and Andy Williams had to come get her to help give herself up. That is just too cool for school," he gushed.

"Well, you know how much Jeremy and I love our place way up higher than everyone—it is a neat feeling. And Cal could exist nude all winter in a proverbial glass house if you do it." I egged him on, only half teasing. Jeremy and Cal loved clothlessness equally, and Jake delighted in the exultation of our men in that state as much as I did. Seeing that much gorgeous silky skin in such anatomically proportional relief was something we would never take for granted.

"Don't forget, Uris reputedly wrote his epic, 'Trinity', up there, too, Jake. Jeremy found that in Uris's diary at Ransom Center on campus when he was researching the man. He dedicated the book to Jill but never did come clean about it all, the hypocrite. Why don't people just get over the monogamy hang-ups they have and get along? Everyone would be better off, you know," I opined.

Jake got it, and we snickered at the stupidity of such thought processes. Too many people thought a hard dick equaled love, and that depending on who the hard-on was pointed at determined fidelity…how off base was that? Hormonal impulses simply and plainly did not equate well to matters of the heart. He and I were living proof of the concept by the solidity of our relationships. Even if we were just anecdotal. By our calculation, America had a huge inferiority complex judging by the divorce rate.

Just as we were about to close the deal on the Ajax Mountain property and solve other pressing social problems, a sharp crack of thunder jarred our chat. Flickering of the lights ensued and finally, loss of power. Being in an internal room in Brack's medical complex, the darkness proved pervasive. Our penlights streaked the dark room as we awaited the auxiliary power sources to kick on.

"Wow, that must've hit a transformer," Jake said as he found his way to the bank of emergency closets on the side of the room, extracting flashlights.

The whole city had been under intermittent storm and flood threat the past month as the Hill Country of central Texas remained ensconced in the turbid trifecta of weather systems training over the area. El Nino had developed strongly to the west off the Peruvian coast since the spring and such an event always imbued volatility into our local forecasts. Just two weeks before, the tranquil rivers surrounding us had become raging walls of flash flooding, wreaking havoc on the surrounding multi-county area.

After the several day hot respite during our downtime, we were now experiencing another wave of training rain systems accompanied by thunder and lightning. The emergency generators were working overtime these past weeks in response to numerous challenges to the power grids.

We knew the ER complex would already be boosted by the power backups, but acritical parts of the complex where we were could take a while sometimes before power resumed. We made our way to the hallway and proceeded toward the treatment bays, intending to check triage status due to the sudden weather emergency onset.

Remarkably, the admissions center remained fairly quiet and we thanked the break between spring and summer terms as the probable reason. The staff had things well-controlled and the generators hummed synchronously amongst the ER sections. We weren't needed, as it turned out, and administration verified our release from duty until the next day, so we exited the area for the locker rooms to change and head for home. I needed to assure the dogs were safe and not flipping out by the thunder rolls, though they were typically immune to the phobia some animals experienced.

Jake pulled up abruptly in the dark and deserted hallway connection, looking toward me, "Hear that? Something over that way," his acute hearing regularly tested everyone, the sense attuned to things most people relegated to white noise. "Over there, Luke—I hear something strange." Thinking he was noticing a sizzling breaker or dripping ceiling leak, I followed his lead toward the hallway door marked "Maintenance".

Upon knobbing the door open, our eyes gradually acclimated to the surprising form of one sexy little janitorial supervisor, Tevin. He was presently busy humping an exposed set of buttocks. In the small of the recipient's back there was tattooed a blood red cross, inscribed with John 3:16. The attached upper end of the person's pasty buns descended beyond our view. Tevin, not to be flummoxed by the interruption, grinned at us and continued the slow slide in and out the welcoming hole.

Jake and I stood transfixed, staring at the spectacle, jaws surely widely gaping as we focused on the thick fatness of the diminutive maintenance man's piece. Out-sized for his body—the man stood barely three inches over five feet tall--- he seemed quite at ease showing us what he had. He even turned just a tad sideways to allow better angle for us, not changing pace in the slightest. His small dark hand reached down and raised his work shirt tail up to his chin, wedging it there, exposing a kinky-haired flat stomach and muscled pectoral pair covered by indigo skin.

The hand returned to the cheek siding the crack where his whopper was pumping methodically in-and-out. "Wassup, docs?" he asked, as if we were nonchalantly passing him in the hallway. No sign whatsoever of chagrin, the mighty mite beamed at us while demonstrating his best feature. The endowment, thickly veined and rigid, showed at least eight inches between pumps, never exiting entirely. While we watched, the engorgement factor seemed to increase the big thing's girth by another half. It liked the publicity, apparently.

The attached torso attempted raising up but the little palm squelched the action, deliberately pressing it back down into the shadows. "Stay down, bitch," the order plain. The person did so.

To us, he quipped, "Check it out, dudes, Little Tev ain't no wallflower now, you can touch 'im. He'd be likin' that, truth tell—go 'head, check it."

The two of us, no wallflowers either, were still taken aback by the brash behavior here inside the hospital confines. Jake glanced at me, looking for my reaction, and seeing my obvious interest in the proceedings, he riveted right back to it, obviously enthused by the exhibition. We fed on each other's attentiveness as moments passed, and upon additional urging by the sybarite in front of us, Jake's hand tentatively reached toward the conjoined junction. I inadvertently licked my lips and reached down to my own responding crotch as his fingers explored the hard slippery piece in its progress.

That pretty much sent the little guy over the edge and he backed out, exposing the eight inches already visualized, plus an extra two more buried until then. Uncut, with a nicely helmeted crown, the thing was definitely happy to be looked at. Tevin fairly levitated at the act of ejaculating before our singed eyes. The piece bounced on and off the butt just vacated, spewing sperm copiously over himself, Jake's hand and arm, and the entire expanse of the recipient's lower back. Some hit the surrounding closet space.

Obviously missing the squeezing heat of the chute, the honker re-entered almost immediately, sliding back in to the hilt. This evoked masculine groans from nether regions below at the re-stretching of the abused orifice. Finishing the cum-se-quence, the root spasmed visibly until it spent itself.

The grin had never wavered; Tevin delighted in this im-promptu performance, regaling us from his vantage point of ecstasy, "Day-umm, that shit bein' jood, dudes…keep on with that rubbin' doc--- don't stop that hand, now, man— 'dat be helpin' this thing. Got…day-umm!"

Still completely at ease with the verboten scenario playing out here, Tevin reached up to access a towel on the closet room wall within his reach. The shit-eating grin finally dimin-ished to a satisfied smirk as he handed it first to Jake. "There been some thunderin' and lightnin' goin' on inside today, too, ain't there, doc-dudes? Hopin' we don't spring no leaks --- that could be serious," the man fixed his gaze on the spatters presently dripping around and off things. The man was incorri-gibly unflappable.

I looked at Jake. He pointed at the still bent over and un-named torso, head still hidden somewhere in obscurity. Un-seen and un-seeing. Whoever it might be more than likely did not desire 'outing'. The logic suddenly dawned on us and we decided the better part of valor would be to vacate the premises. Post haste, and quietly.

To that point, we had neither one spoken out loud; it seemed wise to keep it that way. Other passersby could open a door and bust us any second, so we skedaddled toward the locker room. Opening the door to our private area, we stepped inside. A last glimpse backwards pictured a now disconnected shorty, wiping himself down, dong waggling languidly and still drib-bling contentedly. The door slammed shut, leaving us safely unscathed by association.

"Can you believe the size of that? And who the hell was in there with him?" Jake was beside himself with curiosity. "Could you believe the way he was draggin' that boot?"

"Well, Jake, you can sure testify it was real--- I nearly came watchin' all that. Just too chicken shit to get into it here. You've got huevos, dude," I assured him.

"Yeah, for brains, maybe. Damn, we were lucky no one walked in, weren't we," he replied. It wasn't a question.

"No argument there, for sure, but that was damn hot," and we changed, leaving by the side door into the continuing deluge. There was a story to be told, and our respective partners were avid listeners.

* * *

Juneteenth arrived hotly humid and partly cloudy. The storm systems had dissipated over the past few days, again, leaving the city time to dry out and patch itself up following the maelstroms that had wreaked havoc all around us. Being so elevated, our home had avoided any damage other than broken tree branches and shredded umbrellas. Many lower lying homes and businesses had suffered flood damage and more.

With the dawn, we kept an eye on the gathering multitudes below in the meadow, preparations already unfolding for the upcoming commemorative march, speeches, charity run, R&B/hip hop concert, family-oriented games, etcetera. The minority communities of Austin had combined with the left-leaning white population to put on the immense undertaking and we anticipated tens-of-thousands in our 'front yard' as the day progressed.

Jeremy was ready for our role-playing part, appearing downstairs in his MLK singlet with official entrant number clipped across the back before 5:30 AM. We were excited to join in the festivities and looking forward to the concert. Our best men, Cal and Jake, were on their way into town to join in, as well, and all of us planned to partake fully in the showcase that epitomized Austin's liberal-leaning roots on the red-letter day.

When the boys arrived, we descended to the big field, now populated by multi-colored booths, gaming areas and a large elevated stage, erected a few days before for the music makers. Vibrant banners and pennants decorated the ground zero zone. Multi-hued people filled the grassy expanse even before 7 AM. Behind the stage there arose a monolithic screen used to play video accompaniment for the artists preforming later in the day.

The staggered starting times for the 5K, 10K and 20K runs were calculated. Our longer run began first. We four were entered as a team, shooting to set PR times for ourselves thereby maximizing our charity donations. Each had shanghaied friends and co-workers into backing us and set a tiered scale of contribution for incentive to excel. Anything sub 1:10 (1 hour and ten minutes) as an individual finish time would max out our donors. We were resolved to do so.

The track, while beginning at the springs, wound around the running trails of Town Lake--- aka Lady Bird Lake, nowadays--- and the numbers entered made for a crowded race, typical for the aerobically obsessed town of Austin. We got a good start and bunched together the first 5 or so miles. By the second loop around the race course, there was mingling with the 5K and 10K entrants. Bottlenecks were counted as 'natural hazards' so contestants who desired a competitive finish were forced to strategize through the choke points.

We had gotten separated from our buds but knew them to be close-by due to our comparable gaits. Jeremy and I were comfortable in our stride and on schedule for breaking personal records as we approached the 10-mile mark. While taxing, we were pacing well. Planning for the upcoming bridge passage with its notorious congestion during multi-tiered races was on schedule.

Upon hitting the mid-point across the Congress Street bridge, the logjam intensified. Even with our plan, we were slowed to almost a halt. Breaking our stride was frustrating, as rhythm provided the best measure for continuity in long-distance racing.

We soon discovered the reason for the extra slowness forced on us. Ahead, we discerned a flock of people bearing signs and placards who had swarmed the narrow bridge and now blocked the greater portion of its width. Closing in, we were able to decipher the home-made posters.

Most bore Bible verses, but others boasted vituperative slogans decrying not only the namesake day, but many minority-based issues. 'Stop hijacking the rainbow' was a favorite, followed by 'No Socialism'. Right amidst them were the Leviticus-shrieking crowd with their 'faggots burn in Hell' and 'God hates queers' messages. There were worse ones, but what stood out to the race contestants were the carriers. To a person, almost all wore masks of scowling spitefulness. Most were noticeably out-of-shape and suffering in the heat of the day. Police contingents arrived within moments, already on stand-by. The rabble was herded unwillingly to one side in making way for the racers.

As we were all running for charities of some sort and not injecting political undertones into the event, it baffled us as to the motives on display. Jeremy punched me as we were escorted past a particularly rabid knot of protesters, gesturing at them, "Look, Luke, see who is in the middle right there. See--- the lady holding the 'I Am Here: You WILL Hear Me' sign?"

I hadn't focused on any of them until then, choosing instead to ignore the contingent and focus on the race. But looking now, I spied the person he was indicating: the pear-shaped, video-streaming woman from a few weeks back. The rude person who had accosted us on a morning run. "Damn, honey, that is just sick, huh?"

I then noticed the lady was holding hands with, and flanked by, a man helping her hold the demanding message aloft. It was none other than Brack's resident Southern Baptist hospital pastor, Marcus LeJeune. The man was a demagogue of magnificent lung power and preach-ability. The man was on par with the best-- or worst-- of his sect. Vocal as a religious-liberty mouthpiece, the man had rendered himself persona-non-grata with just about the entire staff of the University Medical Center. Heaping self-righteousness and insults at every turn and providing precious little in the way of Christian love along his way. His radio talk show was apparently lucrative for the man of God and he kept up appearances by 'volunteering' at the hospital. His Christian duty to serve, he claimed… most of the hospital would much prefer if he would shirk it a little more than he did.

The man, while not as obese as a majority of the group, was alabaster pale, wore extra-thick, over-sized black-rimmed glasses and sported a tacky comb-over hairstyle which was presently plastered in long orange-dyed strands over his bulbous head. The man's bug eyes were particularly so today what with the humidity and the vehement verse-spewing bombardment aimed at the runners.

Just then, a tap on my shoulder alerted me to Jake and Cal pulling alongside us. Jeremy filled in Cal on the Elderella lady's antics and Jake excitedly pointed at the Pastor LeJeune. "Luke, quick, look there--- LeJeune's got his hands up holding the sign…look down at his lower backside when he turns."

I panned down to the area. Through the ugliness of the exposed fat rolls, with his hands elevated and swaying to-and-fro as we passed him by, his lower back was bared. In the doing, he was showing the world his strong Christian character: a blood-red crucifix emblazoned with John 3:16 tattooed across the transverse of the cross…Jake and I stared at one another in shocked recognition and then burst into peals of laughter.

Cal leaned down into our faces, "What IS up with all this, dudes? You two enjoyin' the hate, now--- or what?"

Jeremy, equally mystified, pow-wowed with us three, scarcely able to tear himself from his desire to approach the woman again and confront her duplicity head-on. He absolutely detested hypocrites, and wasn't shy in the least at calling such tripe out into the open. Well, I thought, wait 'til he and Cal hear this.

Jake and I took turns reminding the boys of our weird encounter in the maintenance closet at Brack a few days before during the power-outage. Between fits of laughter at the 10-mile mark of a half-marathon, it proved difficult. We finally got to the description of the tattoo we had seen on the bent over 'bitch' who's face had never been visualized. The delicious knowledge that the deceitful Pastor LeJeune's very distinct marking had been recognized in such an illuminative manner was priceless…

Wonder how many get-out-of-jail free cards this might require…for that matter, wonder how many he had already used? Hmmmmm.

Though we missed our PR's due to the hold-up, the four of us felt fulfilled and absorbed the disappointment. We wondered if further hijinks might play out by the antagonists. After finishing the race, we four recouped up at the house. Showers and clean clothes made us whole again, then we re-joined the day's events.

Roasted turkey legs and margaritas later, the band-hands were setting up, techies were revving up the big screen and we lounged on the big blanket toted down with us. The blanket next to us passed a cannon- sized joint our way. After us, it went winding amongst the other partakers. The mood lightened nicely. We laughed some more about the two-faced bitterness of the LeJeune couple while conjecturing the upcoming speakers. There had been numerous factions and activists sign up to address the crowd and we all anticipated some rip-roaring talks considering the issues being debated... or sound-bited. The speeches were the political platform of the day's forum.

"Wassup, doc-dudes?" The familiar voice perked both Jake's and my ears up. We looked around as Supervisor Tevin waltzed over to our spot. "How's it hangin', the lights all on today?" He was wearing nothing but baggie cut-off jeans and flip flops. In thug fashion, the pants hung low on the small man's hips, but no drawers showed underneath them. His attractive little ass cracked like a sunrise. The little lech certainly knew how to broadcast himself. By the outline down his leg, he was succeeding in his mission. Cal leaned over to me and queried, "Where's the imagination there, now?" He wasn't dissing the man. His feeling was to show what you got, but the blatancy was unusual. Even through the oversized leggings, the humongous piece appeared just that--- humongous. Cal's own endowment exceeded the package, but at 6'6", his was lessened by the difference in proportion. I knew of each by firsthand knowledge... but that is another story entirely.

I whispered at Cal about Tevin's identity as Jake introduced him out loud, surprised at seeing him. Inviting him to sit, we hawked the nearby blunt as it floated near again and within a minute, the little guy chatted even more easily with us. He seemed pleased at being invited to stop, apparently expecting sheepishness on our parts due to the closet episode. He was disabused of the idea as our men openly discussed it, obviously aware. After absorbing the openness, he warmed to joking about the situation, even alluding to the ID of the Pastor involved, though still not naming him. Seems that money had been involved and a repeat rendezvous hoped for--- discretion was likely a requirement for that.

A few more tokes and the tripod guy was forgetting his reticence, "Yeah, the boot be worked over, now, but it takes deposits...and does those withdrawals, too. The wrinkled dude comes lookin' a couple times a week for this good stuff," --- pointing at the bulge--- and I noted other eyes following that point to its target. "Always put dat bootie in the darkest closets and then it just be OK. That storm day, all the lights were out. Had to light us up wit' my phone to get goin' that time…I don' like the seein' it too much, but the pumpin' bein' fine, now. Ask the doc-dudes, they seen it all with those flashlights," still proud of the action.

Then, Jake hit on something I hadn't thought of, "Hey, Tevin, when you lit it up, did that video switch on, too?"

The grin said it all, "Hell to da' yes, I got that streamin' now--- trannie friend o' mine done paid for that shit. Likes seeing my stuff all worked up, so's I got double-down payday on that. Shit yeah, set dat over on the wall inside that door and got ten minutes goin' on--- 'til you boys come in an' knocked the damn thing on da' flo'. Lost it, then," again, pleased with himself. Recording his stuff for posterity, no doubt.

"OK, bra, that is hot. You gonna let us have a copy of that, too, right?" This from Jeremy, who had been listening closely. "We missed all that action, and our boys been filling us in on what's packin' down there--- we're ready to check it out, how about?" We all followed the idea forming as he spoke, and concurred.

It worked. The shorty took the attention as an ultimate compliment, coming from Jeremy, "Yeah, I can be doin' dat, a'ight. I can pass that shit over right here, right now, got ya' phone?" Jeremy pulled it out and in a minute, the deed was done.

"We be strokin' to that, Tevin, thanks Bra," he wasn't kidding. Jeremy had already laid the babies twice--- and that was just by hearing the story. I imagined Cal had likewise put it to Jake, too, knowing those two. But, the true value was to come… soon. "Hell, it may just hit the silver screen someday, if that be OK…?"

"Sho 'nuf, big man, that be dope, now. A'ight," he was fine with just about any exposure of the downstairs dweller. Who says the way to a man's heart is through his stomach?

Cal and Jeremy had been up to the house for a minute and we had finished off our third margarita. Tevin had wandered off in search of the next conquest, showin' off the wares, knowing that he would be making choices in the quick future. Three people had nearly waylaid him just in our vicinity and we snickered at the man's hutzpah.

The Juneteenth speakers had throttled the crowd up incrementally and all were finally awaiting the keynote by Lonnie Lynn, Junior. Fresh off the production of Selma, the man was integrally involved with the 21st century Civil Rights Movement, the successor of Emancipation. Austin had been lucky to corral the singer, poet, actor and philosopher into addressing the progressive enclave here.

As the stage cleared and the mayor introduced the man of the day, the guys returned. "Just in time," J-Man said, and we settled in for it.

L.R. 'Lonnie' Lynn, Jr., aka Common, wowed us by his message, espousing the essence of American ideals as embodied in the Constitution, signed into being by the Founders. The man informed us that the new generation coming up after the Millennials would be adopting that namesake, as well. The New Founders were destined to take our divided country onward as originally intended, he intoned. Toward the realization of the dream: Life, Liberty, the Pursuit of Happiness with Equality for All. Rule by the Majority with the Protection of the Minorities. In Peace. The rest of us, he told, must prepare for their coming of age by fighting tooth and nail for the rights under attack by the forces committed to assailing them.

He finished as the crowd, in unison, voiced their standing approval. And the bands kicked it up to entertainment level. We four decided to vacate up to the house and enjoy the concert in the comforts. On the way, distant chants from around the bend and down toward Town Lake filtered over the music. Jake and I diverted to check out the source, pretty certain of what we would find. But Cal and Jeremy herded us both away and back up our stairs.

"It's who you think, all right, boys, but it's already been taken care of," they grinned. Like Cheshire cats.

From our deck, a bottle of the good red was cracked. Our men assured that an occasion was upon us. We listened to the good music, but our ears were cocked toward the lake. Sure enough, the sounds of loud speakers bit into the hip hop song, and the gang of rabble-rousers from the bridge appeared. Nasty signage still proclaimed their twisted and decidedly un-Christian values. Crude and thoughtless discord spread their lies as they waddled toward the concert crowd. The hypocrites halted, almost directly below us. Pastor LeJeune and his wife led them, controlling the message.

Cal toasted Jeremy as we watched their looks of smugness. The huge HD screen backing the stage abruptly tracked, as if on cue, to a shadowed haze. The music video had changed to a very blurry image of rhythmic motion in shades of blacks and whites, in time with the band's beat. As we watched, the focus sharpened and gradually grew into a large black penis plowing a pallid white, flabby ass. That ass, boasting a blood red crucifix with John 3:16 in foot high relief plastered across it brought a collective gasp from the crowd as it blasted the eyes of the thousands present. It was a religious lesson none would soon forget. Parents screamed at kids to look away. Others gawked and cat-called the hard core flick playing out before their surely lying eyes. And the band kept playing... kind of like it were planned. Somewhere, Tevin was a star.

The fundamentalist faction slowly became aware of the video footage and dropped their offensive cadence to gape as well, until only the pastor and his wife were left bellowing into their bullhorns, still not facing the big screen. With perfect timing, the screen image flipped to a new image of the revered pastor, himself, on his knees. Not praying, but attempting to perform fellatio on the same oversized black organ. In a most ungodly manner.

The bullhorn and the female screeching accompaniment

wavered and fell silent, gawping like the rest of us at the re-enactment of a broom closet hookup. The audible sounded above the suddenly pianissimo hip hop song, "Suck that, bitch, just like you always suck that big, black dick you love… filthy bitch."

The flick tracked back to the planned accompaniment and the band ratcheted up again…

* * *

"Hooter Man!" Jeremy shouted up to the roof, "You're late! Get down here boi, quick!" He almost never raised his voice, so I knew something was definitely up. Too, he had used my uncommon nickname---Hooter--- as he did only when appealing to my intellectual side. My obsession with the majestic avian predators, owls, existed on a purely physiological plane. To understand everything about them. Jeremy had extrapolated that to the wives' tale involving the wisdom thing… go figure.

Putting down my treatise by Avicenna, the eleventh century Muslim Physician and Philosopher, I stood under the mist system to cool down, then dried off, flip-flopped up and wrapped the towel around my speedo. My fiancé preferred tan lines and milky white ass staring at him when he was in the mood, which was almost always, so I used the beat-down Austin sun rays to stay in tone. Coppertone.

Descending to the second floor balcony entrance into our bedroom, I was met by a bear hug and a face lick, "My man, It - Be - Done, Baby! We are on the road tomorrow. We're gettin' married in the morning, wassssupp!?"

"Blow me, JK… they did it?" I was astonished, even though we had been awaiting a ruling for the past three days. The trepidation had been killing us. Our suitcases and dog stuff were already in the trunk of the Benz in expectation, yet the news made my skin prickle. Jeremy swung me up over his shoulder and we took off down the stairs, both dogs celebrating whatever in their following--- anything constituted a party for the two.

Seeing the break-in TV bulletin real-time made it true. Picking up my cell, JK handed it to me and I speed-dialed Jake. Answering on the first ring, the two howled into the receiver together, drowning our ears in gibberish. After the cacophonous opening, we traded congrats, agreed to meet on the road at daylight and convoy to Colorado cross-country. Pitkin and San Miguel Counties were about to be changed forever.

June 26th, 2015, C.E. A 5-4 decision, Obergefell v. Hodges was close but decisive nonetheless. There would probably be repercussions for months or years. But the shoe had dropped. The call ended upon Jake's note that he was being piggybacked. Code for 'about to be ravished'…the line went dead.

Jeremy took the cue and my speedo was ripped in half on our way to the floor. We couldn't wait for the onset of the misery.

Three days later found the four of us ascending in a rainbow-striped hot air balloon as the dawning sun peeked over Ajax Mountain. The pilot, a lesbian friend, guided us to 14000 feet above sea level, then resumed her day job as an Episcopalian pastor. Cal's and Jake's vows reinforced their basis for honesty and openness in everything; the rest would fall into place. Very simple. Lifelong commitment was hardly new when the two soulmates had been on that road for eight years. The future looked rosy, and the boys told us of their plans for a summer in Cal's hometown, bonding and reacquainting with the large family he had grown up among. Their honeymoon in Aspen had been planned as a cosseted period to acclimate to the status America had belatedly allowed them.

We all trekked together through the splendor of southwest Colorado a day later, dead-ending into the box canyon that hid Telluride town. Our log home had been opened, aired, and readied for our arrival by friends and neighbors of the mountain community. The county clerk, true to her word, stream-lined our license and certificate-processing in the quaintly handsome, period red brick San Miguel County Courthouse. County Judge Rickenmeier proved himself welcoming to our application.

Marise, the same presiding Episcopalian pastor to do the honors for the Marshall-Broadhearst ceremony honored ours as well, at the pond side setting outside our home. Mountain Columbine bell flowers were rife around the waterside. My denizen hoot owl of the old blue spruce shading our balcony, welcoming to us since we had moved in six years before, called out during the small ceremony at the time of mountain dusk. Twinkling white lights entangled with the bell flowers were everywhere. Neither the white lights nor the blue and white flowers signified virginity. Only contentment. Our wedding eve dinner party at Allred's on the Peak matched the altitude of our best men's moment at 14000 feet, a pre-planned idea. The private party of forty toasted the life of misery heretofore denied.

The plan was to change the ever-loving religious sufferers' self-proclaimed curse to one of positivity and optimism... it had only taken Jeremy and me eighteen years of companionable bliss to break through the ceiling.

America had taken one small step toward minorities and a huge step forward for Humanity…to paraphrase a time-honored space quote. The Kell-Cevennes family had, indeed, arrived. Sky-high.

Ahem and Amen…

Chapter 2
Tride and True: Enduring Embers

With a nudge and a yawn-smothering smirk Jeremy poked me in the ribs and falsetto whimpered at me, "wake uuu—uup," as I ironically continued to drive and he awakened from traveler's daze. Always his way--- deflect the obvious by that distracting charm. Even after 18 years I was not immune to it. The fact of which he remained well aware.

Approaching the Animus River crossing in Durango, we had made a good way toward our destination: Telluride, up-mountain. "Tride" to the familiars, Olympus to the low-landers. Beautiful and rustic, hidden deep inside a box canyon up in the San Juan mountains of Colorado, for all who know of it.

We had fallen in love with the place years before while visiting friends who kept a getaway lodge in the small community. It was Elysium. A mixture of old mining town, bucolic and unpolished, and a more recent bohemian skier's colony. Excellent music venues with an ongoing upscale restoration of the historical texture in refined, urbane mountain style. New and old money had established their presence in the high mountain retreat that so captured sooo different many.

A plain and rough log home with windowed loft master bedroom, rock fireplaces, peaked roofs and wonderful views later, Jeremy and Luke had nestled our way into a quietly replete existence every bit of time we could manage between our two full lives most of the year. Not that we were complaining. Only calculating.

He checked over his shoulder at our two better halves, Suture and Elvee. Both rescue canines lay contentedly sacked out on the back seat, good travelers that they were. Then, he nuzzled over to encircle my right arm in his, rasping in his best Mae West voice, "Where the hell are we...honey?" His other hand reached down between my legs and groped my junk lewdly, making slurping sounds in accompaniment. His full lips enjoyed sucking dick as much as any two I had ever before witnessed or experienced.

I knew this by firsthand knowledge as well as second and even third hand evidence. His nomination to the Blowjob Hall of Fame was all but secured. I hardened at the thought of those close by, talented full ones. On earlier trips they had swallowed my dick in healthy similarity to this present driving pose. What he lacked in kept promises of shared driving pledges was more than atoned for by the doling out of his primo blowjobs... I forgave the intermittent lapses and naps. Besides, he always woke up horny.

Just about my first revelation regarding him decades before was that he was one giant horndog every time his eyes opened from a sleep state. Power nap, siesta, slumber, REM, any suspension of consciousness. Of course, wakening with a raging hard-on every time could account for some of the lustfulness, yet I ever wondered at what was sifting through his subconscious right before waking up that made his big boners such a given. Again, not a complaint, said my smile.

But, I digress. His sensuous dark lips closed determinedly around the head of my cock, bringing me to attention in more than one way. When toes couldn't curl, knees could still lock. The gas pedal became suddenly heavy under my foot.

Knowing full well of his DWM (Driving While Milking) penchant, I still jolted involuntarily upon contact with the talented trio of his tongue and lips. He could bring me to a climax in less than a minute if need be, but preferred to prove his steel-trap control by slow, deep, throatful mouth strokes. The big manipulator...

From my spot behind the wheel, his masterful head felt sweetly exhilarating and my big piece curved into the deep reaches of his throat, spasming every time my pubes got lipped. He always knew where a dick was on that scale of numb-to-cum and perpetuated the teetering feeling at the pinnacle of Mount Climax for about as long as he desired.

Cars and trucks passing us in the other direction surely must be able to see his dark, shaved head rising and rolling over my lap from their oncoming vantage point, though only in fractional snapshots. My erection was amplified by the thought. I rationalized that their short glimpses could leave them only perplexed, shocked...or jacked.

As we crested a hill and descended, Jeremy let me crest as well and I throbbed a high country load down his waiting throat. Proof is in the puddin' as per the avowal. Mouthing of the phatted worm went for several minutes longer and I gradually sat back on the seat, slowly bending my knees. The gas pedal grew gradually lighter.

No longer needing to stop for coffee to keep me alert, we continued the progressive upward slope as the snaking road ascended toward Tride. The boys in the backseat snored on, lulled by the motor and turning wheels. We made more good time onward to the awaiting nest.

True to form, with throat coated and libido slaked, Jeremy regressed inward to contemplate the origins of sperm, or something, while I settled in for the sylvan riverside course inclining over the winding miles to 12,000 feet and our tucked away bower. I simmered reflectively, hearkening back to the first sight of the man-of-my-life now nestled, introspecting beside me...

* * *

...Reaching for the just-now espied third volume of a long sought obscure anthology, the wooden ladder holding me abruptly jerked, twisting beneath my tip-toed feet. Losing my balance but still grasping the book, I cascaded downward in a slow-motion fall to the side of it as I glimpsed a little girl under the ladder, either by cause or effect, right in my line of descent. Futilely grabbing at the ladder to break the impact during the plummet, I next found myself jarringly cradled in the tensed, nutmeg-toned arms of the sexiest man I had ever laid eyes on.

Jeremy stared back through smoky grey eyes, evincing conflicted emotions in that moment as he sized-up the present scene. The little girl had deftly skittered to the side out of harm's way, now feigning ignorance of any incident at all. Even the bumping of my wall ladder, as she had bolted away from her father a few seconds before. Now, her rapt attention was bent toward a fascinating treatise by Sophocles... the tiny, pig-tailed figure did everything possible to blend with the wall.

The man's surety of his child's safety overrode any other feelings and he focused on her. After quietly reassuring the imp and firmly instructing her to stay put, he turned and for the first time ever, floored me by the wafting effervescence of his smile. Introducing himself awkwardly, he offered an apology as well as a concerned look for my own status after the near hard landing. The darkly sexy creature's breath enveloped me in a piney burst with pesto flares. Totally mesmerized, I held motionless for fear he would put me down.

Hardened to a traditional southern male psyche, I had neither expected nor hoped for such an occurrence. Leading an already full life, there was contentment in it. Or so I had thought. Nevertheless, actually falling into this man's arms on our first meeting did happen and It will remain etched in my mind even as my dying moments someday flash past.

The proximity of our faces persisted for long enough to want more and short enough to leave a craving. I sensed his reticence to let go, as well. He stood me on my feet after a lasting, searching pause. Following a relieved yet clumsy chat, we both dazedly went our own ways. Jeremy's daughter, Elle, and he, off to another part of the used bookstore. Myself to the check-out counter.

Other patrons rubbernecked in our direction through the startling scenario and some picked up on the inelegant moment we had shared. Several apparently evangelistic witnesses to the quasi-accident traded supercilious comments. How condescendingly smug, I thought. Had a bad ending resulted from our near miss, then these people would have no doubt easily inferred 'God's Will for fags' from our meeting. Since same-sex serendipity had happened, however, they found need to titter about the breakdown in societal mores. As things stood, mere mortals would need to ascribe judgement in God's absenteeism for this gay, interracial moment... but, by all means, keep praying. Blind pigs do find acorns now and again.

Heading to my neighborhood Starbucks on the way home, I entered the coffeehouse in a bemusedly euphoric state and was bewildered to see little Elle round the corner ahead, eyeing me shyly. Her hunky Dad emerged soon after and totally disarmed me by his affectation of another coincidence. He bent his neck deliberately up and around the room, making note of a 'no-falling-ladder' factor...and, "Oh, my gosh, do you like coffee, too?" Then, "Do you come here often?"

While grasping the transparent come-on, the smooth manner and drop-dead gorgeous smile weaseled its way past any defenses I could erect and the two of us laughed some more over the strange meeting shortly before. I could still feel the ghost of his touch on my arms and legs. Elle very maturely absorbed the charade.

No one ever believes the truth of this account, so we have since claimed meeting at the gay cult genre Erasure concert the following evening. I conveniently happened to have an extra ticket after a friend had cancelled on me at the last minute and shyly offered it, hoping for his company. Since he accepted, we offered the alternative scenario from then on. I still send an annual thank you note on that concert date to the friend who had fortuitously cancelled, providing Jeremy and me our first date.

In spending that evening together laughing over the wild sets, the erogenous music, the onstage antics, plus the excellently weird crowd, our undeniable attraction budded and grew apace. Subsequent dinners grilled on my veranda, dining out at intimate bistros, theatre tickets or basketball games all became common threads for us. The elf, Elle, would announce her and Jeremy's arrival when we made plans for dinner at my place in all the rushed exuberance of a 7 year-old. She adored the dogs, and they her. Always curious about her Daddy's and my connection, the little girl visualized things before we two did, more than once surprising us by her adept skills of observation. And her wry deductions.

Jeremy dourly informed me one day that Elle would soon be leaving for her mother's home in another state for the upcoming fall school semester. It was a better situation, he had explained. As he was still by himself, working full time, and his ex-wife had remarried to a lawyer, Elle's presence there provided stability where Dad could not. It obviously affected him deeply, as good fathering fairly oozed from the handsome man. The bond between the two was unmistakable.

After she had departed, Jeremy began showing up unannounced at my house more and more commonly as he covered his feelings of separation, inveigling his way into my emotions over that ensuing year. Much as we could both feel the vibe between us, it was months after that before either allowed another wedge of the puzzle to fall into place.

Over beer and oysters at a happy hour in Drydock Oyster House the month of the succeeding May, I slid another of the slippery delicacies past my tongue just as he leaned over to plant me with a male-on-male kiss. Right there amidst the boisterous atmosphere of straight world, testosterone-driven afterworkers. With classic Jeremy hubris, he proclaimed for all to hear that he wasn't shy and didn't stutter: this here, pointing at me, was the man for him. So there we were...the ensuing silence was deafening.

He moved his closet into mine that night.

We busted those 'born-again' cherries in multiples, brazenly breaking down the remaining wall in animalistic ritual. As only two seeking males may do, let alone understand.

His dusky masculinity overwhelmed my senses and mutual melding took precedence in the silhouette forever emblazoned on my being. His creeping, cat-like approach, dimly back-lit in an engraved mental video of my legs rising by his muscular insistence, spreading and opening for a fell swoop lubricated slide fuck. We were hooked, both tongue and dick...for life.

Only one twining figure writhed in ecstasy during that carnal introduction. We fit...

* * *

... I passed the uphill miles to the mountain home while zoning in our past. His boyish breaths pushed out muffled 'pfffings' as he slept, as close to a snore as I have ever heard from him. A very endearing accessory virtue, this is a bounty by which I benefited every day. We neither one pushed the other to search a quieter refuge by such nasal habits, thankfully. It was a matchless pleasure waking up to each other. Opening my eyes to those smoky greys was incomparable. As I contemplated the Fates, he slouched against me in repose, my arm resting down his chest and stomach, angelic as a Nubian Botticelli.

The unfolding of the gateway into the mountain-ringed valley was an experience we had enjoyed as a couple since acquiring the hideaway six years before. Soon, I knew, the panorama of the highland vistas encircling us would exert subliminal force on his subconscious and the haze would lift. The mind's eye be very powerful and this shared pleasure had imprinted on us.

Having traversed the upland way two months before as we achieved the almost two-decade goal of marrying, this trip would be inaugural for us in that state of being. Sure enough, the man of my heart awakened and raised up while staying under my arm. We shared the re-entry to our honeymoon milieu oohing and aahhing at the breathtaking scenery.

Winding our way through the shimmering aspen and spruce setting of late August saturated our mental spaces with a redolent solace. It was amazing how the passage of time and the fullness of human bonding addends raw carnality with supple, familiar affection. Our fleshly attraction had not ebbed in the slightest, but our fondness added fervent flavors alien to youth. We basked in common aspirations and goals, ably learning to let the chaff go. Some call it wisdom. We dubbed it 'streamlining'.

At the final turnoff from the avenue traversing Telluride town, we curved up the sawtooth ascent past streets rowed with high-pitched roofs. Gables thinned to widely spaced massive mountain chateaus with exposure to panoramic vistas, and we followed the cobbled way past a trickling of more and more sparsely remote log and rock edifices. Ours resided on a dead end lane higher up than most, its charming log cabin aura pervading the surrounds.

A large second floor triangular geometric of glass dominated the rest of the log lodge, with the lower level fronted by floor-to-ceiling glass encasings as well. The rock chimneys anchored it to the side. Mature evergreens variegated with aspens and Japanese maples all balanced the nestled effect. The entire place vested comfortably into the notched mountainside which terraced up to towering crags far past the tree line above.

The two loungers from the backseat rallied now and combined with JK's contagious rambunctiousness. The three set to announcing our arrival by a vocal chorus of discordant onomonopia which served to thin the wildlife in the doing. Soon to return, of course.

We opened up the many windows to air the place out, uncovering furniture and items protected during our absences, then unpacked both belongings and staples hauled along to enhance our time here. The denizen owl of the ancient blue spruce came down to check out the commotion, familiar with us from previous invasions.

J-man readied the over-sized fireplace for our ritual opening-night blaze which both canine and human residents anticipated. He stacked 4-5 days' worth of splits in the adjoining roughhewn built-in ledges. My fetish for night sounds and by extension, open windows, made our reliance on the great room and master suite fireplaces a given. The cool evenings were kept barely at bay by the beloved heat sources. Sprawled around the hearth we heralded the coming idyll.

Bolstered by hot buttered rums, the evening unfolded harmoniously with firelight sex and conspiratorial banter. Afterwards, amidst entwined contentedness, night sounds once again gained sway.

* * *

Early on in our relationship Jeremy and I had established the daily pre-dawn physical pursuit regimen that still anchored our routine. Entailing multi-mile runs over well-trodden loops and trails close by our Austin home, we had set in motion the basis for the conditioned lifestyle still enjoyed.

Even in the rarified liberal enclave which we purposely chose to inhabit downland in Texas, our then uncommon jungle fever relationship stood out. At times it created a stir. Between the variety of hormone-governed university students and untamed local fauna, I held on to a plethora of memories which recurrently bubbled into virtual dream reenactments ranging from the mundane to the profound to the comical, and others in between. Running shorts and Tiger trainers (now evolved to Asics) were and are our sole attire during the long warm seasons of central Texas. To be certain, this proved to be a double-edged sword depending on circumstances, but we preferred the state, perpetuating the style into the present...

...Lazing in semi-somnolence on our first Tride mountain dawn, I was recalling one particular morning down home earlier in the spring. Suture and Jeremy had darted ahead in chase of one another. When I rounded the turn behind them I viewed a cartoon image of the two, askew in confusion as they attempted avoidance of a charging guinea hen. Wings raised and spread, the monster had the two totally bamboozled. Though only spitting at them with rank-smelling saliva before disappearing into the underbrush, the 'attack' left us doubled over by the humorous image of the wee, fluffed-up bird terrorizing grown man and dog. Their standard of courage under pressure had been established.

As running shorts had provided our only cloth source for cleaning off the viscous spittle, we ended up running al fresco. Between his notorious après-sleep boner and my own morning sex drive, that state did not lend itself to platonics very well. Jeremy had wrapped me up within a hundred yards and proceeded to bend me over a large tree stump. As he twanged the 'Deliverance' banjo theme, we had succumbed to fucking ravenously there on the wooded path. JK slapping my ass like a bronc rider on a wild mustang under the lightening sky.

Upon climaxing, the sun's first rays broke the horizon. We sensed presence. Raising up from the convenient log, we realized we had unwittingly staged our wantonness for three UT cross-country team members. One cute kid stood staring, slack-jawed, as a 1970's 'male-rape-by-inbred-hillbillies' plot unfolded before his eyes in interracial update. The tree bark pasted by cum to my oozing piece was telltale. The other two had obviously lost focus. At least from the look of the throbbing boners in the process of cumming--- by each other's hand…

…As I basked in the penile rigidity provoked by that steamy dream sequence, something in my inner defense mechanism clicked on my instincts and the sexy 'le rive' interlude faded. I blinked open to the too-close image of the real-time snuffling, glistening black nostrils attached to a long, black-furred bear snout presently arising outside the screen of the open window just beyond the smooth dark shoulder of Jeremy's sleeping form. My sudden jerk to wakefulness brought him to an abrupt sitting position, facing me, and I flashed on the just-relived situation involving the spitting guinea, measuring it against the current one. The dubious history of his response under pressure involving riled stray chickens did not bode well for the coming bear encounter.

Reacting rather than thinking, I clambered over my surprised horndog, slapping his confused face with my morning wood in the effort to slam shut the window, barely rescuing him from the man-eating beast. Upon grasping the situation, Jeremy only faked the heart attack he otherwise would have experienced should I not have intervened.

In truth, black bears are notorious flakes and this one substantiated the adage as she scampered excitedly away upon the noisy interruption of her 0-dark-thirty ursine curiosity lark.

Ahh, the price we pay to exist with nature. Well worth the cost, as Jeremy and I personify that concept through the ease with which this and similar disquieting episodes lead so often to excellent follow-up sex. After 18 years, it granted food for thought, but for now we simply sucked face and stroked, viewing the faintly pinkening sky while contemplating our promised land. And Denver omelettes.

Enduring embers, my ass. Stoke the fire.

Chapter 3
Stick Shift

The knock sounded again. It was louder and longer— five taps this time--- and Jake fuzzily resigned himself to the fact that the honeymoon was officially ending.

Broderick was nothing if not meticulous in carrying out the responsibilities entrusted to him. This morning, it was his mission to see to the closing of the boys' Jerome Hotel suite and the send-off of Cal and Jake to the lowlands in their cross-country trek for Cal's youthful hometown of Rome, Georgia.

The butler had initially endeared himself to the newlyweds upon acquiring the balcony suite in the Jerome four years before when his tactful manner and able judgment had intervened with a boisterous stalker outside the hotel. The ski bum had decided to act the over-zealous, unwanted aspirant toward Jake as he had approached the old hotel on a frigid day in January…

… The youth, who had virtually run me over on the saw-tooth halfway down the mountain thirty minutes before, had showed himself again on the street in Aspen town. I was taken aback by the untoward behavior, but even more so by the quasi-malicious undertone to his comments. The accusatory attitude combined with a blatant attempt to hook up had bothered me.

Earlier, up the mountainside, I had stood, awed at the sheer drop down a bumpy, ski-sculpted surface before me. Navigating Devil's Drop had created an obsession. Until then, the black diamond run had virtually laughed at repeated attempts, thwarting my developing skill. This time, attacking the rim determinedly, I had descended. My skis sliced decisively, arcing around the deep edges marking the icy humps. Suspended seconds passed and I hit the traverse, upright and in control. Supremely exhilarated and totally absorbed by my victory over the challenging mogul pattern, I curled around for a pause to soak in the triumph, oblivious to the surroundings.

A masked snowboarder had whooshed from around an adjoining corner and almost broadsided me as I basked there, catching my blindside without warning of any sort. Not a full-on collision, the clipping of my ski and hip had swept feet out and upwards, twirling me in a 1080 to the snow-packed cross trail. Landing flat on my back with a thud led to several more rotations before plunging into a powdery snowbank. I lay still a minute. Then, sensing no danger, nor even sound, I had extracted myself from the fluffy stuff and arisen to assess what just occurred.

The miscreant had hit-and-run, never even slowing to check for collateral damage left in his wake. The behavior was typical for the discourtesy that traditional slalom skiers associated with the upstart variation introduced late in the last century. Many ski enclaves had banned the newbie addition to the downhill sport for years, but Aspen had finally given in to the pressure to open up their slopes. The burgeoning infatuation with it demanded acceptance. Acute increases in 'drive-by' accidents subsequent to the decision had the conventional ski community second-guessing that.

Dusting the snow from my insulated spandex body suit and ribbed parka, then adjusting my bindings, I set out. Scanning the steep backdrop one more time with satisfaction, I lazily slalomed down the expanding concourse serving as meeting point of multiple different ski runs in the descent to bunny slopes and lifts.

Packing my skis, boots and accessories into Cal and my shared locker at mountain base, I donned hiking boots and hoofed it for the hotel. After whisking off my knit stocking hat I shook out crimped curls, finger-combing the tangles. My thick, sun-burnished auburn locks were a source of both pride and wild unruliness. At their present length during my sabbatical from hospital duty, Cal caroused in them. They provided a ready handle for his caveman predilections. The man would no doubt drag me around by them if he thought I would allow it. I lit up a small blunt on the way, mellowing almost immediately.

Cal should be descending soon, himself, after wrapping up the board meeting he had overseen through a working lunch. The mountain peak restaurant was a sought after venue for many business deals, 360 view persuasive by the panoply. The site worked magic convincing uncommitted investors and calming combative board members, Cal had discovered, so it commonly served his purposes. I had grown bored earlier with the monotony of CPA-driven proceedings and stolen away for a loner run down my nemesis, Devil's Drop. Ha, I gloried: my former nemesis…

The turn on to Main street brought the Hotel Jerome into view. I admired the venerable structure with its old-world architecture, so archetypal to the town in which it flourished. The coziness of the innards had drawn me to its intimacy like a newborn to a teat. Cal had sprung for the exorbitant cost, indulging my yearning. We had discussed the possibility of acquiring another property way up the mountainside but both of us were reticent to forfeit the luxury of the central location in such an establishment. The option was being mulled.

My doctor's salary would have been totally inadequate to land the three-bedroom suite but in Cal's successful software company we found the wherewithal to procure its understated refinement. There were more opulent places around the town proper and outlying areas, but the history and magnetism for the jet-set crowd had instilled its ambience with something indescribable. The class and elegance won us both over and we exulted in our abode away from home.

As I drew within a block of it, I thought I heard Cal's deep voice call to me but on turning, I noted a flaxen haired man approaching, hurrying to catch up. The face was unfamiliar and I was curious.

"Fly boy, you ought to be more careful," the man was saying, and I looked back in front to be sure he was addressing me. "Yeah, dude, I mean you…you 'bout caused a 'tastrophe. You new on your skis?"

The person's long blond hair shimmered in the late afternoon sunlight and bounced around his head as he walked. It hit me that the bad-mannered snowboarder up the mountain must inhabit this body. I decided to ignore him and keep walking on to our place instead of addressing his continuing insolence.

"You always this rude, fly boy? I'm tryin' to talk to you--- you just gonna walk away?"

OK, I thought, what was up with this guy? "Do I know you, mister," leaving out the question in my voice, as I had no wish to converse with him.

"Well, I dunno, but ya' just about wiped me out on Devil's Drop comin' off the mogul stretch. That's a dangerous thing you pulled, man." This uncouth person spun a yarn better than Bill O'Reilly.

I didn't stop walking, preferring the haven of the hotel with its buffer of patrons over an open street encounter here with a complete loser. It crossed my mind to wonder if he was packing a gun. His ballsy approach to the truth had my nerves jangling.

"You know, Sir, the ski board has a meeting in a week. If you feel the need, we can review the remote cams up there and set straight what actually occurred. You seem to hold a perverse perspective on reality if you think I'm responsible for your loony-tune antics. I'm late for my evening—take it easy, now." I tried not to sound overly confrontational. This alpha-male projecting himself was not generating good vibes with me at the moment.

Catching up to me, the almost good-looking man handed my arm, pulling me around to face him. A sneer of a smile jagged across his hard features and he attempted what he apparently felt passed for dialogue. "Fly boy, I'm just trying for friendly here. You should slow down a minute and give me a chance. The evening is just starin' at us. We could have some fun together if you just let it go a little... the view from this end is booty-licious, dude."

Having had enough, I shook his hand off my arm, making certain he knew I wasn't in the mood for anything he might have in mind. "Well, thanks for that back-handed compliment, I guess, but what are you talking about, stranger? I don't even know you. You act like all this and then try coming on to me...? See the dichotomy, maybe?"

The blond didn't understand the word and wasn't chastened in the slightest. Taking the brushed off hand he placed it directly on my left cake. Wow, I figured, this guy has got balls, I'll give him that. They sure weren't my type. What's more, I detested being treated in the manner of his come-on. What a turn-off.

With a strong hand of my own, I turned on the guy, no longer guarded in my own approach. Wristing the uninvited grope, I raised it up to his face level. Directing my most severe doctor visage at him, he was informed, "I have performed amputations on better-looking hands than this...and some were just as functional. Please keep that in mind. I've told you that I have plans this evening. If you'll excuse me, Sir, I am home." With that, I placed the hand on the side of his face, dropped my own, turned on my heel and stepped up the stairs.

"Oh, so how long you in town for, fly boy? The Jerome's pretty high-falutin', so probably not too long, I'm bettin'. You can come crash at my place if you want. I'm real fun, now, I'm tellin' you. And I like a challenge," the man persisted.

Good Lord, I was amazed.

Then, it dawned on me. Turning back and looking down on the ski-bum, I tried a different tack, "Did you sideswipe me on purpose up there—Dude?" Borrowing his own vernacular. The snarky smirk told it all, and now my ire was up.

"Fly boy," he went on, unfazed, "I done seen you up there comin' out the Sundeck, pulling that sock over those curls and decided we should get to know each other." He came up the steps in a quick bound, then, like I had somehow made an inviting motion of some sort. Though he was my height, at six foot, the guy outweighed me by probably forty pounds. I didn't like the forwardness, mostly because of the history on the slope between us. I stepped up, preparing to… well, I'm not sure what I was about to do. Though I knew I should just disappear into the familiar confines of the hotel.

The leer was back. He must not check himself out in the mirror while smiling, I reasoned, or he wouldn't do it that way. It imparted an undertone of malicious intent and made his otherwise attractive features appear malevolent. The unwelcome hand was reaching out once again and I was about to get definitive with him when another hand extended between us, gently persuading me backward.

I glanced over my shoulder to find Broderick's benevolent countenance within inches of mine, "Doctor Marshall, it is sooo nice to see you have arrived, sir. Your party is waiting in the library. I have your blazer, here, sir. May I gather your wrap before we retire inside?" He oozed old-world charm and I almost kissed the man. Pulling off my parka, the savior efficiently shrugged me into the proffered sports coat.

Assigned to our suite upon closing the deal with the hotel, the seasoned gentleman took personal care of Cal and me, becoming extended family in the interim. He had obviously discerned my predicament from indoors. The intervention was especially welcome and timely.

The interruption had confused the blond man; his hand backed down. "Well, now… Doc, is it? I'll be. Cute butt and he has a brain, too. OK, I'll just be checkin' in with you in a day or two, Doc, and we can get it goin'," he didn't take hints well, I noted. I slipped past Broderick and took note through the cut glass door that the cultured gentleman stayed, addressing the forward jackass. Broderick's facial features betrayed nothing, but the blonde's reflected re-enactment of a bad silent movie. It looked to be a sad-sack theme. A black cloud hovered above him as he retreated down the steps.

Deflated, but I was pretty sure not defeated, the snowboarder disappeared down the street. I was indebted to Broderick from then on…

…Laying in the big poster bed, the previous three weeks washed over Jake as he stretched his leg out and down alongside his husband's, engendering a reactionary flexing of the supple, ebony leg now touching his. In only semi-consciousness, Calumet's leg lifted over Jake's and his thickly muscled bicep slid under the mane of ringlets that had sprouted to impressive length over the extended honeymoon here in Aspen,

Colorado. Much fuller and longer than when on duty in the ER of Brack, back home in Austin, it now sprayed riotously over the pillow. Cal was totally turned on by the mop of curls, expressing his preference for the state of disarray often and with physical reinforcement. His fingers were constantly fidgeting in it and that was reason enough for Jake to let it grow.

A soft voice spoke in tandem with the next round of persistent knocking. This time, Cal ascended from subliminal depths, rubbing the long leg up and over his husband's ample endowment which began swelling by the act. Yawning, Cal scooched over the top of the white boy's torso, dragging ten inches of engorged phatness across a flat white belly in the doing, then plodded through the living area to the door. Upon opening it, Mr. Broderick ensured that more than the ten-inch crotch snake was awakening by jostling the tall man's shoulder, pushing him gently backwards into the foyer.

Cal turned back to the warmth of his lover to awaken more pleasantly. Following inside, the unfazed butler soft-stepped over toward the open kitchen. Checking that the coffeemaker was brewing on its timer, he made his way around the suite, breaking night's dominion by opening curtains, checking suitcases still partially filled, and perusing closets for upcoming packing-versus-storage requirements. When not in residence, several closets were locked to privatize certain areas. The inquisitiveness of visiting patrons eager to fill the empty periods of the vacated place necessitated such. The couple's winter wardrobe resided on premise permanently.

Andre appeared next, heading into the cutting edge kitchen for preparing the final breakfast of the honeymoon sojourn. Soon, the smell of toast, egg soufflé and bacon wafted over morning boners in the en suite, energizing Jake's dawn function of working up Cal's piece to full-bloom. His mouth engulfed the limber shaft, slowly inching the thickness to a swollen level of turgidity in mutual craving. Neither awakening newlywed was concerned about the proximity of the silently functioning men carrying out routine duties. Perceiving the action through discreet eyes, both older gents had deduced that their vicarious awareness was aphrodisiacal for the jungle-fever couple. Bashfulness had never been a measured emotion in this suite, at least when the Marshall-Broadhearsts were in residence.

Climax was achieved before long, marked by the deep moan betokening it. Creamy jism overflowed ready taste buds, seeping onto the ebony skin underneath. All of which was assiduously tongue-scoured. Jake was like that... Not much remained and the boys stirred from positions held during the erotic episode, slipping satedly into the shower area where they cleaned up for the coming road trip.

The anticipation of the cross-country drive was bittersweet, for while the couple enjoyed traveling together almost as much as their best men, Jeremy and Luke, loss of the honeymoon intimacy was palpable. On another level, Cal was excited about spending the coming months in his hometown. Contrastingly, Jake was trepidated by the prospect of so many new family members with whom to acquaint. And hopefully befriend.

Breaking fast with Broderick and Andre, conversation dwelt on upcoming plans for all four. The major domo and chef, extended family to the boys, were always on paid contingency when the couple were not in residence. Private plots were already conceived and hatching.

By half past eight, the boys had been packed up, escorted to the touring Benz in which they traveled and wished well until they should again return to their Roaring Fork River Valley home.

* * *

"Cal, it's down to 30. What do you think?" I was monitoring the console as it continued to portray the four tires' present condition. The warning picture had flicked on two hours before, alerting us to an aberration in the right rear. Detection of a slow leak had been noted, and since then the pressure had decreased by 5 psi. Enough to worry. I felt that the stop by the side of the road after lunch may have been the onset for the problem. Wanting the guidance system programmed for the trip, I had forgotten it had to be done while the transmission was in park position. GPS coordinates couldn't be pinpointed in a moving vehicle. Exiting the interstate and pulling to the gravel shoulder, perhaps the tire had picked up a nail or something.

"Well, Mr. Driver Maestro, we aren't in danger of going flat at that rate, so why don't we shoot for stopping at…skimming the digital console map…here—Atoka, Oklahoma. It's about 30 miles further. Should be no problem. We'll stop at a gas station and see if we can get it looked to. You good, baby?"

My man was always conscious of my moods; the concern therefore concerned him as well. He stretched his long legs out, subconsciously rubbing over his package in the doing. I followed his fingers out of the corner of my eye and he picked up on it. "Eyes on the road, Horndog Sally. If you need some of this, there'll be time for it when we stop," he grinned at me as I licked my lips. We were both highly libidinous and fed off one another on multiple occasions almost every day. Traveling provided obstacles, but nothing unmanageable. And, there was the novelty factor. I could wait…that is, if he stopped with the rubbing.

Visualizing a nice blowjob in a roadside bathroom, or the like, I put my hand over on top of his to either stop his action or help him out, unsure which.

The smoothness of the ride was not adversely affected by the tire, only the responsiveness. The miles sped by as we maintained attention via NPR and Monster/UltraBlue energy drinks. Twenty minutes later found us passing the billboard announcing, "Welcome to Atoka, Oklahoma". Below that, a caption boasting 'Player Piano Capitol of the World' let us know of the excitement we were in for.

"Jacob, there--- on the right just ahead--- one of those mega truck stops." I loved when he got all formal with my name. It meant he was horny. "Hmm, 'Love's Travel Stops'--- I think I'm liking this place already. Think there'll be any service?" The hand was back on the crotch.

Snickering at his own incredible wit, we pulled in. Finding a parking spot close to a sign marked for autos, vs eighteen-wheelers, we exited to look around. Several covered bays were lined up far to the side of the main building and we entered an office adjoining them. The area seemed deserted so we peeked through a side door to the first bay area, nearly knocking into a coveralled figure bent over an open-hooded SUV. The gender was obvious as he wasn't wearing a shirt under the coveralls and the shapely pectorals extended nicely into lithe arms busily unscrewing something unseen deep inside. The door barely swiped the slim rear end but the unscrewing halted. The torso raised up from under the hood and a bushy-headed man popped up in reaction. A quick smile assured us we hadn't pissed him off and Cal introduced us, requesting someone who might service the gradually deflating tire.

"Well, sho'nuf, folks," sizing the two of us up, "we can do that. Didn't LaShondra get you helped out in there?" The man appeared to be late twenties or early thirties, and his friendly manner evinced a convivial personality.

"Nope, no one inside," Cal responded, "want us to go back in and look again?" I could see he would rather not.

"Oh, it be a'ight, men, she probly's on break. And everyone else be off today, 'counta the piani festival. Whatya' see is whatya' get, I s'pose... Ain't no biggie, I kin help ya'll. Gimme a minute to finish screwin' this nut and I'll do ya'll two," totally oblivious to his double entendre. Now grinning ourselves, we watched the solidly built man then adjust the free-ranging, sizeable bulge beneath the coveralls. The action caused a second thought about the obliviousness...

We backed off while he turned and leaned back into the engine. Unsure if we should wait there or go inside the office, the voice from under the hood read our minds and instructed, "Just hang there a fas' minute, gents, I be 'bout ready to service ya'll. You said it was just that blown tire, now, co-rect?" The air suddenly wreaked of innuendo and we looked at each other in puzzlement, but did as told, checking out the firm globes, covered but imaginable, within feet of us.

Cal pantomimed a lewd hand action over and around the roundness poking up at us, licking lips in lascivious exaggeration. I couldn't help busting out at his typical over-sexed, demonstrative nature but laughed even louder as the cheeks suddenly backed into the hands, causing contact. The man-of-color arose again, more slowly, not pulling away from Cal's touch. Cal didn't break contact either.

Turning once more, he eyed my man in a way that left me wondering whether Cal was about to be clobbered or fondled. Just a fraction of a second provided answer to that as he glanced around the bay, then right back at us. His fingers went up to the clasp on the coveralls, unhooking it. With a fluid motion the entirety of the mechanic's wardrobe fell to his ankles. He grinned back as we took in a rapidly rising thick dick, pendulous balls weighing the big thing down as it engorged to almost the size of my husband's. The man seemed justifiably proud of the organ. His own lip-licking ensued and the more-than-ready auto worker gestured for one of us to feel free to 'kick the tires'.

Both of us went into action simultaneously. Me to my knees and Cal handling the high round butt of dark-skinned hue similar to his own. My lips clamped hungrily on a fatly swollen head that needed attention. I could tell this by the pearling of precum which smeared my tongue almost immediately. I swallowed the pungently odoriferous whopper all the way to the kinkiness at the base, enjoying the feeling of my throat filling up with guest dick.

The dick conspicuously agreed, swelling even more. I heard the two men above me intimately discussing the work I was doing, a few expletives lacing very imaginative descriptions of my method. Interlaced with sucking sounds that complemented the words, I knew the two were tongue-tying it up there and my own piece wiggled its way out the front of my shorts. I lubed up with the excess saliva sliming the thick shaft. Cal's honker dick bounced off my head a couple times forcing me to alternate my mouth action. I never liked disappointing available black dick meat.

Next thing I knew Cal's big hands grasped my buttcheeks, prodding them upward. The intent was for double-dipping. Damn, I thought, this rest stop was better by the minute. Dropping my shorts and spreading my legs for easier access, my man slicked the tens and slid up me with practiced ease, hilting me to the delectable eggs underpinning the snake. All this time, both men remained lip-locked and I set into a rhythmic pattern swallowing the new friend with whom I was familiarizing.

The low-hangers took to caroming off my chin with each opposing thrust and the three of us made some music right there in the light o' day… dead center of Atoka, Oklahoma's Love Stop. I don't think any of the three of us came up for air once during the next minutes. Right up to when the un-named service-center worker grumbled out a throaty message signaling the eruption that hit my tonsils. That sent both Cal and me over and three loads emptied close together--- two unseen and my own splotching the cement floor. We came down gradually, savoring some male-on-male togetherness. Then the two studs backed out their dripping pieces from me, checking the handiwork as they did so.

"Umm, umm, Ummmm, umm, umm…" was about the whole of the intellectual banter voiced between us as we looked again at reality. The working man was audible in his illustrative acknowledgment of a job well done. He grabbed a hand towel from the floored coveralls, using it to thoughtfully wipe my mouth of excess sperminess and followed by efficiently cleaning the rest of our soiled selves. This dude was proficient, I noted.

As if to punctuate the scene, he slapped my just-poled butt and spoke. "Now, men, did I hear there was somethin' deflatin' around here somewheres?" Cal had pulled himself back into clothing by now. He then reached down to the floored shoulder-strap of the big-dicked male and pulled the coveralls up in a clean motion that put him back in business, just like that. The two watched me dress more slowly, enjoying the ravished anatomy.

"Be just a short'n, travelers, and we'll have you back to rollin'," the friendly man absent-mindedly informed us. Cal tousled my head and we made our way over to the restaurant across the parking lot for a snack. I could feel dark eyes boring my backside as we walked and enjoyed the unstated compliment. But wondered if the escaping baby-juice was staining my pants.

Sure enough, a half hour was all it took before we were back in the office to settle the bill and get on the road. LaShondra was still nowhere to be seen and the mechanic conspiratorially confided to us she was shacked up in an eighteen-wheeler over across the way in the truck bays.

"No doubt two-steppin' dat boot", he said, in his inventive mid-western vernacular. I asked to reconcile with him on the repair work and the bush of hair topping his head jostled back and forth as he laughed that he was surprised I wasn't charging him. The work balanced out, he told us. So after a bit more butt-slapping and well-wishing, we parted, leaving the man to his own devices.

In the car, Cal stared over at me, "Damn, Jake, what the hell just happened, my curly man?" We laughed through the re-hashing of the unexpected scene in the 'Player Piano Capitol of the World'. Click and Clack waxed eloquent on NPR, entertainingly advising how to fix callers' cars, and their lives, via radio…we could have advised the brothers on a few things.

Over three leisurely days we wandered our way eastward toward Cal's childhood home. Dinner in Edmond, Oklahoma, with friends; brunch in Eureka Springs with others. Finally, detouring to purposely cross the Edmund Pettus Bridge in Selma, Alabama, we found ourselves on the homestretch toward Rome, Georgia. Staying the last night in Tuskegee National Forest to regroup so as to knock on Cal's family homestead before the next noon, we visited Booker T's and George Washington Carver's gravesites, then toured the famous Airmen citadel. The day concluded by our settling in for dinner at the hotel restaurant found there.

The old Tuskegee Institute campus diminished in our rearview mirror by dawn the following morning. Cal filled me in on some family history and detail, coloring it all with a few interesting stories, in preparation for truly meeting the family into which I was now officially married. On their turf, that is. Having met several members already, though in other cities or when they had visited us in Austin, this would be a test for us both. We wanted to make a good impression in our newly wedded state-of-being.

NPR's World News Round-up announced eleven in the morning at the time the big S-550 touring sedan edged into the ancient oak-lined, pebbled entry lane leading up to the old antebellum country home on the Coosa River. Cal's quiet intake of breath let me know of his gratification for the view as we rolled toward the well-maintained home place, memories no doubt flooding his mind.

We envisioned a buxom and beautifully lean woman with short, spiked hair standing on the spacious, honeysuckle vine shrouded terrace. Sophie, Cal's little sister, called over her shoulder as she waved to us. As we pulled closer, several more people exited the door to stand with her in a welcoming familial gesture. It warmed our hearts. The reception informed us of at least a modicum of acceptance. As a same-sex interracial couple in a state known for its poor track record at acceptance of non-conformity, it spoke volumes.

The sleek automobile purred to a halt before the waving, smiling group, growing in numbers as we got out. No sentiment of distaste hit us as Cal came around to my side. He grasped my waist and pulled me close in presentation to the throng. I was supremely embarrassed to color over in full blush as the introductions were made. Unintentionally, I had set in motion a 'family memory' for the future by the involuntary flushing effect. The brothers and sisters latched on to the quaintly Anglo-oriented proclivity, identifying me as a non-threatening innocent by the reaction. In a family filled with nicknames, I was branded 'Red Hot' on the spot.

Their answers to unspoken questions as to what sort of person I was had been put to rest without much doubt. The physiological weakness proved endearing to the very people I hoped to win over like nothing I could have ever voiced. As the realization struck and Cal leaned into me, arm around my shoulder, we all entered the big old front entry chitchatting easily--- this was much better than I could have ever hoped.

Sophie, Cal's only blood sister, who had initially awaited us on the veranda, buddied up to me in a sisterly manner, nonchalantly filling me in on the day's planned events now that the eldest brother and prodigal son had arrived home. With his husband. Her easy personality and ready smile took me under her wing as she drew me toward the kitchen, proceeding to find out about me and my story without any inkling of the 'interrogation' I had feared. Nephews and nieces, brothers and cousins wandered in and out while two sisters-in-law included me in conversation over preparations for the soul food feast obviously in the making.

Even so, I was overwhelmed at the hubbub. Way too many new names and personas deluged my senses. It all left me in need of Cal's familiarity but my man was somewhere else in the big old home, himself inundated by the sheer volume of attention.

Sophie and a precocious five-year-old niece sat me down in the kitchen nook, continuing a comfortable banter meant to include. I was disarmed by the effort and gladly accepted a glass of mint iced tea. Sitting back to a wall, I gathered my wits. The activity hummed around me. Grasping the inclusion attempt by a number of family members, I gradually loosened up a bit, settling in to more listening than talking. Very beholden to them for a reprieve on the curious questions, nice though they were. Absorbing the cacophonous camaraderie pervading the homey kitchen, I quietly dissembled while sipping my tea. What a beautiful family. I was ready, I told myself, for whatever came along now.

* * *

Within seconds of hearing the latch lock into place on the plywood door, the mound jumbling the inside of the sweatpants nonchalantly positioned itself within eyesight of the 6-inch oblong cutout joining my stall to the next one. Darkly veined hands fingered the rope tie at the waist and with faked patience untied the loose knot, allowing them to drop silently to the floor over the worn, sockless and laceless cross-trainers. No clothing was visible on the darkly smooth stomach above the sexy bellybutton.

A frayed jock only partially tamed the s-shaped black snake within. Rid of pants, the long meat willed its way tentatively toward the hole, the same fingers further liberating the leg lizard from its frazzled confines into a supple, growing organ. Curlicues of pubic cover and smooth low-hangers of hefty size filled the view through the hole in the wall as I considered my dilemma.

I silently grinned in contemplation of the problem 'unfolding' before me. Here I was, on my knees, padded by shorts and drawers. My limber white dick dangled at half-mast between my thighs, popper bottle within hand's reach. A fat black dick swung free through the cutout hole, inching higher in progressive engorgement, evidently eager for some good head. And yet, I hesitated tapping the over-sized uncut cobra barely four inches from my lips…

…The same lips that had partaken of the fragrant herb so frowned upon by much of society only an hour before when a new brother-in-law had tempted me while out collecting my wits from the familial onslaught occurring inside the house. I was claiming a short respite on the back veranda when Coy had appeared, sauntering toward me out of the wooded depths of the shaded backyard bordering the riverside. He was sucking lazily on a fat blunt.

The dark-skinned beefcake eyeballed me smugly and asked if I were just a little bit freaked by the token white boy status I presently held amongst the gathering family. That made me laugh, but he persisted, letting me know that maybe I could understand the feeling black folk commonly dealt with in the lily-white world they navigated. Food for thought, for sure. Then, he proposed to increase my paranoia level by offering me a hit...

Really, now, what's a man gonna do? I took the blunt and inhaled deeply of the smooth creeper weed, of course. We chatted amiably, sharing several tokes as my nerves calmed over the ensuing minutes. Coy's laid back manner indicated prior achievement of his desired mental state: basically blitzed.

Breaking our quiet reverie, the door opened suddenly and we were busted by Sophie who burst out on us calling her brother's name, in search. Startled, we exhaled the guilty evidence directly at her, my discomfort on distinct display by another abrupt flushing.

She surveyed the scene, asking, "Well, now, what you two cute stuffs doin' out here?" Kindly opting to defray my visible angst, she smiled knowingly as my cheeks burned. Then she further endeared herself to me, signaling to pass her the doobie. By taking a hit with us, she let me off the hook. It worked. This woman was smart, sassy and obviously intuitive.

My new favorite lady reminded Coy of the need for a run to the grocery store in town before the soul food barbeque later in the evening, instructing him to, "take this here boy along, too, so your stoned selves both make it back home OK." Sealing my gratitude, she winked at me, flirtatiously stuffing a paper into my shirt pocket, adding, "Here's the list." And with that, she disappeared back into the house.

Finding ourselves on the road into town a little later, Coy told me he had to stop in the bank for a few minutes, could I get the list? No problem, that. I stonedly floated from the car toward the grocery store as he turned in the other direction. Breaking the age-old rule of 'no grocery shopping while high', I wandered every single aisle of the store gathering the items listed, plus some... twice.

In high focus, I collected the filled bags to the trunk and settled inside the car to await Coy's return from his bank errand. And waited... and waited... and waited for the no-show Coy. After half an hour, my mind was wandering. I picked up on a darkly shaded alley to the side of the store not noticed up to then. Had I been in the city, I never would have done so but here in the sticks my sozzled curiosity bested me and I stepped out of the car.

Following through it to the back corner, I turned at the rear alleyway and spied an untamed bush-shrouded door with the sign above it weakly blinking the announcement, "VIDEO ARCADE". Wow, I thought, Mecca for the horndog world invades Smalltown, USA. A few not-quite-guilt-tinged minutes later found myself unsealing the fresh popper bottle and choosing a skin-flick video in the small cubicle locked by a slide latch. The scene was now set for the previous 'problem' sexily rising before me...

...The underground hip-hop music fixed a sexual pulse throughout the seedy arcade as I kneeled before the glory hole, nasty lyrics suggesting my next move. I debated my instinct to do what I wanted to do: suck the pretty dick through the hole. Slurping sounds close by alerted me to the fact that the dick sucker in the booth on my other side was tripping on a fat piece which had no doubt locked itself into the adjoining cubicle for just such a purpose...damn.

I could hear the raspy, falsetto voice of the tranny two stalls down as she begged the long, hard, corn-holing cock to, "Nooo... please, Daddy, oh noo, please, Daddy, don't do that, it's too big... oh, please Daddy, Daddy, oh, please, please don't--- I can't take all that big dick, Daddy...ohhh, please Daddy, please...ohhh...ohhh... ...ooohhhhh...Yesss, Daddy, fuck that pussy, Daddy...give me that big cock...Slam me with that, Daddy, ooooh go, Daddy," in the worn refrain performed one more time...double damn.

What the hell, I thought? Where was I, anyway? And what was this pretty piece doin' here in front of me? It sure seemed to be under no illusions as the beckoning head reached an arching fullness, teasing me. This encounter must be preordained, I rationalized. By that fully twisted logic, I succumbed to the subliminal aura of the sex-infused atmosphere, greedily sliding that big, fat pre-cumming brother-in-law dick all the way past my tonsils. And there I sat, skewered and motionless, absorbing my big, fat indulgence for as long as I could.

Finally needing to breathe, I backed off the handsome prick, exhaling as the thing cleared out of my throat until just the delicious spongy head remained between my lips. Looking down my nose at the long black shaft, I took the time to uncap the popper bottle and inhaled to boost my efforts. I teethed a bit on the head of this hot man's straight out 9-1/2 inches of uncut dick as the rush enveloped me, then curved it back down my ready throat as Coy pressed from the opposite side. Hearing him audibly hit on his own jungle juice bottle, I spit the big thing with saliva and settled into a long, deep, in-and-out motion, sliding to the rhythm of the nasty music. Damn good dick.

I have always loved how my tongue feels when smoothly enwrapping the elastic swelling on the underside of hard dicks. Repeatedly following this one's swollen undertube all the way down the length from the helmet head to the kinky pubic pad and smooth balls, I gradually worked the foreskin back with each stroke, liberating the pliant, rubbery softness of the curves on that extremely suckable crown.

Freed from the overhanging skin and ten times more sensitive, I squeezed it hard between my lips and he shuddered. With each smooth swallowing stroke, I kept pulsing that squeeze. His knees buckled, nearly giving out. Boy, I got off on that feeling. Talk about the driver's seat…my mouth was the stick shift.

He attempted to keep the entire length deeply seated, grinding his pubes as far through the separating wall hole as possible. I lightly bit down on the root while flattening the corona against the back of my throat at the same time, answering his pushes. My hard dick sproinged up and down in unison. Both of us tremored to the pleasure of this action and I lost track of everything but the ongoing connection between us. He could feel how much I was lovin' the dick and began reminding me of it... "ya' cocksucking bitch."

The filthy synthesized music playing in the background kept the action on beat as we zoned with it. His pelvic gyrations matched my sucking. Encouraging mouth-only contact with his cock, the boy demanded me to reach through to finger the asshole. Good idea, I agreed.

My slippery fingertips stroked and probed and slid from the wavy pucker of that manly asshole over the elastic swelling between it and the stud's scrotum in time with my mouth motions. I fondled private contours and G-spots as I cupped those pendulous nuts, rolling them between my thumb and fingers. The added attention all over the area enhanced the thrill. His low moans couldn't lie.

Uncounted minutes took us both slowly up that stairway to the breath-holding moment when dicks ooze that first glob of creamy cum and then rocket out four or five jets of sizzling, gooey jism. We both did that.

I swallowed most of his, the rest overflowed down my chest; mine splattered the wall. The downhill edge of ecstasy extended 'for-fucking-ever' as we lingered over slow, teasing strokes punctuated by jolts of bolting energy in that joined state, neither desiring it to stop.

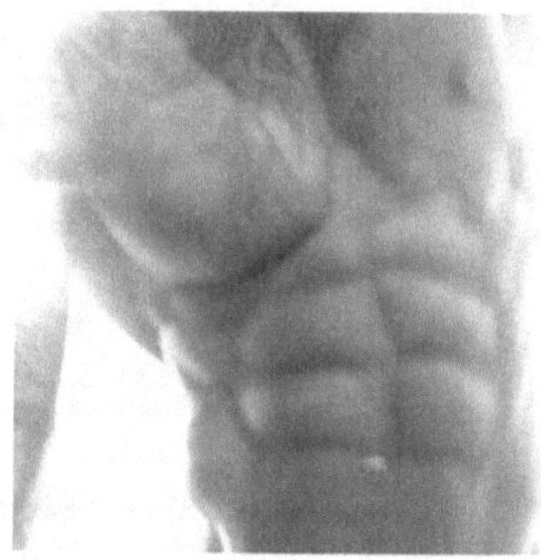

Letting him finally pull back and loose, I peered upward through the good-sized hole, catching the streaming picture of his sculpted cocoa body from that sperm-dripping, quivering cock up to the ribbed stomach, on up over those firmly nippled pecs to the hangdog smile smirking down at me. Eye-to-eye.

At that moment, it dawned on me this boy just knew he had me cornered. After all, from his viewpoint, how could I possibly have known who was attached to the succulent dick I had just made cum? Like a low-down cheatin' slut...sucking anonymous dick.

What a stonehenge. Did he think I hadn't seen his sweat-pants?

Coy embodied the personification of a horny devil. Tall, athletic and adorable-- a sensual satyr. The mischievous stance with fingers coated by sticky webbings of his own leftover cum in need of wiping, the brother projected cocky certainty of his new control over me.

The over-confidence persisted as he commented lewdly on my oral and lingual skills. Mistakenly, he as much as admitted premeditation of our present scenario. From the sharing of the joint to the opportune reminder from his sis of the store run, to his 'bank errand' and no-show appearance at the car. The objective had been clear. To him, at least. Little did this country boy know that he was out of his league.

He next affected a remorseful visage, informing me in no uncertain terms that he, "wouldn't be able to lie to Cal about what had just happened...unless...," and here he hedged his bet: he seemed to be mentally tallying my indebtedness, calculating what he might be able to extract from me. A complete crock, I reflected.

My wholehearted and immediate agreement about not lying left him totally flummoxed. "Just not sure when to tell him," I assured this Lothario. Reminding him that he may not be aware of the fact that though I may have felt some ambivalence for our unusual hook up, I certainly harbored no guilt over the job well done. On the contrary, I had enjoyed it immensely. As, I added, had he…

This unusual tack monkey-wrenched his whole plan. It was not a strategy heretofore encountered. Coy's modus operandus had always been successful domination over his five brothers' extracurricular sex partners by first luring the unsuspecting prey then threatening to 'out' them. Pretty cheesy, the tactic would not do in this instance. As he was now realizing. The boy just wasn't yet familiar enough with either his twin or me.

Before tying the knot, Cal and I had been lovers for more than eight years. We'd been 'out of our closet' for all that time, and open to side thrills from the outset. By mutual agreement. No, that just would not do here...Coy was on a learning curve.

I let Coy down gently by telling him that while I was uncertain which of us had experienced more pleasure by this bookstore blowjob, we could probably agree that rarely had bonding between new brothers-in-law begun better… I would be glad to provide him with more good head whenever he might choose. And, Cal would get off on watching. Win-win.

On the ride back to the house we were bombarded by the heavy scent of cum and poppers saturating us and our clothes. We blithely deluded ourselves that the problem would be improved upon by lighting another skiff. Not really, but we enjoyed smoking it anyway. Opening paper towels and some Febreze, I attempted to at least reduce the odors. Confidence in my man's even-tempered reaction was one thing but I certainly didn't want anyone else guessing our lascivious deeds.

Be warned, Febreze does not substitute well for Handiwipes or disinfectant. Or good old soap and water. Nevertheless, upon darkening the farmhouse door, the two of us managed to pull off a studied innocence worthy of Pope Frank himself.

I told Cal all of the hot details after the inaugural family dinner over sex-in-the-dark. He came three times, while Coy whacked his big piece, listening from the next room.

Meeting the family, indeed…

Chapter 4
Tride and True: Mighty
Diamond Beat Down

Jeremy meticulously tongued the remnants of cum from the slowly subsiding arched, white, big- headed dick still quivering in the afterglow of the morning blow job to which I commonly enjoyed awakening. "I think I'll hike down to get groceries," he garbled, "that pasta recipe I mooched from Andre when we were in Aspen has been on my mind and it sounds good for the dinner party tonight. OK by you, BaddDick?" He lightly bit my shaft for punctuation of his query. Both of my heads popped up at the nip and I winked an eye open to signal my agreement, verbalization beyond me what with the wrong head still in control of my mental faculties.

The sex maniac that was my husband smeared the cum from his own piece to his fingers and watched me eye his deliberate action, wiping my smooth stomach with his slippery hand as he sensuously raised it to his lips. A lop-sided grin wordlessly expressed, "Oh, shucks, I couldn't resist." Then, he licked them clean, one at a time, for my benefit. His nine-inch party-sized prick was just barely receding into the sexy cowl of foreskin following his own eruption. The taste of cum hitting his taste buds always sent him over the edge. His distended dickhead was still peering familiarly up at me in its cyclopean manner, conceitedly admitting to satisfaction at again succeeding in its preferred mission of pumping out babies...the good news was that I had no uterus.

After a minute I spoke a reply while absentmindedly rubbing his beautiful bald head, "I have to go over into town for a few things so let's meet for lunch on the deck, if that works," receiving a nod in response. We basked awhile longer together, enjoying the sunbeams dappling us through Apollo's dawn appearance. "Oh, J, don't forget to ask Adolpho if that '07 Spanish Reserve has come in yet while you are there—y'know how much Sheila enjoys that vintage."

Rolling out of bed, we donned running gear, roused the pooches and invigorated ourselves by immersion into a chill morning 10K running loop around the lodge. The presence of the grazing elk by the pond next to our home signaled us that the bear residents were elsewhere this morning and the way was safely clear. An hour later, showered and coffee'd, we headed down our mountain trail to the piazza that centered Mountain Village. Jeremy turned and tongued me adios, then headed toward the grocery co-op with the mutt brothers in tow for company. I split off to the public gondola connecting our side of Telluride Mountain to town.

Reaching the gondola station in a few minutes, I hopped on a circling car along with old Mr. and Mrs. Chastain who were heading my direction. We conversed cordially as the glass capsule rose smoothly over the village on the constantly circling chain track. The couple were long-time residents since the ski craze days of Tride's revival during the mid-latter twentieth century. They had epitomized the Sexual Revolution of the 1970's, living together in 'sin' for sixty-five years before finally surprising the township by a secret trip to the alter one crisp autumn morning several years before.

Claiming high-altitude sickness complicated by senility, the two had confronted their oncoming mortality, deciding to solemnize their love affair for financial security reasons. They now puttered between the two mountain communities as locally celebrated leftovers from the Love Child generation. Everybody cherished the eccentric nonagenarians. The two had latched on to Jeremy and me soon after our settlement on the mountainside six years before. Marveling at our 'new-gen gay jungle fever status', the two completely ignored the fact that we had been a couple for more than a decade prior to adopting Telluride town (aka: Tride) for our second home. We loved them the more by the fact.

As we peaked the summit and began the descent to the town proper, the old hippies told me of their intent to stock up at the green cross emporium, the newest marijuana shop in town. I smiled at the thought of the two floating in a dazed geriatric haze back over to their rock home close by ours. Drifting mountain breezes commonly carried evidence of their partaking to the neighbors surrounding them. They serenaded us with the sounds of Bob Dylan, Jefferson Airplane, Arlo Guthrie, Joan Baez, Janis Joplin and other music icons from the era. We thereby grew to value the lost tunes from the heyday of their youth. The indigenous elk and moose populations took particular note of the music, showing themselves commonly during these mountain concerts…but, then, maybe it was just the smoke that drew them.

Landing on the square of Telluride town, we strolled the few blocks together to the sign of the green cross announcing all such stores in the state of Colorado. Leaving the two at the front door of the 'apothecary' as they called it, they extracted a promise to stop back by after my errands so they could introduce me to a new addition on the menu in the place. "We simply love the vibe of it," old Mr. Bart assured me.

The mid-morning bustle of the thriving township always startled me after the quietude of Mountain Village. I weaved a way through tourists and locals on my itinerary for the morning, smiling the whole while as I contemplated the future with my man through the eyes of the older couple I had just left. I hoped to arrive at their place of being in similar devotion to one another. Aging seemed much less a battle if the road was shared with a kindred spirit, as the Chastains certainly proved.

Engrossed in such thoughts, I stopped in Overland to gather the new sheepskin pillows and rug ordered a couple weeks back, hit the pharmacy for items on my list, then made my way up Colorado Avenue toward the old refurbished Opera House to pick up tickets for the Mighty Diamonds reggae concert scheduled for the coming weekend. I had reserved two tickets for Jeremy's birthday evening. He delighted in the music genre amidst which he had grown up. My plan was to surprise him with them after the dinner I had planned. Turning in at the side door to the box office, I smacked flat out into a tall, Marley-esque dreadheaded man just exiting. The deep-voiced Rastafarian raised two humongous hands in surprise and regret for his miscue while I excused my own self to him for not paying closer attention.

We backed off from one another, each appraising a new entity heretofore unexperienced, and my eyes surveyed the unusual figure before me. The man stood several inches more than six and a half feet tall, with long limbs clad in black, green, yellow and red clothing and a dangling feather earring of sculpted silver. His definitive Dreadlocks hung thickly tangled to his midriff. Though arrayed neck to ankles in the colorful loose-fitting hemp clothing, his litheness showed through in obviously magnificent proportion, especially for an older man.

The baggy, low-hanging drawstring pants were quite plainly the only material covering him from a narrow waist downward to his sandaled feet, as evidenced by the long silhouetted shape of a very fleshy endowment stretching halfway to the level of his knees. His blackness was ebony-personified and the singsong lilt of his sotto voice hypnotized as he excused himself. It did not escape my notice that his deep black eyes also took stock of my person in return.

Jeremy would be absolutely infatuated by this iconic throwback to his childhood, I surmised, and I asked the giant if he might be involved with the band for whom I was presently procuring admission. His immediate wide and easy smile informed me it was so and I expressed my good luck at meeting someone associated with the esteemed group which pre-dated Bob Marley's Wailers. I had hit a nerve with him. The man beamed at my acknowledgement.

True to Jamaican mannerisms, he reached out that amazingly large hand and placed it square on my chest, letting the outstretched fingers slowly slide down my shirt in recognition of the compliment…my junk lurched at the unexpected familiarity. Again, his eyes noticed. We each promised to look for the other at the concert and I joked that I would try to focus through the smoky haze habitually encountered among reggae audiences. We parted congenially and I hurried inside to secure the tickets as if by delay they might vaporize.

Packing the front row tickets into my wallet, I emerged from the opera house to the brightness of the mountain morning and immediately soaked in the permeating scent of primo pot. Unable to not follow my nose, I turned the back corner of the beautifully restored 19th century brick building and found the Rasta Man lounging on the park bench in the small public garden meant for intermissions during concerts. He was spread-legged and reclining, the fleshy silhouette unmistakably pressing against the airy cloth. It apparently expected me. His smile broadened in an instant and he beckoned me over.

The bags crinkled under arms and my free-hanging piece smiled in its own right, snaking down one pant leg as I approached. Not sure what could possibly occur in the public spot, I enjoyed the chafing of it against the denim of my jeans. Reaching him, he extended a lanky arm. Long fingers clutched a fat blunt and offered to share. Thankful for Colorado's liberal laws enacted the year before, I took it and sat down next to him on the bench, inhaling a filling toke of sweetness. No words passed between us for the moment, hormones relieving vocal necessity. I watched as the hemp-covered silhouette spoke volumes. We communed in silence while passing the burning fagot back and forth, both of us grinning in keenness of something beyond consummation at this time and place.

Highlighting our comprehension of the point, a trio of pre-teens and a mom rounded the corner at that moment. The pretty blond mother cast a disapproving glance at us almost immediately. Lawfulness was one thing, but social acceptance proved quite another. We decided to vacate our bench, quenching the blunt on a wooden slat. Our legs reluctantly closed as we tacitly arose and meandered our semi- hardened selves away from the group toward the street behind us.

Finding our way to the less traveled residential street in back of the opera house, I broke the silence by asking if he might like to accompany me to the emporium a few blocks distant—remembering the earlier promise to the Chastains. My acquaintance nodded his acquiescence, then grasped my hand in introducing himself, "Ambergai Gee, IV, at your service, Mon."

I repeated the name, captivated by the poetic musicality of it and responded with my own, "Lucas Cevennes, at yours as well…Mon." The mimicry elicited a deep chortle of a laugh. He stretched one big hand down, nudging the proud outline, thus defining for me the specific service in mind. Actually, both of our minds. He was not the least embarrassed by the noticeable turgidity. In contrast, I worked to abashedly poke my own responding tumescence to the side and under a sacked pillow.

He didn't miss my discomfiture and drawled wryly, "If ya' be gottin' it…an' by ma' lookin', ya' do…then ya' wanna be flauntin' it, not hidin' it, now, Lucas Mon." For the first time.

Not quite there yet, I again acknowledged his laid back state of mind, yet still hoped for a bit of diminishment before arrival at the sign of the green cross. My Islander roots were only an in-law thing, Jeremy being the one manifesting a similar comfort in his sexuality. While charmed by the candidness, I was unable to proclaim it. Mr. Ambergai Gee acceded to my modesty in gentlemanly fashion and kept pace with me as I guided us to our destination over the next minutes.

Entering the lamp-lit coziness of the emporium, I spied the mature couple in the far corner by a window, lounging next to the fireplace in a couple of easy chairs. They, the other patrons and especially the staff, perked up at our appearance, all clearly beguiled by my companion's persona. The Islander stooped under the doorway upon entering, metaphorically budding into his fullness of character, dreadlocks swaying to the reggae song playing in the background.

Old Bartholomew Chastain motioned us to adjoining armchairs and accepted my introduction of Ambergai Gee with practiced aplomb, elegantly introducing themselves in an old-world fashion that impressed the Jamaican. My friends and new acquaintance took immediate liking to one another, Annalise Chastain fairly purring at him in her San Franciscan Haight-Ashbury accent as she rubbed her hands up and down his sinewy arm. Her long, manicured, lavender nails owned him by the action, like a cat owning a new couch with its claws. The 'good vibe' alluded to by the duo earlier turned out to be a subtly refined hashish bud and the delivery by a smokeless contraption referred to as a 'Volcano' augmented the comfortable progression of our conversation.

Ambergais melded effortlessly into it and we mused on the upcoming concert. The Chastains decided they simply must get their own tickets and after a half hour of congenial repartee, excused themselves to do just that, vowing to have the lanky Rastafarian to dinner while he was in the area. Mr. Gee graciously accepted, saying he was actually due to traverse the well-known gondola mode of village transport to 'conduct some business' and also look up an old friend he knew to be in residence on the far side of the mountain. We stood as the bohemian couple took leave of us and then settled back in for a bit more relaxation via the left-over bud.

By this point, I felt a comradeship with the tall man. It almost seemed as if we had known each other from a previous time or place. We visited the sales bar on the far side of the room and purchased some goodies for further recreation later, thereby concluding my to-do list for the morning. After sharing one more house bong bowl, Ambergai decided to travel with me over the mountain. I thought to introduce him to Jeremy if time and circumstances permitted. My man would be as taken with the mysterious songster as I and the Chastains had been.

At the gondola station, the loading staff ogled at the otherworldliness of my travel companion, watching with fascination as the man folded himself fluidly in through the sliding glass doors of the car. A family of visiting tourists tritely backed off entering the communal glass enclosure with us, barely concealing their distaste for the unusual characters exuding the odor of herbal essence as he and I did. We were both relieved at their action and settled on opposing bench seats as the doors slid closed. The rolling ascension up the mountain whisked us higher. Ambergai's long legs necessarily were bent and spread in facing me, knees way higher in the air than my own. His face expressed an unspoken approval of our moving picture that was the mountain and, I hoped, our aloneness.

Hardly had the glass capsule departed but I noted his long fingers slowly kneading the protuberance inhabiting his roomy trousers. I couldn't be sure if it was purposeful or simply absent-minded activity yet the growing tent-like affect left no doubt as to the pleasure it provided him. He became engrossed in the beautiful panorama unfolding around us as we heightened. My captivation matched his but from a totally different perspective. I couldn't yank my eyes from the swelling crotch within a couple feet of me and my plane of mellowness only served to focus my infatuation. Softly questioning me on the surroundings as we rolled along, the Rastafarian at some point noted my attention to his nether region. I suddenly glanced up to his grinning face and piercing black eyes, realizing my totally overt fascination. Busted, I thought.

Reviving the scene aborted earlier behind the opera house, the limber legs gradually inched further apart and the ebony fingers wrapped around the covered pole now arising in stimulation to my almost drooling interest. Next thing I knew, he had pulled loose the binding tie of the hemp slacks, raised his slim hips and in a practiced move, lowered them in a descending swoop all the way to his sexy ankles. The effect was immediate. His humongous black cock bounced out as they slid past his knees and arose like a dragon unfurling its wings, slapping his belly and then settling to hover before me in quavering expectation.

The excessive length of his foreskin rolled back steadily as the full engorgement of the behemoth progressed and a beautiful dark rose-colored dick head fastened on my eyes, demanding what it wanted. Craving was apparent on my face and my piece had again snaked down one jean leg leaving very little to the imagination. Ambergai's free hand reached over and fingered the swelling, never taking his eyes from mine as he instructed, "Lucas ma'Mon, now would be a vera good moment ta' be doin' some flauntin', mi a guessin'," his smile and singsong lilt softening the firm order. In a short second, I unbuttoned, unzipped and removed the binding pants obstructing both legs and other stuff, tossing them to the side along with my shoes. For good measure, I pulled my turtle-neck sweater over my head to complete my bare-ass state and then relocked to his magic eyes as they twinkled with intent.

Caring little if the cars swinging a couple hundred yards in front and behind us could visualize inside ours, I kneed the floor and commenced what I might have done in the small courtyard earlier: licking the enlarged and waiting monster bouncing before me. I took my time slathering the fat shaft with saliva, working my way up then down from corona to scrotum, swirling my tongue around the hugely fat balls as I worked. My face got slimed in the doing as the turgid prick re-peatedly caromed off it and I rose to engulf the head in a slow swallowing of as much as I could fit down to my waiting ton-sils. He obviously got off on my rotating action while impaled on the thing, jabbering quietly in an amazingly sensual aborig-inal dialect of some sort.

His sandaled foot rubbed against my boinging dick and the friction raised my ante way too quickly. Not typically a pre-ejaculator, I nevertheless popped out a quick load all over that attractive black-toed foot. He peered down at the production, "Ya'don't now be a-thinkin' that you're bein' done, now, ma' friend...mi a-sayin', right?" The consternation on his face dis-sipated when I informed him that I was simply warming up and he settled back to allow my ministrations to proceed.

So softly he could be thinking out loud, he rejoined me with the added instruction that should my excellent work cause a load of his own to flood my mouth, I shouldn't be concerned and by no means should I pull off the dick—he enjoyed slow deep-throating action right through to the second spewing— his words, not mine. So I took him at his word.

Sure enough, after a couple of minutes of rhythmic bliss he exhaled roughly with a rumble and, indeed, flooded my oral cavity to overflowing with hot, sweet Jamaican jism. I never changed tempo. The second load scorched my throat minutes after that, causing my trigger to snap by the taste and I thought of Jeremy's similar trait, wondering if there was an infectious factor spreading to me. Then, I swallowed the whole of it as my own load oozed over my hand to the floor. Climax during a pot high is exquisitely heightened--- anyone that doubts it need but try it. The two of us knew the truth of it. First hand.

Ambergai tapped my curly head like he would a bongo as he intoned, "Ya' better be a-gettin' ya'self a mite more presentable ma'good suckin' Mon, Lucas, else there be a few more a-knowin' about how ya'be a-doin' mi so good, now..." punctuating the final word with a light pop to my noggin in alerting me to the proximity of the summit station approach. I whipped my clothes back on just in time to see the large opening into the station pass by me.

I also noticed the slowly deliberate fashion by which my companion's big piece was covered in hemp once again, almost as if he preferred to allow inspection of his jewels as a tease. One of the blond boy station handlers got a nice strobe shot of the root and pubic curls in our passing, his teenage eyes widening by the view of it. Ambergai smirked at me, "Let it be said again that for those who've got the goods, they oughtta be flauntin' it, now, and it's all a-been done before this, ma'Mon." He didn't bother tying the rope belt.

In a few moments we had passed through the station filled with bikers and hikers, among other mountain enthusiasts, and begun our descent toward Mountain Village and home. I straightened myself further and watched as the tall older stud lowered his pants again, letting me know of his need for further plying. In the lowering, he extracted a finely rolled joint and lit up, handing it to me after sucking on it and pointing to the rising stickiness of his Rastafarian prick as encouragement to get going. I gladly slurped that re-hardened thing as he enjoyed the scenery, toking on the joint throughout. Passing commentary and encouragement continued while I kept myself occupied. We landed at the base station in a happy state of highness, mine including another throat full of Caribbean cum, sweet stuff that it was...

Parting at the town piazza, me with my bags and he with his proud piece jouncing satedly in those baggy trousers, we promised to meet up at my place after he had taken care of his business. Jeremy would be enthralled by my morning. I was hoping his had been half as productive.

Upon banging open the heavy wood door with hands full, I waltzed giddily into the chef's kitchen we had updated several years before to find Jeremy pressing out fresh angel hair spinach pasta. Dancing, nude, to the tune Dreamboat Annie, a bottle of Guinness Stout sat close by, half empty. He smiled lasciviously upon my entry and snickered as I emptied my treasures on to the marble island top, paying particular note of the THC-laden gummy bears and similar lollipops procured just a short time earlier.

He grasped my buttcheek and pulled me to him as he 'welcomed me to his lair'. Tonguing me hungrily, he crinkled his nose upon recognizing familiar flavors. "I smell the cum of an Englishman, honey," he teased. I was looking at the wine rack as he did so and immediately honed in on the unchanged state of it, begging the question of where might be the evening's vintage he had been tasked with picking up while at the co-op...? "Ummm, well, the delivery hadn't arrived by the time, umm, I was leaving, and Adolpho--- you know how he is--- just said come back later to get it," he adorably prevaricated.

Knowing of his penchant for purloining sperm from the Latin man's impressive package, I translated that salvo into the fact that it had fled his mind after slipping into the 'receiving area' in the back of the co-op building. 'Receiving', no doubt, actuating the double entendre: Jeremy had given the straight young Italian another mind-blowing head job.

Cheshire cat grin later, he confessed, and pocketing my wallet I headed for the door. Determined to have the particular Spanish red wine for our guests at the upcoming meal in a few hours, I promised to fill him in on my 'mouthwash' story upon returning. Dashing out, I intended to catch the sommelier before he disappeared: a proven post-cum pattern of the free-spirited youth. I had learned the hard way by previous similar experiences. Yet, far from perturbed, I looked forward to chatting the cute boy up while fulfilling my promise to Sheila for the coming evening.

Indeed, my fears were proven justified upon nearing the co-op's rear exit fifteen minutes later, spying Adolpho sneaking out to an early afternoon highland hike, per his habit. I often teased him that he had occupied the body of "Heidi, Girl of the Alps" in a previous life due to the common communing with high mountain meadows. He admitted his weakness with ready good humour.

"Adolpho—wait up," I hollered to the unassuming Adonis. The boy halted, turning to confront the person hindering his escape and hang-dogged at me when he recognized my approach.

"I wondered if you were gonna get by before I split, Luke," he guiltily excused himself. I forgave his transparency as any doting parent does a spoiled kid caught in the act.

"You should've sent it with JK, you brat," I scolded, grinning. He colored immediately, guessing Jeremy had surely told me of the earlier liaison between the two.

He knew me better than to think I would be pissed. My ambivalence to the concept of monogamy was well known. His own penchant for screwing with the fairer sex, who more commonly demanded 'higher standards' and fewer wild hares made him fall into the traditional mien of the 'busted' trademark. Blushing deeply, he unlocked the door and ushered me back inside to the coolness of the bodega where he stored his stocks. The bustle of the fronting groceria hummed beyond the quietness here and Adolpho gave me an endearing hug in thanks for not badgering the subject. Gathering up the six bottles of the gran reserva, as ordered, I patted his bulging crotch conspiratorially, "I know; I know…who can ever resist his mouth?"

At which he colored over a third time and sheepishly admitted, "I think I'd be gay in a second if he wasn't hooked up already...ain't nobody that good anywhere." His wistfulness made me smile again, knowing of my good fortune. I shooed him off with a hand wave to the peaks above, dismissing any need for further discussion. He and I could chat another time. The hills were calling him.

I stopped by the bookstore next door afterwards for a paper then meandered my way up the trail to our place, perusing the news. The dogs, Suture and Elvee, were camped out on the front porch as I approached. Their tails furiously cleaned the smooth wood surface, having sensed my person from a distance. That was curious, I thought, as Jeremy seldom let the boys out without his attendance, enjoying their company as much as me. Entering the door with them, I caught the lyrics to The Cure's Wish CD, from our oldies collection, rhapsodizing through the log house.

The fresh pasta sat heaped and draining in the colander inside the big copper sink, newly prepared pesto mixing aromatically beside it. Fresh snow peas, baby white mushrooms, onions and a trifecta of colorful bell peppers sat draining next them, all neatly cleaned or diced and ready for roasting. Lamb chops and mint leaves for six marinated in the fridge. My man was a chef extraordinaire and I watered at the thought of the dinner to come. Ditching the wine on the rack, I shed clothing piecemeal on my way up the cut log staircase to the upstairs master en-suite, wondering where Jeremy had gotten off to and ready for a nice soaking shower.

I lit a fat blunt from a few nights previous on the way up, still reading an op-ed article. The enjoyable effect of the herb added to my persistent state of highness. At the middle landing I discerned the presence of two voices from the bedroom above, over the music. It slowed my ascent. A distinct and newly familiar sotto rhythm traded sentences with the individual sexiness of Jeremy's. As my eyes assessed the view at the top of the stairs, my dick began a perceptible stirring at the sight of a delectable pair of butt globes arched in front of and accepting the silky, bare Caribbean dick that I had recently practiced on in the gondola.

Of course, I reasoned. Jeremy must be the 'old friend' Ambergai Gee had alluded to at the emporium and he had arrived while I was collecting the vino…oooh, how hot. My eyeballs were scorching; even the wild curls on my head were standing rigidly transfixed. The pair had no idea I was voyeuring and I stripped my drawers off to free my straining, phattening, and fixedly interested cock. Spitting into my palm for slickness, I enjoyed stroking while seeing Jeremy's rarely fucked beautiful asshole suck in the huge thing now ramming him steadily and deeply.

It appeared as if the Jamaican dick had cum once already from the froth surrounding the stretched hole which I could view periodically when the black log showed itself. Had it indeed cum, Ambergai intended to multiply his pleasure if his continued efforts were any indication. The angle couldn't be better and my visual allowed for every single stroke.

With the passing moments, the reggae artist became more vocal. By the comments, he let me in on a chapter which had occurred between the two on the island of their past, expressing nasty descriptions to which I had heretofore not been privy. My man had apparently taken this dread dick regularly and to climax back in his youth. It filled in a history I would never have guessed.

I watched as the two rotated together, ending with Jeremy's back hitting the mattress. Those large dark hands stretched wide the pretty chocolate thighs and calves I knew so well. Ambergai's huge dick never vacated the seldom-used tight asshole in that motion. My topman was certainly enjoying the ably pumping piece judging by the mewling coming from his throat. His pleadings not to stop put me past the point of return and I stroked sperm on the hardwood beneath me. I continued fondling myself as I remembered the blunt, raising it to my lips and inhaling as the action continued.

The Rastafarian somehow sensed my presence and turned his head toward me, "Oooh, ma' J-boy, the plot do seem to have a-thickened here and now, ma'true baby bitch boy— here is the other Mon-half we were a-speakin' about, and mi a-guessin' he is now a'thinkin' ya' are familiar with this here dagger daincin' down in the purty hole it's a'fillin' again afta' so long. Da' vera hole getting a' cabin-stabbin da'way it knows this big Dad likes to be havin' it." He reached for the blunt in my fingers after that rant.

My husband peered up and around the slim waist sprouting the dick he was accepting and literally beamed at me. "Oh man, Luke, this here is happenin'…oooh…. by your own fault. Oooh… This fat- dicked ole' Rasta is hittin' this ass, now… oooh—you shouldn't have oughtta got it goin'… oooh… on its way here—this Jamaican Daddy can…oooh… go for hours doin' just like this. Oooh… I am knowin' all this, baby…oooh, fuck me, big man."

Ambergai reached another audibly dubbed eruption at that moment. He pulled the spitting head out for a split second, verifying to me what he was doing to my stud. I didn't take insult. The two had no doubt determined my response beforehand, as evidenced by their picking of the big rough cedar bed we shared to do this deed. I left for a second to retrieve a pre-rolled doobie from our morning's visit to the 'apothecary'.

Upon returning, I found the two men separated, Jeremy's familiar fat piece resting languorously on that ripped belly which sported creamy gobs in proof of his enjoyment. His strapping legs were now bending down over the bed's edge. The RastaMon was leering my direction and signaled with his besotted eyes that I was next.

His on-point rigidity never wavered, the perfectly proportioned thick and straight dick still suspended like an expanded cobra waiting to strike. By the time we had shared a deep hit each, the two studs had positioned me like we were on a mission and the missionaries were ready to do penance—or maybe I was…I get confused on that. Regardless, two gorgeous black men spent the next hour putting it to me, unloading on and in me until they and I had 'got enough'. Let me just say, it was more than plenty.

Afterwards, our multi-person Rainhead equipped shower saw me practice scrupulously detailed hygiene on the satisfied bodies sharing the marbled enclosure. The luxury was all mine as I rigorously detailed each beautiful mature man's body, methodically scouring, buffing and polishing every muscle, organ and crevice. Jeremy filled me in on the past adolescent and youthful years living on Blue Mountain as he had discovered himself. I learned of him becoming the man who loved me and to whom I was devoted.

Mr. Gee offered contrast, nuance and levity to the descriptive tale. Finally, we toweled off, collectively groomed stray dreadlocks, oiled down glistening bodies and descended to the low beamed great room that centered our log home. I cracked the wine open and picked music for the evening. 'Gai, as Jeremy called him, had agreed to stay for dinner. He readied, then lit the big rock fireplace, and Jeremy worked his magic in the open style adjoining kitchen, watching his mentor across the room.

As Apollo descended and waned, we three sat comfortably on the front porch sharing wine and tokes of our various smokables. The three neighbors and friends joining us for dinner strolled up to our perch. They were welcomed by the sentinel canine denizens and each accepted a first glass of the full bodied red of the evening. Both women and the older gentleman joined our discussion of the Island life, Blue Mountain, Kingston, Jamaica, and reggae in general. We all got to know the most interesting dreadhead be-tangled personage to darken our door and shower in the entire time on this mountain. Jeremy's dinner merited scrumptious delight.

Afterwards, we sat out back around the fire pit watching the full moon rise over the craggy guardian peaks. Three musically-inclined guests pulled out their drums, guitar and jazz flute, and the majestic embodiment of the original Mighty Diamonds added his vocal wares to the welcoming of the autumnal equinox.

Amidst the amazing private performance, Cat G pulled me aside and let me know that her lady, the Ms. Sheila Escovedo, was entirely taken by her fellow Creole-Jamaican's surprise appearance. And, I was assured the gran reserva fulfilled her evening.

Jeremy and I basked in our happiness and luck as the Milky Way blossomed all around us. Suture raised his fat-headed snout to the moon, adding his howling two cents to the overture.

Leaving us in stitches.

Chapter 5
Stick Shift: Fivespeed

Admonishing silence, Cal held his big hand over my mouth as his bent elbow kept my knee raised and trapped. Impaled on my man's 10-inch piece, flat on my back, both legs were up and spread. Toes curled. His other hand sexily prodded my ass ring at the point of that big dick's entry.

His favorite way of getting off, he had always told me. Locked to my eyes, feeling his dick slide in-and-out of my ready hole with his own fingers, climbing that ladder to eruption all in one..manly..motion. Over and over, of course. 'Til it delivered the babies...

Well, who was I to stop that action? My own dick lay hard and squashed between us, rubbed tantalizingly to its own climax just moments before with only morning sweat and now, my own cum, as lube.

Though a mite uneasy, I settled back on the pillow and felt his palm follow as he enforced the order for quiet. "You'll wake everyone in the damn house, my good bitch."

Having just loosed my load, I smothered my misgivings and let him have at it. I could always feel the approach of his explosion by the swelling goin' on in there while it pummeled my channel and by the swelling goin' on, it was gonna be a fruitful one.

It had been sinfully fruitful for me, watching what was happening now as I lightened up and followed my instructions.

The creak of the floor alerted Cal to another presence; the same presence which had witnessed my own gusher and vocal pleasure moments before. He lifted up enough to turn his head and see Boy, that way too curious nephew, screaming silently and grinning ear-to-ear at the view of his favorite uncle laying pipe with his white boy husband.

By reflex, Cal plopped his uncut meat out in surprise, though quite unable to stop the climax he had just achieved. Cum sprayed over both of us, and like a man confronted by a suddenly bursting faucet, he did the only thing one could do-- he plugged the hole to stop it. All the way back into my now excessively-lubed hole. Throbbing pulsations squeezed his perineal muscles and pushed more sperm to the exit point...up me.

"Boy, what in Hell you doin' up in here? Shut the damn door, pissant!" Cal never raised his voice--- not ever--- so the boy wiped the grin away and pushed the door shut as Cal turned back to me. Still inside the room...

Unbeknownst to either of us now, he watched as Cal's cum trickled, squirted and dribbled all over the damn place--- the bed, us, the window behind me and I think in my eye as it began to sting a little. My inner grin matched the thought-to-be-departed Boy's.

Cal didn't bother retracting the appendage now safely, and warmly, hidden back in me, assuming the little interloper had scrammed, but looked down with recriminations covering his face as he asked what the hell was I thinking by not telling him we had company at 5 AM on a Sunday morning?

I licked his palm with my tongue in reply and he backed the hand off my mouth in sudden realization... a sheepish smile flooded the big man's handsome face and we giggled at the look of things.

But that dick didn't move an inch. Except to continue spasming. It felt good. If anything, it occurred to me, it was more engorged upon his awareness.

Boy, silently incognito, stood stock still, mouth now gaping wide open and eyes as big as saucers, locked on one particular spot. Cal's thick piece had oozed its slimy way out of my ass and now bounced lightly on and off my junk. What a visual that must make.

With a start, he came to his untainted senses and turned as red as a dark ebony boy possibly could, yanking the door back open. He then raced out, bumping the door hard against the wall in the doing. Typical Boy: sneak up-->spy-->surprise-->shock-->Oh...shit Retreat! All one flowing emotion. No telling where he would end up.

So much for a quiet, down-low Sunday morning "fuck and re-fuck". What we labeled the early service. I eased loose, rose, and brought a warm wet wash rag to service my man as we laughed about the present innocent peccadillo and re-hashed my previous afternoon's less-innocent grocery run with Cal's twin, Coy.

As I had known would happen, when I relived the scenario with Cal last night in bed he responded with a massive boner, not jealousy. Neither of us embraced that useless emotion. Three successive orgasms filled me as I related the story of how I had encountered Coy's pretty piece at the old video store while he slowly, methodically pumped my bones... and listened. Cal loved my voice and said he could get hard listening to me recite Bible verses. A whole new meaning for getting religion, I guessed, as I conjured the image of Coy...spent and smirking down at me through the glory-hole the day before. Waiting for my reaction to the fact of his own bodily attachment to the dick just 'anonymously' sucked in the smut shop behind the grocery store. He had thought I was unaware. How little he knew me. So I had enlightened him.

Reality had foggily descended as we later made our grocery-laden and cum-bestained way back to the house in the country. Blitzed, but much better acquainted. Desiring to cover our conduct upon arriving back with the cooking list needs, Coy and I had acted just that--coy-- about anything out of the ordinary during our trip.

The womenfolk were chattily bustling when we entered the house. They noticed only the arrival of the necessities. Remarkable how often people see what they want, I reflected. When I declined reimbursement for the goods, wanting to help and belong, they were touched. Saved by the bill...

Over a delectable soul-food dinner, Cal and I had filled everyone in on our lives and doings, absorbing the life experiences of the family in return. We were well aware that our 'elopement' a month before had probably topped anything more possibly jarring to the family's sensibilities following that news. The old downhill slope looked pretty good to us by that yardstick.

Though we had already 'come out' years before, the effect of a new SSM couple in the country haven where Cal had grown up had proven startling to the oldsters, to say the least. Our decision to visit over the summer months had sent the emotional gamut ranging amongst them from chinwag to complacency, yet we felt relieved at coming.

Family members were accustoming themselves to the news at various paces. Coy and Boy in the lead of the acceptance faction, the rest resolving their stances on the matter as they could. Or would. Cal's other brothers had proven variously OK, mute, smart-assed or, in Doy's case, derisive, regarding our nuptials. It had been noticed, however, that the married members: cousins, nephews, nieces, sisters and brothers were, to a person, accepting of the newest couple in the large family group.

A few of the older generation and the single men were a little less so; the kids could care less. The younger generation was very simply electrified to have the presence of their idol, Calumet Alfrederic Blackhearst II, or Uncle Cal, for the present time. Their own local celebrity amongst friends and schoolmates had been secured by the actualized personification.

The family had been gratified and mollified as Big Bro Cal, the gregarious, athletic, successful 'elder' of the younger Blackhearst generation had established himself in the bigger world. Presently controlling a software company encompassing multiple and expanding major metropolitan areas around the country, all had been beneficiaries to his largesse over the recent years.

Now, to have him back amongst them even for a few months made for a more direct coming-to-grips with the 'elephant in the room' issue: his new marriage. By merit of both Cal's and my self-confidence and self-acceptance, tinged by some ingratiating self-deprecation, we made it plain that we were good. What could, or should, anyone say?

What with my unaccepting family ("He is a man, gay... and black?") and the then-unknown reaction from his, we had decided to wed and honeymoon at our high-country hideaway, close to our best men and far from any negativism.

Aspen had welcomed us. The rest of the world could put up or shut up.

* * *

"Are you and Uncle Cal gonna make oreos?" Five-year-old Vivian wanted to know. She had been informed by Boy of our liaison that morning and now couldn't quite figure things out.

"No, honey," I told her, "we are not going to make oreos. I am much too young to be a mother."

Not solving her puzzle in the slightest, the little cutie went on, "If you do, will they be my family, or someone else's?"

"Viv, don't you have enough cousins to keep up with already?"

"Well", she replied sagely, "I just want to be ready in case I have to watch out for them when they come visit."

"Do you think you will have to watch out for them if that happened?"

"Well, Daddy told Mommy that if it happened a long time ago, they woulda been drowned in the creek."

Perplexed, I didn't really have a reply for that, on several different levels, so assured the tyke that should Cal and I have any children they would more than likely be orphans. Who didn't have a home. That was the way people like her uncle and me ofttimes made families, I explained, affording loving homes to unfortunates and strays, thereby fulfilling one of our natural, age-old, village-community roles in helping the world address a societal conundrum.

"But will they be orphan oreos?" Vivian had to know.

"Well, honey, they could be oreos, I guess, but whether they were or not wouldn't make any difference. We wouldn't make a family on that basis. On purpose, anyway."

"So they might be oreos but for sure they will be orphans, right?" The little girl was persistent. Seeing my confused look, "I just need to know what is gonna happen here."

She sounded so adult I couldn't help sniggering.

"Help me out here, Uncle Jake, how 'bout?" Vivian was obviously very serious about this concept but I was just as seriously not the person who was going to discuss birds and bees with this five-year-old girl. My mental picture of her earlier Boy-translated mental picture was already disturbing enough…

"Skunks," I said finally.

"Skunks?"

"Yes", I explained, "we are going to have skunks. They are beautiful, snooty and nobody ever messes with them."

* * *

I remained utterly intrigued by Cal's family's male names. We were all sitting in the family room one Monday evening watching baseball, the brothers all here enjoying the Braves stink up the national television airwaves. Thank goodness for beer and Bob (Marley's ghost). Cal and I were the popular ones, having come stocked from Aspen, where the green cross thrives.

Coy, Doy, Roy, Loy and Voy. All junior to their big bro (Coy was younger by two minutes), two married and three not. All could be mistaken for each other. They were all chips-off-their-Dad's block, the patriarchal head of the family, deceased these past six years.

The senior Cal, or Professor, as he had been more commonly known, and his wife Cassandra, had wanted a distinct but connectible link for their five sons following Cal II, and knew they would have the chance as the family tree was over-populated by males and twins. Very few daughters.

Their solution had been simple enough. It was one they borrowed from Francis Ford Coppola's majordomo. The iconically prolific overseer for Coppola's Belize Maya Mountain retreat for more than three decades. Cassandra and Calumet, Sr., had been close friends over the years.

The man was iconic throughout Belize for the fame of his marijuana production operation. Mr. Marley, himself, had been a common visitor to the estate over the years, among others. Snoop Lion, Sting, Prince, Seal and Heidi, Iggy and Lenny had all frequented the palapa-themed compound. It was even reputed that Anna Madrigal had once stolen fertile seeds during a stay.

He was prolific because he had fathered seventeen children by two wives over twenty years. Both wives had co-existed amicably, happy to share the child-bearing burdens and wifely duties. Through the passage of time, the old chief steward had kept the whole family united.

Every child was named Fred or Frederica, as were both wives. No roman numerals; no added letters. Just the name. Oh, and for good measure, so were his five Rottweilers. The local jaguar, coney and tree iguana populations detested them.

Even his weed lines were Fred-derivatives: 'Fredling Fly', 'Fred A-stare', 'Fred Flintstoned', 'Alfred Ganja Khan', 'Fred Jiggleitalittleitllopen', 'Fred-Lb rightover'. And more.

Somehow it worked. Majordomo Frederick Mansard Lansing bragged that he never feared being ignored, nor losing his mind. One name was all he need remember. If he ever lost memory of his own name, he figured, well, it was just that time... To top it all off, he was willing to wager at least somebody of the troupe would carry on the name.

Cassie and Cal had employed their own peculiar twist on the theme by middle-naming all five successive sons Alfrederic, just like Calumet, Junior. Therefore, Coy-Al, Voy-Al, Roy-Al, Loy-Al and Doy-Al.

Their only sister, Sophie, had the effrontery to be born into the world with indoor plumbing and paid for this by a lifetime of signing official papers as Sophonsiba Rill Blackhearst.

As a child, she had called all of her brothers Al. In contrast to the Belizean, she deduced that any sibling she might call would mix it up with one of the others and thereby, thankfully, ignore her. Worked to a T.

At the seventh inning stretch, all six brothers deserted the cutting-edge 72-inch Samsung curved-screen to the starry night out back for their own game-update report. They did a better job than the pundits, and with their looks and scant wardrobes as impetus, I opted to join them.

Personally, I still missed marching bands at halftime. Oh, wrong season...scratch that.

Women-folk had long since departed the house for the safety of a baseball-sparse venue so a fraternity-like mood ruled now. Spitting, farting, burping, scratching, and the like, prevailed in this atmosphere and we were bonding the more as a result. Peeing on the grass was acceptable, as well, and I heartily joined this exercise in one-upmanship from as close proximity as possible without being splashed. The view was worth the risk, I posited, even if I didn't quite measure up.

I found no better luck telling them apart by this method, however. They were all hung like Cal and Coy: huge, thick and uncut. On the bright side, as drunk as they were getting, no one would likely fall down...third leg and all. Tripods are notoriously stable on their legs.

Yup, good ole' filial bonding. One of Cal's and my primary intentions in descending to the flatlands for the summer. Sophie was already won over to my side. She had always wanted a sister-in-arms. Ahem.

Cal reminded us of the 10 mg THC gummy bears and lollipops. He led the sweet-lovers inside to test them. I had become absorbed studying constellations heavenward, a favorite pastime in the mountains. Loy and Roy both preferred the professionally rolled joint to chewables and I saw them light up from my vantage of the porch swing. Their flame distracted my star-gazing.

The younger twins not only looked alike, they also spoke alike, cussed alike, walked alike, thought alike and finished the other's sentences. When they were younger they had developed a 'language' of their own, as twins do, and were commonly observed conversing quietly or heatedly together. Nobody the wiser about the content.

Very curious words and body-language soon captivated my attention as I experienced the artful display firsthand. I watched, infatuated, as they discussed something of apparent import together. Both were clad in only cutoff jeans. My salivary functions could not keep from evaluating the handsome shadows they cast in the waxing gibbous moonlight.

After a peculiarly gesticulative exchange the duo suddenly signaled in my direction. Then they turned and approached, offering to share the old-fashioned method of partying, as they called it: two-toking. Loy turned to Roy and demonstrated their unique take on the old shotgun toke. The innate sensuality exuding from the two during it made the tent in my running shorts rise a bit. What total unassuming studs.

I arose and stepped down toward them in the yard, happy for the attention. With the 'demo' toke consummated, they sidled to me in tandem. Loy put the lit blunt inward between his lips and leaned at me inquiringly. Roy came up behind as we partook and parked his crotch between my asscheeks. Large hands brazenly wandered in hormone-driven search over my butt and groin.

Pretty hard to miss that offer, I mused. Being a suck-up for muscled black dudes, brother-in-law status notwithstanding, I bent slightly into the sausage fattening back there and took a deeper hit from Loy as he braced my head with his other hand, kind of pushing the issue.

My shorts lasted above my hips like two seconds past that. Loy did his best to keep me from noticing the ploy by perpetuating the shared lip-lock, but Roy didn't just lower them. He ripped them off by brute force. One yank and I was butt naked between the two. Their cutoffs slid to ankle height and the nice southerly breeze wafted northward over a lot of exposed skin.

Loy took out the blunt but continued the lip-lock, joint-unaided. His tongue took over, stabbing my inner cheeks and throat in foreshadow to what more was coming. Roy hawked my bare ass with a glob of saliva, using his fingers to spread it up inside my chute.

The next move proved debilitating as he weaseled that big-ass ebony dick, recently evaluated under moonlight as it had pissed, right smack up into my white ass. I pushed back invitingly, arching the globes.

Loy's tongue still enforced distraction and I moaned as the Mandingo pair set into a mutual gyrating dance very obviously practiced before this interlude. Hmmmm. My mental strings were picturing the two conjoined by dick as they practiced perfection in another time and place...who knew, I fantasized, what went on between them? These boys spoke a common private dialect. Why not fuck a common private dialect, too? The unmarried state suddenly suited them.

They audibly purred while they pumped, in a resonating hum, so similar in sound that I really couldn't tell one from the other, ending up in 'sense-surround' mode through their susurrations.

The men were absolute animals in the taking of the forbidden fruit (smile) out there on the moon-drenched lawn. As they shifted from one position to the other I lost track who was doing what to whom. I take that back. I was the one getting plowed. And watched, though unbeknownst to me at that moment.

I felt like I came each time they bred me, sensing the swelling releases fill me again and again, but it wasn't so. My cock stayed rock hard, bouncing off my abs the whole while. The two were ravenously insatiable. The number of loads were simply in plural… the twin action only settled down when we heard Cal call to us from his and Coy's soundlessly assumed seats on the porch swing.

We had over-stayed the seventh-inning stretch, he joked... The top of the eighth was on… "What the Hell are you bitches and ho's doing, anyway?" My man voiced all this as he and his twin stroked to our beat.

Experiencing the boys' private vernacular repertoire, I felt I had just solved the sexual Rosetta Stone. Damn, the twins spoke that sensual jargon well... Was I ever lovin' me some new family.

Seeing stars was just frosting on the cakes.

Chapter 6
Stick Shift: Eagle's Nest

"So, you think that God is a civil engineer, Jake? Really?"

"Not what I said, Sophie." Bemused, I tried again. "It was just the joke I was telling you-- I was saying the contractor told the engineers that." The magic gummy bear may have been a bad idea for this girl, I thought.

The 10 mg THC infusion added to the sugary animal shapes up in Colorado must be made for those of thicker blood than these flatlanders. Aspenites became nice and mellow whereas several down here had acted out a bit strangely.

Two of Cal's brothers had taken three each during the ball-game and disappeared soon after. Without a word. That was three days ago and we had heard nothing from them since...hopefully they were OK.

"Well, tell me again, then. I didn't get it, boii," Sophie drew me back to reality. She glanced my way from behind the wheel and threw me an easy smile. The trademark sparkling smile of the Georgia Blackhearst family. I'd recognize it any-where and saw my better half's face etched all over those perfect pearly whites as they flashed my direction.

"OK, then. But keep an eye on the road, Soph," I told her, as we flew down the old farm-to-market road. She was a good driver but got easily distracted by animals, I had noticed. We were passing a herd of red angus on her side and they drew her attention more than the road sign on my side warning us of a curve and another announcing Opelika, Alabama, eight more miles. Puffy clouds pocked the sky as we enjoyed the comfortable harmony between the two of us, out on a day trip together.

"Two engineers and a government contractor went into a bar," I tried it over again. "All three had agreed that God must be an engineer, but they disagreed on what kind he could be. The Electrical Engineer claimed that the electrical genius behind the design of the human body--- 'why, just look at the intricacy of the nerves and spinal cord and heart and the amazingly complex brain'--- made it a given that He had to be an EE Himself. The Mechanical Engineer countered that, no, with the amazing functions of the muscles and tendons, bones and joints and ligaments, He had to have been an ME to design that."

"Their government contractor buddy came back from the bar with three beers and overheard them. He then insisted, well, no, God HAD to be a civil engineer to devise the human body. The other two looked at him like he was crazy and asked why he would think that?"

"Well, he said, anyone could figure that out...who else but a civil engineer would plan a recreational area right through the middle a waste disposal unit?" I grinned inwardly as I remembered Cal's best friend, Jeremy, first tell us the joke at the top of Ajax Mountain last Christmas morning. The first run of the morning-- nothing but fresh powder below us. A good day, I reminisced.

Soph looked stymied. "I still don't get it, Boii, break it down for a country girl."

Hoo-Boy, I thought. It was a gay joke, after all, and we were in a deep red southern state. "OK," I said. "Think like a gay man, Sister Souljah. Three gay professionals. Talking about the complexity of the human anatomy over a beer. The cynical government contractor, who spends his days trying to fix the goof-ups by the engineers and construction companies he deals with overhears his engineer buddies talking and immediately links anatomy and how gay men like backdoor sex...recreational area...through a waste disposal unit...get it? "

"Eeeeewww," the pretty woman with richly red-spiked hair gagged and puffed out her cheeks. "How gross is that? That is not funny, Jake."

"What, do you mean to tell me your boyfriends have never taken the Hershey Highway, Sophie?" I laughed, because I knew of her sexual proclivities. Her history with men was quite splotchy.

This was the woman who swore she wouldn't get pregnant--"fo' sho' that"-- until after getting her degree and buying her own house, away from her brothers. But, she was very nearly as hormone-driven as any of the boys in the family. This woman was in constant 'hyper-drive'.

Something did not compute, here. But far be it for me to pass judgment, so I just changed the subject as she refused comment about the Hershey Highway-- I knew she got the reference, though.

It was just last Saturday morning that I had come into the kitchen while Boy was reciting what he had learned at school the day before. Sophie and Vivian were intent on the pancake batter but were listening to the precocious boy at the same time.

"Milk, milk, lemonade, 'round the corner, fudge is made." sing-songing the words while he pointed first to each boob, then to his crotch and then a round-house curve of his arm, finger pointing to his rear-end.

Not awaiting their response, he raced off to the other room, leaving the two girls to wince and Viv to point her finger down her throat. But they got it...hence, the Hershey Highway.

"There's the turn-off coming up, Soph," I said, as we approached the sign for Auburn University. We had happily planned this day trip for a week, so we might get away and enjoy a somewhat culturally-oriented day alone together. No brotherly or spousal interference.

Cal, my lover for eight years and new husband, Sophie's older brother and mentor, had concurred with our plan while the other brothers, aunts, uncles, and family 'graciously' backed away from including themselves. Go figure, we thought, snickering.

* * *

Our day trip had begun rather tumultuously earlier in the morning. I had just returned from my morning run, still before dawn. Waxed and winded by the heavy humidity down here so close to sea-level, I heard Goldie, the next door neighbor's big boxer, ramp up to a fit of barking over in the Brown's garden area behind their house.

Next, I heard old Farmer Brown kick up a cussin' rampage that would have done a nickel-whore-in-church proud. Hearing a familiar bleating sound, I pretty quickly figured what might be occurring so went to jump the split-rail fence separating the two farms.

Coming up behind the elderly farmer, I saw Goldie in the setting moonlight backing down the Blackhearst family's pet goat, Aloysius (say: Al-oo-Wish-us...). There were asparagus tips hanging out of the Nubian goat's cheeks and even though he was in a defensive posture of head down, front legs spread and ears hard back on his head with horns bristling, he was still munching those tender shoots. Both dog and farmer were having none of it, brandishing teeth and shotgun at the outlaw ungulate.

Aloysius suddenly saw the situation as a losing venture and whirled, leaping the small fence surrounding the backyard garden, lickety-splitting into the spectral cornfield behind and towards the pine woods beyond.

Goldie was off like a rocket after the thief and I managed to get my hand up on Mr. Brown's shoulder as he was leveling the shotgun for a birdshot barrage at the reprobate goat, forgetting the fact of friendly fire for the boxer.

Pulling back in surprise at my touch the old man swung the gun around on to my belly, calloused black finger close to the trigger. He charged up his epithetical bombardment again, this time at me.

"Ya' nigga-lovin' rascal, what ya' doin' puttin' that varmint on my Elsie's 'gus patch?" Trying to settle the old fellow proved difficult, as he needlessly explained, in high-volume detail, how it took three long years to get a good crop of asparagus, and "that damned devil of a goat was damn well gonna pay with his damnable hide this time. If ya'll wasn't gonna keep the damn critter on a damn leash than me and the little missus was just gonna be eatin' us some got-damn goat meat pretty quick, here."

The dog's fading barks let me know that the two animals were out on a chase like to last awhile but at the same time, out of birdshot range. So I soothed the cantankerous old coot as best I could to get that double-barrel pointed away from my belly-button.

He did settle down after a minute, at least to a decibel range softer than a rock concert. I began helping straighten up the cherished asparagus plants just as the 'little missus' stepped out the back door.

"A good morning to you, young Dr. Jake," she greeted me. Her ever-present smile won everyone over, without exception. Even curmudgeonly husbands quieted down in her calming presence.

Profuse apologies for the goat's pilfering elicited physical and vocal brush-offs from the tiny titan of a woman. She explained that so much asparagus had been picked and pickled by this time of the season that the couple could exist on the delicacy quite a long time, now, thank-you-very-much. Besides, she added, "that billy is a whippersnapper-- I love that big old goat."

After making sure all was under control, she warned me against catching cold, which confused me, and extracted a promise to stop by for a coffee-chat soon. Maybe after I was able to shower and dress, she concluded amiably. Which solved my confusion, considering my running outfit. Then she warned her husband to mind his manners in front of me-- and his tongue, too, if he knew what was good for him. She had apparently overheard what he had called me a bit ago. With that advice, the smart lady took leave of us, disappearing inside the screen door once again. Farmer Brown and I went to work attempting to raise the battered crop, each of us meandering silently in our own thoughts for the moment.

There was no problem on the name-calling, I mused. Old people had very few filters by their age. In their mind's eyes, they had 'graduated' from the societal mores system, feeling no compunction to guard their thoughts as they once had done.

Standing helplessly by a few years past when last visiting my folks, I had watched as my own elderly step-father rudely accosted a departing restaurant diner. Boring in on the man's size 50 waist, he had expressed hope that the man had left us some... food, I supposed... as we were entering for dinner. All I had been able to offer was a wince and an apology. Would I be the same upon reaching that point in life? My mind wandered further during the old farmer's temporarily chastened state, continuing the effort at repairing the abused vegetables.

Mr. Brown and my father notwithstanding, ladies of advanced age tended more to matronly lenient acceptance than older men. With that in mind, I hoped for my female hormones to pick up the pace in my elder years, as is common for the male gender. Just not at the expense of my masculinity or testosterone levels, mind you. That was too precious a commodity to do without. Especially in light of my other half's sex-drive.

Cal had about the highest level of libido I had ever experienced. It never ceased to amaze me at his wherewithal to pop a hard-on under almost any circumstance and in any venue. Desired or not. Not that I was complaining. His handsome piece achieved rigidity quicker than any prick his size that I had watched harden. And it came quicker than any, too, when need called for it. Hell, the man had grabbed me just an hour ago as I tried to sneak from bed to go for my run, insisting on his early morning blowjob before departing.

Then again, when we were not rushed, the stud could last three hours with a towering pipe, quivering in anticipation at three inches past his navel and two inches out from his ripped stomach, curving gently upward and usually throbbing to a beat of its own as it awaited further attention from yours truly.

I loved teasing him. He was extremely careful not to offend people by the tenting effect he proffered the public in every day clothes--- his junk could not be hidden in most any pants or drawers, short of using a drag queen's truss. I knew the exact buttons and triggers which set the beast into motion...a fact of which he was well aware. Therefore, he insisted on ground rules for us when we went to public events. Ha, on that, I laughed to myself.

More than once I had seen him tent the front of his pants hugely, much to others' notice and his own exasperation. He suffered embarrassment at the expanded state, while I simply reveled in the reminder of my man's prodigious capacity and staying power. Just the thought of it made my juices flow. I would need to address that premise in a few minutes, knowing his morning wood would not be sated by a single blowjob. My junk lurched a little and I fantasized amidst the asparagus's phallic shapes. Still trying to raise the stalks from their hoof-flattened wilt, the thought crossed my mind that someone should market plant Viagra.

At that mental profundity, Farmer Brown ended the brief reverie, making his presence known to me again. "Boy, you musta forgot yo' drawers by the looks o' things," pointing the now elbow-cruxed shotgun barrel in the direction of my crotch.

Indeed. I looked down and realized my Cal-induced semi-boner had not done me any favors here. Nothing but running shorts and running shoes provided me cover, and as hung as I was, very little was being left to the imagination just now. Thank goodness Mrs. Brown had gone inside.

Attempting adjustment was futile without a jock and the old man cackled at the picture. "So, white boys might can't jump but at least some of them pack a bunch, huh? How d'ya' get that whonker out'n the way when the time comes? With that Cal-boy of your'n, I mean. Must get a mite crowded 'tween the two o' y'alls' belly-up matches. Everybody know what that boy's a'packin'. Matter o' public record since the state finals wrestlin' match back in his high school days, a- yup." At that recollection he straightened up, staring off into the morning darkness with what would seem to be a sentimentally wistful gaze. Wow, I speculated, what could that be about?

Making promises for further amends to Farmer Brown, I decided it best to vacate the scene. Dick flopping. A little abashed, I reached the doorway to our bedroom in a couple minutes, still well-heated, and warming more so to the thought of climbing under those covers with my Daddy.

The fleeting idea of showering was quickly squelched. I had been well-conditioned over our years together to the assurances of my man's preference for me in the semi-ripe state such as existed following physical exertion. Even emanating the faint odor of 'eau de billy goat gruff', I knew Cal's reasoning: "If I wanted a woman or a damn ho', then I sure know where to look--don't be comin' on to your man smellin' like a flower, now. You listening, white boy?" After several years of personal disgruntlement over that particular, I had finally acceded to his appeals. At least on occasion. I had to admit that musky male aroma certainly whetted his appetite.

I snuck through the creaky door and just about reached the covers to climb in when a wide awake Cal emerged from the still pre-dawn shadows where he had been purposely waiting. Rousted earlier by the commotion and on the verge of barging outside to save my ass, he had listened and detected little real danger. When the 'little missus' voice had entered the conversation, he had decided to wait, considering the boner state at his abrupt awakening.

So, now, capitalizing on my appearance, a strapping bicep suddenly materialized between my salty thighs. From behind and underneath, the smooth forearm flexed up onto my stomach. In the doing, my half-mast cock was pincered between us. Feeling my anticipatory swelling, he growled pleasurably at our mutual need, whamming me down onto the mattress in one fluid movement. Trapped by familiar ebony musculature, I succumbed easily to the 'foreplay', such as it was.

His full lips locked onto mine, the beautiful arm slid snake-like up my stomach and crotch. The attached hand matched its mate on either side of my head and he buried his long, talented tongue far into my mouth. It still stole my breath away at the intensity with which he took control when ready. I had long ago linked his aggressive sexual nature to the legendary lust of Attila the Hun after success in battle. Taking the spoils of war. The analogy aided my understanding of the origin of the term, "booty".

Before my liaison began with Cal, through the post-pubescent era of my youth, I had styled myself a total top man. Being well-hung in the whiteness of the WASP world, I had no problem taking the dominant role and playing it to the hilt, though my experiences were sparsely numbered before I was 'schooled' by Cal. I liked being in control. As a strong alpha personality, it fit my persona. All through undergrad school, I practiced what I felt was my natural predilection.

Upon introduction to Cal Broadhearst nine years back at a frat party, no less, I became acquainted with his world of sex. That year, at the Spring Break interim of med school's second year, our paths had crossed. I was borderline frightened by the man. The divergence in our thought processes then were a challenge for me on several levels.

Cal was most definitely straightforward in his designs with relation to us. At the same time, pursuit of a medical degree was not something from which I allowed myself much distraction. Luckily, my man had intuited these sources for my wariness in regard to himself. Deliberately altering his archetypal method of conquest, he had suspended the demonstrative bravado so commonly successful to that juncture in his life. Instead, patience took precedence in approach to the goal he had set.

Within the year, he was in my pants, in my bedroom, and in my Life. To the present day, the only challenges to Cal's anal virginity had been my tongue and his proctologist. He had never been topped.

Sure, my tongue had tested his virginity through the years. He melted to putty upon my lingual ministrations. I could've probably pushed the envelope and gotten into his ass had I tried at those times. The desire to do so had been strong in the beginning. My own personality had demanded such, in fact. But, thankfully, I had apprehended the folly of that path. Having tasted of his sexual prowess, I discerned that the quickest way to relegate 'us' to irrelevancy was to take that role with him. The lustre of his masculinity would be irredeemably diminished.

He was a total man: the man who wanted me. And, yes, other men on occasion. But, others were solely sexual sorties. It was a fact with which I was confident enough to be comfortable. Always and forever would Calumet be My True Top. And I, His Bottom. Any way he preferred.

While we both effectuated sex with some select others, by mutual and non-jealous consent, my heart was ever with this man. Never could I have pictured that for myself, but the puzzle fit together. We were united. Our first and last rule was honesty. Nothing else made sense. Or mattered.

On the subject of lingual ministrations. Millions of women would keep their men happy for a lifetime with that single maneuver. If they could only do so. But it is a male thing: passively aggressive yet non-threatening. Women have serious blocks at even giving good head and ho's hired for fellatio wear thin very quickly: too ghetto. Too unfulfilling. On the other hand, almost any top man would choose good tongue-to-ass action over, yes, even fellatio. Because a major G-spot exists there.

Take it from me, the way to a man's heart is not through their stomach-- it is by the lingual backdoor entrance. The Hershey Highway. Just practice good hygiene...Hershey is only euphemistic. Hopefully the fairer sex will never find enjoyment in this act. The entire gay world might be dealt a serious setback. Fo' sho'. Shhhh, don't tell.

Meanwhile, back at the ranch, Cal wended his smooth, sinewy legs in between my own. Gradually inching mine apart, per his wont, the sexy mouth never left my lips. Rock hardness ruled as our dicks entwined and tongues dueled. He bit my lips, tantalizingly, one at a time and repeatedly.

Finally getting our legs separated from their mates far enough, his man muscle spongily probed for that opening. I always kept some Palmer's cocoa butter within arm's reach on the nightstand and found it while he continued the teasing. The butter coated both him and me and I shivered at the impression of the giant piece posturing to take me once again.

Ebony arms hooked tanned knees as the head popped my sphincter. Our animal grunts along with his staccato instructions and pleadings took over as his prick slowly, persistently, slid up into the hinter regions of my channel. Upon 'bottoming out' we ceased rhythm and held close for what seemed forever as my ass accommodated its guru yet again. His tongue in my mouth played the perfect decoy.

Cal knew the ecstasy of delayed satisfaction well. He found my desire upped by a power of ten when taking time like this to own me. Once established, he was aware he could proceed in any way he preferred from there on. At this time, on this morning, he preferred chest-to-chest rubbing while his fingers wrapped through the spaces between my toes, extending my legs and his arms out to the sides. He knew toe spaces to be my #1 g-spot. Growling deep into my mouth, he suffused us both with a vibrating buzz.

The rhythmic motion of our coupled state enfolded and held us captive by its power. Not a thin dime could have been fit between our bodies. With my legs and his arms out and away from our torsos, Cal took us to the place we knew as our own. Nobody and nothing could rival this link. Over the years our experimentations had perfected various methods for mutual bliss. Even so, this man still surprised me.

My fat dickhead pumped cum from its eye without warning following one particularly long, throbbing, stroke. I felt his climax pulsate inside me when my constricting prostate signaled him. The vibration shifted into a long sigh of total release, both of us sagging together as juices flowed.

After long minutes, our still interlocked tongues messaged each other of continued viability and we groaningly retracted from one another's bodies. A mischievous smile pervaded my vision by nose-closeness.

Cal abruptly licked my face from chin to mouth to nose to forehead and sprang up off of me, shower intentions obvious. Dragging me along, we disappeared into the steam for purification rites, not noticing the stealthy figure skootch out from under our bed and, quiet-as-a-mouse, slink away evincing the smuggest of smug looks...

Things that make you go, "hmmmm."

Following a very laid back breakfast, Cal revved up his tablet while we cleared the table. He had scheduled a webinar for mid-morning with his board-of-directors and a group of potential new investors. Business-like and detached in his pre-occupation, I shouldered my backpack to depart. A perfunctory butt pat and cheek peck sent me and my sis-in-law to the door.

In contrast, Boy bounded up to both Sophie and me, demanding lift-up hugs and little boy cuddles. This hadn't been a part of his new, grown-up image for the past 6 months, as I was later informed. His aunt was tickled by his reversion and when he nuzzled my neck goodbye he whispered in my ear, "I love me my Uncle Jake", totally blowing me away.

The imp hadn't granted such a title for me up to then and my heart grew three sizes as we two loaded into the Range Rover to head out. She was likewise surprised, and heart warmed, by her eldest nephew's vocal acceptance of me into the family. We considered the lovable innocence of the scamp while chatting amicably over the first hour of the drive...

* * *

"Well, if he is, he is going to have one long, hot wait," said Sophie, biting into the warm panini sandwich over lunch at the Museum of Art cafe.

The young man had been nonchalantly lounging on the rock bench in the adjoining patio since she and I had sat down for lunch half an hour before. I had commented again on the very conspicuous mohawked guy to Sophie upon our running into him for the fourth time in as many hours during our campus visit.

At the Raptor center, he had been locked-in and absorbed throughout the lecture on birds-of-prey which both Sophie and I had put first on our list to hear. Seated two rows in front of us in the small outdoor amphitheater, his caramel skin glistened with a light sheen of sweat in the hot mid-morning sun.

The deep red mohawk kind of stood out in the group of 20 as we listened to the ornithological expert discuss with us the raptor species in general and the Auburn War Eagle in specific.

After the talk ended, Sophie made note of the man as if he were a woman wearing her same dress at a cocktail party. "That color doesn't do much for him and the green and yellow tie-dye pants make him look like a Kwanzaa banner," she noted tartly.

The hair color almost matched her own hair tip color, so I failed to see her point. I took in her waist-tie, full length draped caftan, the zig-zag pattern of yellow, black and green very attractive on the exquisite young woman I called Sister. It was startlingly similar to the outfit the young man wore. His muscle shirt was a black-ribbed, dressier type. The two could have been cast members of the Cirque show traveling the southeast US who we had seen as a family in Atlanta the previous week.

Cal and I were big followers of the Cirque du Soleil shows. We had spent a week in Vegas the previous fall just to see the four resident Cirque shows on the Strip. 'Zumanity' had given us both raging hard-ons, what with its emphasis on the sensual. The steel-barred set of the soft-core prison sex scene had burned him a boner that took me hours to put out after the performance.

The MC had been an amazingly well-put-together transgender in hip boots and a fluorescent, sequined, two-piece leather outfit who had wielded fluorescent whips which shot phosphorescent sparks into the air each time she had disciplined the next-to-naked Chippendale quality male 'prison' performers. Clad only in leather thongs they gamboled over props closely resembling sex slings. It was extraordinary and left both of us horny for days. We saw it three times...

This exotic boy had an uncommon air and flair about him. As we got up to leave the raptor talk he turned and smiled, half-bowing in Sophie's direction. She was aloof to the gesture, having taken affront to his outfit. I noted a strain of jealousy over the happenstance. Hmmm, surprising.

When we visited the Arboretum next, there he was again. Very convincingly engrossed in the flora and fauna of the exceptional garden, he only acknowledged us with a quick nod as we walked out the exit later on our way to the Smith Art Museum.

Now, as we sat at lunch after touring the good quality 'Great Masters Exhibit', we again acknowledged the man's sultry presence on the sunny outdoor veranda just outside the plate glass divider. Sipping an iced Starbucks drink, Sophie was a bit more than put out: the striking man had passed us several times while ostensibly contemplating the stellar art.

Not only did she feel that the youth had copied her look, stealing her thunder in some way, but he had made a point to shadow her at each stop on our day's excursion. As we finished up our light lunch we weighed the odd situation.

While he wasn't threatening toward us, and the venues we had visited were public, the fact that he had seemingly copied our schedule did seem somewhat weird. As she collected her things, she again referred to the copycat-dresser outside. "If he shows up at the Vet College I am going to call in the law," she declared. A bit draconian, I reflected.

Sophie was alluding to her appointment with the dean's selection committee at the Veterinary Sciences College, the underlying impetus for our planned trip today. Not yet ready to announce her intent to enter veterinary medical school to her family, I was honored at being confided in. She had requested accompaniment to her interview. My background in medicine and marine biology had been right for advising her in a course of action.

Asking if I would be OK for the couple hours while she was busy, I assured her I would have a great time wandering the campus and exploring the Ecology Park. We planned to meet later at Heritage Park by the university entrance for our return trip to Rome. I was quite comfortable on college campuses.

They were my natural niche, as I had discovered early on in life.

Sophie left me at the Auburn University main entrance. Before driving away in the Rover, she warned me to be on the lookout for the interloper, as she had now dubbed him, promising to be careful herself.

On my own for a bit, I felt liberated. Wandering the scenic route through the storied tree-lined campus of the old East Alabama Male College, as Auburn had been titled at its pre-civil war inception, I studied the landmarks. The history was intriguing for me and I stopped frequently in making my way toward the Ecology Park.

Entering the Park, I looked around only perfunctorily for the Kwanzaa man, expecting to never run across him again. After all, it was Sophie who need be on guard. Checking my phone, I was relieved to see no messages from her. I delved into the well-planned ecology park so cleverly sequestered on the old southern campus.

The university being in between summer sessions, the place was almost deserted. I enjoyed the solitude and removed my button down shirt in the afternoon heat, letting the warm breeze caress my skin. The well-known eagle's nest was where I headed. A teaching replica, it had been specially designed and placed on the site for public enjoyment. It was huge. Five adults could act the part of eaglets and hide down in the deepness of the inner cup. The old oak trees overhanging the site shaded the nest. I had to climb in and check it out.

Its inner surface was lined with something akin to feather down, providing a super-soft surface for kids to experience a real-life eagle's nest. Very interesting. I settled back in leisurely repose and luxuriated in the softness, stretching and gazing up through the tree branches.

The hot, still day and intermittent dazzle of sunlight through the overarching branches soothingly beguiled me with mental images of huge eagles landing on the edge, offering freshly caught eaglet delicacies for my culinary delight. Dappled sunlight sprinkled me with sunbeams...

Some of the downy lining floated loose, tickling my lips and I brushed it away in drowsy lassitude. Then, thinking to check my phone for messages in case Sophie or Cal had attempted contact, I roused an arm into movement toward the device. Upon fluttering my eyelids open, I started at beholding a dark figure hovering above me. The effect both blocked the sun and banished my grogginess.

There, directly over and only a few feet from me, was the Kwanzaa boy. Curiously studying me as I lay dozing in the nest. A feeling of creepiness skulked in, gooseflesh arising. I gawked at the mohawked male, my fluster contrasting his curiosity.

"What the fuck are you up to, dude?" I demanded. He half-smiled, without showing teeth. Provocatively, Mr. Mohawk placed his now bare foot on the lump fronting my shorts. I backed up on the curve of the lined declivity and pushed his foot off. "Dawg, you need to chill. Really, what is up?"

No answer, at all. He cocked his head to the side and reached forward, fingering my wild, curly auburn hair, mussed and feather-flocked. The red-topped man raised up erect again, now bracing himself by well-developed arms on either side of the nest. Like a gymnast descending on the still rings apparatus during competition.

Clearly athletically-honed to a peak of physical condition, he posed in arm-horizontal position, supporting his body in a feat by which true Olympians could have been satisfied. He pointed his toes downward, targeting my slightly askew bare legs, aiming for the gap between them.

My disturbed feeling ebbed as I observed this amazing demonstration of bodily discipline, detecting no danger signals emanating from him. His feet reached my legs and lightly nudged them further apart in a very seductive move. I allowed it.

Noting my altered body language, the mute gymnast remained suspended over me. Those toe tips continuing to prod my inner thighs. A full smile slowly shaped his full lips. Beautifully even white teeth gleamed at me. Sensing an opening, he let go his arms to the sides of the nest and reached down again, unclasping and unzipping my shorts.

Taking hold of the lower hems he swept them off in one smooth motion, pulling my legs to vertical in the action. My briefs went next and my woozy endowment began swelling at the sensuous turn of events.

He loosened the hold on my legs, guiding them to either side of his widely planted bronzed feet. Picking a few feathers out of my hair he ogled down at my now naked self. That smile of his grew and so did my dick.

His foot came up onto my crotch again, this time bare skin contacting bare skin. It wasn't the foot that was engorging, though. In a fluid motion, the Kwanzaaonian pulled his black ribbed muscle shirt off and untied the yellow and green loose-flowing britches. They floated down to his ankles and he stepped out of them, kicking them aside.

His perfect caramel-skinned elegance was now proudly on display, poised over me. On his chest and stomach was emblazoned a naked black angel, wings and arms fully unfurled. Covering a set of astonishingly handsome pectorals, the wingtips disappeared into his deep armpits. The black angel's feet tiptoed on the root of his cock as if just alighting there... Green, red and yellow ink perfused the body art. I was both stunned and riveted.

No hair covered his skin even in his groin and pubic area. His tool phattened before my eyes and while not the size I was used to in Cal, the thickness was more than that of a beer can; the balls were tightly drawn and plump. It kept on levitating. Shamelessly.

And, the man definitely liked that I liked his angel...if you got it, brandish it...

Mohawk Man's smile burst into a full-fledged grin and he raised his head to survey the surroundings. It was mid-afternoon and though no one was around, who was to say that would persist? His perusal reflected that thought but he looked back down, arched his eyebrows upward and lewdly licked his lips. Then he just about fell on top of me.

My guess was that his concerns for interruption were now allayed.

Wide, flaring nostrils snorted in a breath of air and the aroused man raised my tanned legs widely up and over my head, burying his tongue in my ass. It made me gasp.

Kwanzaa stud didn't waste any time, spitting on my rectal sphincter and swabbing it in readiness for the Coors-can prick I was now fixed on. How did we get to here, I thought?

Oh hell, who cared...the man was totally hot and shimmering in sweat. Though not exactly handsome, he exuded an animal magnetism that had me wanting all of him. Right here. Like I had a choice in the matter.

His big dick suspended itself at my ass pucker, prodding it in slimy warning. In contrast to my caretaking Calumet, this wild Indian with the red mohawk mane blasted into my inner sanctum, brooking no dissent. Of course, I didn't raise any, but the shock of the painful entry made me shudder. I groaned out loud. He hesitated momentarily, allowing my adaptation to the thick intruder.

Even through the sex-infused wantonness in his black eyes, the man/boy managed to show me he wasn't trying to hurt me. He just liked it this way. He wound up and delivered me a pile-driver fuck, rocketing the massive thing in and out of my ass while pushing my heels up, toes touching the down-lining over my head.

I stroked and fondled my own dick and tipped his angel with my fingers as I focused on his whole figure. The cut arms stretched out securing my legs, sculpted torso taut by exertion, over-developed dark nipples crowning the killer pecs, massive brown shoulders and neck muscles on magnificent display. This stud was supremely proud of his physique and in full command of it all, enhancing the damned effect.

Ultimately, Mr. Mohawk pummeled me to the point of no return. Making one final wind-up of a plunge, he exploded into my chute, delivering a copious load I could feel both saturating me and spilling out. My own prick pulsed cum by involuntary response.

Collapsing on me, dick deeply implanted, he panted in the heat of the afternoon. I experienced the feel of his hard body heaving on me, dripping euphoria. That prickly mohawk tickled my nose.

How. Fucking. Hot.

His breathing evened out to long, deep, cavernous intakes and outflows as he gradually gathered himself. Hoisting up off just my stomach and chest, leaving our bodies enmeshed from pubes on down, the boy was not yet allowing that still rigid cock of his to retract from my ass.

Rather, he reached over for his pants, pulling an iphone from the pocket. Raising it up behind his head, the stud pointed it down on the both of us in our present state. The thick root of his piece showed about three inches of its bulky stalk protruding from the point of entry, our torsos providing backdrop. How kinky, I thought. A new take on the selfie...

When he'd clicked several different angle shots, careful to leave our faces out but unable or undesiring to avoid his trademark red mohawk, he settled back on to my torso. Enjoying our communal satiation, Kwanzaa Boy leisurely finger-painted in the cum congealing on my flat, tanned belly. His mouth, near to my ear, sublimely purred at me. How feline.

Raising up again, the mysterious male teasingly flicked my nipples. He then handed me his phone. Grinning again, the youth purposely began tensing his dick in my ass to prove his continued influence over me, or maybe just to watch me squirm at the feeling. I was captivated. The moves this being had...

As I wiggled under the spasmic onslaught, the boy pointed to the phone in my hand and tonelessly mouthed the words, "your numbers" at me, intending for me to enter them to his device. Hesitating for only a moment, I acquiesced. Then, on second thought, I snapped the pic of his angel. From my vantage point, the amazing figure art appeared to be coming to rest on both of us at the moment. The smeared cum imbued an impressionist painting effect... He sniggled his delight.

Reluctantly, the sexy mulatto at last began gradually inching that girthful piece out of my hole, in direct dissimilarity to his blast-like entry. A sensual pop announced our separation, as if I needed that to know it, educing a 'great bigger' grin of triumph from the suddenly very boyish fucker.

With that, the stud pummeled my hard stomach with half a dozen play punches. Looking me directly in the eye, he pointed to his chest and pantomimed, "Me, Bam." Then touched my chest with his fingertip, evincing a 'pssst' sound through his teeth at the moment of contact, mouthing, "You, Sizzle."

Bam sat back, gathering his clothes and iphone. He then stood, nakedly waggled his dripping dick over my stomach to dribble a little bit more sperm on me and rubbed his fingers through my sticky spunk. Smirking, he licked it off.

He cocked hand to head, thumb at his ear, pinky touching the corner of his mouth, and lip-synced Carly Rae Jepsen's title, "Call me maybe". Then, he lightly vaulted the side of the nest.

Gone.

A minute later, I heard a cacophony of elementary age voices and jumped from my reverie to don my clothes, mentally imaging a caramel-colored, red-mohawked, angel bejeweled naked Indian flashing through the wooded environs of the Ecology Park, junk bouncing all the way...those kids would never forget it. I knew I wouldn't.

Cal would totally cream over it.

* * *

When Sophie pulled up to the curb at the entry gates of Auburn University an hour after that, I was greeted with a girly shriek and mouth-covering gestures, informing me of her successful interview at the Dean's office. She would be notified for sure in a week or two but things looked good. We shared the giddiness as she exuded happiness, explaining to me all the details.

On the road awhile later, Sophie suddenly spoke up, "Oh, Jake, I never saw or heard from that strange Kwanzaa boy again. I forgot to tell you. Did you ever hear from the weirdo?"

My phone vibrated and chimed at that very moment, signaling me of an incoming text with photo attachment.

"Not a single word," I opined.

Chapter 7
Tride and True: Pound Cakes

Damn, those feet were big.

Exiting the downstairs doorway of Telluride Hardware and Feed Emporium, I was absorbed in my thoughts when the hefty hooves ruined my concentration.

The Nike Cross-trainers were not new, nor were they rare. Rather, the presumption of the size of the dwellers within them was what captured my attention. While many would dispute the notion that big feet infer a full set of like-sized appendages, I beg to differ. Living with size 13 and 17 extra-wides in my home, and aware that the largest feet on record in the NBA, Roy Tarpley's, whose size 25 immeasurably-wides still held the Ripley's record for something, I knew the veracity of the general concept. Just google that name, and add the word dick.

I traipsed up the stairs before me while my eyes stayed glued to the ground supporting those big'uns. Upon reaching street level, I broke away from them reluctantly. That reluctance melted, however, at my realization that the biped being they supported was an entity rarely encountered in the wild… or Telluride town.

A gangly, obsidian-skinned, double image of the foxy musician, Jon Batiste, stood with impressive feet planted, knees slightly bent, arms akimbo, nostrils flared, stomach flatly absent, onyx eyes checking me out.

Oh, he was licking thick dark lips, too, I noticed, upon raising my own eyes from the nicely bulging crotch to encounter this overtly cocky Pan-like creature. His first words stuck with me. "You be the Doc with the bookends, a'ight?"

For a second, I thought I was being mocked. His face was not looking directly at me, rather at an angle, which made the cock-eyed scrutiny seem other than sincere. It morphed quickly to mischievous when his brilliant white teeth broke out from under the tongue licking those succulent lips.

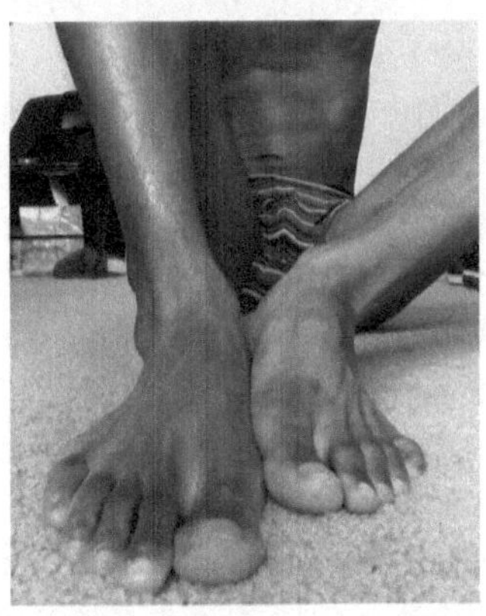

So I responded in kind. "What's up with those 'bookends', bra?" Though noncommittal, by my downward nod, he grasped the fact that the comment referred to his feet. I was gratified the guy had noticed me, but still unsure of any intent, stuck to an impersonal tack.

"I seen ya' with those two fly mens a couple days back—ya'll was in the bistro where I'm workin' right now. Kinda stood out. And, your hands was playin' all 'round those studs…Wassup with ya'own self?" Ahhh, now it came clear. My men and the proclivity of mine which was hardly held in check here in the liberal bastion of the mountain town full of 'misfits'. It did define me, I supposed.

And nobody overlooked my men. Both mature studs made plain our close-knit connection by their own body language, maybe more than I did. I will admit, my hands did tend to rove over their 'fly' presences…

Both big, deeply pigmented hands made the next statement: one wrapped around the bulge I had been assessing moments before and the other fisted itself toward me in a friendly bump request. The smile dipped on one corner as he clarified his intent. I bumped back and his fingers blossomed in retraction.

God, I loved the innate sultriness so many men-of-color radiate. Especially when they are tail-chasing. This one was manifesting the trait exceedingly well, I noticed, and my junk pitched upward by the comprehension.

Did I mention that the rascal was pinching a short, fat blunt between one dark thumb and long forefinger? He motioned me around a corner into the adjacent alley, using the blunt as a carrot. Little did he know that the bulge was much more my 'carrot' of choice. Or maybe he did know. Either way, I followed like I had a nose ring attached to his jeans button. I was feeling an oncoming event. No one was around that I could see, so what the hell?

Mystery dude lit up as he hoofed it, and the smoke left a definable trail to the back corner. He drew me leftward into a narrow dead end, his body language conveying a certain familiarity with it. A throbbing undertone of base drifted down from the small open window above us. The window vented a bar behind the wall the man stopped to lean against. The accompanying melody imbued the small semi-enclosure with an erogenous channeling of Grace Jones' song 'Walking in the Rain'.

Turning around to me, he cocked his leg up, foot on that wall, balancing on the other. The enwrapping hand still lightly massaged the noticeably bigger bulge. This act and the smile said a lot. The blunt went to his lips, lit end pointing inward, offering a more intimate share of the herb. I answered by matching my mouth to his.

His full lips were moist. They brushed mine as we anteed things up a notch. His dick-rubbing set of digits altered to out-reach, grasping my package. The thing blossomed in time-lapse as he unbuttoned my 501's. Only spreading the opening, he then leaned down and grasped the edges of our sweaters, slowly raising both of them over our heads in an upward mo-tion. His tongue licked my taut abdomen all the way through that progress and as both cleared our heads, he engulfed my mouth, tonguing it open.

My heavy dick punched its way out from the front gap in my bunched boxers and poked his sable belly. Day-ummmm, I gasped. This man was able and steroidal in his tightness, and I think I felt a fucking lightning bolt jolt my dick head. He traded our places with his hands on my waist, now pushing my back up against the wall.

That versatile tongue vacated my mouth and descended once again in the reverse manner it had licked me up, this time guzzling down over my cock. Stopping only upon reaching my loins. The back of his throat provided a perfect endpoint and he ground into me greedily, teeth biting the phatted root.

Experienced in the trade of cocksucking, the veteran raised up off of me as he recognized my too quick approach to the precipice. "As good as advertised, sexy man," he hissed in my face. Did he mean me, or himself, I wondered? His crotch contacted mine and I honestly didn't really care what he was packing by this time. The head was good enough. He appar-ently meant me, since he was back down on the dick in a fast second. Very clearly ready for the load.

He rivaled my Jeremy in his talent. Not. But, a distant sec-ond, no less. With only a few dozen full strokes, I came. He anticipated the timing, backing off of it for a moment. Watch-ing me spurt the first two jets of jism up to my own mouth level, it roped my lip. His devilish grin sent shivers up my spine. This was a bad boy, I suddenly apprehended. He managed to get his mouth back over my dong quick enough to swallow a full helping of protein, despite the watching, and I luxuriated in the hot wetness while his tongue cleaned up. I licked my lips.

We sat still for a minute, then the doppelganger unhurriedly stood up. He had loosened his pants and freed his piece while sucking. To let it breathe, I supposed. On rising up, I felt a limber cock rubbing up my calf and thigh. Next, delving under, then pulling against my scrotum. The warm member sideswiped past my asshole on the way. It rasped along my stomach, then pressed between us as he sucked my face now, passing me some cum-laden saliva, as nasty as he could.

My dick had no chance to wilt, springing back up between his own smooth upper thighs to his balls after he passed over it with his own on the way up.

He stopped oiling my mouth with his, "Don't be lookin' down there at my junks. Not 'til I tell you…Doctor." Uh-Oh, I thought. Intoning that title wasn't a real good omen.

My questing born again hard-on managed to contact his perineum and close-by asshole. The hot stud rubbed suggestively over it, teasing my just-erupted and still oozing piece. "Dat ain't gonna be happenin', beastie-boy…dat hole be a exit only. Get it gone from ya' head, now," he warned. But, he never moved from the contact.

My dick opportunely dry-pumped the spot while he lit up again, trading tokes to the slow grind rhythm of the on-going Grace Jones medley. 'Nightclubbing' filled the surrounds and we absorbed the sexy beat between us.

Blunt now down to a nub, the no-name cocksucker placed it on the tip of his tongue and pushed it as far down my throat as he could. I downed it, hoping it wasn't all I soon swallowed. "You 'bout to be my cravin' bitch, oreo-man. Seein' all that creamy white boy ass 'tween yo' two mens got me goin' t'other night. I'm a-wantin' to feel you all up on the insides." He didn't stutter in my ear at all.

Ooooh, that sweet talk always gets me. And, it just got better. He pulled out a little packet, white powder familiar. Handing it over to me, he told me "O-za Kay-za, bottom boii. On my mark, now, you gonna be removin' yo' mistaken boner from unda' ma' nuts, where it done been fakin' itself out, and you gonna go to descendin', slow-like, with yo' damn eyes closed, and durin' the trip you's gonna be thinkin' 'bout how you's gonna 'sprainkle' this all along my shaft after you's be slickin' the thang all up, good and nice—it gonna be stickin' to it a lot better that way. Then, you's gonna be lettin' me lift those creamy legs up and I'm gonna crack that private li'l cookie jar you got goin' back there, bitch." As this all sank in, he dipped a good scoop up on a long pinky nail and sucked it in one flared Batiste-like nostril, staring at me while he did it. The other hand's fingers searched out my pucker.

My dazed perceptions got the message, "And keep those damn eyes shut." I understood and I was ready.

"On mark.......Beee—yutch," was all else he said.

I followed the precise instructions, taking care to rub my dick all the way down his thigh and calf on the way for my introduction to the mystery piece rubbing between us. I kept my chest sliding down against his cum-laden chest, too. Getting down to a crouch, eyes closed, I searched for the hard prick with my tongue. Sucking it into my curious mouth upon locating the piece—it wasn't too tough to find—I said a mental 'Hi' to the long, smooth stalk. It went in easily, an insistent push the only evidence of his hyped desire.

The nice dick was cut, with a huge flanging head that explored the inside of my cheeks on the way in. I spent a good several minutes slathering it, liking the feel of the full bush surrounding the pole, contrasting it to the total smoothness around Jeremy's dick. Unable to deepthroat Gai's full eleven inches precluded that huge one from a common comparison to this one. My mental state of stoned was now enhanced by an extra small bump from the man's proffered pinky 'spoon' and, knowing what to do, I did. Sucked it in. The powdered pinky then erogenously rubbed my inner lips and teeth, leaving them tingling. My sucking was improved by the application. I doubled down on the rhythmic stroking.

When the music mix segued to Grace's 'Pull up to the Bumper', I managed to focus, letting loose my new favorite dick of the moment. "OK, you can open those eyes, now, boii." He was certainly keeping watch on the effort from above, slapping my face a few times with it, slobbering me up.

I carefully poured the remainder of the packet, as instructed, along the top ridge of an utterly stunning upward curving deep black penis. I had never seen such a darkly hued dick before and up close as it was, it appeared blue-black. Large, tortuous veins scrolled down the sides. The huge swollen crown kept threatening to throw off the powder by its happy jumping. I was forced to roll a finger around the top curve of the base to control its excitement, but finally managed without wasting too very much.

I next spat in my palm and slimed my waiting hole with it, reaching between my legs from my crouch. I couldn't wait to put the beauty where it obviously belonged. For the time being, anyway.

Standing, I allowed the mystery man to hook my knees, one by one, over his elbows. Strong arms lifted upward, pushing my back up the ancient brick wall. Our noses met. "I'm goin' in for some cookie dough, now, bitch." The throbber aligned right nicely in its curving anatomy. We both studied the other's eyes for emotion as it slowly, surely sank inside my juicy asshole. "Those pretty bitch eyes sure are getting' big…Doctor… and I'm thinking it ain't all because o' that powdery frosting on top o' my fine black dick…huh?"

Nodding, I felt the curved end reach its length—only slightly shorter than my true man's—and we sucked face while it was getting acquainted. My arms wrapped around his neck and drew him in to me. Liking the feel of the brillo bush tickling my ass globes, we grinded together as Grace broke into 'Use Me'. It was hot. The cold weather made both our nipples extra hard but the heat of our hooked bodies kept the chill at bay.

"Tell me what they call you, Dick Man," as I stared at him fucking me.

"When I pump yo' ass full of sperm and send you home to Daddy with it drippin' out, you call me Ezra—Ezra Pound. You gonna have me a baby and I am gonna have visitation rights, now, you got it, bitch?"

As we rocked my socks off there against that wall, I felt the scorching connection between us where the ultra-black dick was poling my ass. It was being rubbed. By fingers not belonging to any of our hands. All four were currently busy upstairs.

It was startling, but felt jood. Ezra felt it too, and our eyebrows both arched up. Looking back over the slim man's shoulders, we spied a miniature, nappy-headed ebony male kneeling down between Ezra's legs, checking the action and adding to it. He looked up at our altered movements and threw a familial grin up at our surprised faces. Couldn't care less by his intervention. "Boy, I told you to wait in the car, didn't I?" the big-dicked man demanded. No response. "Well, didn't I?" Nothing but crickets.

Grace broke into 'Nipple to the Bottle' and it dawned on me the rhythm between us hadn't changed. Neither had the small alien hand stroking our connection point down there. Ezra looked back at me, shrugged and grinned, like, "What can I do?" We picked up the pace.

The connection between us was palpable and I devolved into the music and the strokes. Ezra pounded my ass for ten more minutes, telling me all the disgusting words he could think of, most comments ending with "bitch". I bounced with the flow and crested before he did, spewing cum all between us again, smearing our bellies and chests.

That finally did it for the slim man, and I felt the sharp punch of his fat black dick into my gut where it seated itself, convulsing unseen shots of cum up inside me. The midget's alien fingers excited the whole effect.

Ezra Pound sucked my lips into his while he groaned at all the various sensations. Forbidden thoughts pulsed through the both of us…and maybe a third. In the midst of it all, we felt hot stabs of prickly hot goo erupt over both our asses; our eyebrows jumped again. So did our dicks.

We pumped together long past the climax point, feeling the erotic drippings underneath our connection, broiling in the blissful afterglow. The leer and evil-esque look had been replaced by satiation and he kept up the tonguing for several prolonged minutes. Extra fingers were still busy massaging the last pumps of his dick, keeping the slippery action going down below.

"You are pregnant, bee-yutch, and I be the Daddy, now—what's those two mens o'yours gonna be sayin' bout that, do ya' think?" He posited, rubbing my nose with his. And smiling.

"They're gonna want your number…Ezra Pound. You free night after tomorrow?"

Chapter 8
Stick Shift: C.S.P.

I watched, rigid dick in hand, as the smaller man squatted before the handsome stud who hit the vape cig between his fingers in obvious expectancy of some good head. Both men's ebony skin aided their blending into the shadows, which added to the mystique of my visual.

The diminutive dicksucker knew his way around dicks in general and this 'cocksucker palace' in specific. My nickname for the upscale bath house here in Atlanta was pretty apt as I had found out over the early part of the evening. Much communal and public dicksucking had already been witnessed as the hours unfolded, amongst many other anonymous, gratuitous sexual activities. A total turn-on.

My husband, Cal, had been correct in his depiction of the place as we drove to the big city the day before, taking a room at the Four Seasons off Peachtree Street for establishment of a base to pass an urban weekend bent on debauchery.

'Variety is the Spice-of-Life', as was once originally stated…the two of us were keeping the old adage viable.

We had enjoyed our first evening at the hotel restaurant on the loggia overlooking downtown Atlanta in casual but stylish fashion, laughing together over intimate discussions in anticipation of the hedonism to come.

The wait staff had been sized up during dinner in imaginative delight. A couple of convivial hours were spent conjuring lurid scenarios, assigning pretend tendencies, preferences and down-low plots to them while enjoying the full-bodied Cabernet we both preferred.

Ecdemolagnia. Definition: The practice of lascivious pursuits in cities other than one's origins.

We always laughed at the ridiculously strange word learned during Mardi Gras several years before from a jaded older gentleman. In the heart of the French Quarter close to Preservation Hall over a chance dinner at Petunia's on Toulouse Street. The retired English literature professor from Loyola University in New Orleans had dined alone at a table adjacent to ours. During a pause in our conversation, he had gestured and leaned toward me, stating the word into my ear. Having observed Cal and me during dinner, the older gentleman had apparently been daydreaming on our particulars through an elderly mind full of dirty fantasies.

Enthralled by the wiry old gent, we had accompanied him to his last-century, old-world residence overlooking Bourbon Street for an after dinner glass of port and kept contact with him ever since. He had grabbed a place in our hearts at that moment in time. We corresponded back and forth to the present day.

Pulling myself back to reality, I focused once again through the ready-made hole between the dark cubicles expressly cut for voyeuristic purposes. The two men of color carried on with their meeting, well aware of watchful eyes as they enjoyed themselves.

The smaller dude settled contentedly on his knees and proceeded to lovingly deepthroat the tall, lean big-footed man who relaxed, naked, back on the wall as he exhaled the vape hash smoke. The beat of house music set his tempo and the ex-perienced sucker fed himself a hit of amyl nitrate to 'up' his game.

I could see through to the next booth over as I watched and saw another pair of eyes taking in the action, as well. My closed but unlocked stall door creakily opened and a hand reach out tentatively, searching for my junk. Never the wall-flower, my knees spread to allow the probing and I sat up on the small bench above me to give better access.

Greedy hands gave way to slurping mouth and I, too, re-clined back on the wall to enjoy some oral work while continuing to view the ongoing masterful blowjob next door. My own cocksucker was well-suited for the task and I lightly shivered as he swallowed my shaft and pre-cum in a long, slow dive that ended with his nose nuzzling my crotch, rotat-ing on it in pleasure...for us both. His tongue worked inside the deepness of his mouth and throat while he stayed impaled there. I sighed at the ability he demonstrated.

Getting to see the sensual tactics practiced by the couple while I was being serviced was exactly what I had come here for. I reveled in the slow ministrations by this un-named mouth boy. And, boy he was: mid-twenties, at most. The dark-ness kept me from the details but what I could see of him portrayed a young face with bushy 'fro topping it and slender-ness below his neck level bearing out youth. He was enjoying my over-sized white prick as much as the dick sucker I was studying next to us servicing that huge one. It seemed the two were in sync with their rhythmic strokes, which increased my enjoyment by the fact. The boy offered me his popper bottle after a deep intake of his own and I accepted gladly.

Other eyes were watching the action between us and I heard various sex acts playing out close by in other stalls over the beat of the implicitly sexual music egging-on the activities. What a vibe. Begging, dirty instructions, animalistic grunts and pleading groans all perfused the shadows and amplified the testosterone-saturated atmosphere. I could sense the blood-pumping hardness of many boners as I watched the one and felt the other. Hedonistic heaven.

The statuesque man next to us, focus of my attention, began an agitated increase in activity. Locking his hands over the sucker's head to guide the efforts, he finally unloaded a nice load to the smaller man's tonsils. Keeping his big piece lodged to the limit, the man pumped cum in multiple squirts, marked by the thrusts I saw.

After enjoying the climax, the tall man extracted the thing and slapped the sucker's face by wagging it back and forth across cheeks and nose. His little server loved the 'frosting' on his face and tried smiling up at him but couldn't quite do so with the 10-inch piece wiping the smile off with each swipe. Then, he was finished. Turning, he slipped out the spring-braced door to other pursuits. I was satisfied from his show and looked forward to running into him elsewhere. My bigfoot man.

The dick boy between my legs continued on in ignorance of the exhibition next to us, oblivious to just about everything except for my dick and his popper bottle. Good for me. I leaned back and closed my eyes in enjoyment of the pleasure being delivered, slowly rubbing my palm up and down my stomach and chest. I wondered why I hadn't moved into this place years ago.

The little pro worked my piece up to shooting several times but the swelling alerted him and he disappointed the big dick over and over in extending his control over it and me. Finally, ready to let me jump the juice, the skinny boy backed off. Turning his curved little pre- greased butt to my dick he plunged down on it all in one motion. This maneuver had obviously been practiced before as he squeezed until I couldn't handle any more and gave homie the prize he had been holding at bay until then. I released in bliss, feeling the baby-laden essence roll around warmly on my mushroom head, making me tingle by the heat.

The cute boy didn't want to give up the dick and stayed there, planted, while he stroked his own cock, contentedly bouncing up and back on mine for stimulation, then suddenly constricting hard as he erupted, hitting the opposite wall in an arc of milky plasm. Five or six more spurts followed as the kid gritted his teeth and butthole, adding to my after-effect. I was glad to have stuck around...

We lifted together, allowing the extrusion of my 8-1/2 inch piece. Still turgid to the point of bouncing up and slapping my belly, it then settled contentedly on his glutes. Dripping left-overs onto the sexy little small point of his lower back. He jumped like he was burning and turned around laughing, then hugged me and promised to look for me again later on--- I stood out in the dark, he told me. So it was a 'date'.

Assuming he meant due to my stark paleness in contrast to most of the clientele, I smiled and blew in his cutest little ear, leaving the cubicle in search of a hot shower and my husband...bigfoot.

Temporarily satisfied to voyeur my way through dark hallways lined by locked private rooms, loaded with feet of turgid meat and audible as hidden booty-traps, I wandered my way down two levels to the festive pool area and then on past to the humid, communal tiled shower room.

With the only light filtering in through the glass entry door, I could barely make out the multiple groupings of partakers in luscious iniquity, variously peering low to see couples on the tile floor writhing in joined frenzy to steamy corners where orgies carried on their sexual tirades against the disapproving outside world, skin-to-fucking-skin, heads-to-tails, mouths to groins or other body parts, all while apparently overlooking the cleansing function that the shower had been meant for...not. This pleasure room was a multi-tasking buffet of a sexual Mickey-D's. With eat-in-only services.

Finally locating an unused showerhead, I feasted on the live, rowdy porn flick around me, luxuriating in the cleansing steam and soap, half-hard throughout by the lewd party.

I definitely over-stayed the recommended three-minute shower as several beautiful examples of suckable dickmeat meandered past my spot. Some lingered for a test-run, which I happily provided. A couple of mouthfuls of cum and a third or fourth shower later, I sashayed past two phosphorescent cock-ringed boys in the midst of mutual explorative efforts-- almost a Cirque show of coordinated body movement in itself-- and vacated to the next erotic 'bumper car'.

The big darkroom on the level above had a constant stream-ing nasty video screen meant to trigger activity in that place dominated by the wall-to-wall mattress. Like a trigger was at all necessary.

I found clumps and piles of black-skinned hunks or black-on-white hydrox blends, all intermingled in snake-like, writhing bunches and joined in an amazing array of sexual di-does. The overwhelming odors of maleness on top of sperm pervaded all. The beat of the ever-present explicit lyrics and music blended the environs.

Inviting hands attempted to draw wanderers into various plots and schemes but I was curious to see if that tall ripped man of exceeding masculinity from the third floor cubicle was anywhere to be found. Hottest man in the place.

A huge dark hand fastened around my ankle and its viselike grip forced my attention. The attached man was a giant of a guy, seemingly endless in his length from the horizontal per-spective he presented. No one else was with him and he apparently intended that as he brusquely shook off a hand on his own leg. Pulling me down to him, I just barely resisted, drawn to the man's size and girth. Jumbo. A towel loosely draped his crotch and his cue ball head ogled me. The big-boned wrist was equal in size to my ankle and his bicep easily out-sized my thigh.

His towel was tenting very invitingly as I hit the mattress. The plus-size dude didn't give me a chance to say anything, not that I really attempted it. The big body covered me in a split second. The man sure seemed to know what he wanted.

Those hands entwined and dwarfed my own, spreading them away from my body and successfully stifling any imagined resistance. Beautifully full, sensuous lips engulfed my own and his tongue snaked its way between my teeth almost gagging me by its size. God, I thought, what is between the man's legs if his tongue can do this?

In covering me, his left leg had bent, kneeing my stomach as an anchor. His calf pinned my aroused piece against my smooth flatness. That did nothing but engorge me more so. I worked at getting enough breath into my lungs as his gargantuan chest pinned mine.

He withdrew his tongue and backed off a bare inch to peer down at me, eyeing me as he growled, "Who's your Daddy tonight, Bitch?" My answer was almost squelched by the quiet vehemence; I gave in to the moment and the fantasy.

"You, Daddy," I barely squeaked. I felt that muscled calf rhythmically spasming over my hard dick. To the music. Oh, wait...that was not the man's calf...

"Bitch, you gonna need to be tongue-cleanin' my ass, now," he informed me, and I trembled a bit as I contemplated both that and the size of what I had mistaken for his calf. I wanted a look down there but he guessed my thought and let me know, "You don't-Even-need to be nosin' around down there, pretty bitch, I don't want you passin' out-- at least before I get all up inside'n you, pussyboy." The sweet-talk gets me every time. I smiled, remembering my best friend, Luke's, similar weakness.

Apparently deciding against my eating him out, at least for the time-being, he loosed one huge hand and reached for his towel. Unwrapping a knotted corner, Jumbo withdrew a small vial of white powder, rolling it between his fingers in front of my face. "See this bitchboy?" he said, 'I needs a bump before I remind you of the trailer park, pimped-out, ass-lickin, punk-ass bitch that you are."

With that, he warned me not to try getting up and raised his humongous set of pecs from mine. His knee stayed planted on me and he unscrewed the little bottle one-handed. A long fingernail provided a spoon for a small mound of the powder and he adeptly snuffed it into a flared nostril, inhaling deeply to get it all in, some escaping down on my nose and lips. I could feel the stuff as it lay on my face and noted the tickly prickle that was cocaine powder as it numbed my skin.

Seeing my dismay, he assured my it was 'only coke—nottin' better', as if that should relieve me, but he then took the matter up a notch and rolled the fingernail over, emptying the residual directly on my lips and rubbed his pinky over, around and between my lips to my gums. Not good, I thought, but a little late to refuse.

His smirk assured me of his deed as intended and he raised himself further, allowing a gap between my crotch and his. I got my first glimpse at the wrist-thick log hovering buoyantly an inch above my erect cock and would have been fearful, I think, had I not felt the beginning effects of the coke infusing me with a desire I hadn't known before.

Even as I eyed the monster, an anonymous ebony hand reached for it, slicking it thoroughly with Vaseline. I was awestruck at the seeming smallness of an otherwise large hand partially encircling it and buzzed with anticipation now as the big bull sprinkled an extra little pile of powder on the foreskin and ballooning head poking from inside it, using that multi-tasking finger to spread it over the whole greasy thang.

The mystery hand disappeared and I felt my ankles being pulled apart by other unseen hands until I was spread-eagled under that prick. One foot had been pulled on by a foot fetish freak who set to driving me crazy sucking my toes. I watched as Jumbo, slow-motion, lined that thing up with my asshole and met the sphincter lightly, looking up at me as he held it there to allow a minute for the powder to absorb.

"Are you ready for a good, deep fuck lesson, Bitch?" His steely breath filled my senses. Not waiting for nor wanting a reply, the giant pressured forward steadily with the object of my new-found need stretching my gut as I couldn't ever re-member. The magic powder blocked any pain, but not the stretching sensation.

He drew my eyes to his and literally drooled on my neck and face. Both of us shared the plugging in of that beautiful dick until finally sensing the tickle of his pubic curls and mega balls against my round butt. I also felt more than one unknown hand massaging and exploring that dick-buttocks juncture and my whole ass was soon fully smeared with lube. This Daddy-tonight re-inserted that huge tongue back into my mouth and proceeded to undulate those huge hips as we melded into the act.

The knowledge of observers to this and the feel of multiple fingers following our progress heightened my first-time expe-rience of several unaccustomed sensations. Jumbo's tongue searched my mouth from my gums to my teeth to my own tongue to my tonsils and I silently begged for this to never end. My eyes were locked on his as we joined in a fucking of deep-in-my-gut places not plugged into before. Those dark eyes widened each time he dead-ended up inside me, and I faintly noticed outside sounds complementing the fingers feel-ing our fuck. Close-by but faraway voices play-by-played our action.

"Feel that big bare-ass bumped-up dick hittin' that slut-ass nasty-ho' pussy," one said, "this white bitch be needin' that dick--he ain't never gettin' enough o'that pimpin' dick, is he? Everyone know what a low-rent, ass-slurpin' pale-butt slut cunt cocksucking, big balls licking, faggoty, cheatin' punkass, cum-smellin, raggedy, loose-hole cunt he really be… a'ight?"

My racing mind and heartbeat numbly registered the rant as I took that beast to the hilt and pleaded this big daddy for more. The hands increased in numbers and places visited and I detected familiarity to the nasty-ass 'conversations' going on around me. I found it hard to concentrate on anything more than the dick and tongue invading my married self.

Never wanting this to finish, the music registered dirtiness describing me to-a-T and I moaned in ecstasy amidst the wholeness of this coke-fueled fuck on so many planes.

A hand took my wrist and pulled it to a long dick pushing in-and-out a close by asshole, bare and slimy, while voices kept up the chanting gutter talk. I lay engulfed by that demanding muscle tongue and listened to the words between the raspy, whispering topman whose dick I was fingering hit the ho's hole next to us. The whimpering bottom needing the dick, bad.

"Pumpin' this bro-ass pussy like it likes, aren't I, you cheap cunt bee-utch? That phat black ass takin' this slippery cock you love so much with that deep, pimped-ass hole beggin' me to cum up in it while you feel that big dick plow that sissy-ass drugged-up badboy cocksuckin' prissy-prancin' whiteboy nigga-lovin faggot over there, c-o-r-r-e-c-t. bitch?"

"I bet you thought this big dick faggot-fucking booty-bustin' throat and face-fucking sweet dick daddy forgot this black bubblebutt slut cunt cocksuckin', lipstick-wearin' sissy-ass bro-hole, huh? Well, I gonna tell you how I be fuckin' you right here with these perv-lovin' bitch cunts wishin' they had this dick pumpin' their nasty slimed-up sissy pussys just like you and this white bitch be gettin right 'chere and right now, huh, babypussybitchboy?"

The sexy perverted harangue made me feel at home in a weird way as I kept my fingers probing the slippery prick pushing on that begging hole. The couple obviously wanted my hand there as an extra hand gripped my own ass, encouraging it to share the fuck-action with them. I was enjoying their fuck almost as much as my own.

Other fingers followed the giant's and my gyrations, finding spots to rub and probe, wrapping us two in a greasy sheen of whole-body slipperiness. My huge dick daddy took to fucking to the beat of the rap music and my pelvis responded by rolling into it with each punch back up to those tickly pubes and I listened to the rutting pair in my reach as they fulfilled needs obviously unfilled 'til now...

"I'm gone' put you back on that couch downstairs, bitch, in front of everybody, and grab the back of your nappy-ass head with my large man hands and pump my massive nigger-bro cock in-an-out your bitch ass faggot sissy cunt throat, as my big beautiful cock start to swell in your throat with all these cocksuckers wishin' they was you. I will facefuck you hard and deep and right before I cum I will pull my massive pretty dick out o' your beggin' bitch-ass throat and slap you in the face and head with it and then spray cum all over your sissy ass bitch face and watch while everyone watch you enjoy the warmth of my juice splash all over yo' punk face."

"Then I'm a gonna sit back and watch as you take your sissy bro hands and wipe it off your face and lick my sweet cum off your fingers then crawl your bitch ass over and suck the rest of my cum out of my large fat cock. Then I'm gonna command your punk ass to lick and suck my balls and lick my manly ass, all of which will give you as much pleasure as it give this man fuckin you now."

"Little bro bitch nigga, you gone' discover why bitches are MY bitches for as long as I want them to be! I'ma turn your faggot punk sissy ass over and put you on your knees and you gone' lay yo' head on your folded arms with that sweet bubble ass in the air and your ass pussy fully exposed to everyone, you cheap-ass nigga-ho, the small of your back arched up and your belly touching the couch, nothin' but ass in the air."

"Then I slide up to your sissy faggot punk ass and rub my large fat swollen-up dick against the opening of your sissy ass pussy, and again I just put the massive head in that tight ass pussy hole and stroke you a inch at a time until you are begging for the 10's."

"I will fuck you slow and deep so everyone sees what a punk-ass begging sissy you really are and then I pick up the pace and thrust my massive man meat into your faggot rear pussy and you will call me daddy like this white bitch next to you do for everyone that wants his cheatin' ass sissy white hole."

"You gonna be calling for all the gods you know, bitch, 'cause I'ma pound your punk sissy faggot ass just the way your punk ass dream of gettin' your ass fucked by every big dick you can get holt of, and the way I always fuck you. You are as near to heaven as any living being has ever been, and bro-bitch, that is why I am your big dick faggot-fucking throat-choking, sissy making, massive dick giving daddy, and don't you ever forget it, BITCH."

My butt-punching jumbo man was feeding off this hot-as-hell bitch-rant as much as I was and suddenly rose up, pulling his whoppin' big piece right out of me, shooting sperm all over my whiteboy stomach and chest and face, anonymous hands reaching in to catch it. Then those hands guided the mother-fucking thang right back where it had been inside me and he lay down on me rubbing his cum between us while the duo with my fingers on them continue to fuck each other.

The big man growled throatily in satisfaction and then reached a fat hand up to my chin and turned my cum-bespeck-led face sideways toward the nasty-talking fucker next to us: there be my husband man, grinning at me as he rhythmically dicked his little brother's ass. Doy-Al's. His real life younger brother. And my derisive brother-in-law...

Doy had been condescending to me from the day I had darkened the family doorway in Rome, Georgia, and try as I might, he remained the single brother of them all that I could not win over regardless of my tack...here he lay, pincered by my loving man stud of a husband, Cal, my beloved true-me Daddy, and my only love, with his beautiful 10-inch man dick buried deep in the brotherly ass now so obviously being enjoyed.

As my jaw slackened in disbelief, my man and Doy-man both stared over at me in my spread-eagled hard-on state, my big erect cock sticking out from the side of the gap between my jumbo fucker's belly and my own. In my coke-induced euphoria, I saw the brothers grin in sexual satisfaction as they viewed my pretty dick start spewing cum all over the mattress and the two of them, while my rigid-dicked topman continued pushing his huge dick in and out my asshole.

The pleasure was indescribable so I will suffice it to say my man and my disapproving bro-in-law came at the same time, watching me writhe in ecstasy. Cal's hand felt my ass with his fingers as I spasmed through my climax and the pretty dick of Doy's pumped juice, too, while enjoying the breeding by his older brother...satisfied smile written all over his handsome face as he stared me down.

Many unknown hands finger-painted all over the canvas of our four-way joint orgy. We all just lay, sagging in exhaustion after the sensate feast just experienced. Cal's big strong hand slid sensuously up my slippery side to my lips in replete communion and I licked the juices from them rather than biting them, as Doy had apparently predicted. Doy was grinning ear-to-fucking-ear as he declared victory, ignorant of Cal and my solid bond.

Through a now re-invigorated confidence in he and Cal's brotherly link, Doy-Al communicated a distinctly new vibe between the two of us as he fingered his full, cum-spattered lips then reached out and touched my mouth and Cal's fingers with family juices, coating me thoroughly. We had achieved détente… He felt he had won the battle here, but we all had won the peace and I now relaxed in full knowledge that Doy's disapproval would be forever in the past from here on out.

Good thing I am such a non-jealous, sharing bitch, I thought, as I completed the circle with my own fingers touching my nasty, sharing, brotherly duo.

Jumbo Man never stopped pumping me slowly and deliberately and we three basked in the afterglow while my temp-daddy methodically gave up two more loads to my probably pregnant hole. The feelings perpetuated sublime contentment and I was fulfilled in much more than a single way...Da-y-ummm!!!

Loving me some more of my family... and their friends. With my man.

Atlanta rocks.

Chapter 9
Tride and True: Mighty
Tungsten Tuberosity, Part 1

"OK, now I think I get it," I responded to Jeremy's detailed explanation about the idea for his Hallowe'en costume being 'assembled' for the coming weekend. I continued massaging the meaty, dark-skinned foot resting across my lap as we chillaxed intimately on the rich mahogany leather divan in the cozy low-beamed great room. The fire log was still glowing with heat on the nippy early evening, as borne out by the comatose dogs before the crackling fireplace on the sheepskin rug newly covering the hearth. Oh, we were butt-naked too, but not goose-pimpled. So, yes, it was still blazing comfortably.

I dearly loved the stark contrast of my husband's big feet, the top surfaces matching the color of the couch while the white undersides were paler than my own skin. The dichotomy had always stoked my curiosity by the puzzling two-toned affect. While sexy as hell in my eyes, the color scheme just seemed upside down to me for some reason.

Jeremy tossed kernels of popcorn into his mouth by launching them in a high arc and catching them on the descent, a satisfied look permeating his face now that I seemed to grasp his concept. I couldn't help eyeing the thick sausage reclining in the crevice of his nearby groin as I watched his adept hand-to-mouth action. My fingers contemplated dropping the toes and upgrading to that master piece.

Damn, I thought, this man still had me whipped even just lounging here, innocently smushing BaddDick. His nickname for my cock. While J-man feigned ignorance of it, the intermittent pressure exerted by the foot alerted me to his recognizance of my piece's taut posture…

"Ya'know I couldn't just use 'Gai's band's namesake, honey. It would feel sacrilegious or something. So, since tungsten carbide is the second hardest substance known to Man after diamonds, and the hardest metal," he accentuated the last two words with a noticeable prod to my crotch, "it just seems right."

Jeremy had a funny way of rationalizing sometimes, I mused, kneading each toe methodically while mentally visualizing the intricate outfit gradually coming together for the upcoming ghoulish celebration Saturday night.

Different pieces of it lay spread around the house and porches. It had been plainly tough to understand when he had first described his intent, and I was still perplexed at the complexity of it but I wasn't letting on about my doubts at this point. He was approaching exasperation with me after days of explanations, so I had decided the better part of valor was to simply claim comprehension and await the final product for its full effect. Pictures versus a thousand words, I had deduced…

Mighty Tungsten Tuberosity: why was my man naming a costume, anyway? Loosely translating to 'hard rounded protuberance', the mixed metaphor and double entendre just didn't lend credence to a spooky factor for the Tride Mountain Monster Mash Bash scheduled to occur up in the old Pandora Mine this Saturday night. Wrapping my mind around it had left me a bit abashed…smile. Pun intended. I sniggled inwardly at my own wit.

Jeremy glanced my way at that moment, a popped kernel bouncing off his wide nose. Supposing my smile indicated a completely different subject—and no doubt the same one on his mind-- he wrenched the size 13 hoof from my hands, dug those toes at my midsection and in an athletic motion pivoted his sinewy body around until I was suddenly holding the sides of his smooth bowling ball head instead. He went to licking on my now freed hard-on. I certainly wasn't about to argue that decision.

His excessive hormonal displays were never really surprising to me at this stage of our relationship. I had received superb head in the confines of aloft jets beneath sleeping blankets, grocery store bathrooms, and tennis court bleachers at midday over the years. There had also been that time at a symphony performance when the electricity went out. The symphony kept playing via battery-lit music stands and I had cum during the cannon shots of the 1812 Overture. Formally attired for the concert, it had given a whole new meaning to the word cummerbund.

I never tired of the attention and felt gratified that my man was attached to my dick as much as he was to my ring finger. He had, after all, fitted both our fingers and our dickstaffs with matching— yup, indeed: size 10-1/2 and 12 finger rings and 2-1/2 and 3-1/2 inch diameter dick rings— 24 K gold-dipped sterling silver bands on our wedding night.

Very attached to both, I wore them now, and my man wrapped his hand around the precious metal cock ring as he commenced with his second favorite pastime. Swallowing turgid dick. Mine fortunately topped his list and I laid back now, feeling the hot mouth and tongue set to work riling me further up. Apparently Jeremy had additional ideas in mind, too, because the other hand's middle finger wriggled its way directly up my puckered asshole, edging my prostate and expanding things.

He gradually switched to swirling his fingers over my stomach in increasing arcs, ending up at my nipples, while inching his knees up under him and thereby narrowing the gap between his dick head and my hole. The steady mouth strokes distracted me until the tip of his piece tentatively brushed against the ass ring he desired. Those nipple tippling fingers erotically reached up to his mouth, collecting enough spit to smooth the engorged dickhead's entry into my warm and waiting chute. His favorite sexual pastime...fucking.

Jeremy was the only man I had ever known who was hung enough and limber enough to be able to suck my dick while sinking his long pole into me simultaneously and he pushed it now while continuing the oral action. The sensations were wonderful and my eyes rolled back in my head as he penetrated more deeply.

Upon bottoming out at the thick-rooted nine-inch mark, he held stock still all at once, letting my ass get used to the filled feeling. His pelvis arched backward while he pulled my globes along with the retrograde rotation. As I was still acclimating, the thought of his gentlemanly nature ingratiated me more to this indulgent action.

That is, until opening my eyes to the view of big Ambergai Gee, our houseguest, peering down at me from over Jeremy's shoulder. I realized then that the reggae man had snuck in without a sound, coming up on my man from the rear. That must've presented an alluring picture...Jeremy's high, round, curved melons were unignorably perfect.

He was now doing his own penetrating, right up into the opposing buttface of the arched pelvis whose house anaconda was piercing my ass. The knowledge that that huge prick of Gai's was sliding up into my stud man completed the ménage-a-trois. We had been refining the technique since the temporary addition of the mature Rastafarian to our happy home.

Jeremy continued bending his beautiful butt in acceptance of the familiar dick and upon seating itself completely, we three reveled in the state of things. The two of them began a slow, rhythmic, undulating pattern which progressed to a blasting three-way fuck. Damn, I was a lucky man, I thought, amidst the pounding. All of us were of similar mind as we enjoyed the conjoined intimacy.

Gai's hands grasped my man's waist as he deeply stroked the ass that he had broken in as an adolescent so many years before. The tall, older man's dreads tickled his back. Jeremy's mouth rose up off my dick, meeting my lips as we sucked face amidst the double fuck. I could feel the spasms of J's dick pulse through my innards with each forward stroke by the Jamaican. Both worked their way to climax until the heat of an erupting load suffused my gut and a cascading effect capped us, all three groaning in a collective cum of paroxysmal pleasure.

Mr. Ambergai fell forward against J's back, the long dreadlocks brushing up and down over my face now, in post-coital satisfaction. Jeremy tongued me deeply as the sensations ebbed. All three of us lay in flushed fulfillment during the regaining of our grip on reality. The two big dicks stayed right in their warm holes and mine wasn't wilting a bit. Jeremy fingered it possessively, gathering my creamy globules.

"Methinks ma'two pussy boys be vyin' for ma'ttentions by the way mi keep a'findin' the buttcheeks a'tuggin' at ma' eyeballs on each o' ma turnarounds, now," Gai contentedly drawled. Jeremy turned and looked up at his mentor, noting that he didn't miss too many chances. We tended to find ourselves in this situation rather frequently nowadays.

Ambergai Gee had invaded our sanctuary since the autumnal equinox weeks before, inveigling himself into our routine, our music playlist, our diet and, of course, our big bed. We were both good with the company since variety was, indeed, our spice…and most assuredly made the most of the mindbendingly beautiful ass-stretcher between the man's legs. Either one of us was likely to come upon the other sucking on the insatiable tool and each such discovery inevitably led to variations on the three-way such as had just finished… horn-doggery abounded.

As we backed off and toweled each other, the subject of the Hallowe'en party re-emerged and we queried our friend about any intent regarding his attendance. He responded circumspectly once again, as he had when we first told him of the annual bash.

It seemed the Jamaican community did not view Hallowe'en, or All Hallows' Eve, in the same manner as we Americans did. He had informed me of the solemn and macabre history it symbolized in the Caribbean nations. The religious as well as the pagan undertones of the day and night still took precedence over any light-heartedness. Even to the point of high anxiety for many. Morbidity and mortality were more commonly associated memes of their season.

All Saints' Eve. Dia de los Muertos. Day of the Dead. Samhain. All were a part of the three day Allhallowtide observance for remembering the dead. And preceding that, the harvest festival. America had managed to divorce itself from the seriousness of it through the generations. Ahhh, the low expectations of casino capitalism…

We hoped the man would commit to attending, even should we not know what way his presence might manifest itself. Hence, our enlivened curiosity. Settling back to the spacious sectional sofa with hot buttered rums, I nestled into Jeremy's body while receiving one of his exquisite head rubs. Gai (we pronounced it: Jye) took his place at the opposing end, proffered a size 17 foot toward my lap in replacement of Jeremy's and we popped in a DVD to enjoy 'vegging' for a while: the old spoof cult movie, Hocus Pocus, starring the divine Bette Midler.

Early exposure to massage through a favorite aunt had been refined by devoted practice on other favorites in prophetic anticipation of Jeremy and, recently, Gai, the two men I now fondly kneaded. Besides, the huge appendages of both the men in my home provided exceedingly sexy ways for bonding…as evidenced by my almost constant half-hard state. The men seemed to enjoy both the attention and my sexual readiness. So we were all happy.

Half an hour later, when replacing one huge foot for the other in my lap, we all jumped upon hearing a sudden rap on the front door.

Being dark, and the weather in flux due to a descending Norther, we had not expected company during the evening, but Gai retracted his leg, arose and nudely made his way over to our entranceway, big languid dick dangling and rocking as he did so. Our heads both bobbled with it as it bobbed back and forth… go figure.

Twisting the knob, he shamelessly opened the heavy wooden fixture and smiled seductively outward as we heard a soft, refined exclamation, "Well, now, Sir Ambergai. Don't you just look so…healthy?" We recognized the articulate manner to be no less than the personage of the Lady Carlotta Saxe-Coburg, a neighbor from one of the opulent chateaus down the mountain. Jeremy pushed me up in front of him, pulled on a pair of baggy boxers and threw a like set at my face in an unspoken instruction, then went to greet the unexpected guest.

She stood under the porte cochere, still mesmerized by the au naturel state of Gai, perplexed as to what way to proceed. Jeremy rounded into the doorway, chesting Gai aside with a big hand and inviting the true Lady into our log home. I looked out through the wood shutters of the tall windows behind the couch to the pebbled drive, spotting the Pierce Arrow touring car Carlotta most commonly used for travel, discerning a barely visible driver through the gloom of the misty evening. The precision classic automobile idled almost noiselessly, answering the unheard nature of the neighbor lady's appearance.

I reached over and gathered up the three fluffy robes next to the fireplace where we had dropped them after the shower following the sexcapade earlier. The dogs finally roused themselves to the intrusion, sleepily going to sniff the English peer now entering our domain. She acknowledged them each with a pat and I wondered if she might replicate the action toward we men should another nude male happen upon her.

Lady Carlotta did relax somewhat upon the breaking out of the robes, though noncommittally eyeing the fact of Gai's insistence at leaving his untied, the big piece still lolling visibly. Such a Jamaican, I thought. The human anatomy's visual presence seemed a granted state in his island mindset and I busied myself corralling the boys back to their hearth sites as cover for my grin at the candid display.

Carlotta wore an evening dress of black silk, cut low over one shoulder, dark hair coiffed up and framing her attractive face, ringlets escaping, showing off her long, swanlike neck and simple pearl choker. Obviously coming from a dressy affair, her matching black high heels wrapped in crisscross style up around slim ankles, complementing the understated outfit. The woman exuded great fashion sense. A faux silver fox stole hung low around her arms and no jewelry adorned her aristocratic long-fingered hands. The effect only accentuated the class dripping from her presence.

"Upon leaving the Devon's dinner party," she was saying, "I had Paecup drive up directly to see you boys." Ambergai extended a long arm and taking hers to his elbow, led her into the warmth of our home, sitting her down in an overstuffed easy chair close by the fireplace. The man bowed, as did his proud island dreads and long dick, then backed away.

The picture of the well-dressed lady and the dread-locked, partially robed, dick-dangling giant with humongous clodhopper feet waltzing through the room nearly had me bursting with laughter as I channeled Bilbo Baggins and the elven queen of Lothlorien. My man, seeing my look, stepped decidedly on my foot as warning to curb it…ahem, he signaled. So I bit a lip and behaved, snugly securing my own robe belt. Darn it.

"Because of the disturbing subject of conversation over the digestif," Carlotta went on, "I wanted to check on you boys to assure myself that all was well with the three of you." Her glance over at Gai made me think she might as easily have said, "the four of you." Curious, Jeremy questioned her concerns and she continued by informing us that there had been an alarming development from high up the mountain. As our secluded home was one of the most highly placed, she had worried over our well-being, she told us.

It seems that Adolpho, the wine sommelier, while hiking the high ridge earlier in the day, had come across a dreadful scene. An apparent bear attack had left a tourist couple visiting the area sorely ripped to bloody pieces, the lady brokenly apprised us. The bodies had been so disfigured that the sheriff's department had only made an identification by dental records in the past hour and word was now spreading around the small, close knit mountain community.

Miss Carlotta had stopped first at her close confidants, the elderly Chastains, to make sure of their safety, before coming to see us. Hmm, I pictured the Lady popping in an hour earlier had she not stopped there…Gai's excitatory state then would have made her present discomfiture seem tame by comparison. I had to again curb myself at the notion of Gai nonchalantly plopping the homunculus out of Jeremy's ass and opening the door in that imagined moment… Slap that thought from my head, I warned myself. This was serious.

While relieved to hear none of our neighbors had been victimized, we were all three horrified at the prospect of man killer bears marauding through the area. Gai, ever the gallant, disappeared for a moment, reappearing with a snifter of Drambuie for the Lady. She accepted graciously. We discussed the ramifications of the development and decided it best to proceed carefully until the murderous beasts were tracked down and relocated.

It was extremely rare to have black bears act aggressively, unless cornered, so we were all taken aback by the violent episode so close to us all. Adolpho was apparently very shaken up, per the sheriff, Carlotta informed us, and Jeremy went to call the boy he was so fond of, to ascertain his mental state. I hollered after him to invite the young Italian to come stay with us for the time being, what with the man's flimsy house a mile away from ours. The place was very remotely located.

Carlotta settled herself by sipping the sweet liqueur and we gradually led the conversation away from the catastrophe, attempting to further calm her frayed nerves. Gai's protuberant dangling did seem to draw her attention periodically, I noticed. I asked the English woman if she had heard anything pertaining to the coming costume soiree set for the old mine up the heights on the other side of the mountain. She answered that the 'constabulary', as she referred to the law, was assessing the situation for the safety implications over the next days. Depending on what occurred, she surmised, would affect the decision of the event going forward or not. But, of course she planned to attend.

Peering out again into the deepening dusk, I noticed the driver leaning on the long hood of the touring car smoking a cigarette and asked if Carlotta wouldn't prefer him to come inside under the circumstances. She concurred this was a good idea so I went to invite the man indoors.

The handsome young man appeared surprised at my request, usually being content to stay with the automobile that he babied and cooed over, keeping its pristine condition up to standards. Nevertheless, he acquiesced to my invitation. After turning off the engine, we came into the warmth. Gai, again acting the gracious host, brought the chauffer a balloon of Louis XIII cognac.

Paecup couldn't disregard the haphazard dress of the tall man and was not immune to appraising the startlingly large, fat piece the two of us were usually so content to have flop around. The Lady herself seemed resigned to the uncovered beast by now, still sidelonging it every so often. The driver inadvertently licked his lips at its sighting and I wondered how long it would take for the RastaMon to acquaint himself better... introverted, the man was definitely not. And, his interest in the young Russian was palpable. The big dick waggled just a little more than need be when delivering the best cognac in the house, I observed.

We spent another half hour catching up on the community news and considering details about the 'episode' up mountain, then decided it was time to call it a night. Jeremy offered to accompany Lady Carlotta home but she informed us that Mr. Andropov was 'quite accomplished in the pugilistic arts'. She felt quite safe with him escorting her, thank you.

So we bid the two out to the Series 36 dual valve 1927 model icon of touring cars, delivering the Lady into the plushness of the embroidered Italian leather seating and the gold trimmed interior. Paecup secured her inside and took the driver's seat as they gracefully purred away down the mountain into the darkness. I licked my nose as a large snowflake alighted on it, contemplating yet another of this high-born woman's peculiarities. Who else might have a handsome Russian chauffer named Paecup Andropov?

* * *

The windows had all been secured and draped, the doors all double-locked, then rechecked, before we had retired upstairs to the polished cypress king bed we called our own. I lay, head on Jeremy's stomach, gazing into the dying embers of the bedroom fireplace. Listening to Gai's low breaths and feeling the slow rise and fall of J-man's familiarly slow, deep sleep breathing, I luxuriated under Jeremy's warm palm on my bare back. It was safely comforting as I brooded over the probable final minutes of the unknown tourist couple torn to shreds on the top of the majestic mountain I so loved. I didn't want to associate it that way from here on.

It must be close to 3 AM now, a common time for me to awaken. I internalized things during that dark-of-night time: mountains from molehills were conjured in the sterile stillness of the hour. It required effort to keep in mind that the conjured things would be reduced to nothing...mental ashes...by the breaking dawn. I missed the night sounds with all of the windows shut tight this night. The silence stifled me. My man put up with the peculiar need for openness and outdoor sounds, even in the dead of winter. Its susurrus hypnotized me to sleep and I wanted to hear those reassuring sounds now...

Out of the stillness, I picked up on a light scuffling outside our French doors to the balcony. At first I thought it to be the lisping scrape of overhanging tree branches. But the sound persisted in regular pattern and I quickly determined it was animal or human generated. A slow grating accompanied the soft noise and I experienced a wave of gooseflesh warning of something not right.

Raising up carefully so as to not waken the sleeping Islanders, I separated myself and left the bed, tiptoeing to the double doors. Tipping back the blackout curtain so rarely used, I scrutinized the darkness outside. The sky was low. No moon or stars lit anything what with the weather system enveloping us. The first snowfall had magically changed the world out there. Everything was shades of silver and gray, shadows and dark spots pocked the several inch white blanketing.

The trees stood guard in stark contrast and I could make out a set of some kind of tracks just outside on the balcony. Unable to tell anything more, there suddenly came to my ears a soft 'pfflumph'. I inferred something or someone having just jumped down over the bannister around the corner, landing in the snowy covering a floor below.

It was disturbing, especially with the marks in the snow just feet from me. They led around the corner toward where the sound had arisen. My goose pimples multiplied. Padding over to the side bay window alcove preferred for reading, I pulled back that curtain and was further dismayed to envision what I thought to be a bent figure loping away into the woods surrounding the house. It moved with a limping shuffle and the figure seemed large…bulky. And dark. A bear, I ventured? Not something I wanted to see after the gruesome occurrence the afternoon before.

It occurred to me that the 'mountain' in the dead-of-night might no longer be a molehill.

Unbeknownst to me, the Jamaican had quietly awakened, watching from the bed behind me as the ominous limping figure disappeared into the shadows. The wise man's eyes narrowed to slits at the sight and he shuddered silently before resuming a sleeping position, forcibly controlling his breathing.

Not brave enough to venture outside under the circumstances, I scoped the perimeter for ten minutes or so before the chill to my skin subsided. Seeing nothing more, I nevertheless canvassed the darkened house. The dogs dutifully followed me as bodyguards while checking all of the doors and windows for a third time.

The boys normally sounded off at anything unusual and as they were both quiet, I concluded that my imagination must have transfigured some familiar night creature out on its nocturnal curiosity trek. After all, bears were common visitors… Suture and Elvee had long since ceased signaling their presence, sensing no inherent danger there. Probably not a good thing under the present circumstances.

On the other hand, however, it hit me that the elk were absent and I had heard no night hootings from the owl, either. Both were uncommon events. The elk liked our property due to the salt licks I put out regularly and over next to the pond, under the protection of the looming mountain, there was fresh hay during the winter. I had just put out two bales the day before. And the big elk were not there. Things that make you go, 'hmmm'.

Well, I was 'hmmmmming' all the way back upstairs at these contradictions, slipping back to the warmth and security of my lair. Weirdly, the dogs both climbed up and in, also. That was unsettling in itself. And eerie. Jeremy turned over on to me and covered me in a sleepy embrace. I fell into an uneasy slumber.

The next morning dawned dark and smotheringly quiet. No breezes, no animal sounds. No tittering birds. The snow muffled almost everything. I arose from under Jeremy's muscled arm and torso where he had protectively cloaked me hours before. Whether consciously done or not, I was unsure, but I had melted into his smell and warmth. Now, I hated leaving the cocoon. And the boner.

The Rastafarian was gone. Rumpled bedsheets and an indented pillow were the only trace of him. While this in itself was no great cause for concern, it added to my angst. The amiable Rastafarian had admittedly proven mysterious in some ways during his weeks with us. The man would awaken at times in the night and pull one of us to him in a possessive bear hug. Never voicing a word, just seeking intimate proximity, we had presumed. Other times he would perform a deep-of-the-night blowjob on one of us. Something that never occurred in the light of day. He was big on the macho thing.

Some mornings, the Jamaican would slip out of bed an hour before my 5 AM arising and we would find him deep in contemplative repose somewhere in or out of the house. Still other times, the swarthy gent would sleep far into the morning, getting up in a blurry state of mind, seldom communicative at those times. No set routine seemed strange to both of us, as we were very habitual. Not in our pastimes, mind you, just our awakening and retiring patterns.

I showered in cool water to jumpstart myself, toweling off as my man entered to take a turn. He nuzzled me on the way in without a word. The quietude of the snow and the repressive atmosphere that I felt was apparently affecting him, as well. Pulling on clean jeans and my preferred choice of turtleneck sweaters, I descended to start coffee and put on an Enya CD. It matched the pensive morning mood.

Ambergai Gee was not in the house from what I could tell. That was unusual as he had demanded dick attention from one of us sometime during every morning since his arrival. Hm-mmm, again. Jeremy followed me down after a bit, looking for coffee, still sleepy-eyed. His warm-up bottoms barely covered his crotch and the residual morning engorgement was sticking down one leg, straining to be seen. And noticed. Nothing else covered him except the towel around his neck. He stopped short upon eyeing me and I marveled at the absolutely stunning physique of the man I called my mate.

At 44 years old, not a strand of body hair, except a trapezoid patch above his endowment, marked his entire body, no crease or wrinkle indicating age. I teased him that he was a black Dorian Gray and kept an eye peeled for the alter-ego painting that surely must be absorbing the years… seeing him like this every day was a most treasured indulgence. That he returned the affection made me feel I inhabited a novel—real life couldn't be this good.

The morning horndog squinted across the room at me, gestured down at the now ascending tent inside the warm-ups and made plain his expectations. I listened to Enya plaintively lyricize as I pulled off my sweater and descended to knee level by the time I had reached him, by now adept at the assumption of my favored morning position.

Coffee percolated on the counter as I rounded down on the now extruded boner, its hardness rising to mouth level, foreskin inching back from his fine spongy crown. I settled into the awakening callisthenic which the black stud needed, either passively or actively, every single day. In eighteen years, I could count the number of times on my left hand that this man had not erupted in an ejaculative 'good morning' and still have fingers left over.

My right hand was occupied cupping the hairless balls, massaging the cum up through the cumchute, of course. His marriage ring was sexily encircling the entire package, per usual, and it grounded my strokes. Within three minutes, the erect nipples hardened under my fingertips, signaling his coming spurts. I kept time to Enya through the explosion and shudders.

Following his hard smoothness downward to the sensitive toes, skimming him all over with my fingers and then working my way back up, engendered my own eruption. I had early on discovered this one human that could set me off without touching myself. The oversized white dick of mine just pulsed it out as I enjoyed his body under my hands. He leaned down to cup the babies, razzing me that someday he would get pregnant by the method, like an immaculate conception. He licked his fingers lasciviously while basking in my touch of him.

Yup, between his need for sucking dick, mine firstly, and my own weakness for the art of fellatio, we certainly sucked a whole lotta of it.

Good thing his little girl had knocked me off that ladder so many years back. Little Elle was now grown up and had Elle, Junior, to love on. The image of the pigtailed imp with no front teeth brought me a full-mouthed smile. And it be hard to smile with a mouth full of dick, especially the size of Jeremy.

I wondered why the hell girl babies weren't accommodated by numeric nomenclature the way boy children were: Junior, the third, the fourth, etc. Seemed mighty strange to me, and I was glad Elle had broken down that particularly stupid wall. We couldn't wait to have the two best girls in our lives present with us in a couple more weeks for the Thanksgiving period. Even if it did restrict our lewd ways a smidgeon.

We both gulped down cum at the same moment of eyeing one another, sending us into gagging fits of giggling. We were openly aware of our idiosyncrasies and took amusement from sharing them. After refilling cups of coffee, we conspired together on barstools faced toward the steepening mountain outside our windows, feet entangled with the other's.

Commenting that Ambergai was nowhere to be found, I later related to him the disconcerting occurrences of the night. Jeremy was mightily perturbed that I hadn't wakened him, as if that would have helped anything. My knowledge of his reactions under stress were well documented and the last thing I would have wanted was to see him confronting whatever I had espied in the effort to act the hero. Which he would have done. I kept my mouth shut.

We went upstairs to examine the scuffed patches in the snow on the balcony and then followed around to the side, viewing the abrupt ending to the markings. Prints on the handrails and a pronounced depression in the snow below appeared telltale. So, I had not been imagining things up here. By the evidence, it was likely that I had, indeed, seen the large, limping figure disappearing into the woods, as well. Now, my prickling skin was contagious—J-Man 's forearms were goose bumped, too.

Not finding our long-haired housemate on the landings around the house or on the property raised my hackles further and I insisted we make a call to the sheriff. JK wasn't quite as upset over his friend's absence. "He leaves for the boondocks on a regular basis to do his secret things, wherever he stays. I think it's religious stuff, or something," he posited. But he ultimately agreed and we called anyway.

I hand-walked Elvee and Suture with their hated extend-a-leashes. The boys felt the devices were instruments of restrictive torture. Not desirous that curiosity might take them roaming, they had to accept the control for the time being. The duo found multiple other tracks in the snow, but it was hard to determine similarities or differences now. Following the prints of the limping figure's path up to the point where the rocky heights held no snow at all, I lost them. Though it did solidify the proof.

There were no size 17 footprints to be found anywhere. Of that I was sure. And, still no sign of the elk… On the way back in, I spotted a branch on a big evergreen tree contrasting in red and found a piece of snagged material. Some sort of coarse burlap. I freed it and brought it along.

Coming back inside, I was elated to find a revived, crackling fire. Jeremy was busily working on the long strands of hemp he had collected for the planned costume. He was weaving and braiding the pieces into some sort of wigged-dreadlocks using his outstretched legs and toes for anchors. I was beginning to see the described endgame in real time now, at least somewhat. The collection of bones and wiring, along with various other pieces, still proved baffling.

Jeremy looked up excitedly and called me over while I was liberating the furred quadrupeds, "Hey, Luke, look at this, honey." He held up a big leg bone, which I had seen before. Unsure where or by what method he had procured the thing, I was staying clear of questions there, as well. It was a true human tibia, that I knew after examination. "Look close—see, right there below the bony knobs—the ones you call tuberosities, right? There are teeth marks. Something's been gnawing on this one," Jeremy was hyped over this discovery.

"You don't think a critter took a few swipes at it during the night?" I asked innocently. "It was laying outside the past three days, J."

He responded with a conniving look, "Yeah, my boii, but these gnaw marks were made by human teeth, Luke." He was dead serious, so I looked closer. There was, for sure, mostly blunt indentations and no sign of 'wolf teeth' marks, the big hooked teeth that look like a vampire's, which all non-humans have. All predatory animals, to be precise.

"Well, Jeremy, that does look unusual, but what about baby animals or herbivores, or something like that?" I was still playing devil's advocate. Jeremy wasn't having any of it.

"My dude, you may know anatomy, I will give you that, but I grew up in 'The-Jamaica-Lond'," devolving into the sing-song Island lilt left behind years before, "and I am telling you, Luke, these are human teeth marks. I'm gonna show the sheriff." When I pulled out the burlap shred after that, we both hummed the 'Twilight Zone' discord theme.

The visit by the law a bit later turned out less than supportive. The deputy merely glanced at our evidence and barely took note as Jeremy related his gnaw-tooth theory. The little tinhorn half-heartedly took the material shred I showed him. When he laid it down on the porch outside the front door and proceeded to ignore it, I pocketed it. He didn't even notice.

'Deputy Fife' was shutting the conversation down, letting us know that the bear culprits had been sighted, were on the run, and expected to be apprehended very soon…translation, "Fuck you very much, we have everything under control. And, keep the dogs in the rest of the day, too." I half expected to hear him tell us 'little ladies' not to worry our pretty little heads because HE was on the case.

I had to step on Jeremy's foot this time. He was puffing up in his indignity. Had the deputy not excused himself, the steam would have been visible from my man's ears…I knew him too well. We were both frustrated by the inattention afterwards but finally concluded the need to just blow it off for the time-being. So we lit up a head high doobie. Sure enough, the whole thing became hilarious within 15 minutes. And Jeremy's costume assemblage was back on.

Chapter 10
Stick Shift: Flapjack

Lulled by the sonorous pre-dawn sounds wafting through the open bay windows over the big bed, I drowsed half-in and half-out of sleep. What a wonderful place to exist, I reckoned. Particularly by the knowledge that the trajecting flashback was reminiscent of our trip into the big city the previous weekend. The memories of steamily sultry events witnessed and experienced at the 'cocksucker palace' would hopefully be recurring…

My resultant early morning wood throbbed under the weight of Cal's slumbering leg as it draped across my groin. His arm bended over my chest, his face softly nuzzled my neck. Amazingly neutral morning breath sighed from him while he dozed possessively over my butt-nakedness.

A very endearing house rule, I loved the fact that he had lobbied hard for the pact stipulating no clothing in bed on the inaugural night of our relationship. He was a semi-nudist as it was, preferring only saggy boxers when home, never anything tighter. Frontal opening usually gaping, he preferred the freedom of air-cooled skin whenever possible. Big, wide bare feet were a given.

As it were, considering the silky smoothness of his superbly toned body, such a predilection was to my benefit. Boasting less than four percent body fat, the sight of him never went unappreciated. My mind's eye now contentedly pictured us tangled in skewed bedsheets as if I were peering down from a perch at the ceiling corner. What a lucky man I was.

Gradually rousing myself without any body movement other than some isotonic tensing and releasing, Cal faintly responded to it by a soft, purring change to the rhythm of his breathing. Coming up from the deepness that was his sleep mode, he licked his lips and "shooshed" a breath at my neck in exhalation. I heard his twinkle through the tease, "You my sexy baby, dude-boi?" I managed a contented, "Hmmmmmm", from behind a closed-eye half smile.

In another few moments, "Baby, you gettin' me goin', now. You keep up that slo-mo pulsin' down there and you gone' make me cum, you know that, right...? I'm 'bout ready to climb up into that, bay-bee," he whispered in my ear. I loved when he reverted to the local patois of northern Georgia, in lieu of his normally articulate manner. It made my dick harder...but wait... slo-mo pulsin'...?

My hands were presently raised up over my head. We both stiffened together at the sudden discernment of an unbidden presence sharing proximity. Sleepily benumbed tactile sensors abruptly alerted to the nappy texture roosting in nether regions. Sitting bolt upright, Cal exclaimed, "Small Boy---Dawg!" he reached down to the narrow space between us, awakening the slumbering nephew who had evidently snuck into the bed sometime earlier and now lay in the thick of our entwined legs.

The youngster worshiped Cal and since his uncle's return home, had latched tightly on to him. The absoluteness of his innocence, while disarmingly endearing, could be unnerving at times. The boy was wont to seek cuddling with his superhero uncle... I was surely included only by default.

Cal, while deeply attached to his sister's boy, drew the line at the sanctity of our bedroom. Especially upon awakening to his endowment rasping against the slumberous, bristle-headed youth as it was now... "You little bugger, whatchyoubedoin-downintherepissant?"

The little nephew popped up, surprised at the vehemence, and leapt out of the tiny gap where he had wedged between our bodies. Skittering to the floor, the rascal raced out the cracked door, slamming it on his escape. A winsome giggle faded around the corner as he went...

"Damn," Cal hissed, "that little mess is gonna get on my last nerve. Damn it! That's the third time, the little mole." He reclined back to the mattress, drawing me down with him amidst some more overly-earnest cluckings.

A few extra, forced hrrrumphs later, the swollen heat of my man's dripping curve inched up my hip and rubbed hornily on me. It never took anything more than a brushing touch from any part of this man's body to raise my fervor. The desire for a slow-ride before breakfast came unnervingly easy. My buoyant cock bounced expectantly as I stretched out my enjoyment, feeling my tubular underdick whisp rhythmically off the smoothly dark hard belly next to it. I nibbled the earlobe and blew lightly for effect. He shivered his notice, enwrapping my lips with his own.

It almost bothered me, this hold he had over me, but I smothered the feeling as I pushed his leg over and crawled up on to his flat lap, intensifying the stud's already boinging tumescent state. His foreskin rolled sensually back from the phattened head. He froze as I lifted up to get the ten inch pre-cumming monster-of-my-eye targeted to its preferred location.

Cal peered around my waist to assure Boy's absence, then groaned as I descended over the one-eyed 10's 'til our white-on-black melded. Squeezing the cheeks strongly and deliberately--it made him nuts-- I began a slow canter motion, all the way up, then down, in hopes of inducing long, rolling spurts.

His large and manly hands cupped my rounded globes in a pretension of control but his rolled-up eyes told a different story. I had this man... It only took a few dozen full, slow, deep strokes before I was rewarded by the hot, goopy, sliminess of release. He rumbled at me, "puleeeze don't stop that honey, puleeeze don't..."

Fat chance of that. I kept up the motion, right through his vulnerable after-cum spasms while he winked one squinted eye open to see my own eruption. He knew perfectly well the effect his implanted, spewing dick had on my prostate. The rotations roiled my sensations to climax, adding to our mutual satisfaction. He reached the big-boned fingers of his hand to my mushroom head and swirled the goo marking me as totally dick-whipped. Just as he intended.

We fit. And, we knew it.

Boy pogo'd up and down by the stove, impatiently demanding pancakes from his aunt's griddle. Holding a plate in one hand and fork in the other, ninja-turtle do-rag flapping hilariously, he was impossible to avoid laughing at as Cal and I exited our upstairs bedroom, descending after a buddy-shower wake up following the morning fuck.

The Boy's loose white boxers, in mimicry of his idolized uncle, provided the ball-of-energy's only other covering. The little man took satisfactory note of Cal and his like outfits as we sniggered through his antics. Cal's own sagging, over-sized boxers mostly hid his recently sated snake behind only a minimally gapped opening due to its sleep mode, now. God, what a hunk I had married.

Attempting nonchalance was not yet a tactic mastered by the lovable tadpole and Sophie smiled at the seven-year-old's transparency, instructing the boisterous boy to hold his plate for delivery of the blueberry-stuffed flapjacks.

Even at the early hour of 7 AM, Cal's younger sister looked ravishing. Her short-cropped black hair, blood red-tipped and spiked, accentuated the two-piece red and black spiraled spandex body suit. Her ab fab abs and body smoothly filled the outfit and her make-up free beauty rendered regular mistakenness for Halle. The lithe young seductress was completely at ease in her skin and amongst her six brothers. My acceptance into her sphere had pleased me no end. She and I communicated.

She was well aware of the effect she had on people. Those negatively affected were most commonly treated to a vamp-like act for the shock value. In our presence, she exuded a motherly affection honed to an art ever since the loss of the family's matriarch several years before.

Cassandra Broadhearst had doted on her husband, Calumet Senior. When he had succumbed to a horrific head-on collision with a drunk driver years ago, the aristocratic woman had faded in desolation without her soulmate. Bodily wasting diminished her to only a wisp of her former self and the lady passed in her sleep, leaving an indisputable legacy of elegance rarely seen outside European aristocracy.

Boy concentrated on getting to the breakfast table without spillage and succeeded in joining Vivian, his little sister. The mini-him version of unassuming liveliness now patiently awaited pancakes like the small lady she could occasionally pull off.

Mostly, she worked at keeping up with her older brother. The two shared a natural curiosity and frenetic pace typical for Blackhearst children. Soph glanced at Cal and me as we took notice of her mannered patience and explained, "Viv just let me know she is expecting 'an incident' any minute...she wants to be ready." Perplexed, we wordlessly asked 'what was up' by our faces and she added, "I have no idea--she just does this sometimes, you already know. I am sure we'll find out-- she sees everything. So, just watch out, boys. Come get your cakes."

Cal's butt pinch let me know of his 'done-already-got-'dem-cakes' double entendre. I smirked a wordless reply.

Cheek pecking my sis-in-law as I took the offered plate, I scooped up a glass of orange juice. Having heard and seen Cal and my interaction, she playfully poked me in the ribs. 'You gettin' pretty used to the mood around here, aren't you, boii?" She teased more, pointing out my own, Cal's and Boy's matching boxers, "Only took a month... welcome home, little big bro."

Cal grinned and quipped, "Come on Sis, you know I'm keeping him barefoot and PG, and I don't want a lot of crap in my way when I'm ready, right?" as he bit into his honey-slathered breakfast jacks.

"Well, big Daddy, you sho' didn't seem to have any o' that problem an hour ago, now, did you?" She tilted her head in the direction of my tush as she waited. My expected face, neck and chest flush was a source of delight to the family and it surfaced right on cue. Soph loved doing this. In my status as the token white member of the family, the weakness was regularly provoked.

The Blackhearst siblings were all close, and each exhibited elevated sex drives. The tendencies were recognized and accepted quite matter-of-factly. They all had been brought up understanding the healthy benefits of a full sex life. I, on the other hand, had been raised in a puritanical household. Sex existed only in a world of sinful wickedness. The adage, 'to Hell in a handbasket' had to have been derived in my childhood home, I felt sure.

Procreation was the only use my folks and siblings had for the frowned-upon pastime. Those totally debasing moments when I had been caught in the act of jacking off during an extremely awkward adolescence indelibly scarred my psyche. Expressions of mystified disbelief at my continuing 20-20 vision persisted amongst my family. God must surely have a supremely stiff alternate penance in store for me, I had been warned. Hence, the obdurate flush reaction at mention of the subject.

Cal's family had collectively entered me into 'active rehab' as a counter measure for defraying the psycho-babble holding me hostage from that upbringing. I was gradually responding. But the blushing thing remained a source of high hilarity, all the way down to the five-year-old Vivian. While obviously never talking of sex (well, not intentionally), even the little girl practiced multiple methods of sparking my discomposure. Darn it.

Just then, a bang and a crash mixed into a rush of masterfully phrased profanities erupted down the long hallway from the other brothers' wing of rooms. Vivian straightened up and put her fork down, hands in her lap. "Here it comes," was all she said, and we all watched the hall doorway. Within a few seconds, Doy's bedroom door screeched open. Running footfalls sounded in the hall and we all gaped as a very naked and aroused unknown Hispanic youth erupted into view. He was highly agitated and in a hurry.

Doy came barging down the hall after him, heated words heralding his appearance. This Broadhearst brother was a volatile personality and easily riled. Right now, he was hot. And naked. And, boy was his dick handsome when he was pissed off...I hadn't noted how much until this moment. It was dribbling spunk as it preceded the rest of the brother's body through the doorway, making for a startling focal point to our breakfasting group.

The typical overhung male family jewels waggled from side-to-side, suspended in mid-air and raising hell. The rest of Doy followed the dong around the corner and we saw that his face matched his wiener... Swelled up, pissed-off and blustering. The girls just lowered their heads but us boys were looking. Cussing and waving, Doy pin-pointed the skittering chasee, "You fuckin' asshole thievin' bitch! Get the fuck out my house! Steal my shit and I'ma tear that ass up--- get the fuck out!" he insisted. The olive-skinned young man twirled in anguish, sputtering ill-attempts at apologies. All were very flatly rejected by the erect Doy. He spewed expletives and saliva non-stop as we observed, enthralled.

The smaller visitor abruptly snapped to the realization he was on display in front of us all, kids included. Blooming to deep shades of purple--- a fact that warmed my white boy heart--- by the humiliation, the young man attempted covering the teeny-tiny up-pointing sprig of a fully hard dick. He even managed to eke out a stilted request for his clothes.

Doy was having none of it. Grasping the short stalk, he manhandled the object of his anger across the room. Opening the glass storm door, the wincing trick was yanked through it, cock first. The see-through covering allowed our visual as the boy hesitantly contemplated the wide open space, clearly not comfortable in his outdoor state of nudity. The slamming door slapped the naked little butt down the steps, a high shriek punctuating the contact. After one last mortified glance back, he disappeared from sight around the corner.

Doy turned on us, dick still fully erect, flopping madly, low-hangers bobbling. I suddenly felt like a character in the 1920's anti-drug propaganda flick named, 'Reefer Madness'. "What? What the fuck ya'll starin' at? The little prick thief tried to lift my wallet right when I was pokin' him, goddammit! Had my iPad and iPhone already packed up and hid, too. I knew I shouldn't trust the bitch-- anyone with a two-inch dick is always a thief. I always tol' ya'll that! Shit, I'm just glad I didn't give the ho' but two loads, or he woulda' prob'ly got the damn TV, too." Suddenly remembering, he turned back and yanked open the door, "Where'd you hide my damn phone, wench?" But the boy seemed to be gone already.

All this had unfolded while Doy's pretty piece carried on dripping an obviously interrupted load-dumping moment. We couldn't tell which was pissing him off more-- the thievery or the messed-up climax. His thick nine-inch piece continued haranguing us by its wagging, upward arch, and the cum-laden 'cussing' it was still spewing proved demonstrative.

Cal and I couldn't stop pivoting between both erupting heads, trying to keep up. Sophie rolled her eyes, then reached over and handed her brother a dish towel. Viv just shook her pretty little head sagely at Boy and opined, "I know, I know."

Doy, still pissed, disappeared down the hall and into the bedroom. Emerging again a minute later, hands filled with the trick's clothes and shoes, he strode barefoot to the door. Exiting, his pretty little bare ass bounced cutely behind him as he hollered for Aloysius, the family's Nubian goat.

We tried to finish our fast-cooling pancakes and make sense of the situation in the post-tirade calm but found the brouhaha too funny to ignore. All but Boy and Viv lost our appetites. Typical kids, they went right on enjoying breakfast, quickly dismissive of the imbroglio. The three of us were more entertained over the happenings and I was particularly vocal about the mini-dicked boy's blushing episode. Cal and Soph allowed that his was far worse than anything I had exhibited. I was satisfied.

My man finally had enough and left for his study to do some work while Sophie and I cleaned up. Little Viv thoughtfully worked on her iphone and Boy wandered outside to follow the happenings there.

A half hour later, Soph was on her way out the door to several of her day's errands, still amused at the incident. Viv hadn't looked up once from her phone, completely absorbed, so I thought to check if the goat friend of mine was still alive.

Nobody replied as I descended the back porch steps calling, so I headed over to the neighbor's yard where the social goat commonly slunk off to for "talks" with the Missus Brown. The two had an understanding of some sort. I had overheard some engrossing goat-on-woman dialogue more than once.

The goat was tied to a tree on the side of the house, pawing at the little trick's clothes as he dug asparagus stalks from the pockets and inside the wrapped clothes where more had been stuffed. In digging out the delicacy, of course, the clothes had been very thoroughly pawed and gnawed to shreds. Clever, I thought, but why hadn't Farmer Brown had a fit over this, per usual?

Next, sticking my head around the front corner of the old farmhouse, I noted the absence of the Missus' car, answering another of my questions. Stepping between the hedge and the side of the house heading back to the goat's picnic site, I heard a muffled sound from the open window and drew closer to see inside.

There, lazing back in an easy chair, spread-legged, head lolled all the way back, arms on the armrests, was a still naked Doy. Moaning to the tempo of an ongoing blow job being expertly administered by a busy Farmer Brown. Ha, I thought. You Go, old boy. The man was assiduously bent over Doy's full dick, slow-sucking the thing, oblivious to anything but that good hard-on. Can't blame the old guy for that, I thought. Doy sure had no problem with it, by the look of things.

Interested, I stuck around to voyeur a bit. Another surprise, I reflected. These country folk sure were innovative. And un-inhibited. At least the menfolk were proving to be. The older man knew his way around a dick, to be sure. He worked the thing for several minutes before Doy finally warned the old gent to get off it. They and I watched as that dick popped off several good arcs of cum while Doy gripped the chair. I quietly backed off, returning to our house. Things that make you go, "Hmmmm." As my best bud, Luke, and I always say…

When I entered, there was Vivian, now busily punching buttons. She looked up as I opened the door and waved me excitedly over.

"Viv, I didn't even know you had a phone. When did you get that?" The thought had struck me a bit earlier after leaving to look for the goat.

She grinned at me conspiratorially and pointed at the screen, "Uncle Jake, this is Uncle Doy's spare. I took it out of that man's pocket when I saw him put it there and I hooked up the iPad to skype-- look what came up."

I was amazed as I came over and viewed Doy's shadowy bedroom the hour before breakfast. The five-year-old tech wizard had ably set the scene. As I watched, Doy and the kid awakened from the night, some inaudible pillow talk going on. The boy went into the bathroom first, then Doy did so afterwards.

The little trick proved mighty curious while alone, poking through various drawers and pockets. He had just snagged Doy's pants as the younger brother opened the bathroom door, re-entering to his desired pursuit of hitting the sweet butt noticeably distracting him. Doy missed the trick's cleverly strategic drop of the pants close to where he positioned his head for the upcoming reaming.

Doy got lined up behind and slightly out of the picture frame. The proceeding action was heard but not seen and the next minutes showed no hard core porn shots--- thank goodness--- due to the angle. The backdoor work Doy was doing was quite audible and at the nine-minute mark, I watched as the boy reached out for Doy's discarded pants.

He skillfully shielded the act of removing the wallet, just the way Doy had accused. As he put it into his own shorts pocket, Doy apparently opened his sex-blinded eyes and caught on. All hell broke loose as Doy knocked the kid from the bed. The youth crashed to the floor.

We all knew what had followed.

Wow. No wonder little Viv had predicted the future. She had watched the whole set up by the skype connection. I could never have thought of it, let alone carried it out. The 'when' and 'why' of the matter didn't occur to me...

A little later, with Viv moved on to the next plan for her five-year-old agenda, Doy swept in the back door looking much relieved and much quieter. Still completely nude. Happy to find his missing iPhone on the bar, he settled at the kitchen table, half-hard dick lolling to the side on his thigh, uncaring for his exposed state. He told of his packing of the little thief's clothes and shoes with the asparagus. Aloysius had thoroughly enjoyed the filling treat, he informed me.

Unable to help myself, I had to ask how he had convinced the old farmer to part with his precious crop. Doy smugly replied, "we bartered for it." At ease in his nudeness as he was, I should have anticipated the openness. Seeing my expression, he replied to the unasked question, "Hell, Jake, that old dude? That wasn't no deal. He gots those blue pills he takes and I lets him suck my dick sometimes. I traded him on the greens--- it was all good. He was wankin' that big ole' man dick off when I left, like he likes to do, so..." He winked, stood up, wagged his happy dick at me, slapped playfully at my crotch and disappeared for a shower. With his phone...

Cal wasn't going to be interrupted, even brushing off the shoulder massage I used to tempt him a little later into conversing. Mumbling about deadlines and such, I retreated back to the kitchen. Viv was in her room singing along with some Nickelodeon kid's show and her usual companion, Boy, wasn't anywhere to be seen. It struck me that I hadn't seen him since leaving out the backdoor after breakfast. I better find the rascal or he'll have gotten into something no good, I figured. I was, after all, the responsible adult for now.

Perusing the backyard surround and the barn, as well as Aloysius' picnic site, and still not finding the boy, I untied the goat and was about to search the front yard when I thought to peek in on the farmer's blue-pill morning progress. Doy had left him jacking earlier and I was still curious. As I peered in the window where Doy had previously enjoyed the 'mature' blowjob, I was disturbed, but not surprised, to find Boy standing in the doorway just out of view of the old farmer who was busy watching what sounded to be a skin flick by the musical accompaniment. Brown didn't seem aware of the fact in the slightest, spellbound in his stroking...

Well, that ain't happenin', I said to myself. Scurrying around to the old farmhouse's backdoor, I let myself in, came around the corner to the hallway where Boy was and lightly smacked his little ass. He jumped a foot into the air. One 'busted' shriek later, he was off and gone out the door. Knowing that didn't go unheard, I sucked it up and cleared the next corner into the bedroom.

"What is up, Mr. Brown?" I said as I cleared the doorway. The old gent didn't bother withdrawing his hand, instead scoffing my way. Continuing to raise and lower the happy hand gripping the nice sized pill-fueled piece. The farmer was clearly pleased with himself at the state of his arousal.

"So, the pretty white boy with the big whonker decided to see how a real man works it, huh, docboy? Well, set yurself right down there and get a eyeball full. This big ole dick won't be a'leavin' much room fo' anythin' else in yo' head once ya' get to lookin', boy," he gloated.

I snickered at the hubris, inwardly setting aside the secret hope that when I reached his point in life's tenure, I had the hutzpah to exhibit similar bravado. At the same time, I was curious enough at the scenario that I didn't immediately excuse myself and back out. Remembering a bit earlier, while voyeuring Doy and the farmer's session from the window vantage, my piece had actually responded.

Feeling then that the response had been more due to the recipient's involvement, hunk that my brother-in-law was, I was a little taken aback now as I felt mini-me warming a mite to the older gent showing off before me. Tentatively, I edged a few steps forward into the den, hearing the cheesy background music accompanying the man's old-fashioned video sex flick.

"So, the pink boy pro man likes to watch, don't he, now?" Farmer Brown stated matter-of-factly, furthering both my chagrin and my dithering. I wasn't certain at all that I was where I should be, but the present plot here was sublimely motivating… the old guy motioned with his free hand and I hesitantly shuffled closer.

Now, just slightly out of arm's reach, the old cuss crudely slurped a nasty smacking sound and leaned forward, taking the initiative. I stayed where I was. His fingers wrapped around my lengthening piece and he glanced up, "I been thinkin'" ta taste me some paleface dick, now, ever since you been showin' it off that mornin' last week. Let's try that thing out, boy," and with that, he leaned even closer and abruptly sucked the head of my piece into his Doy-approved mouth.

What the hell, I thought? If anything, maybe I'll help out the old codger and sometime down the line remember the act in reverse, should I reach that side of the equation... it was going to happen, some day.

So, I acquiesced, and moved into the sucking orifice, letting my dick swell inside the toothless mouth. It was warm. The pleasure, surprisingly, grew my hard-on in a minute. The old mouth did, indeed, know its way around a dick. I thought the thought for the second time in one morning. As it occurred to me, I flashed on his comment the past week when he had cryptically mentioned 'that episode' involving my Cal from back in his high school days... now my curiosity was peaked more so.

Before I could contemplate further, however, a set of fingers squeezed an exposed white butt cheek backing the scene below me. I started at the touch, my hand grabbing back at it. A glance over my shoulder revealed one very aroused bro-in-law, Doy, standing within close adjacency. His re-invigorated cock stared, one-eyed, at the unsqueezed twin cheek.

A leering grin let me know my bro-in-law was still on the prowl, probably still seeking satiation after the thievery entanglement's earlier frustrated climax. After all, I knew, these Broadhearst brothers were endlessly edgy...multiple orgasmic events were common among them.

"Give it on up, Jake, and enjoy it—Brown be a veteran, and I be knowin' you already done been seeing him in action. Seen ya' watchin' a while ago...didn't think I did, huh?" He put it in head-on perspective. Those squeezing fingers checked out the produce like a matron at a fruit stand, kneading and testing my firmness, searching the dimples and dents.

I couldn't deny my enjoyment of the dual action going down, now, and succumbed to the unfolding set like the slut that I was…why deny the facts? I let the hand round down and inward to the crack between my cheeks, trying to stay upright for the continuing good mouth work, but at the same time, liking the big, venturing fingers.

Turned out, I needn't have split my attention, as the big fat black dick on proud parade sidled right on up to me, whippling back and forth across my anatomy, letting me know of its intent by the doing. This was getting interesting, I decided, and turned my neck more, so Doy's approaching lips could better access my own.

Seeing our lip-lockage, the farmer's mouth uttered a garbled comment between strokings that approximated his enjoyment at the sandwiching effect. My thoughts exactly, I silently concurred. I accepted the long tongue into my mouth, sucking it in and reaching my own hand around to explore the tantalizing torso attached to the dick rubbing my backside.

I had to halt the oral progress by palming Brown's head as the ministrations were too good. Though it didn't release me. The mouth only sat still. I luxuriated in the heat and scaled down from an eruption. Doy, the formerly derisive brother-in-law at the outset of our summer here in Georgia had come around admirably since we had shared the CSP experience in Atlanta. The stud now waxed on about that scenario in between face-sucking.

You the BITCH, now, ain't ya', Jake?" he began, "Done satisfied the jumbo dick that night at the club, now, didn't ya, cunt-boy? Ain't been nobody able to satisfy that whopper like you done…Everyone got to see how you take big black dicks in that place and no one do it better than a white boy in a black house, for sure.

You took at least three damn loads from that giant, and that's just the one's I heard an' saw, ain't they, Jake? You been practicin' on all this Georgia dick since you been here, huh? And Cal happy to be a'sharin', by what I'm seein'. I ain't lost no big bro, now, just done got me a new white ass to add to my barn, ya' think? Let's see what ya' can do with this'n, Jake," he warned me.

With that, Doy plugged into my asshole in one long, deep pile driver stroke. Spit-slippery while he had talked. It made my big dick throb up in the old farmer's throat and without notice, stimulated an acute eruption, spewing cum all in the old guy's mouth. I surprised him by it, and his mouth slipped off momentarily, squirting jism over his face.

Doy was leaning over my shoulder and viewed his implanting effect, telling me in certain terms that I better just settle in for the long haul, 'cause he'd already had one interrupted ending this morning with the little dick thief. He wasn't doin' another aborted effort. His hands secured me in position by the shoulders and the farmer realized he was in for a show, so took my throttle back in his mouth for the long drive...such metaphors spelled out the long-ass fuck I 'endured' over the coming half hour.

Doy was prolific in his longevity, no doubt. The man embedded a quick cum load into me just by the recall of feeling the giant's jumbo dick in the bath house the night he played next to me with Cal's dick all up in his own ass. I took the gargantuan dick while feeling Cal's dick flood Doy's ass twice before I even knew who was doing what to whom. I hadn't been allowed to look...

Likewise, Doy had had his hand on my ass, feeling the jumbo dick poling me, stroke by stroke. Now, Doy was fantasizing the memory, as was I, and his quick spasming informed me of the fact. Plus, it warranted an act of minority-ownership, by his reasoning.

That was just the warm-up, as my ebony in-law proceeded to attest his versatility, now playing the top man's role masterfully. He fucked me every way possible in those confines without ever breaking the old man's contact with my cock, as he dosed me multiple loads while spelling out in vivid detail all the things he'd seen me do, was doing at that moment, and was gonna be doing to me in the future.

By his communicative prowess, my sexual social calendar appeared prolific in his summarization of the dozens of past, present and future attempts at, or to be attempting, my impregnation…fat chance, I thought. That impossibility was a solid given. However, I wasn't about to argue under the circumstances. In truth, I liked the allusions.

The farmer literally got a mouthful with an earful as he pacified himself on as much big, white prick as he had ever thought to do. The retiree was privy to all the excessively nasty plans the Broadhearst family of brother's apparently held in store for their communal Anglo brother…Cal would surely acquiesce, I was told.

As if to solidify the 'contract', who should appear at that moment in my peripheral vision but my man, Calumet. He had missed me and come looking. Look what he'd found, he grinned… his main squeeze familiarizing with his family and the neighbors… in very friendly fashion. Imagine that.

Doy deposited un-numbered baby loads up my ass, then in gentlemanly fashion, stepped aside as my Cal plugged into the cum-deluged asshole. I was poking the chute up and back in my attempts at qualifying for Ripley's believe-it-or-not records: cumloads in a row. Stand back, Barry Manilow.

Cal, always my knight, succeeded in raising my flagging bone upon perceiving the familiar 10's, and we surged together in conjoined bliss while the now-transfixed farmer and Doy wandered their hands over, around, between and amongst our molded bodies, aiding the prolongation of our honeymoon.

I'm unaware of anything approaching reality in quantifying that sex session. It was true, though, that the dicks in my ass numbered two, the dicks in various mouths were not limited to three, and the dispensation factor allowed Catholics for consanguinity trespasses couldn't have kept our pace through the next hour.

Cal's careful, deliberate deep-stroking forced a final emphatic ejaculation from my overworked cyclopean eye. Feeling me let loose, my man planted a crescendo of pumping spurts, coating my insides with one more possessive orgasm. We hung together, dick inside, his hand pressing on my tight belly. Lips and teeth hickied my ravaged neck and big bare feet remained planted widely outside my own.

The picture must've been stimulating. When both of our eyes re-opened and focused, we watched Farmer Brown's aged but sturdy piece ooze out a very mature load. Tears escaped the sated man's eyes as he peered up at us, confirming a triple back-to-back for the first time in years…

"You boys be beyond fly'," he growled. The old man never thought that would happen again. He had been satisfied enough, he said, by the blue pill re-boot. "I can live with this remindin'," tapping his head with a finger, "and leave the flicks in the drawer." Flipping his wilting piece, the old guy sagged back.

Doy chimed in, "Well, Skeezer, don't hide the video streamer— look-it here." He sat on the side chair, viewing the device brought by Cal as he had slipped in. Our whole episode was still playing, realtime. As we watched, Cal reached over, flipped the keypad a couple times and brought back up a live-feed skype link. None other than Jeremy and Luke, our studly best men from Austin, were grinning, wide-eyed, amidst their own climax through cyberspace. Enjoying a birds-eye view of our impromptu orgy. The stroking evident in the reverse feed showed their vicarious involvement.

"Cal, how in hell did you do that?" I asked, incredulous.

Waving at our closest friends, he looked at me, "Don't ask me, boii. Viv did all the work over to the house. I just brought it along looking for you," he laughed. "She's the Wiz at this stuff… just keep the damn thing locked up."

Doy promised the old farmer we would download him a copy… Day-Umm, was I meetin' me some neighbors, now.

Chapter 11
Tride and True: Mighty
Tungsten Tuberosity, Part 2

Three days had passed since the bear incident and we had still not seen nor heard from our friend, Ambergai. The evening was coming on, the fireplace was lit, the dogs were in their normal position at the hearth and Jeremy was enjoying the hearty soup I had made earlier, sopping up the last remains with the French bread accompanying it. His feet were raised toward the fire and the wind was whistling around the chimney flue above. Another weather front had delivered a second snow and we were heartened that no more tracks had been found on the balcony, or our property. So far as we could tell. Still, the culprits had not been captured and everyone on the mountain was nervous.

Jeremy was also fit to be tied over the non-decision about the next night's party. He had spent a good part of the past week working up the costume he was 'wearing' and there now seemed to be a good chance the bash would be cancelled…I kept him medicated with gummy bears to defray his angst. Which also kept his dick hard.

The hard-on thing actually hadn't been too much of a feat, considering the addition of the handsome young sommelier, Adolpho, to our home. Jeremy and he had a close bond of friendship. Upon being invited to relocate to our more solidly spacious log home, Adolpho had expressed reticence to the proposal, but had not refused. A veritable lone wolf with a teddy bear personality, the grizzly mountaintop discovery had nevertheless thrown the young entrepreneur, assaulting the boy's sensibilities in the most sacred of his spheres: the high country.

A drafty lean-to, called home, secluded and vulnerable to formerly non-threatening black bears capable of breaking down the door had ultimately convinced Adolpho that he should vacate it for the sturdier confines of ours. The Italian boy had accepted the offer. Arriving the same evening with a large backpack, extra hiking boots and his mountain bike, the attractive youth had taken refuge in a spare bedroom downstairs.

His state of mind had been frazzled when we answered his arriving knock. After unpacking the few belongings brought along, the young man then begged off from further conversation due to a need for rest, he told us. Even the pooches failed to draw him out. We left him to himself.

Adolpho persisted in a stubbornly taciturn approach toward us the following morning as we gathered in the kitchen. While we understood the boy not really desiring to relive the ghastly scenario on the top of Telluride mountain, he inexplicably accepted our hospitality in typical single straight-boy fashion. Which is to say: he didn't. Not even expressing appreciation for a 'port-in-the-storm'.

Upon exiting the bedroom door, it appeared he had donned almost every piece of clothing in his sparse wardrobe. It crossed my mind that if he could've gotten the second pair of hiking boots on over the first ones, it would have happened. I detected several symptoms common to PTSD.

His flannel plaids contrasted oddly in layers and were made more mismatched by the haphazard buttoning job. At least three color schemes blossomed around the neckline, long underwear showed beneath that. I observed that there were multiple buttons missing on the outer one so that might be the case with those underneath. We could discern uneven tails sticking out at the waistline, all untucked as they were. The bulkiness to his otherwise slim waist and legs led us to believe he had layered the bottom half as well. Barely ten words left his mouth as he almost gulped three cups of double espresso, which did nothing to relax the almost frenetic body language.

"That was just strange," exclaimed Jeremy upon the boy's hasty departure on his bike down to the wine shop he owned. Coffee time, normally so laid back, had been awkwardly tense with Adolpho. The attractive man was unshowered and greasy-haired, his eyes bloodshot… and he smelled. Not in a good way, either.

To that point, we had only known the well-groomed and outgoing youth. Both a good conversationalist and a cleanly put together, if un-imaginative, dresser. I allowed that he was a single straight boy and we only knew him from his work-mode world, so there was that. "But, honey, he never went in to work like that before…ya'think he needs to talk to a pro about what happened?" Jeremy had said, and we had worriedly wondered together about the situation.

With our busy agendas preparing things for winter, readying for holidays, settling some matters back in Texas, plus expectations of Jeremy's girls' visit in a few weeks, neither of us had the time to stew over it for long. Add to that my man's intentions with regard to finishing up the costume he was obsessed over, and the concern for the disappearance of our friend Gai, who had left without a word days before, right after the eerie nocturnal visitation, and we decided to just give Adolpho some space. We proceeded in our schedules.

A meeting over the mountain with our lawyers relating to the Austin, Texas, property and gathering needed supplies for the anticipated visit by Jeremy's girls—girls most definitely required items uncommon to gay men--- took the bulk of my day. It culminated that late afternoon with a bulky trip on the gondola, having filled an entire lift car with my purchases. Storing everything at the station over three trips from varied stores finally found me bushed and alone as I ascended for the home crossing.

Totally immersed in planning an itinerary and mentally ordering our extended stay, along with mulling the Texas issues, I gazed vacantly from the glass enclosed car. Reality yanked on me as I suddenly realized that below, three black bears, a mother and two cubs, were loping across the snowy meadow. They made their way from a copse of spruces toward a rocky abutment covered with bushes and aspen trees. The three vanished into a shrouded cave or hollow through an aperture between two large boulders.

After the fact, I realized that the mama bear had been carrying something in her mouth and as the gondola continued upward, away from the scene, I thought I noticed a pinkish trail in the snow coloring the tracks left by their passage. The last rays of sun disappearing over the far west peak obscured whether it had been sunrays and light reflections, or something more ominous.

Arriving at the Mountain Village Station, I hired one of the boys just leaving his shift there to aid my traverse to the lodge. Even with two of us, it was an ordeal managing all of the packages and sacks up the lane to the house. As we trudged up the last stretch, we found Jeremy in discussion with 'Deputy Fife' on the front steps. He was gesticulating in a fashion which led me to know the homecoming was probably timely.

Sure enough, as the station kid and I climbed the steps, JK's chest was puffing up in a display of animosity unusual to my easygoing man's nature. A full head taller, his face was bent downward into the law officer's and he was tersely cold in expressing words I couldn't quite decipher. Having seen enough, I pushed between the two, forcing their separation. The banty rooster of a law officer retreated off the porch and down the steps, red-faced. Obviously determined to have the last word, he whined, "Well, you just better mind that you do that, boy, and just so's you know, your dog is a coward, too!" With a cap-straightening huff, the wiry little fellow glowered at me, as well, then turned, stomping his little-booted feet down to the big cruiser awaiting him.

"Little dick bent out of shape, huh?" I posed, as my stud glared after the disappearing vehicle.

"That's about it, for sure. The little snot-nosed prick," he gritted out between clenched teeth. The faintest of smiles arose as I reached up to kiss him hello. "That little turd started pullin' my chain because I had too many questions about 'Gai and the bears, I guess, so I told him that he and the Sheriff sure did seem to dither and cower in the face of adversity… How does that make my dog a coward?" He was perplexed by the simplemindedness of the man, but that level of ignorance made me laugh out loud.

He lightened upon noticing the blonde ski-bum kid standing there in bewilderment at the scene. "Sorry, Bryce, pay us no mind, now…" looking at me he gestured we could continue it later. Gathering all the bags and packages inside, we were broadsided by the wonderful smell of simmering rabbit fricassee. The young man almost salivated his acknowledgement of the dish—absolutely no idea what it was, nevertheless he was orgasming at the smell.

Jeremy and I laughed at the boy's reaction and my man mopped his 22-year-old tow-headed waves in familiarity. I wondered at that and watched as the two exchanged pleasantries like old buddies. 'Six degrees of separation', I thought…the early Will Smith cult-genre movie with scenes exposing that stud's naked stuff crossed my mind. Casting Stockard Channing and Donald Sutherland, the story had posited the theory that every person in the world from the Pope in Rome to the lowest untouchable in New Delhi could follow a random chain of connection separated by no more than six people… to me, a mind-boggling concept.

My look brought an edifying reply from J-Man, "We met a month back, going down on the lift together while he was mountain biking…" Jeremy then looked at the boy and asked if he'd like to stay for dinner. "There's plenty—it's like a stew, and Adolpho should be home anytime to join us, too." The kid responded vigorously in the affirmative, perking up at Adolpho's name, which left me speculating if the energetic reply was even food-related. Six degrees, indeed, I thought. Though the delicious aroma on its own would have been justification aplenty.

I took the multiple items upstairs while Jeremy took the other things to the kitchen, bedrooms and storage pantry. With the puppydog-eyed blonde's hypnotized aid. I laughed to myself as I pictured the boy on the gondola with my man, full well knowing his effect on men and women alike and the ends to which they would go upon first meeting him. I fully agreed —the man was irresistible. The phrase: 'going down in the lift together' easily could have taken on a different meaning if Jeremy wanted it to. And this boy—Bryce, did he say? —did meet pre-determined qualifications for happenstances Jeremy encountered.

I was repeatedly rendered glad to be void of jealousy, what with the hormonally heightened realm Jeremy thrived in. Since the 21st century had augured in the era of jungle-fever proclivities more common amongst the younger set than ours, I had found that the movie-star looks of my husband kindled a startlingly sexual undertone with these millennials. I couldn't count the number of times that younger men—and women— had thrown themselves at him in the most de-basing of manners. Panting and drooling seemed to be the typical counteraction to Jeremy's animalism. The man simply could not hide the drop-dead sensuality, nor did he much try.

From the 'magic stuff' drawer in the side table by the bed, I removed four 10 mg THC-infused gummy bears and a body-high joint. Making my way downstairs, the creak of the front door floated to my ears. Reaching the landing, I glimpsed Adolpho's apprehensive face peering tentatively up at me. I welcomed the attractive youth and let him know dinner was just about ready. Like he could be in any way unaware by the savory aroma. The lip-licking look let me know he was famished. The nervous swipe of his dark shoulder-length waves let me know he wanted to discuss something. So I drew him into the great room. Sitting by the fireplace, he broke into a gushing tirade of apology for the way he had acted earlier in the morning and previous evening. My quick acceptance of it and the lighting of the joint, followed by a couple of tokes each, had us chatting amiably as we always had. I was happy to see the boy letting it go. His relief was evident.

Freaked by the experience on the peak the day before, as we'd surmised, the boy was also upset by the vehemence of the police interrogation. It had cowed him—he even wondered if he, Adolpho, was somehow implicated in the mess. 'Deputy Fife" had third-degreed his ass while at the police station for several hours. He told me that the sheriff and the other officers were all talking like this was a murderous rampage by a person or persons rather than the bear-mauling being officially put out by their office. There had even been a reference to the reggae musician's name. Ambergai Gee.

No wonder this boy was totally messed up, I thought. First, coming upon the bloody scene, then being treated like a person-of-interest, then having to stay alone in a lonesome up-mountain place such as his own, unsure of what or who may have him in their sights. And, what the fuck was this crap about Gai?

When Jeremy had called him, Adolpho continued, he had first hesitated at the chance to join us. He had revolted himself by the thought that my man might think he would take the offer for sexual reasons…silly straight man. The convoluted reasoning they employed when it came to their dealings with gay men. Jeremy might be a lot of things, but by no means was a lech or perv among them. My man had a nearly two-decade track record of upstanding character traits, by my first-hand knowledge, who happened to be overly-endowed with both bodily and psychologically magnetic qualities. Inherent to his being. There was nary a less-than-gentlemanly bone in the man's body. Including the nine inch one.

Never did he stick that beautiful thing anywhere close to where it wasn't invited. The man had proven the fact umpteen times over the years. Horn-doggery and lechery were not worthy of comparison. Jeremy epitomized the difference. I assured Adolpho of all this over the coming minutes and we went to the kitchen to gather things for the upcoming impromptu stew fest…it was making everybody hunger-cum, if that was even a term.

Popping open a couple of Belhaven ales, which I knew the young Italian enjoyed, we finally thought of helping Jeremy and young Bryce finish unpacking things. Where had they gotten themselves off to? Those turned out to be prescient thoughts. Upon opening the second bedroom door, our curiosity was answered. Adolpho was, while I was not, surprised to find the two locked in a sweaty fuck down right there beside the bags they had managed to get placed on the bed before ripping each other's clothes off. Literally.

Bryce's shirt was in two pieces on the floor, his jeans were tossed on the potted plant by the window, shoes were nowhere to be seen and his Under Armour briefs were hanging in multiple pieces between the lampshade and the credenza. My man's clothing was similarly arrayed around the room. The two were lip locked and tonguing each other through audible groans and moans. The big fat black dick of Jeremy's was buried balls deep in Bryce's ass so that it wasn't visible.

By the spasming I could see going on at that level, it was evident that eruption was now in progress and as we watched in spellbound fascination, Bryce's white boy dick started squirting sperm onto Jeremy's ripped stomach and chest. Naturally, my man's hand was cupped for the reception. Bryce was straddling the prone black man, one leg on the ground, the other bent upon the bed, the boy rocking deeply on the thing in his hole. Jeremy's big hand clenched one of the two white melons he was pole holing, still kneading it as the barely visible root of his piece emptied jism into the hot cleft between the matched set.

Adolpho couldn't suppress the guffaw that passed his lips and the sound brought the rutting pair out of their trance. Jeremy's guiltless grin came visible as the blond ski bum—bum being the relevant term—bumped up from the bottomed-out state of his sperm absorbing crouch and swung, humiliated, around to face us as his ass and dick both dribbled cum. Jeremy's pretty piece spewed a last couple of weak jets upward and onto the round buns just abandoning the geyser.

I just sucked in another toke at the sight, feeling my own piece respond in typical fashion to seeing my own guy in the writhing state of ecstasy I so well knew. I totally got off on viewing or sharing his pleasure. Turning to Adolpho, I offered a power hit and the stoned straight boy reacted by accepting it.

Bryce, not well-versed in our open ways, sputtered his apologies to everyone and no one in particular. Jeremy reached up and seized the still bouncing-- and cumming—boy's cock, squeezing his attention long enough to let him know all was OK. That silenced the kid and he slowly relaxed, finally smiling self-consciously at the three of us. The sexy boy transparently reflected shock that he wasn't about to be beaten or shot. Or strung up.

Rather than that, I stepped into the adjoining bathroom and brought each slimed man a towel and warm washcloth. Adolpho was simply not sure what to make of the whole scenario. No women were present, so he evinced the vibe that this shouldn't be right, yet the telltale tenting to the front of his multiple layers of pants told an entirely different story…

Reading this rightly as bullshit (his take on the matter had always been; "Yeah, right, and male hustler's dicks get hard at the sight of the money…uh-huh…"), Jeremy rose from the bed, wiping the spume off of his delectable self, licking it shamelessly. Then he went over to the Italian and sat down on the side of the bed while he deliberately pulled Adolpho toward him, unzipping first one jean zipper, then a second, and finally, unbuttoning the last pair. Under all this, two pairs of boxers resided, wrinkled and crumpled, against the bronze-skinned youth's ripe groin.

Stoned and happier since his and my talk, Adolpho allowed the action, no doubt remembering what came after the 'unwrapping' part of this process. "Maybe you might be wantin' to cover this all up just a little less for the next time, straight man," Jeremy grinned at him, removing the somewhat shy, but very stiff Florentine hard-on waiting to be unveiled. It had grown up to be a large, curved, cut beauty. And it strayed toward my man's succulent lips. Bryce couldn't look away from it, I noted. Jeremy neatly pushed all three pairs plus the drawers to the triply-socked ankles.

Jeremy's legs were now spread around Adolpho's from where he sat and that mouth drew the dick in like a Hoover deluxe, ebony hand pulling the brown Italiano butt to him, not stopping until just the dark brown curls and the tight balls were visible. And being licked by the long tongue inhabiting the black stud's multi-tasking mouth.

He slowly worked his way around the shaft with that tongue snaking out from the full lips between slurps, until the whole of it was slimed to his satisfaction. Then, he backed off completely, leaving Adolpho's face wearing a look of bereft desertion.

JK turned to me in silent request of a power hit. Which I gladly provided. Then, I provided the straight boy with one and then the ski bum. Finally serving myself, we were sufficiently saturated. The four of us proceeded to perform or voyeur the ongoing group thing. Adolpho's mouth succumbed to the ski bum's tongue and I fastidiously cleaned both the ski bum's and Jeremy's cocks. Between the group, everybody's tongue got a work out and with the delicious smell of rabbit fricassee enveloping us, we swallowed our choice of aperitif…

Adolpho was amazed to find that male tongues were more athletic than those of the persuasion to which he had been heretofore inculcated and ended by actively tangling with his first masculine linguist. Probably not his last. At least, so hoped the young ski bum. And his little bum…I mean butt.

Hunger or sleepiness inevitably invades after orgasm; the two senses being served by adjacent cranial nerves. The former extended precedence in this case. Jeremy's rabbit stew was just what the doctor ordered. I signed the prescriptions personally. The freshly baked, warm buttery rye bread and Depeche Mode's Violator CD provided us filling nourishment and ambience.

After cleaning up both the kitchen and ourselves, taking the dogs out, and banking the fire, the four of us headed to the warmth of our respective beds. Each of us enjoyed a gummy bear as non-liquid digestif…

Jeremy nudged me upon noting Bryce's surreptitious U-turn when he thought we were safely upstairs. The boy slipped into Adolpho's sanctuary for who knows what kind of conversation. The two certainly had the time to hash it out. We both smiled that the sommelier's door opened from the inside on Bryce's approach. 'I told you that boy just needed some good ass, honey," I poked my stud.

In answer, he threw me over his broad shoulders and headed up the remaining stairs, concurring, "Me, too."

Privately in our lair, Jeremy first filled me in on the good deputy's visit, telling me bad things which I had feared and didn't care to hear. In the process, my good man worked himself up to the point that I had to resort to slapping him. With my dick. He was distracted by the subtly nuanced move and forgot the subject as soon as my rigid prick hit his tonsils. Would he never learn, I asked myself? Minutes later the man was asleep with it and my load filling his mouth. I didn't have the heart to take it away. He lay there so angelic and pacified.

For the first time in days, we both slept uninterrupted, falling into the arms of Morpheus as softly muffled sounds emanated from the bedroom below us.

* * *

Hallowe'en morning. All Hallows' Eve. All Saint's Eve. The beginning day of AllHallowTide, the Western Christian Feast days signaling the liturgical dedication to remembering the dead. At least, that is, those dead that were saints, martyrs and all the faithful: those who existed in Purgatory until the Day of Reckoning or, modernly, the Rapture.

All those not waiting there were already sweating in Hell. I had sometimes wondered to myself exactly how those in Purgatory spent their time. Hmmmm. Maybe I would review Mr. Milton's take on it. Paradise Lost. Published in winter, 1667, it came out within a year of the Great London Fire…plenty of pre-burnt and freeze-dried souls to contemplate.

So, anyway, different strokes for different folks, I reasoned, by the variance in ways for observing the date… My mind dwelled on the ancient days' rites, before and after being hijacked by religiosity, as I lay watching out the undraped bay window, head on my lover's smooth, muscled pectoral. His nipple, always erect, tickled my ear. My dick got hard as that nipple wobbled, inviting me with each deep, regular breath. My phattening white shaft climbed the smoothness of his thigh.

Brushing softly downward over Jeremy's luscious skin, I lightly fingered the black prick lying there in wait, turgid as usual. He didn't even stir, also per usual, but that dick sure did. The thing sprang up at my touch. I could stroke the beautiful thing while that nipple continued harassing me and he would likely only awaken to the flood of emissions at the ending, if then.

I was certain his dreams entertained a ribald world where continuous rapture and climax held dominion. What else, I reasoned, could Heaven be about if not that? Could true religious believers fail to understand that their Lord, in all His infinite wisdom, hadn't made orgasm so sweet just to decry it as a curse? The doings of the Devil Incarnate? Any extant Creator was surely getting a good laugh at the stupidity of that illogic. This basic non-sequitur really bothered me.

With that, I slicked up that pretty ebony dick, closed my eyes and climbed on for a classic holiday ride. My hard dick bounced on and off the taut belly beneath it as I contemplated the concept. Rapturously. Climax came with the epiphany that any caring Creator had, indeed, meant orgasm to be a gift. Never a curse.

That curse thing had to have been part of a nightmare of sterile old, balding, impotent men who forced all priests and monks to dress alike, tonsure themselves and act alike, calling it "Holy", so they wouldn't have to suffer alone in their misery…

I opened my eyes to find Jeremy's hand swiping up my load, smiling up at me as his own piece flooded my guts, "what the hell were you thinking about inside that curly head, Luke?" We pulsed pleasurably together in our personal religious atonement exercise… call it gay communion.

Yup, the old geezers were just pissed because they didn't have Cialis back then. We sure would, when that time came…

A soothing communal shower later, we two descended wrapped in towels to find our adorable pair of guests cuddling together on the fireplace hearth, apparently comparing tongues. Lip-locked as they were, it was a bit difficult to tell. The two freshly showered and combed boys looked up as we entered with our coffee cups, shy at the interruption. Hard dicks poking unshyly from the fronts of their towels told another tale, for sure.

Adolpho appeared much more at ease now—multiple orgasmic experiences tended to do that to a person—and his pinkly cherubic cheeks attested to the fact of the successful addressing of the gay question regarding he and Bryce... entwined bodies seemed to bear the fact out.

Limerence would appear to be in ascendance, if body language was any indication...Jeremy and I exchanged self-satisfied glances at the overnight change. The two were absolutely beautiful together. Let the bitter, rancorous, oath-keeping, sanctimonious side of the spectrum marinate themselves as they liked. Just leave the rest of us enlightened ones the hell alone, I philosophized... These two had melded under our roof and considering our own disparate beginnings along with a solid two-decade track record, naysayers may happily go fuck themselves silly. With my blessing.

While meandering through a congenial breakfast of granola, yogurt, berries, honey and buttered toast, we four compared notes for our hopes in the coming evening, should the Mash Bash materialize. Jeremy laid out his da Vinci-of-a-costume and I described my own makeshift personification of a cubic zirconium, at which all three chuckled in the visualization. The boys went off to their now-shared bedroom to pow-wow over their own. We gave them free rein over the abundance of extra clothing and other packed-away contents in the down-stair closets, should it be of help.

The best laid schemes o' mice and men...oft go awry. An apt quote, with much truth to it.

A short hour after that, the door banged at us in announcement of visitors and the dog boys went racing to it, yipping their proclamation. Upon opening up, we found two grim-faced law enforcers, aka keepers of the peace, in the forms of none other than 'Deputy Fife' --- we didn't really care to know the man's name--- and his boss, Sheriff Hamlin Delmar. Rod thin and irascible, Jeremy and I had always found it hard to believe this progressive community had actually elected the cantankerous old codger into office. Nonetheless, it would seem to be so. Here he stood.

The two scrutinized us both from head to feet there on the porch. From our perspective, a whole lot longer was spent seeing the skin parts then the towel covers…just sayin'… The transparent projection of disdain for the minimally clothed, biracial duo with whom they apparently had business to discuss was plain.

Ever the raconteur, my studly man pulled me closer to him, draping his long, muscular arm over my bare shoulders. He looked from the wizened little deputy to his stern-faced boss, all the while smiling cordially so as to clarify things. His body language spoke volumes. Out loud, he looked down on the uniformed face of the law from his six-foot-three frame and innocently inquired, "What may my husband and I do for you, Sir?" The ironic sarcasm fairly dripped from his mouth.

Deputy Fife visibly chafed at the action and words, but in an attempt to keep things professional, Sheriff Delmar ignored the obvious yet benign provocation. He cleared his throat and tipped his cowboy-style hat, "Well, Mr. Kell, we are trying to locate a gentleman who has been reported to be staying at this address: a Mr. Amber…Ambergay…errr, Amberger Gee, IV. We have an interest in speaking to Mr. Gee and are hoping to do so now, that is if you might be of help."

Taking the cue of the calm example set by Jeremy, I butted in, "We would be glad to, Sheriff, but for the fact that we, ourselves, have been perplexed by his disappearance three days ago. DOCTOR Kell and I haven't heard a word from him, and we're both quite concerned." In my most professional voice, I added, "May we ask as to what the matter might pertain?" Ignoring the query, the law man obtusely deflected by asking if we would call and let him know should things change and we did hear from him. "Of course, Sheriff, and we would likewise appreciate the same courtesy should either of you. The man is a dear family friend."

Jeremy was enjoying making the little deputy uncomfortable. He upped the ante by airily smoothing his free hand over the patch of peeking pubic hair showing above his towel, thence upwards from bellybutton to pecs, offhandedly tweaking his nipples lightly...the insouciance of this action was punctuated by never taking his eyes from the deputy's, who couldn't look away.

The behavior rattled the man, leaving him nonplussed and blushing. Evidently on a short-leash, Fife was unable to bring the power of his badge to bear here in the presence of his overseer. My man had read the situation perfectly. He had been livid at hearing of the tactics used on Adolpho at the sheriff's office and more so when Gai's name had been bandied. His unspoken retort here to that treatment by only body language was proving classic.

Memory of the deputy's demeanor in this same spot the previous day had left me with the impression of a pugnacious pug, shrilly barking his power at my man. Today, the man was more the picture of a submissive cocker spaniel upon being caught peeing on the new carpet. I had to control myself.

The 'conversation' was apparently at a conclusion and the lawmen curtly backed down the steps, turning to re-enter the waiting cruiser, then disappearing down and around the bend as we stood watching. Jeremy reached down now and spanked me on the butt, deadpanning, "Well, now, that went well, don't you think?"

I let go the laugh I had been holding and we went back inside, wondering what that encounter had really been about? The landline we kept in case of lost power was ringing in the kitchen and upon answering, I heard elderly Mrs. Chastain's voice on the other end. She had seen the police cruiser pass three times on the way to our place the last three days, she told me, and couldn't hold her curiosity any longer.

Worriedly, she asked whether we had had any word about Gai, rightly guessing that the official visits might be related. When I let her know what had happened, she and Mr. Chastain, who was also on the line, regaled me with their own news: there had been another bear attack the previous afternoon. They had just heard from Lady Carlotta that the three bears allegedly involved had been tracked down, tranquilized and corralled at a wildlife preserve on the next mountain over, just this morning. The good news was that the bash was a go, they added, and were we still attending?

Concern for our friend was overshadowing our focus but I assured them that we didn't want to miss it… wait a moment, my mind suddenly reeled as I caught the comment, and I asked the old couple to back up a bit. Had they said there was another death-by-bear?

"Oh, no, Luke, there was an attack— another outsider again — but it hadn't killed the man, only maimed him. He is at the San Miguel County hospital now, comatose in the ICU. An arm and his…thing…had been ripped off. Poor soul." she added. We ended with mutual hopes for any news regarding our missing dread-headed friend.

Hanging up the old-fashioned solid state rotary desk telephone I looked at Jeremy in disbelief. "Wassup, Luke? You look like you just talked to a dead person," he asked with concern.

"JK, there was another attack—over on the far side—yesterday afternoon. I think I saw it—or, at least, the after part."

I recounted the sighting of the three bears while on the gondola the previous day and the pink trail I had been unsure about in the snow. As I filled him in on the other details and the telephone call, the first things in our minds were: why hadn't the sheriff spoken about any of this? And, where was Gai? He was, indeed an 'outsider' as Mrs. Chastain had called the victim. We were now officially freaked.

The next hour saw the two of us hurrying over the mountain to the county hospital, burning up our iphones calling everyone we could think of in search of details and answers. Nothing proved forthcoming and we fretted.

Getting admitted into the ICU proved tricky, as we were not relatives to an unidentified comatose patient. I finally prevailed on the nursing staff that even without privileges at this hospital, I may be able to offer help or advisement due to my ER status in several Austin and Texas hospitals. That worked.

Upon first viewing the close-cropped person-of-color lying almost full-body bandaged, my relief at the lack of dreadlocks was mitigated by the poor stats he was exhibiting. The right arm was obviously missing at the shoulder, blood seepage was evident around the midsection and every orifice plus some newly forged ones had been plugged by supportive devices. I conferred with the clinicians on duty.

We discussed a new regimen of innovative shock remedy interventions developed at the burn center in San Antonio and recently instituted at my medical center. The protocol was accessed and begun. Regardless, the prognosis would remain grim for the patient due to the copious loss of blood and severe hypothermia suffered before being found. He had been over-long in the snowy exposure.

I promised to keep in touch on the case if they would like and returned afterwards to the waiting area. Jeremy was uncharacteristically fidgety and very jumpy. In surprise at my touch he nearly bolted from his seat, "Damn, Luke, you scared me—how is he?" He had convinced himself that his older mentor was the victim and tears appeared when I let him know it wasn't so. He blubbered awhile into my shoulder, then we thanked the nurses and left a number should they need it.

Leaving the quiet confines of the small mountain hospital ER, we made our way back to the gondola station. The discussion between us was one of reciprocal assurances that Ambergai Gee, IV, was a hardy and resourceful soul of much experience. He hadn't just fallen off the proverbial turnip truck. We resolved to keep positive about his wisdom and abilities.

Our pep talk relieved us more than we could've hoped, knowing we were right. Bucking one another up, we arrived at the station to find no less than our friends Sheila E and her spouse, Cat G, awaiting a car. The chance meeting provided a needed diversion from the fraught past hours, so joined them on the trip back over the mountain.

The svelte, cutting edge couple were relieved to hear that, at the least, no bad news had been learned about the singer with the Mighty Diamonds, though common concern stifled the normal upbeat tone when sharing time with these special ladies. The two were partiers. Sheila was glad the bash was still on. She and Cat were scheduled to perform, they informed us.

We hadn't known, as the surprise was not to be unveiled until they were introduced, last-second, by the imported San Francisco DJ. They swore us to further secrecy by spilling it that a close friend and maybe two were flying in later in the afternoon to join them, and we both zipped our lips in mimicry of losing the tattle key. Little could we know…

The music was going to be unbelievable this evening, Jeremy whispered to me when Cat also let it out that the theme was 'Music of the Night'. The knowledge raised a spectre of The Phantom of the Opera, and it seemed appropriate what with the old mine venue. Both of our spirits were lifted and I was happy to see a smile perfuse my man's face.

We parted from the couple on our different ways up the 'hill', their chalet in a secluded glen a mile from our log home, trading promises to meet later during the celebration. In climbing homeward, attempted levity boosted one another more so by teasing about the coming hijinks sure to occur at the Mash Bash and comparing guesses as to the refurbished venue in the old Pandora Mine from the nineteenth century mining period. Just about nobody was privy to the upgrades undertaken there and only vague hints had slipped out. The girls must've known something, but hadn't spilled the beans about it.

Absorbed with ourselves, we missed the hushed approach of a sleek silver automobile from behind and nearly died of startlement when the short tap of the horn signaled its presence just feet from us. We twirled around in midair to see the capped visage of Paecup Andropov grinning by his surprise materialization. Dropping back to the driver's window brought the razzing and unmerciful quips marking us as 'pussy-boys' for our comical shrieks at the interruption.

"I'm guessin' that Lady Carlotta isn't with you considering the low-rent thug talk, Paecup," Jeremy teased back, regaining a semblance of dignity. "How's it hangin', bra? You gonna be seeing us up at the mine tonight?" He obviously liked the Russian man and we had agreed to try to get more acquainted after the previous impromptu get together at our place.

"Ya. I've been invited to escort her ladyship this evening and been forced to acquire appropriate attire for the affair. My first Amer-ee-kan par-tee," he informed us. "She is quite a lady, and the be-est employer I have ever had— will you two be dressed, as well?" Apparently, he meant costumes, but the difference in backgrounds muddled the terms, I noticed.

Ha, I thought, will we ever. We assured him it was so. The man then offered Lady Carlotta's greeting and asked if we might acquiesce to joining the two in the travel to and from the bash, seeing as the gondola would be no doubt stretched to capacity by revelers. She had sent him on the errand to personally invite us.

We were delighted with the offer. The idea of Jeremy's cumbersome get-up was presenting a daunting challenge for traversing the mountain and our Benz was not nearly large enough. So, we merrily accepted and climbed in, allowing the Russian to carry us the rest of the way to the lodge. We were already nearing the time for beginning Jeremy's assemblage. The afternoon was getting away from us.

Inside, the cabin of the auto dazzled in its aristocratic appointments and Paecup pushed buttons which caused the drop of a small marble serving table and the appearance of a compact refrigerator below it. Another button rendered a partial rotation by two of the six facing Italian leather seats toward each other. Foot supports arose to push us into a position we had not experienced in a car—except maybe a remotely similar contrivance in the new Benz Maybach S600 Pullman, test-driven back in Austin.

I facetiously inquired if the Geisha girls would sit in front with him, to which Paecup replied, straight-faced, "the girls would always enter from the boot to avoid contact with the passengers, until the proper time…" Jeremy snorted at that.

The efficient chauffer then asked if we would prefer refreshment before unloading. Jeremy's disbelief was evidenced by his wryly faux-formal comment, "Why yes, good man, I do believe I will have a single malt and a couple small bumps before we deplane." We were feeling mirthful, now, at the unexpected ride and opulent 'accoutrements'.

That is, until Mr. Andropov clicked three successive switches which ejected tiny silver spoons from the facing seat back, each heaped with pure white powder, a bit floating extravagantly down to the marble surface. "Would the Sirs prefer Columbian, Bolivian, or perhaps the absinthe—that on the right?" We exchanged shocked looks and Paecup chuckled in the rearview mirror at us, "We keep the traveling sedan well-stocked, monsieurs, per the Lady's instructions.

Jeremy almost choked in trying to respond and I finally managed, "but Paecup, who might the third spoon be for, exactly?" My provocative tone brought the quip, "Uh, boii, that would be for moi, but only should the two gents desire a short interlude before our parting…"

That did it. Jeremy unhooked the small spoon on the left, raised it to his flared nostril and inhaled in a sharp intake, rubbing the sides together while raising his head, like he knew what he was doing. My turn to be astonished.

He turned to me, checked to make sure Paecup was watching in the rearview, then blatantly licked my face from chin to forehead, "Honey, we shouldn't act like thankless guests—get the middle one." His grin, as usual, disarmed and reassured me. He grasped the middle spoon himself, held it up high, affirmed with the driver, "the Bolivian?"

Then he wedged shut one of my nostrils, raised the engraved spoon to my other and directed me to, "suck...... Honey, don't blow, it's a euphemism..." I replicated J's technique and caught sight of the Russian man ejecting his own private dispenser next to the steering wheel. He raised the chauffer's copper spoon there and did the same with a cheery Russian exclamation meaning, "Salud", leaving us to share an extra bump each by the remaining spoon. Absinthe. Hmmm.

We all sat chatting for a minute while 'absorbing' the party favor. Then, pulling into the pebbled drive, we floatingly unloaded from the vehicle, skipped up the steps and entered.

The Russian man was stripping as he crossed the threshold. Jacket, tie, cap, all disappeared over the couch; his shirt, undershirt, pants, boxer briefs, socks and shoes next left in quick succession, ending with him spread-legged, proudly naked and boning up in split seconds. The rising member was very ethnically Slavic: big, long, thick and uncut.

Jeremy whistled his appreciation, "you move fast Paecup. What else are you good at?" In reply, Paecup reached out and thumbed my man's pants down to the floor. I proceeded getting myself undressed, enjoying the show. His face contacted and followed the contour of the strongly built ebony body as he lowered the jeans.

Slowly and with intent, so as to feel as much of the beautiful physique as possible, his nose slid from the thick neck downward between the mounded pectorals, over each ripple of the six-pack, all the way to the exposed crotch.

Since Jeremy seldom restricted himself with underwear or drawers—he did sports straps occasionally—he had only to lift each foot out of the leggings and raise his bulky crew sweater over his head to be stunningly, rigidly nude. His nine inches matched the white Russian. The thing levitated bobbingly upward over the parallel plane, foreskin coyly shrouding the bare edge of the spongy, curving base of the corona.

The fat, round, snug nuts hugged the flaring base like lovers and it was a very good thing that I was familiar with its details as I managed only two blinks before it nestled to the short curly pubic curls in the back of that deep throat. Slavic nostrils deeply inhaled the muskiness emanating from it.

The man must have studied Houdini's techniques for breath-holding, or perhaps the dick stroker simply had the lung capacity of an orca. Either way, I nearly passed out as I watched through my own held breath while waiting for him to back the thick thing out of his gullet.

Basically, it never did. Through the whole head job. Jeremy stood staring directly into my eyes the entire time, his sexy gray eyes dilated with the go-fast bump and glazed by the blissful longevity being accorded him via the cavernous throat. He shared the effect with me.

Obviously possessing no gag reflex, Paecup's throat had visibly expanded by the outline of my man's swallowed shaft embedded in it but the pro never once winced, hiccupped, or hesitated in the delivery of the most unique blowjob I had ever witnessed. Or that J-Man had ever experienced. Jeremy, gentleman that he be, later denied it was so, in deference to me, but the truth was what it was.

What the sucker did do wasn't actually sucking. As the distended dickhead stretched down that throat, Paecup set his swallowing mechanism into a repetitive glugging motion. The effect caused a continual wavelike effect of his Adams' apple to roll for minute after minute.

Over and over the super-sensitized spongy head was massaged in this unusual manner until an 'arrrggghhhh' escaped from Jeremy and the dick I loved began pulsating to the throat rolls. The extreme throat action forced his eruption without a single other stroke.

Jeremy's eyes rolled up in his head, his fingers clasped the close-cropped blond hair, holding the man in place--- as if that was necessary--- and the giant orgasmic release quaked through my man's senses.

Every perfect muscle in his body appeared to be on high-tension squeeze mode. Had I only walked in at the moment of climax, I would've thought JK were suffering a grand mal seizure…of utter euphoria.

As my pleasure rose in seeing the prolonged effect Jeremy was deriving now, I could feel the pre-cum drip from my own dickhead. It stood straight and long in quivering readiness for my hand to stroke it, but I suddenly felt hot lips wrap around the tip and nurse the drippings.

Being so intent during our entry, we had failed to notice the two young men sharing our home lounging together on the recliner by the fire. The two had stayed silent, voyeuring us through the entire occurrence. But upon seeing the unique climax and my own ropy oozing, the two had soundlessly crept from behind, settling before me on their knees. Obviously intending to prevent my drippings from messing the clean floor…

Now, the duo set to licking and massaging my hard-on, making it jump by the pleasure. I watched as they enjoyed themselves, each exploring the other's tight young body as they slobbered over my piece.

My eyes quickly raised back up to the paroxysmal satyr before me just as he gazed over at me again, conveying gratification. My longmeat soon gave in to the fervor and he vicariously shared my cresting, as I had his, only moments before. The boys' newness to each other and their youthful libidos allowed for a stroked mutual boy-orgasm while licking and swallowing my juices. They lip-locked together around my shaft and then sprayed all over each other in their enthusiasm.

Four sated men stood or knelt in a sheen of man-goo--- oh, wait, make that five men--- we all four watched the still impaled Russian erupt in multiple jets of Eastern Orthodox bliss, too. I think that made for a straight flush or five-of-a-kind, or something.

With some more time we came up for air, savoring a most excellent pre-Hallow'en rite. If they were watching, I figured those saints and martyrs must be cumming, too. That's it. I had finally hit on what all those inhabitants of Purgatory do, whiling away all that time in their long wait for the pearly gates to open up: they voyeur. Pearly—get it? But, I digress.

A little embarrassed— like, not at all--- we five enjoyed the big upstairs shower together after Paecup's 'short interlude' and planned for the coming evening. The new couple accepted an invitation to join us in the Pierce-Arrow. Paecup extended one in Lady Carlotta's name, knowing she would love the company of four virile men.

Jeremy leaned on the steaming wall jets under a cascading rain head while I massaged the sore muscles after all that constricting and contracting. I counted myself a fortunate man.

We finally descended to sort out mixed up clothing, playfully bombarding our new driver friend with his uniform. My black stud kept up his teasing of the Russian, "Nice of you to stop Andropov a load. Now Paecup your uniform and get back to work." Tucking in his shirt, the chauffer bounced down the front steps to the auto, waving that he'd be back... I felt like a scene from the Walton's, all four of us on the front door deck waving good-bye to Paecup, half-waiting to hear a voice from the open upstairs window call down, "Goodnight, Jonboy..."

How homey we looked. Except for the facts that Jeremy was butt-ass naked, dangling, and the two boys were draped all over each other in just towels, there was no discernible difference between us and the old TV series family. My wisecrack, "Well, let's go in and have a little helping of 'the Recipe'," got some mighty weird looks. Jeremy and I got it, anyway.

In the great room, we hunkered around the fireplace, as always, nursing some of the Recipe...errr... Old Fashion cocktails. Jeremy had pulled Adolpho into his confidence about the coming costume attraction dubbed "The Mighty Tungsten Tuberosity' and the two were animatedly planning the transport logistics over the mountain to Pandora Mine.

Bryce, meanwhile, snuggled over to me on the huge leather sectional with his drink and asked, "Could we talk, Dr. Cevennes?" Uh-oh, I thought, those words rarely had a good connotation, and I braced for a broadside. Were his parents suing us, or had he strained something helping me haul packages? Was he pregnant? With the recent tragedies, I was kind of expecting something else bad.

"Of course, Bryce, but...what exactly is up with 'Dr. Cevennes'? I mean, yeah, I am older than you and that is very respectful, but good grief, boi, we have been suckin' each other's dicks and showering together...aren't we a little past the formalities?"

The wavy-haired youth colored a little and stared right at me, "OK, sir...uhh, Luke" --- that was better--- "it's just that, well, I haven't ever known real doctors—I mean, as friends— and you guys have been so nice to me and everything..." It sounded to me like he was stuttering through a prepared speech. What was in his head, I wondered? He went on, "It's just that I'm so happy right now, even with all of the shit that's been goin' down, and...well, I'm just figurin' that this bubble has to burst pretty soon—am I gonna owe a bill, or something...?" I burst out laughing at the serious look on this cute boy's face. The others looked over at us, hearing my reaction.

"Well, Hell, Pearl, what are you thinking," I posed, "that you're checked in to the Hotel California?" His blank look let me know that that had gone right over his head, so I took a breath and wrapped my arm around his shoulder, drawing him to me, "Listen, Bryce, I know that Jeremy and I are new to you, and this 'thing' going on with you and Adolpho must be confusing, but don't think for a minute that there is any foot about to fall, here. JFK and me, we are just in love with Life, so when the unexpected rolls our way, we just accept serendipity and make the best of situations. We both are convinced of the 'Tree of Life'."

"Are you worried how your parents are going to handle this —do you even still live at home?" Pulling up short, I shut my mouth like a kissing gourami. Idiot that I was.

Taking a deep breath, I straightened up across from the youth, sticking my hand out, "I am Dr. Lucas Laughlin Cevennes, and this is my husband, Dr. Jeremy Fallsworth Kell. We are from Austin, Texas, and stay up here in Tride for as much time as we can. I am on sabbatical from my hospital for a few more months and Jeremy teaches, Philosophy, at the University of Texas. How do you do? Would you care to join us in Life?"

It had struck me abruptly that we knew next to nothing whatsoever about this young person. That should be changed, post haste. Life is, indeed, a party, but there should at least be invitations, after all.

The young man fairly melted into me at this soliloquy and when he looked back up, a single tear was somersaulting down his cheek. "Yes." Nothing more came out. I realized in a moment that he really couldn't talk, so we just sat there quietly for a little. Over my shoulder, Jeremy's big hand suddenly appeared. Adolpho had stood and come up behind the boy, putting both hands on him.

My superman looked down at the both of us and softly said, "Bryce, I am so sorry. May we know who you are?" Adolpho's dark hands gently massaged his shoulders, and finally, Bryce took a deep breath, "I am Bryce Adams Canyon. I moved here to Tride a year ago after my grandfather passed away in Seattle. I am working to get my degree in computer programming, I love mountain biking and I don't have any family. At all. I'm not sorry about that, it's just what it is, is all." And with that, the tow-headed Adonis leaned into me and bawled.

I think my heart swelled up and burst at that moment. Jeremy, along with Bryce, sat down with us and we all just lost it for a while. Even Elvee and Suture, sensing the profundity, came up and lay down at our feet, communing with the pack.

Hmmmmmm.

My drink tipped over between J-Man and me where I had forgotten it and we both jumped up, shattering the deepness. We went to get paper towels and on our return, found Adolpho and Bryce whispering together. Much as we didn't want to interrupt, the mess needed cleaning up, so we did. In reaching by him, Jeremy managed to trail his middle leg, for once unintentionally, over Adolpho's, and the Italiano reacted by slapping it. The thing boomeranged over and sideswiped Bryce's leg next, and the oppressive atmosphere evaporated.

Wow, I thought as I perused the trio. How funny, the way that families are made.

Chapter 12
Stick Shift- Storge

Cal leaned over me, rippled chocolate stomach muscles sweaty on my lower back and buttglobes, ten-inch manmeat throbbing fixedly inside my glistening bare ass. My arms extended straight down on to the bed, supporting us both as I kneeled before the greek god fucking me.

His long dark thumb still wrapped around my dickroot as my piece pulsed out a few final globs of creamy, burning cum and his long fingers massaged our joined dick and ass connection, maximizing our velvety buzz. His long tongue still massaged my ear, deep into it, as his other hand slowly contoured my tanned pecs down over a taut stomach to pubic shorthairs.

I could see his luscious mahogany gluteal muscle masses rotating in sensuously slow undulating arcs, interrupted by intermittent spasming, as he watched me watch him in the mirror reflecting us from the wall. His low, gnarly resonations were fading as the blooming of his releasing cock relaxed.

The washboard from his manly abs up to the prize-fighter quality pectoral muscles so sexily crowned by the sensitive nipples I loved to suckle were all combining to polish my arched backside. Those hard nipples pinpointed themselves as they waved over me. The congruence of our forms pleasured our afterglow.

Neither of us attempted withdrawal from our conjoinment and the soft nuzzling continued for minutes as we luxuriated in this state that we both cherished. Love is a word so overused, yet also ill-equipped to describe our contentment with one another. Slow-growing natural affection is the basis for all long-lasting, enduring relationships. Love based on natural affection takes time. It requires genuine liking and understanding by each person.

Signs of mature love include acceptance, emotional respect, consideration, commitment, friendship, calmness, kindness and caring. There was a term for this in ancient Greece and Rome. It was called storge. Affection stronger on the day one dies than on the first day.

Storge is the reason our ardour never lessened, even after eight years of experiencing it and four months of post-elopement matrimony. Of course, our innovative variations as well as our allowance for extramarital hijinks aided our venture together. Cal's efforts to freshen us never ceased and the ways he came up with, in the doing, convinced me of my luck. All the time and daily.

When we had first hooked up, Cal and I had discussed the major fault in most relationships and agreed to avoid the trap. Monogamy is such an over-valued, underachieved state of existence. Americans are obsessed by it. We understood that honesty is the first tie that binds when two people match up. If the age-old provocateur, jealousy, can be dealt with then the fruits of an abiding relationship may be bound. Storge.

When episodes developed outside the two of us, rather than compartmentalizing and hiding these from one another, we chose instead to employ the instinctive hormonal stresses commonly pulling on most persons as a catalyst for our shared rhapsody. It worked well for us. The fantasies and variety renewed our reciprocal adoration toward a wholeness few attempt to understand. An epic poem was unfolding before our blended eyes.

From the outset, when I first spotted the tall, sinewy stud up on the bar at the frat party nine years before, he had locked on my eyes while sweeping a gaze around the riotous party room. Jiggling his barely covered, coveted booty, of which he was totally aware, the man never relinquished that stare until the DJ changed the tone to one less raucous. The erotic performance had beguiled me.

After it, the lean six-foot six player had bounced nimbly down from his perch, gliding ably past grabbing, grasping hands all hoping to seize his attention. I marveled at the fact that he stopped a simple inch before bumping me in the far corner from where I viewed the revelry. "Hey, sexy, come here often?" He clichéd purposely through a wide toothy grin as he fingertipped the small hollow where my neck met my chest. I had nearly died of embarrassment and burned to a human crisp all at once.

Propping his outstretched fingers on the wall behind my head, he leaned over and down to my smaller six-foot frame and made a sizzle sound through his teeth. The man exhibited hutzpah, confidence and cockiness enough for three men. His musky aroma floored me. Neophyte that I was, and inexperienced in the ways of social interaction, let alone male-on-male assignation, I sought as quick a way out of the scenario as I possibly could. My girlfriend passed him my digits on her way out, following me...

The drive for a medical degree completely blindered my psyche at that point in life. Only by the fact that spring break had offered a rare lapse in the tunnel-vision engaged for attaining my goals had I reluctantly agreed to accompany a close female classmate to the frat party in the first place.

Calumet Broadhearst reigned as campus stud and b.m.o.c. amongst both the male and female student bodies. His persistently attentive, yet respectful, onslaught toward my late-blooming, loner, bent-on-achievement-self baffled me mightily. Somehow, Cal recognized both my angst at his forwardness and the drive for set goals almost immediately. After the unbelievably sensual come-on from that bar dance intro, the Nubian giant plied me patiently over the succeeding year until I finally succumbed at the 'finish-line' of a cross-country track event in which I had competed.

Long distance running had forever been my personal physical release and could be practiced anywhere. Singly. And with my dog. Though neither talented nor driven enough to make the university track team travel squad, I was sanctioned to compete at home meets, thereby allowing maintenance of my strictly set study regimen.

It was more than eleven months after our meeting before physicality struck us. Right between the eyes. And legs. He fucked me slow and deep against a tree beyond the backdoor to the gym after my clean-up following a half marathon. Calumet had accosted me as I exited the gym locker room, alone, on the way to my spartan Austin apartment. Endorphin release from physical exertion mixed with his endearing congratulations for my mid-pack finish proved too much that day. A sex-starved body finally couldn't hold out longer and Cal, sensing it, piggy-backed me to the hidden spot he knew by the burbling little creek.

The ebony Adonis sucked my face while he stripped me. His hands lightning-bolted my body by strategic finger-brushings and explorative swirls. Long, limber biceps and hairless forearms lifted me by cradling my bent legs effortlessly off the grass against that tree as he masterfully sank the cobra rising from his groin up into me for the first time.

His ranging fingers marked the margin of my virgin butt-hole, both kindling my anus and massaging his own magnificent prick as it entered. We felt our last remaining wall of separation dissolve in a slow rush of elation. The agonizingly patient, almost reluctant act provoked the sweetest pain I had never imagined through every synapse of my being. From tailbone to brain. My toes extended and curled in one arcing motion and our commencement marked the ending and the beginning. Our eyes never once lost contact.

He and me became we.

Cumming simultaneously and almost immediately, his sexual prowess slowly seconded our roiling orgasm over the succeeding moments. Never once releasing my legs, my mouth, nor my tear-streaming eyes, his movements inked our pact. I had been his dick-whipped mignon ever since.

A blown up, framed picture of the memorable beech tree adorns the wall above our bed to the present day, lower branch harboring a chance bluebird, thus manifesting our meme. Nobody else knows its story. Well, until now.

Anything close to acceptable looks, personality and unrequited id had overtaken me very late in maturation. Evolving slower than my classmates, I awakened to life outside a closely controlled evangelistic upbringing only upon Cal's determined assault. My parents detested him, and by extension, me, for our unfathomable union. Eternal damnation had been sealed, said they. I insisted the parties in Hell were hotter. And then left them all to their bitterness.

My ego was a vestigial thing until he came along. The super-ego that the man nourished in me had imprinted solely on him as I grew into myself. Lucky for me, my wild auburn ringlets and pug-nose had captivated this stud who could have taken anyone. He told me it was my mysterious nature but that was hard to fathom. Introvert, more like...or nerd. But who the hell was complaining?

Cal grew up in a locally well-known family with a tenured university professor father and worldly, refined mother who thrived in their graciously bohemian lifestyle. The couple imbued Cal with the natural flare he now evinced as an adult. His dark-complexioned good looks empowered by an astutely imposing mind opened doors that propelled his establishment in the tech world of software development. By his thirty-third and my thirtieth birthday the two of us were comfortably set in our own right.

The loving, growing, accepting family nurtured my eccentricities, showing me a 'joie de vivre' never once anticipated. By me, that is. Cal told me he knew of our coming together long prior to our first meeting and Cassandra, his doting mama, reinforced this in me. He just didn't know what I looked like, he teased. I bought into the idea slowly but now held to it dearly as my permanent rudder.

Cal grudgingly pulled up off of my well-oiled, fucked frame, still viewing us through the looking glass as he did so. The day was afoot and we had schedules to meet. "So, J-man, do you think he will show up today?" His humongous dick lumbered its way gradually backwards as he asked me again about my new patient from the week before who had peaked our curiosities. It was a bemusing story 'Samuel' had stiltedly shared with me during that appointment. And which I had shared with Cal.

"He may, or may not," I replied, wincing, "Oooooh, baby, Bay-bee, that is a long dick, don't take it ouuwwtt...," I begged him. He sniggered and held still, half of the log still inside. Tensing it several times, teasingly, he grinned at me in the mirror. This man knew I couldn't get enough of him, having witnessed my appetite thousands of times to date. I pushed back on it, enjoying some more. "That man is a puzzle," continuing my answer to the question. Samuel Hodge had been my final appointment of the afternoon last week and it took the nurse and me an hour just to get him undressed. "No trust level at all. He wanted me to prescribe him 'the pill' without an exam, said that was all he needed."

Cal continued studying me in the mirror, caught between pleasure and perplexity, while massaging my butt lightly as we listened to the rain pattering on the window ledge. "A pill? For a broken toe?" He plopped the monster out abruptly, without notice, knowing it was the only way... I registered the expected complaint. 'Day-umm', I felt abandoned.

Turning over and spreading my legs, bending them around his while he leaned down over me, nose to nose, we continued. "What did you do?" he asked. I had to focus as I felt his manjuice dribble out back there. This man-boy of mine was copiously prolific: we could bottle and market the stuff.

"Well, the man apparently knows and likes Keesha, the nurse, so I got her to tease him into getting stripped down while I left the room. It worked-- but I think she's going to have to probably bone him to get him out of them today. That is, if he shows. He lost trust again after I came back in and took over.

I had been enjoying a third day volunteer practicing at the Rome Free Medical Center after tiring of the vacation mindset six weeks into our summer stay at Cal's family home. My presence had taken some of the load off the stressed-out, overworked staff and I loved getting back into a quasi-clinical mode. Pro bono work. Good for the soul, I believed.

A middle-age 'boy', for lack of better description, Samuel had come into the free clinic the week before. He was 40 years-old, prematurely graying in his temples and goatee, stoutly built and well-equipped for the farm work by which he sustained himself on the small piece of land outside this town of Rome, Georgia.

Never having finished high school, he had helped around his uncle's land for the first decade after dropping out---school just wasn't for him, he'd stated. It seemed that Samuel, the orphan, just went along to get along. His uncle had left him the parcel after passing away of untreated diabetes a few years back. I wanted to test this blood relative of the deceased man.

Not dumb by any means, he was distinctly close-mouthed and unforthcoming. I had figured that out by his first two minutes in the exam room, sitting on the exam table. Fully clothed. He kept his eye on the window as if it were an emergency exit. "Doc, I need 'the pill' for this dang toe I done bent," he had informed me. Doc Scott always did that for him, he insisted, very plainly uncomfortable in the medical setting.

After sleuthing for twenty minutes, searching for what might have happened to 'bend' his toe, it finally came to light that his milk cow had 'stepped' on his foot a few days before. Guessing that wasn't the whole story, I asked if the cow had had any other contact with him. He shook his head, "No, Doc, she just landed on it for a second, accidentally. After kicking me in the nuts... She din't mean nothin' by it." Ahem, I thought. This was apparently a repeating theme.

So, pretty young Keesha flirtatiously coaxed the shoes and clothes off, cleaned him up a bit and drew a blood sample while I had conferred with Dr. Scott down the hall. The older doctor assured me that he had only examined the man one time, years before, and had never treated any 'bent' toes up to now.

Re-entering the room and signaling the nurse to slowly make her way out, I sought to put Samuel at ease in his now bare-ass state with some of my runner's travails, having broken more than one toe and spraining more than one foot over the years while on the running paths. I had a bent toe, myself, I told him. And it just so happened mine had resulted not from running, but ironically, kicking my horse in the butt to get him out of his stall as a teenager. I was in a hurry; the stubborn horse was not. That big toe remained bent to this day. And ached when the weather changed.

He looked up at me at that and after removing my own shoe to prove it, we compared notes for a while as he gradually opened up. Naked was not a state he liked in what he considered a public setting, as he let me know. I could see at least one quite swollen and bruised testicle slathered in remnants of some dark, thickly greasy substance. Old, used axle grease from the tractor, I was informed. A country cure.

Keesha had been disallowed or disinclined to clean the site and I decided to jump that hurdle in a bit, instead squatting to attend the very bent second toe, also purple and yellow with bruising. Palpation proved it to be only dislocated and we agreed that he would let me to realign it if I would agree to no sedatives.

"OK, big man, if you want to be a hero, fine with me," I concurred. Grasping the toe with one hand while bracing his foot with the other, I quickly extended and rotated the smelly thing in one quick motion, seating the small bones back to normal places.

Flexing it afterwards to assure proper joint alignment, I looked up at him. His surprised look made me laugh. "That's it?" he questioned stoically, while flexing the toe himself in its further testing.

"That's it," I assured him.

As I stood back up, I gestured to his crotch, stating the obvious. "I need to look at that, Samuel," I said. "There could be some damage there." It must hurt like a mo-fo, I figured.

"Naww, Doc, it be a'ight in a couple days. The grease'ud fix 'em," was all I got, but I insisted. Very gently reaching down and cupping his hugely swollen and rank scrotum, he exclaimed and brushed off my hand. This caused him further pain and I had to sternly instruct him in my most severe doctor manner to lay back and let me examine them properly.

Not liking it at all, the man reluctantly did so, and I was able to check things over. Finally. His uncut but sizeable dick was shriveled and somewhat bruised black and blue itself but the testicles were what concerned me. Three times the normal size and very tender. There was also a possible small hernia next to them over his pubic area. Luckily, no intestine was strangulated in the swelling and I reduced it by manipulation back inside easily enough, proving my diagnosis. The action gave Samuel immediate relief and a heavy sigh exuded from him, "Whoa, Doc, what'd you do? It don't hurt near as bad, all sudden."

Not unusual under the circumstances, I told him, the pressure had been relieved. But a temporary truss, a week's lay-off from heavy lifting or coughing, and a week of Epsom salt soaks with honey and lemon on those testicles would let us know if we'd need to do any surgery on him. That word scared him sufficiently enough that we were then able to get the instructive soaks started. A truss and some prescriptions were ordered through the pharmacy next door.

He had looked ready to bolt after it all, again eyeing the window, but changed attitude when the herniating tissue popped back through upon his sitting up. He agreed to pick up the medications and the modified 'jock' on his way out after dressing, through wincing discomfort. I had called the pharmacist to make sure he did so.

That was a week ago, and Cal was now wondering whether I would see him for the recheck today. I finally let my man arise and we drug ourselves to a shared shower where we made sure of no missed spots... After a quick coffee and toast with my sis-in-law, Soph, I bade 'bye to them on my way to town and the clinic.

As usual, the place was thrumming with activity, staff readying first patients, entering histories and filling us doctors in on the schedule. Typical for most publicly underwritten clinics.

About forty appointments, including two minor surgical procedures later, Dr. Scott and I sat in the break room comparing notes. "It sure is good to have someone to share with,

Jake," he admitted, "things run a lot better with two than one. And you big city ER med-center practitioners know how to move, now," he grinned. I ego-preened, respecting the seasoned practitioner's pragmatic, homespun approach to medicine. I remained in awe of the man's wisdom.

The afternoon went well, too, except that Keesha told me Samuel Hodge had not shown himself..."Doc, he's a good man but he don't know what's good for him." In agreement, we just hoped the man was better and that that was the reason for the no-show. City or country, I mused, patients tend to the same foibles and eccentricities.

Come 5 PM, we were just cleaning up, closing records and books, turning off lights and locking up when who should show up but Mr. Samuel Hodge himself. He just about knocked T.L., the cute young orderly, down as he was locking the door. Mr. Hodge was not limping, even using the formerly afflicted toe as a wedge in the door, and demanded to see me. Keesha attempted to intervene and reschedule the farmer for the next day, but I could see what was occurring and intervened to see how he was faring. I was glad he had come in, after all.

Afraid he would not come back again, I assured Keesha I didn't mind checking him. The pretty nurse scowled that she had evening plans and needed to leave. Dr. Scott and the other staff had bolted a bit before, leaving me alone but for the one nurse and orderly. Texting home to let them know I would be late, I let the orderly and Keesha leave for their evening and put my smock back on.

No big deal, I thought, I didn't need the computer system and no controlled drugs would be necessary, requiring multiple keys and redundancies, so I took the much more animated Samuel back to the exam room for his check.

No sooner than I got the exam table rotated for him to use, the man asked, "Doc, you been in town abou'a month, right?" Six weeks, I corrected, glad he was acting so much more amiable this visit. A bit curious but good, nevertheless. I asked

Samuel if he would let me check the toe and the hernia. Only a grunt in answer.

I busied myself calibrating an instrument to avoid scrutinizing him during his (hopeful) disrobement and upon turning around was pleasantly surprised to see my previously reticent patient seated, totally naked. Waiting expectantly. One leg dangling and one knee bent, leg raised with a heel up on the exam table edge. An exceedingly straight toe was just about pointing at me.

Actually smiling, he commented on the successful 'surgery', figuratively pulling my leg as an awkward attempt at a joke. I examined its mobility, noting a freshly clean scent and newly clipped nails, complimenting his quick healing. And, loving the improved hygiene.

His smile persisted as I released his foot and I glanced upward to check the formerly triple-sized swollen balls of mutiple hues. Now, I perceived much less discoloration and a much less shriveled sausage nestled between the pair. I thought Samuel was going to point the almost healed 'junk-package' at me as his palm encircled the bottom of his scrotum, but he just made note how much better it all felt now, jiggling the fat sack in his palm.

"Wanna check it out, Doc?" he asked.

"Well," I answered, smiling back professionally, "Yes, I will need to check those out. But the swelling appears to be significantly reduced." I cupped the duo as they buoyed the nice espresso-colored penis looking at me.

Manipulating the ballsack and palpating the previously protruding pubic mound which was presently much more flattened, I noted a nicely mending area overall. "You heal quickly, Samuel," I told him, "Another week and your whole groin should be back to normal function."

"Could you check it a li'l bit closer, Doc? It's still sore when you do that," as I continued manipulating the fat eggs. What I had initially taken for some residual swelling now appeared to be just well-fatted balls and I was impressed, again. The rise and phattening in his prick verified to me the lessening of pain and I turned it over to check further.

Samuel's jewels now contracted as I jostled them and flipped the nice piece. The recuperating patient changed tack, asking me if I was familiar with "Torchy Lane"?

"Afraid not, Samuel--- should I be...?" Thinking of a London skid row alley, I was pretty certain he wouldn't be familiar with that. He drew my eyes to his face by a light snort and informed me 'she' was a cross-dresser at the only gay bar in Rome, 'Jugs'. She performed there every Friday and Saturday night at midnight. Maybe I should check it out sometime.

Letting him know that I wasn't a night-lifer, I sought to keep the conversation on track. The now markedly engorging dick was rising from its nest of hairy balls and they were not only improved, clinically, they looked to be functioning quite well. It was distracting me.

A gotcha flashed across the man's face as he now proceeded to describe to me the inside of an arcade behind the local grocery store. The back of my neck prickled. He went into detail telling me about his own visit there about a month before when he had met the notorious transgendered dancer, Torchy, where he had, as he put it, "put the hurt to that tranny bitch's pussy." He furthered it by describing how vocal she liked to get, begging for the daddy dick she liked. Which was conveniently staring up at me at the present moment.

"Doc, she likes to check out those booths around us while she be taking this big black dick...funny, she swears you be down on yo' knees suckin' some fly poker the night we was in there hittin' it." He was staring straight at me now, steely gaze wordlessly challenging my denial. And, demanding unprofessional treatment...

I was stuck, hand still palming and rubbing the fat nuts down there. The very pretty, cut dick was bouncing right up at my face, quivering its hopefulness. Reading my hesitation, Samuel gambled on my reaction by adding, "Y'know, Doc-Boy, I was just thinkin' t'myself on t'way here how I din't that much mind comin' in for check-ups now that I'm a-trustin' the pretty man doc. And, besides, lookit how happy Clyde-d'-Glide is rightchere..." deadpanning right down at the now-changing connection between us.

Having had precious little experience like the present situation up to now in my still young career, I calculated the pros-and-cons for a minute. It was true, I had been in that arcade the night he had just described. I had given my brother-in-law, Coy, a long, slow blowjob, on my knees while indeed hearing the Tranny doing exactly what Samuel had stated.

Admitting the sexual being that I had become, I found myself sinking slowly down before the surging prick. The fatty just about launched into my mouth and I too easily let go, sinking down over the helmet-headed, sproinging eight incher. His hands almost immediately grasped my doctor head, lowering my rank by so doing to that of a "cocksuckin' bitch faggot."

My dick was straining at my slacks so I unzipped, freeing my white dick to get some air, and a look at what I was sucking... Samuel definitely liked this as he pushed and pulled on my head. My slurping mouth got pubic hair caught in my teeth as I bottomed down on the over-fat prick.

He put me into a rhythm of his liking, reaching up to my dick with his sexy foot, rubbing and slapping the thing as he warned me not to get too comfortable because I was about to get a taste of 'Torchy dee-light' as he pronounced it. My very unprofessional junk was dripping pre-cum while I thought this over.

Coming up off the table suddenly, the horndog yanked down my slacks and boxers together, twisted me away from him, then got down on his knees to sniff and tongue my Cal-hole. When he'd done lubing it, he stood up, turned me around and pushed my bare, soupy ass up onto the exam table just vacated. Pulling shoes and all off, he tossed them aside.

His fat hard-on listened intently while it's now nasty-mouthed owner told me just what and how he was gonna own my hole "rightchere", as he liked to say. My smock and shirt were pulled over my head and I found myself looking up at my patient, through the V of my nakedly spread legs, his hand targeting the pole-to-the-hole. I groaned as he punctured my pucker, proceeding to rocket that thing all the way in-and-out as he kept up the chant of perverted ideas playing out in his brain. Sounding peculiarly as if they had been previously thought out before the check-up.

As Samuel sped up the already fast pace, I found myself stroking along with him at half speed. He pulled out, only momentarily, and nodded over at a shocked orderly, TL, peering through the door. The surprised worker had returned to pick up a phone left behind. Right in time to see the eruption of cum-spray disappear back up inside me, having established himself. Very pleased with his performance, my buttfucker slowed his pace to one allowing the even spreading of his farm-man's sperm around and up in my lovin-every-second-of-it ass.

I knew I was in deep shit the moment I looked over my shoulder at the young male orderly. That is, until I saw the hands lower the zipper, digging out a very interested-looking piece of his own. So much for the steady girlfriend he spoke about non-stop.

Answering the beckoning motion by Samuel, the young orderly soon replaced the patient's nicely healed dick with his. The youth lewdly conversed with Samuel about my cum-loving, dripping asschute. Primed and ready for a second load. It took only a few minutes before his diluted the first one. Samuel propped up my legs from behind my head, rubbing a still dribbling dick in my hair and face.

Slowing to a more leisurely rhythm, my staff member compared notes with the nasty voyeur/patient regarding my "damn worried" yet "filled-up" butt, agreeing the two may need to test run it again to get it right. "Doc, you should oughta stay ready..."

Pulling ourselves back together---aka, cleaning and dressing---we more sanely agreed to keep this pro-bono boning more under wraps than we had been able to do with our collective junk, parting ways at the front door of the Free Clinic of Rome.

Arriving home to dishwashing, having missed Sophie's dinner, Cal took one look at me, grinned knowingly and commented, "Full schedule today, Jake?"

Leaving the kids and Soph downstairs, my man piggybacked me up to our bedroom and after locking the door as a safety measure, proceeded to teach me the error of my ways...to my play-by-play... of course.

The storge of it all.

Chapter 13
Tride and True: Mighty
Tungsten Tuberosity, Part 3.

An hour passed and we roused ourselves from the spiritual reverie, realizing that 'the car' would be coming by for us in an hour or so. The youngsters disappeared into their bedroom and we two hustled up to our own, spending a talkative shower time, again, just because we wanted to, discussing the situation in which we found ourselves.

Coming out, we put on matching silver lame thongs over our wedding cockrings and donned mountain boots with wool socks, all sprayed silver, then descended to get the grand assemblage underway. Magic lollie-pops for all were laid out to usher the four of us into the mood of the eve but not before Jeremy and I ogled the stunning young pair. Upon exiting their new haven, they were now transformed into the characters of Alexander the Great and his lifelong lover, Hephaestion Chiliarch.

The two were radiant in their simple mirrored attire, having appropriated matching calf-high sheepskin-lined leather lace-up boots from J-Man and my Santa Fe Days. The briefest of matching bikini underwear sporting an over-sew of gold-hued aspen leaves minimally cloaked anything of their lean physiques. Matching evergreen brow-rings encircled their wavy hair. Bryce's flaxen blondness contrasted sexily against Adolpho's sepia tones. Various temporary thigh, belly, dorsal and bicep indigo tattoos complemented the look.

They set a mood of Bacchanalian mindset by the sensuality oozing from their pores and joined the two of us, singly. We figured separate tasks might enable us to keep their pants on and hands off each other long enough to help.

Adolpho aided Daddy Jeremy with the intricately complicated Tungsten Tuberosity, while Bryce helped me clip together the clear plastic wedged shower door guards I had accumulated from the three hardware and bathroom supply stores in Telluride town.

We shaped the pieces into a geodesic diamond shape that would easily fit over my head and enshroud my body from neck to crotch. Heavy-duty clear rubber-banding would hold the contraption in place, attaching to my neck, arms and each upper thigh. We covered the geometric beehive-like surface with a tight-stretched cover of sheer Glad Cling Wrap, then emptied the hundred other rolls of the sticky stuff, wadding them all into loose translucent balls which would be stuffed strategically into the interior, capturing me inside.

Not quite see through, but enough so that it left a shimmery impression of my body, I looked in the mirror as Bryce positioned all of it evenly. The faceted appearance of a 'cubic zirconium' now personified itself. We fashioned a ring of thin, tawny, moldable straws from the hobby shop to snugly encircle my neck, then extend behind and above my head to a rounded hoop wrapped in tinfoil, make-shifting a halo, and I was ready.

I could put it all on and off, with a little help, in a matter of a few minutes at the mine entrance so as to allow free mobility, especially on the ride there. I was sure we would need the room with the five of us.

We came out of the spare bathroom to an extraordinary sight. An entire human skeleton grinned at us, suspended on bony feet a few inches above the ground. As we came in, the spooky wraith began walking toward us, quite dexterously, arm, leg and neck joints working in synchrony.

Shadowing two feet behind it followed Jeremy, the managing puppeteer, supporting and controlling the skeleton by attached equestrian riding crops. His own dazzling body was sparklingly phosphorescent and golden. Head to toe. Every supple tendon, muscle and ligament were on magnificent display. His head and face were similarly glowing, the left half hidden by a skull mask of a pearlescent finish. His eyes had been outlined in Pharaonic manner, above and below in stark black kohl, his lips were blackened as well.

A set of spectacularly feathered silver wings lay enfolded behind his back, curling over and above, then down behind his head from the strapped attachment between his shoulders. As Bryce and I oohed and aahed at the aura of the whole vision, some controlling spring tested the up and outward spreading mechanism of the functional pair, ending in a glowing umbel, as widely arching as my man was tall.

How in the world had my innovative husband ever dreamt this up, let alone brought it to fruition? Adolpho stood at the back corner looking like a woodland elf as he peered from behind the thing he had helped put together, every bit as wowed by the effect as us.

"Honey, you look amazing. I am sooo blown away," was all that I could come up with. "But, I do not even want to know where Mr. Bone came from." The wide grin wasn't giving anything away, as he preened through this unveiling. "How in hell are we going to get you there all in one piece, baby?" I exclaimed next as the size of the final product came into 3-D focus.

"Don't worry, Luke-man, this ain't just a fly-by-night show. I can get this thing on and off in five minutes flat, and I made it so it can even fold up. As long as you can put up with my gilded ass for the night. I may need some help getting the dye off, later. We covered…everything," winking at Adolpho.

"You've got to be kidding, JK, I am not letting you ever wash that off-- you are a damn god. I fully intend to suck my first god dick tonight."

Bryce drew in his breath next to me and exhaled in total disbelief. "How did you two do this?" he finally managed, as he cooed at his new lover behind Jeremy.

"Oh, newbie, you hain't seen nothin' yet. Wait 'til we get up to the mine," came the cocksure reply.

A triple-tone automobile horn interrupted, bespeaking the royal's arrival. It pierced the dusk outside, and we all busted ass into disassemble-mode, forgetting to be curious.

Sure enough, we got Jeremy down to his glowing, gilded self by the time the Lady of the evening arrived up the steps. My golden man glided gracefully over to the heavy arched door. Opening it, he reached a gilded hand out to welcome fingers now be-decked by rings.

We all stood back as first the fingers appeared, then the rest of the Lady Saxe-Coburg inched forward, revealing none other than Liza Minelli in her transformed guise for the special night.

Short, spiked black hair with silver tips mohawked her heavily made-up, blood-red lipped doppelganger Liza face. A silver lame--- how convenient--- full body spandex leotard graced her torso and arms, high neck hugging her tight-skinned chin. Mid-thigh black leather spiked-heel boots stepped authoritatively over our threshold, coming to a sharply loud, staccato halt before Jeremy.

Her similarly black kohl-outlined eyes widened as she perused the puppeteer's 24K envelopment, beginning at his face, stopping for a pregnant pause at the snake-stuffed silver thong, finally traveling downward to the exquisitely sculpted thighs and calves with silver-shod feet. "It would seem that our tastes tend toward a parallel, Dr. Kell," Liza wryly observed, "yet we obviously fill things in differently...don't we?" As Jeremy's clothing consisted of a very minimal few square inches of cover, it was fairly evident to what she referred.

Ten long, silver-tipped aristocratic fingers had arrived this evening, ringed with every sort of silver band and tinkling knuckle charm. They raised up and virtually outlined my man's form like a murder scene cutout. "My, but you do fix up nicely..." she whirred seductively.

Jeremy raised one hand to hers again and turned her slowly to face the rest of us. Until that moment none of us had existed. She arched a single perfect eyebrow in inspecting the three of us.

One side of her mouth rose up, lips parting in a Liza-esque smile-to-kill. She stepped forward. "My God and Save the Queen. Mr. Andropov informed me that we were to have company for the ante soiree send-off but he did not let me know we were up-classing the 'Arrow... This entourage glitters more than a popinjay in the court at Versailles. How did I get this lucky, young men? Do we all wear the same dress size?"

That broke the ice for the bedazzled Adolpho and Bryce, who had never traveled in an automobile of the sort we had described, let alone one conveying the thirteenth person in line to the throne of England. This naughty vixen humanized the whole affair and I brought the boys forward to greet her.

"Lady Carlotta Saxe-Coburg of Annenberg, Saxony and Mecklenburg, it is my pleasure to present to her ladyship the Messiers Cosimo Adolphus de' Medici, XIV, of Florence, and Bryce Adams Canyon, the original, from Seattle." Adolpho reached out to kiss her hand and I thought for a moment Bryce was about to curtsey. Or pee.

He was not prepared, and all four of us broke up seeing his tangible confusion. "Bryce, this is Tride. The Lady is our friend, Carlotta, and we are all about to par-tay together, young dude. C'mon, let's get our game face on." And with that, Jeremy brought out the hookah for the special hash we had procured, while I passed out the vintage Bordeaux with a tray of fruit and brie.

As dusk waxed upon us, the boys donned their black capes with red silk lining, each fastening one another's neck clasps. We all helped load the costumes into the spacious boot of the 'Arrow. The lady was suitably in awe of the Mighty Tungsten Tuberosity, if not a little bewildered. Just as Jeremy preferred. Mysteriously, he poked a large black bag in last, leaving me wondering: what else?

Paecup, in full Russian Cossack garb, grinned at all of us knowingly as he loaded all into the warm interior. Carlotta, now comfortably medicated, was familiarly touchy-feely. Who could blame the woman, what with the succulent manflesh surrounding her? All of the same dress size, I would have to remember. Her court was in session and her courtiers were in thrall. And enthralled.

After a small familiarization period, so we were more knowledgeable of her traveling palace, her next order of business was to instruct Mr. Andropov to dispense the 'international fare'. The tiny spoons appeared and the boys had yet another choice to maneuver through.

Our comfortable banter made the ride around the mountain along the San Miguel River byway through the township intimately enjoyable for all as. We zoomed pleasurably upwards in mental states of jocular camaraderie. Jeremy, in rare form, entertained us in his own gilded cape. I snuggled next to him and the boys balanced Carlotta's sides. To her delight, she got to play more the role of 'Liza Cougar' than 'her ladyship' this night.

Approaching the old entrance to the 19th century silver mine, we were caught up in the traffic coming together for the Hallowe'en Bash. The local police, including 'Deputy Fife' and Sheriff Delmar, helped in directing the parking for those coming by vehicle, looking fairly askance at the opulent vehicle as we passed by them waving.

Several hundred more were streaming up from town and the gondola on costumed feet. We safely secured any evidence of the 'implements of destruction', as we had named the partying accessories, while Paecup navigated to a site separate from the masses, per a perk allowed by Carlotta's friend, County Judge Rickenmeier. We ended up in a secluded cul-de-sac populated by only a few other cars and some security guards.

Upon exiting the car with thanks to Paecup for the safe passage, and a remonstrance to join us soon, we commenced to reassemble Jeremy's and my two costumes. Lady Carlotta was absolutely taken by both, though the Tuberosity was 'stupendously fabulous', as she called it.

Leaving the parking spot and heading for the mine entry point, we began feeling the distant pound of the music beat inside. The sounds reverberated at us from diverse sources, probably vent and adit openings, I figured.

Jeremy had Adolpho carrying the mysterious bag, as his own hands were busy with the 'puppet' controls and Mr. Bone preceded our entourage. The characters we encountered boggled the mind what with the wide-ranging imaginations populating the area, but our own arrival set off a rumble of wonder by the group we brought. We soon had a flock of varied ghouls, celeb mocks and fantastical figures following in our wake; we looked at our own selves like, "What have we wrought?"

The recently enlarged hangar-style gates were wide open and welcoming this eve. Reaching them, we halted. All five of us were virtually afloat, already levitating by the party favors. Now, we were additionally elevated by the pot smoke billowing out from inside.

Jeremy signaled Adolpho, and hunky Alexander the Great unzipped the big black bag, extracting a carefully bundled head cover of woven hemp dreadlocks. They had been painstakingly sprayed shimmering silver and embroidered by hundreds of glittering sequins.

Then, he extracted a snowboard with foot bindings. At least, that is what it appeared. But the thing sat several inches off the ground by some tubular mechanism mounted underneath.

While the duo fit the ornate dreads onto his head, fastening them by some pre-arranged plan, Carlotta passed out to each of us a set of wireless earbuds. The devices would not only diffuse the sounds inside, they should also allow for inter-personal communication with one another while partying. Something new from Harmon-Kardon, she told us. How dope, I thought.

Looking back at my man, I saw him now pointing a small remote at the 'snowboard'. After programming the thing, the board suddenly began glowing, then very slowly rose up about a foot off the ground, hovering obediently in place. He grinned at me, mouthed the words, "UT physics department prototype" and stepped up into the rubber foot grabs attached on to it.

He needn't have mouthed them: the ear buds made each word clearly distinct.

The Mighty Tungsten Tuberosity was now complete. Exclamations surrounding us were audible in their disbelief. This silver dreadlocked, golden-glowing, 'Magic Mike', Cirque-esque character, formerly known as my husband, towered above us all. Balancing on the mag-lev hover board, he looked every inch the image of a Greek God. With a skeleton vanguard.

By some pre-set signal, the trendy hip-hop music suddenly changed to the rhythm and lyrics of 'Monster Mash'.

The Mighty Tungsten Tuberosity, along with the four of us, and followed by dozens more, all made our entrance into the now cavernously spacious re-do of the Pandora Mine. Those partiers already inside were drinking, mixing and dancing. The multitude turned to see Jeremy in his glory as a murmur of acknowledgement spread at the bedazzling spectacle.

He pressed a button and slowly the silver wings spread, arching upward and outward. The effect was breathtaking and silenced the cavern chatter. Then, a growing roar of acclamation built and I took Carlotta's hand. The boys followed suit, and we entered the cavern in ancient Roman Procession style. I felt goosebumps welt up all over my body. Glancing over at Carlotta, we knew we were experiencing the coolest Hallowe'en we would ever possibly imagine.

Inside, the dance floor stretched out over the edge of an under-mountain lake, the gloom swallowing its far subterranean shore. A bartender delivered each of us an order of drinks, sent courtesy of a certain Russian Cossack now leaning on the bar hugging one distant hewn rock wall.

An attractive female buttercup blossomed next to him, obviously into uniformed men, by her look. Paecup raised his pint of ale in toast with a grin, and we raised ours in reply. The party had now increased in energy level and the multitude gradually got over the grand entrance, gathering to smaller groups for the celebration that was the Tride Mountain Monster Mash Bash.

The renowned San Francisco DJ of Castro District fame spun round after round of danceable music, keeping many attendees on the dance floor without pause. We five joined in, Jeremy disembarking from the mag lev to wiggle that thong-enhanced golden booty.

Carlotta was in her element, accepting well-wishes from most everyone as a true royal would expect. Her Gordian knot boys, inseparable and interlocked, kept guard over the lady while magnifying her pleasure just by their presence.

We all danced together with abandon, passing the constantly moving blunts circulating through the crowd. Jermy poked me and pointed at Paecup as he disappeared with his buttercup. Another of the man's 'short interludes' must be occurring. Good for him, I rooted.

Jeremy lowered his wings and came over to me, drawing us away from the others, as a slower song allowed the revelers to catch their collective breath. He removed both of our earbuds, nuzzling into my ear, "I am in love and lust with you, Luke. You make me real." The beautiful man once again made me feel like the first option.

Congregating together at a side bar for a break, we watched the lights gradually dim over a few minutes. While ordering another drink, the ladies, Sheila E and Cat G, mounted the far steps to the stage, followed by two male figures with whom they were conversing and sharing a joint.

JK pulled me along as we wove our way toward the four on the stage, vagrant hands reaching out to touch of the Tuberosity passing by. It looked as if the silver lame might be stretching its limits in recognition of the attention…which caused my own to answer in kind. By the time we arrived at the stage, we were both sporting boners and signaled a pact to address the predicament in a little bit.

Climbing the stage, Jeremy turned back and squeezed my hand. "Honey, it IS Robert Cray and Prince—I knew it!" Some band members had begun setting up for a live concert. The four music world heavyweights continued conversing, somehow not causing a riot by their presence on the stage. Only in Tride, it crossed my mind.

Cat spied us and came over, giant grin congratulating our earlier arrival. "That was some entrance, maestros," she said as she pulled up to us. Sheila E, now following her wife's path, brought the two superstar talents with her.

We were wowed by their affirmation and the group of us chatted over their intentions to smash the festivity with true star power, all together here for a set. I felt a shoulder tap and glanced back to find 'Liza' and the 'twins' next to us. They had been separated from us but had found us. By our questioning look, she lipped, "Dears, you glow."

The music legends all acted like typical humans, taken aback to be presented to a royal personage. They not only joined us in conversation, they even shared a hash vape cig that Adolpho produced from somewhere.

The lights blinked three times, signaling the cavern, and we left them as the band warmed up. Everyone finally realized what was about to be up…almost. Over the next hour, the evening was crowned by the exhibition of bombshell, impromptu talent serenading the audience like none of us would likely ever forget.

After classic songs led by each of the four luminary performers, the crowd was crazy in its preoccupation with the star power before them. Then, the band went low to a pianissimo undercurrent like an on-hold freeze-frame.

The lights abruptly blacked out completely and the only luminescence came from multiple phosphorescent entities and fluorescent devices around the subterranean theatre. Umbrella'd by the golden glow put off by Jeremy, all five of our intimate group were together in front of the stage. Thanks to our earbud communicators courtesy Lady Carlotta, we collectively huddled around one more vape cig share, able to converse privately amidst the cacophony.

J-Man was the first to recognize the new undertone pulse, his senses switching to high alert. The rest of us listened, finally hitting on the fact that the band had picked up an island beat. As the lights phased up into strobe, our eyes latched on to an immensely tall, lean figure with a mike. The character was smiling and pointing directly at us, having picked us out beforehand by our luminosity. We all just about collectively lost it as the dreadlocked crooner launched into a lilting lyric made famous by the Mighty Diamonds. The crowd went delirious.

Ambergai Gee was back…

* * *

I lay across the big polished cypress bed inside our log cabin nestled amid the high mountain vale overlooking Mountain Village on Telluride Mountain, situated in the San Juan Mountains of southwest Colorado, America, Western Hemisphere, Earth. Latitude 37.93 degrees North, 107.85 degrees East.

My legs were pinned back over my head, spread wide open by two huge ebony hands. The long fingers of each encircled my ankles, securing the clear path below. There was an eleven-inch-long, large diameter slick black dick slowly and methodically pumping in, then out, of my excessively lubed bare asshole. It was fucking purposely slow, all the way in and all the way out, to the ridge on the phatted mushroom head.

Each stroke was separated by a pause, necessary to prolong the slowly warming and rising approach to the long-delayed volcanic, eruptive, climactic edge being savored all the more by this manner of the mature fuck. As the big dick anticipated the long, propulsive release of baby-infused, Creole creaminess, it knew the pulses of ejaculatory ecstasy would be passed to me by the energy.

In the coming release, and by the knowledge of the adjacent sensuous pluggings now unfolding within inches of my union, I knew that the practiced patience would reward the people with whom I was inordinately close. All four of whom I desired to share the magnified effect by this way of doing the deed.

I held the dark brown glass cylinder in my fingers as I used the opposing fingers of my other hand to close off the manly nostril of the nose on the man now staring deeply into my eyes. He inhaled slowly, then I switched the like action to the other nostril.

Having just served myself to the popper high, I was reveling in the view of Ambergai Gee and the feeling of his long, swinging dreadlocks caressing my skin. I listened to and felt the slow beavering fuck coming down next to us. My stud husband, Jeremy, enjoyed the same sensations we were as he passed along the feelings to Bryce.

Bryce, who was slobbering hungrily on the rhythmically synchronous Italian curve sliding down his throat to the same pace of the two fuckers. His new life lover, Adolpho, made sure to hold his boy's legs wide open for Jeremy as he matched the two black dicks' rhythm. We desired mutual arrival at the doorway of elusive five-way bliss.

Indeed, after many moments of suspended time passage, the low grumbling throat sounds by the Jamaican set my Jeremy, and Bryce's Adolpho, into sendoff mode. Within seconds, all five of us came collectively, the only sperm to be seen was from my and Bryce's cocks, as the other three spent their loads deeply embedded in the cavities of choice.

Jeremy and Gai vied for the cream afterwards, Adolpho too new an initiate to gay methods for partaking yet. At least in the vision of anyone other than his baby, Bryce. Scooping the pearlescence, the two ritually smeared each other's mouths, allowing the licking clean of both men's long fingers by the other's tongue and lips. The ultimate expression of domination by black men over white men: cannibalizing the next generation.

If ever the religious right feared the expansion of their concept of sinful manifestation, our group perception of gay consummation provided the template.

We all luxuriated in our communalism, sharing collective intimacies as we recovered our wits and backed down from the peak just scaled. Should others desire to understand our bohemie: get high, do a hit of poppers, multiply the effect by fifty while climaxing during a thunder and lightning storm in the middle of a hurricane. One might then possibly understand…it was exhilarating.

Jeremy scooched over to me as Gai arose to get towels and washcloths, whispering nothings-at-all into my ear. I giggled back at him. Adolpho covered his tow-headed blond boyfriend with kisses because he could and we awaited Gai's return.

When he walked back into the room, big dick swinging possessively at us all, we pounced. Bombarding him with questions for which we had been awaiting answers since Hallowe'en night. When he had finally returned to us.

Jeremy, the man's protégé and long lost confidant, took the lead. "OK, my man, Gai, where in hell did you disappear to and why did you leave without a word?" Among the multitude of questions, these two were the most perplexing.

Gai slowly, deliberately, washed and toweled himself as we all watched his big dick. Then he smirked and wordlessly clod-hopped downstairs. Size 17 quadruple E feet tend to do that. On returning, he held a Chimay Blue Ale bottle by the neck, classic blue vapor spreading over the lip of the bottle and descending around it like dry ice. It was an ethereal effect. I bought Chimay Blue just to see it. The ale was stellar, but the vapor effect was better.

Clearing his throat, he asked to light up some ganja so Bryce got a blunt out, minding our patriarch. After exhaling a long toke, he began.

"Ma' pussy boys, ya' all need t'know a bit a' the few t'ings mi does before ya' may unnerstan on th'appenin's around o'late. So, mi a'gonna tell ya, now, Mons. Be listenin' close."

And Ambergai Gee, IV, did tell us. And we did listen, stonedly rapt. But, as I am not him, I will relate it in this language, for ease of unnerstannin', as he would say...

The statuesque denizen of Rastafarianism explained to us that the Rastafari Sect began in Creole Jamaica, during the early days of Western slavery. It was the sole method for the slaves to empower themselves. They adopted some tenets of the Bible and developed their own dialect of English, called Lyaric. They lived by the basic creed calling for treating one's body as a temple: never cut one's hair, eat only that which is good for one, never tattoo oneself...

They did hold to some macabre beliefs, too, though. After vanquishing their enemies in battle, they would save some bones of enemy bodies. Upon going to fight the next time, they pulled the bones out and gnawed on them symbolically. To bring strength and courage.

Like all religions, internal divisions developed through the years over differing interpretations of their beliefs. Squabbles turned into blood feuds. Now, a fundamentalist off-shoot, the Rasta, had deemed the time right for purging the impure.

He said many other things, too, but these ideas were enough to explain to us what had happened. Gai told us that he had gotten word at the opera house reggae concert--- the one Jeremy and I had attended--- that agents of the Rasta fundamentalists had put a 'hit' out on the band called 'The Mighty Diamonds', believing the music group had corrupted the true beliefs the Rasta held dear.

The victims of the mountain attacks, far from being tourists, were instead, stagehands from the reggae group. When members from the Rasta sect had caught up with them, the victims had been chased. They had attempted escape by a high mountain route but were caught and horribly murdered. The two were dismembered according to ritual cleansing rites in demand of atonement for the bands' drift away from the ascetics' beliefs.

Black bears had only happened along afterwards, apparently by chance, dragging away some of the body parts. Their tracks left the appearance of them being the perpetrators of the killings.

The night of my frightful experience in our bedroom, the Rasta had tracked Ambergai Gee to our home. Somehow reaching the balcony entrance, the assassin for some reason had aborted that attempt in the religious vendetta, or perhaps it was only a scouting venture. Regardless, he had retreated, jumping down from the balcony and escaping into the night, leaving the torn patch of burlap clothing stuck to the tree where I had discovered it.

Gai figured he had been startled, maybe by me. But having also seen the disappearing figure, he had rightly identified a threat to his 'family', Jeremy and me. He had resolved to leave us to ensure our safety, and try to avenge the wrong while ridding the threat...

He spent the next days pushing forward to do just that. Using Adolpho's remote, abandoned house as a base, he had convinced another stagehand from the band, who had also remained in the area, to help him. The stagehand had tracked down the true murderers, but had been brutally attacked and hacked in the confrontation.

During this assault, the bear clan had once again shown up, maybe drawn by the smell of the blood, Gai reasoned. They succeeded in terrorizing the terrorists themselves before they had finished their macabre aims. While interrupting the gruesome deed, their presence had furthered the public's fear that marauding bears were attacking humans.

Gai had happened on his cohort afterwards and was aggrieved to find him alive but partially dismembered by the Rasta. He had taken the man to the hospital in hopes of saving him, and then left to go after the zealots.

The day of Hallowe'en, Gai had caught up to the perpetrators and 'brought a end to da' rampage', as he put it. He would not tell us the details of what had happened, only that the threat no longer existed. As well, he had gone to the Sheriff with the evidence, proving what had occurred. The assassins and their ilk would not make menace again.

His critically injured friend had regained consciousness only long enough to verify Gai's account, succumbing in comatose peace soon after. The Sherriff, along with the town officials, had decided to allow the bear attack story to remain intact, relocating the bear clan to a remote area of another mountain range away from humans. The case was now officially closed. The cover up was to persist, the truth never to be told... We were all sworn to secrecy and must agree to hold the knowledge close amongst just us. He had insisted.

Our pact sealed the ending of the whole affair, and the ritual lighting of the hookah hash pipe provided both closure and then levity after the sad tale. In true Jamaican fashion.

Ambergai Gee, IV, informed us that by taking turns bringing the Daddy Rastafarian of the domicile to climax, while the rest of us watched, we could all be sufficiently expiated for our knowledge. Well, we all 'sucked' it up and did the penance. Now, if that didn't seem like the kind of religious ritual I could embrace, then I didn't know what ever would.

Boy, did we sleep like babies that night…

Chapter 14
Stick Shift: Nocturnal Writhings

My pace matched the underground, ethno beat set by the synthesized fusion music from the evening before. It was powerfully evocative even now, as it had been through the recent dark hours after first having experienced it.

"Whyyyya'lookin'back, nig... I'ain'gon' kiss y'ass,
Ya' ge'me out ma'drawers... ya'think y'playin' fas,
I migh'be fu-kin' youu, but gonna nail yo' bitch.
Don'be usin' those finga's, or I be makin'a fist..."
Def-nit a freak t'keep--- in ya'back pocket...
fo' dat--- late...night...creep..."

The raunchy, alluring, lyrical patterns kept me mentally hovering a few inches off the ground as I padded lightly over the dirt path through the glade of woods which marked one of my running routes. It was the first path I had mapped out upon our arrival this summer at my in-law's home, not then knowing my direction or destination.

Since college, this method of scoping out a new cityscape or countryside had been my preferred one for familiarization with an area. Running allowed both introspection and sight-seeing at a constant pace; good for getting the lay of the land and taking in the scenery. A person running didn't as often miss things, good observation being a necessity. And it got the heart pumping. My natural curiosity had drawn me to this loop winding by the river, which I had followed for several miles that first morning at the Blackhearst homeplace two months before...

Familiar landmarks barely registered now as I fairly floated with the subliminal song from last night crowding my mind, tantalizing the memory. I had stopped by my younger twin-in-laws' secluded home then. The screen door had been closed, unlatched, but the heavy oak door stood ajar. I could feel the mysterious beat from the boys' synthesizer before hearing the music or making out their lyrics. The elusive rhythm inhaled me further into the hallway and toward their warren. Peering around that doorway, I had found the boys absorbed in a gam-boling duet. But more than that: a private rave performance of mind-bending seductiveness. Amidst their music-making, both were unclothed and in a shared state of arousal.

The convoluted song was now somehow difficult to de-scribe to myself, disjointed and syncopated the way my mind had stored it. Fleeting yet memorable at the same time, it had a flowing melody like a deep, steady ocean current. Later on last night, upon returning home, I had drifted to sleep in the sen-sual reverberations, reliving the sultry scene in the boys' den where I had entered without their answer.

"Too high t'take a breath, too high t'take a step
Two wrongs don'make a right, three rights--make a left...
Highway t'heaven, I'm takin d'scenic... foll-win' dat road,
   risin' like d'phoenix,
walkin' like a puppet, gots legs on ma'words,
Def' a freak t'keep--in ya'back pocket...
fo' dat--- late...night...creep..."

Their arching, bobbing cocks led their ebony bodies in the intricately complex caribbean macarena with a rap overlay. Swollen dicks touching, tapping, brushing. Their arms and legs, heads and torsos, intertwining and writhing, at once to-gether--then separately--then together again. A dance of incredibly synced quality by the light of flittering candles. Their performance had enveloped me in a pin-prickling, whole body shiver by the optics. I had just stared. Transfixed.

"Tie me to the tracks... by the train o'yo' thoughts,
bellies touchin' skin... by dat twelve-pack bought,
Trigga' finga' itchin', trigga' finga' itchin'...
trigga' finga' itchin', trigga' fixin'ta itch,
ahhhh...nic...nic...nic."

They would not have seen me if they had looked--- and their eyes did, indeed, pass over me--- but the eroticists only had mind's eyes for their strongly synergized choreography and libidinous lyrics. The combined totality cocooned the two in a cloistered place only they knew. No one else was invited. Not sexual, yet entirely sexual. Their movements illustrated a burlesque of libertine expressions, breathtakingly lustful by the display. I could not shake it. I did not want to.

"Rest in peace, say d'gang... 'cause I'm fresh-- wit'---
d'dev-il...
Rest in peace, say d'gang... 'cause 'dey kill------ d'em-
selves...
You--- go, bro--- try-in'... t'get......
fresh..like..this.."

I wanted to know more. The niche into which I had had but a brief glimpse was something special that only twins share. Just like the discreet vernacular of which we, their family, were aware but not made privy, I had now stumbled onto this...this inconceivable secret jive dialect. My senses had enlightened me of something akin to it before now, but the manifestation was remarkable.

"I jus'can't see-ma'self... livin' in a house o'mir--rors...
put dat in t'place where... it bouncin'..off..d'doors.
Trigga finga' itchin', trigga finga' itchin'...trigga' fixin'
  at itch...
Ahhh…nic...nic...nic..."

Cal and Coy, the older twins, had an awesome rapport. Cal had shown me. But nothing close to these younger boys. This performance validated that. It was not meant for anyone but themselves. Li'l Bow Wow would be proud to call it his. And he'd be boned-up doing it. I was smitten and couldn't let go.

Reluctantly, pulling myself silently away, I had left the pair to their private personal devices...forgetting completely why I had stopped in. I sure wouldn't forget what I had happened upon.

Afterwards, upon arriving home, I had crept into bed next to Cal and spooned over to his heated, naked form, my focus still bent to the psychic vibe pervading my consciousness. I had been absolutely mesmerized by that phenomenal aura.

I dreamed a strange province through the next hours with my husband. On the one hand, I knew he was there, feeling him respond to my body, turning and enfolding me in his long arms without reaching a completely coherent state, as he was wont to do.

On the other, I never left that ephemeral creation of Loy's and Roy's, the one envisioned just a short while before. As my man spread me open, entering and making me whole, I vicariously experienced the young twins' own hedonic climax. I knew they were surely writhing together, entwined in a carnal finale as I throbbed together with my Calumet. Erotic, metaphysical unions. Cal and me fucking while dreaming their fucking, while they were truly fucking...mmmmm.

Now, running in the pre-dawn dimness, I was like a man in a shadowy jungle filled by Sen-surround sounds, and fears, and longings. Perceiving some Haitian voodoo ritual playing out in a remote, smoky clearing. I could see and feel vestiges of the boys and the vibe they had unwittingly shared. But I could only hoard the emanations, never catching the source...

In the midst of this continuing reverie, my head shrieked sudden pain. A low-hanging branch had scraped me, I thought, until the flapping of huge wings and swirling eddies of agitation informed me of a sharp set of talons within inches of a second strike. Instinctively ducking and rolling, I somersaulted away from the attack, shanking my ankle in the action. The huge set of wings flapped over and then upward, opposite me, their swooshing dissipating in the dark.

I quickly deduced that Hal, the great horned owl, had just mistaken my head for an early morning snack. The hand-sized claws had raked me. I could feel the blood well up, dribbling down across my face, fuzzling my vision. Hal, as I had named him, was a hugely handsome male more than four foot in wingspan with whom I had developed a connection over the preceding weeks.

Able to mimic a barn owl since a child, I had called to the big predator upon first hearing him hoot. The nocturnal hunter had replied in inquisitive puzzlement and a mutual interest ensued. The big raptor appeared to be awaiting my pre-dawn appearances after that, commonly following as I signaled my routes via hoots and audible footfalls.

This morning had been different by my silence. Perhaps the owl took insult at the snub. Regardless, I had to struggle one-legged to stand upon finding the inability to support weight on the twisted ankle. Removing my singlet to headband the bleeding, I gimped my way toward the riverside. Knowing it to be close by, desiring orientative refuge. Reaching running water in a few minutes, I adopted a good-sized fallen tree branch for a cane and a weapon, should Hal return.

As I descended to the bank below, a low, menacing voice probed at me, "What the hell you doin' here? This here my spot." Scared shitless at yet another intrusion, I grabbed my crutch by both hands and raised it defensively.

The voice personified from the leeside of a huge bald cypress rooting into both dry land and river. I heaved a sigh of relief as I recognized Voy Alfrederic Blackhearst, my fifth and youngest brother-in-law, picking his way across huge roots toward me. "Damn, Voy, you like to scared me to death, man," I winced unsteadily at him.

"Is that Jake?" he queried, knowing my voice in a second. I lowered the stick, then myself, to the uneven ground, wobbly from the bleeding and blurred vision as well as my ankle. The muscular man, obviously relieved as well, came to me and squatted, quickly assessing blood, limp and weakness in a familiar, non-threatening form.

Dawn still an hour distant, we compared notes and I figured out Cal's brother was setting out trout lines at this early hour. His cute wife, Winnie, had developed a pregnancy-induced passion for fresh fish with black licorice, I remembered. Voy was following very husbandly orders...I asked him if the licorice was biting this early.

A close copy of all the Blackhearst boys, Voy was tall and rangy. Darkly handsome and built like a brick shithouse. Reaching to my head, the baritone-voiced fisherman carefully unwrapped my makeshift bandage in the filtered moonlight. His deep armpit cupped my nose and face, overpowering me with the ripe smell of unwashed maleness. Despite my condition, this set my hormones to flowing. I readily drew in his essence as he bent over me to look at the marked scrapes left by Hal's talons. "What the fuck you been up to, boy? These cuts are purty bad-ass." Concern shaded his words.

More fully discussing my predicament, we decided it best to head over to the closest, and sole, farmhouse across the river. He knew the resident, he informed me. Rewrapping the oozing wounds brought further contact between my bare torso and his. Then, before I could say anything, the limber black man lightly hoisted me over his shoulder in a fast rotating lift. I felt my junk grazing his upper back as he waded down into the shoulder high water. The coldness of it shocked me but didn't seem to faze the big guy at all. His uneven strides jostled me awkwardly as he sought solid footing over the couple minute portage. Way too much rubbing and joggling went on between my dick and his superb musculature.

By the time we reached the far bank, the cold water, combined with his firm grip, left my body in a quandary. Should my stimulated package shrivel or explode? Like espresso braces crème Brule, the result proved to be a bittersweet amalgam as the brisk, constricting effect gave way to a burst of uncontrollable engorgement. My balls retracted up inside me while a huge boner sprang up. It would have made me proud under circumstances not involving the persistent bouncing against Voy's shoulder.

I was next startled to find myself twirled again in a half-gainer from his back to the ground. But the thoughtful man, not forgetting my sprained ankle, dexterously put out two very large, veined hands to cushion my landing. One supported my muscled white runner's butt, the other caught the front side, covering and pinning a boned-up piece against my stomach. That damnably smooth shoulder buttressed my side and lower back.

The abrupt absence of motion rendered me to a state of rigid mortification and him to a grinning, grasping support group made up of a single body. "You good, Jake?" he joked, as his hands rubbed up and down my anatomy. Sizing up both my erection and retracted balls inside of one palm, my skewed running shorts provided precious little concealment. Along with his other hand on my buttcheeks, I could do nothing except blush at him stupidly. My typical ten shades of 'Jake-pink', as it had come to be known in the family. I was probably glowing like a blood moon.

Voy separated us by straightening up, now blatantly scrutinizing my disheveled self. Wild, mud-tousled hair jutted from the blood-soaked edges of a makeshift headband, wedged shorts twisted off my embarrassingly inflated, ball-shrunken junk. All of this, balancing awkwardly on one foot. "You keep in good shape, dude," he offered. "By the feel o'ya," teasing me with a wink.

My mental clarity wavered just then and I recognized a dizziness not felt before. The bad ankle disallowed my precarious stance and he darted a sinewy hand right between my legs to keep me from falling as he caught my teetering. While stopping a fall, this only stiffened the distressingly inappropriate response my sex organ so wrongly displayed.

If that wasn't enough, as his hand steadied me, a middle finger strayed into my butt crack. The one-eyed betrayer surrendered, spouting a viscous rope of pre-cum right on to Voy's wrist. "Well, at least you ain't bleedin' from that, too," the teasing continued. Such a diplomat, I thought, through a crimson haze. He hiked my arm up high over his shoulder, cupping my hip with his pre-cummed hand and we made our way up the path to the cottage mentioned before.

In a minute, we were at a small arched wooden door, Voy's knuckles rapping heavily on it as he intoned, "T...T, wake on up, I got a patient out here needin' some tendin' to."

After a few moments we heard muffled shuffling from inside and the solid little door pulled open, revealing a sleepy-eyed young man wrapping a floral robe around himself, squinting through a stifled yawn as the porchlight clicked on. The red hue of the sudden lighting cast an odd ambience over us three and I recognized TL, my youthful orderly from the free medical clinic where I volunteered.

Yup, it was, indeed, my recent after-hours 'co-worker-in-crime' gaping at me through his yawn. This man knew me better than I would've liked. "Well, I'll be. What is up with this?" He glanced from me to Voy and back, not missing the blood-soaked bandage, the connected condition of our contrasting bodies nor my persistent, waggling, full-mast hard on. My eyes were definitely not down there, I ventured an unspoken cliché.

"Seems there be need of some early-morning triage...or something," he quipped, now stepping aside to allow us entry, sweeping a petite hand backwards as he beckoned us. The look we got was priceless.

If mortification had been present before, this turn of events sure notched things up on the scale of humiliation. My stuff continued its unabashed, way-too-happy jiggling as Voy practically hoisted me inside to a big armchair. Thankfully sitting now, I was noticing the light-headedness again. Probably associated with my injury, I analyzed. Laying back, the two men bustled to the adjoining kitchen. I closed my eyes amidst multi-levels of emotional chagrin, attempting to straighten the pitiful excuse passing for running shorts.

With TL's coaxing, I drank a warm tea concoction which I was informed would take the edge off my pains. It did relax me, and quickly. Through the wooziness, I recognized ministrations of nursing and bandaging to my head wounds in the next foggy period of time. The 'aid workers' tended to wrapping my ankle as well, somehow mistaking my buoyant prick for the afflicted ankle several times.

I barely focused while I was lifted and moved to a more comfortably reclining position with the ankle elevated, in a different room. Their soft conversational tones were both efficient and subdued, Voy's deep rumblings contrasting TL's higher pitched sing-song tittering. I drifted off hazily, basking in much less discomfort...

...The haunting, melodic beat of the twins' jungle-rap re-emerged, suffusing my being and I concentrated on the suggestive lyrics as I rested. They seemed so close as to be inside my head. I hearkened back to the starry night in the backyard during the baseball game when the twins and I had shared an animal magnetism fueled by magic gummy bears. Loy and Roy had taken turns fucking me nasty, right there under the stars. My man and his brother, Coy, the older twins, had watched the whole thing from the cover of the porch. Unbeknownst to me. Until we came, anyway.

They had produced multiple loads of cum between them, all three of us collapsing in a sticky mess afterwards. I somehow knew we would repeat the hot episode and with the rhythmus in my brain now, it seemed the two had decided sooner rather than later would be good. Gladly accepting of their attentions that starry night, those pulsating dicks had slowly inflamed my prostate. I was loving the re-enactment now. My cock was presently rising and falling with the cadence of their strokes, ready for eruption any time but desiring to hold off longer to stretch out the pleasure.

The provocative drumbeat lamentably diminished as I gradually recognized the lewd activity for a fantasy delusion. The dream state receded. My awareness re-surfaced and with it awakened the reason for the persistence of the deliciously slow-paced deep fucking effect. My eyes flicked open from my lust-laden trance and I found myself focusing on the Chippendale-worthy form of, not Loy or Roy hitting my boy pussy, but big, married Voy, instead. Adultery abounded. His hands were grasping my calves, splitting my legs wide apart, carefully avoiding my securely wrapped ankle.

I was swaying with the deliberate dick thrusts in some sort of sling. He was watching my gauze-wrapped head and eyes as he prodded deeply with his jumbo-sized prick, feeding off my half-conscious cheerleading. Matching dream state to groggy reality, the measured ass pumping continued in a slowly methodical manner. The gentle behemoth made my erect dick rise and drop over my belly with each repeating push. Voy's concern for any suffering was allayed by my rigidly see-sawing 8's-plus, which he himself had engendered during the river crossing. He now maintained the effect by intermittent light finger-slapping, much to my delight.

Coming up from the mental depth of the dream proved a timely return to reality as I felt my dick tensing, on the very verge of putting out. My hands were nowhere close to it. I heard Voy encouraging me toward that end, telling me he was about to cum inside my impregnable ass, and, 'Oh, shit, that shit feel Good, boiii, that feel Jood!"

His head arched upwards like a wolf howling at the moon as he plunged into a massive explosion, flooding me with spermful gushes. Damn, married men fuck so good. That was all that came into my head as I followed suit, emptying squirts of juice over my own face, chest and stomach.

Big bare feet were planted far apart, pelvis thrust fully forward into mine, and those beautiful arms still restrained my quivering legs. This sixth and final linkage consummated me with the entire brotherhood of the Blackhearst family. My bleary, cum-splashed gaze watched Voy stop, freeze-framed, in an extended pause of ecstatic enjoyment before he finally recovered and descended from that silent howl. Licking full lips and focusing on my copiously splattered form.

I heard a chipper little voice from under the sling, "Goddam, Voy, that is gonna be one phyne fuck flick, baby." Popping up from floor level, a now fully made-up TL arose, beaming in the flowing floral robe, assuring the married man that the angle of that fuck shot would be the best one yet. To be viewed on the occasion of their next plowing, he promised his black sancho. So much for TL's imaginary girlfriend---

hadn't I thought that once before? This diminutive man-girl was brazen, for sure true.

Oh, and it was a good thing Winnie was so hankerin' for that fresh fish and licorice, what with her baby-making pole presently otherwise occupied...

Voy, lascivious grin lighting his face, glanced from the drag queen to me, "Torchy Lane loves her videos, now, my bra..." And with that, he unceremoniously yanked that big dick all outta my ass, spanking her right across the head with it. To her delight and my further stunned surprise.

Cal examined my head scrapes upon being delivered safely home in the next hour, kneading the hair apart tenderly as he heard the low-down about his younger twins' budding nocturnal musical endeavours and wondered at the full morning's happenings. "Hell, Jake, it isn't half the morning gone yet and you done been hyped, scraped and raped...whatever we gonna think up to do for the rest o' the day, my ever-ready dudeboii?"

Smiling sweetly up at him, I inquired if there were any brothers left who I had not yet met?

That got a hoot in reply.

Chapter 15
Tride and True: Caribbean Chicken Delight

"Tha' goat bein' da genuine stud, now, Mon," said Amber-gai Gee, IV. "If'n mi hadda' been so bent-horn hung, den yu'da been feelin' more true-screwed when mi bein' climbin' up tha'pretty ass of ya' own, ma'pussy boi, LukeMon," he sassed, staring up the craggy height looming over the back edge of our mountain vale property.

Fluffy snowflakes fluttered down over my face and I shielded my eyes with my hand, following the man's gaze. At almost 12000 feet high, there was an ironic glare even in cloudy weather.

Upon focusing, I envisioned the outline of a magnificent Rocky Mountain Bighorn ram standing on the edge of a stony outcropping hundreds of feet above. The hugely thick, curling horns imbued the beast with an almost Luciferian appearance. One front hoof was slightly bent and the big ram was sniffing the thin air, searching for something. He looked for all the world like a picture out of 'The Lion King', by his regal stance up on the precipice. Ignoring the fact he wasn't a lion, of course.

Immediately relieved, I exclaimed, "Wow, am I glad to see that big fella. Jeremy and I have been afraid all during the 'bear scare' that something had happened to him. Adolpho hasn't even run across him for the past few weeks, he told us."

This brought a puzzled response from my tallest friend and newest family member, "Ya' meanin' tha' ya' know da' goat, Luke?" He seemed surprised, but he shouldn't have been. He was aware of my penchant for eccentric behavior and relation-ships with animals already.

"That is W.C., Gai," I enlightened the older gent, "He grew up down here years back, funny enough. The boy comes home now and again to check on us and the dogs…and especially the girls." This comment did nothing to clear his questioning look, "W.C.? Now, ya' be a'tellin' me tha' ya' are about nam-ing da' wildlife, too, ma unusual Mon? And, whaddya' mean, 'grew up down here', where bein' da momma, now? Or da' family?"

"Oh, sorry, Gai. It seems like you've been here forever. W.C. Ovis—William Canadensis Ovis, aka, Rocky Mountain Bighorn ram—he's a sheep, Gai, not a goat… The big boy dropped in on us one day about three years back and we adopted him until he grew up and decided to own the moun-tain. He must be in rut and, I'm guessing, back from making babies, now," I thought out loud.

"Dropped in?" He stopped the sectioning of the hay bales being spread, in complete bewilderment at this point. Hay pieces flocked the man's long dreadlocks. We were in preparation for the elk who commonly took shelter under the overhang of the rocks during bad weather.

There were two yearling elk cows patiently grazing a hundred yards away, picking through the snow for any remaining mountain grasses left from autumn. The females would lift their heads our way occasionally, knowing there would be soft padding to rest on once we had finished. While not tame, the cows were familiars, recognizing benevolence in this mountain dale. Gai was still getting used to this elk thing; with this new ram quirk the questions multiplied.

"An', now, I'ma s'posin' dat ya' gonna tell me dat da elk ladies there, a'waitin', are gonna be a'havin' names, now, too, are ya' not, Luke?" His indulgent mockery was transparent, now playing along.

"Yup, that is Wapiti on the left, and her sis on the right is Sambara. They're twins." The rolled-eye look I received was amusing.

I kept pulling apart the timothy hay, mounding it thickly back under and away from the falling snowflakes. It would stay dry here, I knew, so the yearlings and any others showing up would be protected should the snow become a storm. We would sometimes find up to six or seven sharing the rock-shrouded acclivity. The salt licks close by kept them happy, and by eating their bedding they remained well-fed as well as occupied during bad weather. I had constructed a cedar cabin with a small front porch nearby years before and stored the extra there. Inside were upwards of fifty more bales.

Winter had begun early this year, what with the El Nino effect. We were in for a wet and cold season here in the high country, I could tell. So could the other resident fauna, all of whom were busily readying for the weather blitz in their own manner. There were black squirrels and chipmunks busily hoarding above us and several nuthatches and chicadees twittered amongst the tree branches as well.

Ambergai resumed helping spread as he realized I had internalized and patiently awaited my mental return, in the way

Jamaicans are so adept. After finishing the five bales, we wordlessly headed over toward the outdoor cedar hot tub, a six-foot diameter traditional barrel and hoop design. I had planned ahead by turning on the heat mode earlier, so it was already up to 102 degrees F, and almost perfect in light of the elements. We pulled off the cover and switched on the jets.

Bumping and grinding good-naturedly, we stripped and hopped in, leaving our clothing hung from pole hangers next to it. Our easy togetherness was a result of the intense intimacy established over the preceding weeks since this gent had burst onto the scene and alighted in my and Jeremy's midst.

Gai had taken to our mountain lifestyle readily. He had grown up at 5000 feet above the Caribbean Sea level around the main Jamaican island, like my Jeremy. Having been a native-born Hagley Gap, Blue Mountain, Jamaica boy, it wasn't that much of a stretch. The only stretching involved, I was noticing, arose from the bulging homunculus between the man's legs. The hot, roiling water in an outdoor venue tended to trigger it, at least I so hoped.

Within a few moments, as we sat across from each other in the agitating bubbles, the foreskinned dick sure enough peeked his bobbing head from the depths, peering at me in expectancy. "I hadna' thought to put ya' t'more work ma'fine boii, but there's no J-Mon lips to be a'seen, and the little mon here seems t'be a mite insistent..." He smiled and nodded downward as he made me aware, in the charming way I had come to know, that the 'anything-but-little-man' was ready for some slow, deep head.

Exactly what I had been waiting for, I thought, crossing the gap to grasp the hard thang in a second. I must have been drooling, because Gai told me, "Now don'ya be a-rushin' through dis work, LukeMon, we be gottin' us all da' day to get things correct, now, mindya', youngsta'. Slow it all down, and enjoy da' ride, now..." The man's unpretentious animalistic air always wowed me. Surely, the man had been a woodland satyr in a past life.

I found irresistible the way the man gave orders and got right down on the hard piece, my nose dipping below the water surface as I warmed up. Wishing I had a snorkel to stay submerged longer, I nevertheless managed to get a nice, comfortable motion all the way up and down the XXXL shaft, no doubt making headway in my mission. His mellow, lilting banter lessoned me on the best way to get cum from it. I slurped noisily as I came up off the granddaddy-sized cock, diving right back to the root in search of treasure.

Only a scant few minutes passed before I could feel helping hands and the obliging 'little man' begin exhibiting symptoms I recognized to be telltale for an underwater eruption. I backed off, leaving just a grasping hand (almost) encircling the flare, smirking up at the chagrined duo of heads before me. Each were threatening desperate measures should I not get back on it, and pronto.

As the eye opened up, I tongued the gooey globule appearing there and then submerged again with the satisfying nestling of my nose into his pubic hair where I rotated slowly. Only recently had I become adept enough to swallow the thing this deep— and only through diligent practice. The big head squashed inside my esophagus. It delivered the viscous load I had been striving to make coat my throat.

Hating that I hadn't gotten but the barest taste of the sweet Caribbean jism, as it had been shot so far past my taste buds, I had to be satisfied with resuming my efforts. Accustomed to Gai's multiple load capabilities, to which both my husband and I were habituated, my second favorite dick soon swelled up and pulsed me the next load. I bobbed around on just the huge head, tasting the cum to contentment this time.

Ambergai clucked in Lyaric-dialect euphemisms above me as I aced my homework. Finally raising up, I found his wet dreadlocks cascading around me like a fishing net. The seasoned older man abruptly swung his head back, throwing the mess of them backwards, drawing me into his shoulder. I cozily fit under his long arm, fingers on the familiar dark hand finding and cradling my own phat white boy prick. We enjoyed the heat together awhile, luxuriating in the jet action pulsing our skin.

As I had anticipated, upon resting back with him, there but ten yards distant from us stood the big coil-horned head of William Ovis. Studying our peculiar activities, the big ram slowly munched his cud in profound concentration. "Believe it now, LukeMon, tha' we do sure 'nuf have another mon-watchin' freak in da' yard, here. Did ya' by any chance have summin' t'do with dat, too?"

I chuckled at the wit, picking up again on the delayed explanation of William's descent into our lives. Three Junes before, I clarified, we had arrived for a summer sojourn here with Elle and Elle, Jr. The third morning after we arrived, all of us had been sitting right where we were now, I told Gai, when suddenly, a racket far up in the old Douglas Spruce thirty feet from where we sat, interrupted us. As we all watched, there appeared the tiniest, emaciated form of a week-old mountain sheep baby. He tumbled down to the ground, hitting one after another branch on the evergreen, thereby breaking his fall and preventing surely fatal injuries. Upon hitting the grassy lawn, he laid dead-still and we all thought he must surely be that—dead.

Little Elle, Jr, only four at the time, and her mama, our grown-up Elle, launched from the tub, scooping up the miniscule six or seven-pound waif, both pouring crocodile tears over the thing. At the touch and the wetness, the shocked little kid came to and bleated one long, wailing cry then sank into Junior's arms.

All of us went into hyper-mode, opening an air passage, checking vital signs, looking for wounds, gathering warm towels and pillows as we sought to save the little being. We concocted a milk, yogurt, egg, honey, lemon blend and procured a baby bottle from the co-op. The girls proceeded to spend the next three weeks nursing, massaging and basically fostering him into our nascent family.

The little thing revived initially but then reverted to slowly dwindling and fading, so I got online and searched baby-formulas, dietary needs, hydration regimens and such. The information I gleaned did not paint a rosy picture for the orphan, I discovered.

Jeremy and I had next driven all the way to Boulder and the Vet college there. Some fast talking convinced the hesitant neonatal staff into providing some precious sheep colostrum and goat's milk, probably because of our promise of a sizeable donation to the institution... Upon returning, we found the girls beside themselves at the weakening state of the tyke.

Apparently we had hit the mother lode of luck, because over the next week the baby began suckling again, taking the proper formula into its sorely ravaged little body. He made a slow, steady turn-around.

Another month saw the little cuss turn robust, engineering feats of manifest disaster inside the log house, forcing the construction of the cabin I now used for the hay. Upon fencing a good-sized area around it we showed him to his new home. Bonding came easy then and everyone gloried in his woodland faun free-spirit antics... the little booger stole all of our hearts. And, boy, did he grow.

Ignoring the species dichotomy, the name William, in honor of the Goats' Gruff, was settled on. It came from the bedtime favorite of little Elle at that time. She insisted on William over Billy, citing his extreme good looks. We inverted the mountain sheep's genus and species names for a more personal touch, granting him provenance.

"Well," said Gai, following my explanation, "that story be all well-an-good, LukeMon, but for one tiny little t'in. Where in da world di' the bebe come down from, and how di' such a t'in 'appen, now?" He eyed the big animal as if he expected the thing to join us in the hot tub.

I told him that we couldn't ever be certain, but with all of the high cliffs surrounding us, we figured that either he had been a poor-doer baby, or maybe a weak twin. It had been, after all, late in the eweing season for bighorns to drop babies. So maybe, we rationalized, he had been sacrificed by mama and drop-kicked off a high ledge from somewhere in an attempt to humanely--- what a misnomer of a word--- let him go… Nature could seem cruelly hard at times.

We also conjectured that perhaps he had been kidnapped by an eagle. One could have nabbed him and then dropped him in flight. Either way, the spruce that saved his life in heralding his descending arrival seemed imprinted on W.C. Ovis as much as we were. Jeremy and I would sometimes find the grown bighorn cuddled up around the base of it, or scratching himself against the bark, when he would return.

Elle, Jr., learned an important life lesson from the whole affair. For that matter, it also reinforced we grown-ups, about how the twists and turns in Life can lead one on strange paths. When the hairy, bearded, seven-month-old kid reached puberty it was time. He had known before us. Coming to Junior one morning during the Christmas break, the young ram proceeded to bathe the little girl over most of her body with his tongue, doling out tiny 'love-nips' along with it. His favorite friend and playmate answered with shrieks of laughter and little girl hugs.

After that expression, W.C. Ovis had kicked up his heels and bolted to the edge of the surrounding woods. He turned and bugled a heartfelt 'adios' and 'gracias', thence breaking all of our hearts again by answering the call of the wild. Thank goodness.

We all pined for a week. Then began the sightings of him in the upper reaches of the heights directly above, alerting us to his presence and establishment of dominion there by a trumpeting call. Over the succeeding two years, we heard more than one cracking clash of his horns with the racks of bighorn competitors and were fearful for him. But now, he seemed to be in full control of the surrounding area, coming down periodically, in search of his girlfriend, little Elle.

Jeremy and I sufficed for stand-ins, we supposed, but the time he came down and actually found the six-year-old version of his little sis, the two exhibited an amazing interspecies display of prolonged and boisterous renewal. The big ram knew intuitively the gentleness required to be with her. They fell asleep together under the big spruce, curled up together. We have the framed photo in our bedroom to this day. YouTube went nuts over it.

Our little girl had one great show-and-tell back at school that fall... no one could rival it. Now, we were hopeful that a snowy reunion might once again happen with the girls scheduled to arrive in a few days.

True to form, while I illuminated the story to Gai, we observed the ram grow tired of us, losing interest. He parked himself at the trunk of the old spruce. Vigorous scratching and rubbing followed and we induced that he was wiping off the smell of those yucky, now-useless highland ewes--- ho's that they were— by the activity. His odoriferous emanations did rival an old goat, to be sure. We laughed at our anthropomorphic bias, reckoning he was actually just 'sprucing' himself up for his real date, Missy Junior...

Amidst this wooly show, we were abruptly distracted by the voice of my main man rounding the corner of the house. "Wassssuppp, my two fav men?" Jeremy was ebullient even by the standards of his normally upbeat personality. As he approached, he began lasciviously disrobing, a-la Magic Mike, hilariously break-dancing our direction. Upon reaching the cedar tub, he jumped, turned and bent down, sliding his drawerless jeans down in the motion and presenting us a broadly waxing full double moon.

He badly miscalculated Ambergai's wingspan. One long arm reached over and slapped a hard, handsome glute. It startled William by the sharp report. Apparently translating the sound into a challenge, the big ungulate jumped up and assumed a head-down charge posture.

Identifying Jeremy as the source, the curled horns sprang toward him. Totally freaked, my man launched into a backwards somersault. Flipping up and over the side of the cedar tub, he plunged head first into its security. Jeans bound his legs, shoes were still in place. The picture of them sticking up out of the water, hanging over the edge of the tub in that condition, provided a memorable finale to his ribald entrance.

In the sudden absence of any discernible foe to be butted, the feral Goat Gruff just as quickly subsided in his blitzkrieg. Resuming the placid personality of the curious lamb we had nurtured, a now nosy Mr. Ovis arrived at the tub side. The scary headstrong instinctive response devolved to mouthing the jeaned legs still extruding from the vat. Grasping the leggings from my man's shapely ankles, he backed up, pulling hiking boots and pants completely off. Jeremy finally surfaced, bubbling and spewing water, the antithesis of that previously cocky projection.

Failing miserably at controlling ourselves, Gai and I did manage to slap the sputtering heartthrob on the back, helping him expel swallowed water. In the doing, we both got our hands all over the prime object of our desire. He sank back down into the warmth of the jetting water spouts, just head and neck visible.

Covering his sheepishness, he attempted deflection from the less than courageous reaction, quipping, "Try and beat that entrance. The tuberosity lives." In his defense, the hunk truly wasn't as spooked as his body language had seemed. The evidence was borne out by the nature of the response his dick was affecting in my squeezing palm. Gai's hand must have been helping by penetrating his delectable little hole as Jeremy's voice abruptly raised an octave. "Billy's eating my favorite jeans," in a falsetto that broke us up again. We all three watched as the horned devil proceeded to appetize on the expensive boots.

I finally composed myself enough to stand up, waving at the ram and distracting him into sniffing my hand in greeting.

The lovable beast was clearly wondering what all the hub-bub was about. Neither of the two Nubian princes were stoic enough yet to show more than their heads above the froth. Even while viewing my hand being slathered in gentle sheep saliva.

It suddenly dawned on me how off-base my assumption of their shyness was upon noticing Jeremy shudder— and not one that evoked fear. Gai's exceedingly long middle finger had, indeed, successfully implanted itself in the asshole the finger's owner had first entered in its virgin state thirty-two years before. That same dexterous phalange was now stimulating the sensitive prostate gland hugging his colon.

In one fluid act, Gai lifted the buoyant butt, slowly working it closer to the familiar reggae dick. Approaching the still leaking tip, the other hand smeared it, then slowly lowered the sphincter down over the juicy sponginess. The effort met very little resistance. With another shudder and an audible sigh, Jeremy slowly sank eleven inches deeper into the 102-degree water.

As always, when I was near, his eyes locked on mine to share the pleasure. I wrapped fingers around my man's now fully erect piece as it convulsed with each descending inch. Standing up again, my unsated cock bobbed in front of his mouth. It slid over his lips and was immediately sucked into the moaning throat. I patterned with the two fucking men of my life and once again, we solved the puzzle of finding holes enough to go around. This time in the company of a moon-eyed bighorn.

The snowfall intensified and we three melted all that touched us, on contact. Fade to white…

* * *

"I skyped with the boys this morning--- they seem like they're having a great time," I was filling Jeremy in about Adolpho and Bryce. The two young lovers and newly close friends had decided to visit Adolpho's family in Florence and we all missed them. In just the short time since the two had met, a solid bond had been wrought.

Adolpho had finally figured out his difficulty committing to women. He hadn't met the right person. Commitment had turned easy upon setting eyes on Bryce. The amorous Italian had just known. Bryce, also. The rest of the details kind of fell into place. The young de Medici family member, quintessential straight man, somehow rationalized he hadn't shifted lifestyles. The free-spirited young man felt deeply that he had simply come upon his true life partner. Chromosomes had not been a relevant factor.

The sommelier was now on a trip to Italy for business—stocking his reserves for the upscale clientele on the mountain with his native country's superb vintages. He had convinced Bryce to accompany him. To carry the wine bottles, he had been teased. Like bulk shipping did not exist...

Now, however, the two had chosen to present their decision to Adolpho's aristocratic family in the old home country...

"You mean they were accepted?" Jeremy asked hopefully. Having been ostracized by his own folks, a young Jeremy had self-exiled from Jamaica two and a half decades before. He knew of the contention involved in relationships with family firsthand.

"Well, you know how Italian families are, JK," I replied, "They put up with 'youthful indiscretions' up to the age of thirty. Then, duty calls. By that measure, there are about four years left until tithing time. So, I am guessing the jury is still out, baby."

"BeBe?" Gai walked into the kitchen at that last word. "There be a' pair of those bein' in da fronta' mi eyeballs right here, and we's a'stuck in da indoors by da big snow, now. And no beastly spittin' goat a'watchin, so..." pointing to the crotch of his hemps with two long index fingers. He sat down at the big marble island after pouring himself a glass of wine, joining us.

Ambergai was still thinking about the hot tub sex in the snowstorm two days before. W.C. had apparently sensed the testosterone-on-steroids during our session and at the moment of cum, the rascal had copiously spit his cud over the three of us. Interesting end. We had to drain the tub.

"Gai, you know your Jamaica goats were worse than that sheep, mister, and those goats slept in bed with you," JK offered, surprising me by that odd tidbit.

"Ya', but da' goats were precious and got demselves stole if'n they di'nt, an' I'ma knowin' ya'are rememmerin', now, ma' good boy bitch. Dey seemed ta' like ya', alot, should I be thinkin' on it right now." The big man grinned at the thought.

Seeing an opening, I reached in the drawer and pulled out a head high doobie. Good for storytelling, I surmised. I was fascinated by my man's still enigmatic past. Lighting it, we watched out the big plate glass windows at the swirling snow. Over two days, we had seen more than a foot of the stuff. Drifts up to four feet were piling around the base of things.

The malodorous spitting ovine had been spied camping out with no less than six elk cows in the protected grotto earlier, corroborating the seriousness of the forecast. "Looks like the critters out there are sharing a bed, now," I observed, "and I wager the strange bedfellows are suckin' up their differences under the circumstances…kinda like goats and farmers, huh?" Though a bit transparent, my men traded tokes and looks while we enjoyed the wine in the quiet of the late stormy afternoon.

Getting no more rise from either, I resorted to junk adjustment. My minds-eye was picturing a high Jamaican mountaintop and a crowded bedroom full of valuable goats and a young boy. My piece liked the possibilities, especially upon extending the scenario to the arrival of a then-younger dreadlocked coffee-grower. Sure enough, the white dick began growing at the idea. It did not go un-noticed by Jeremy.

Always the voluptuary, he slid down to his knees, pulled my sweats down around my ankles and swallowed the only white cock in the room. Gai came around the corner from putting in an Enigma CD, then eased himself back on the sectional to keep an eye on the action. "Ya be perfectin' da technique dat mi been taught ma' little bitch all back 'der in dem young days, J-Mon," he stated. "Mi bein' vera glad for you's two figgerin' out where t'other one be in all this big world, now." He sounded profound, but I noted that the drawstring of his preferred hemp pants had somehow come untied, and the thick piece inside was showing interest in the present goings on.

As I enjoyed the purposely slow mouthstrokes, Ambergai pulled a small clear packet from a hidden pocket, tapping it with a finger. He glanced over at me and gestured questioningly whether it was cool to put a bit out. "Dat boi, Paecup, donated a tiny bit o'dat Peruvian last time mi been seein' da' mon," he explained. Seeing my nod, he came up on us, scooped a small fingernail bump and sprinkled it down on my hard, slimed piece. Jeremy held my dick head in place waiting for it, then descended on a downstroke, absorbing the powder with his lips. I was served a similar scoopful into my nostril, Jeremy closing my opposing nostril with a free finger while continuing the slow strokes.

Ambergai did himself one as well and sat back on the divan, now stroking slowly on the longmeat centering between his long legs.

He began a story about his fourth wife and him fucking in their mountain farmhouse when a boy burst in the door without knocking. His wife was pissed by it, he said. Not enjoying the sex and worried about another pregnancy, she left in a huff, pushing by the kid on her way out.

The story was coming in subdued tones but with increasing energy as the blow kicked in. He was palpably relishing this reminiscence. As the monster dick stood straight up now, dark fingers stroked its length, matching with J-man's rhythm and the music...

…After the wife left, he told, young Jeremy stared at the big stick in front of him for a long time, then finally crept forward to touch his first manmeat.

My man was all ears hearing the remembrance but never once did he pull off my dick, tacitly good with the older man's memories. His own cock told the same thought, standing up between his legs. He slowly slid his hand down on it, enjoying both our dicks.

I was amazed at the control of the two. There was no ribald three-way unfolding, per usual. Gai continued, now describing the first awkward blow job of Jeremy's career…

…The thing just wouldn't and couldn't fit inside the immature mouth, so a lot of licking and slobbering had resulted. I couldn't help sniggling as he told of the first eruption drenching the boy's nappy head. He had jumped up, totally grossed out, and run all the way home. It took three weeks and a chance meeting on the road down the mountain before the two tried again. Things progressed from there.

Ambergai was elated to find a non-impregnable partner, overly young though he was. After the sucking technique was deemed acceptable, the boy gradually learned about taking dick. That would encompass a year, at least, I found out. At his junior high graduation, he took his first full-blown fucking with a load, and found he halfway liked it. He just couldn't walk upright for a week.

Gai was able to avoid an eleventh child and Jeremy grew up knowing nothing different. With twelve siblings, and parents too busy to find time for all, everything pushed the young man toward Gai, who became mentor, confidant and de facto family.

His own children were by three other wives and all lived elsewhere. The then-wife finally had her tubes tied to avoid anything unexpected, which was fine with Ambergai. By then, however, he was 'stuck' on Jeremy. So everyone seemed ignorantly satisfied.

No one even noticed the development of their bond: Gai hired Jeremy to help around the farm. Their liaison was never discussed. The affection between the pair grew over the years as Jeremy's home life continued to be severely lacking…

…Just hearing the story, I came twice, figuring out the two were re-living it for my benefit. Jeremy popped off each time I did and we both watched the huge cock ooze a rarely seen load as he related the virgin fuck scene. Most of the mature man's loads were deposited out-of-sight…

…At 17, the explosion had occurred. One of Jeremy's older brothers happened in on the two in the middle of cumming--- the big dick in tiny ass, young dick close to shooting. The irony of the affair was that the brother went down on Jeremy, taking the blast of adolescent cum down his throat. Then, the big jerk of a brother went straight to his father with the dirty details. All, of course, except for the part about swallowing his little brother's load. The damage had been done.

Now, a veritable leper in the eyes of his own family, things became progressively toxic. He found he was persona non grata at Gai's home on the mountain—Gai's wife banned him from the place. Gai was forced to give only surreptitious support. Securing a small, secret apartment for him in Kingston, Ambergai had insisted on Jeremy finishing high school in a different parish.

This actually turned out to be fortunate, because the teenage Jeremy had been sorely under-challenged by the mountain school. He blossomed academically those final two years, finding some love and stability with the daughter of a Kingston preacher. He graduated with honors.

Gai, his reggae band and career now taking off, stood in as his 'godfather' for all ceremonies, even serving as his best man when he married the pastor's daughter. So continued Jeremy's 'straight period' and a fast rise, unforeseen before.

Both of our lives may have shaped up differently had not two vagaries of fate occurred.

For two years, my man had lived a fairly satisfying life with his new bride. He became a church-goer and college student in Kingston. Gai's celebrity sky-rocketed and they gradually drifted apart, rarely speaking. Two years in, little Elle was born and Jeremy knew true, unconditional love for the first time in his life. He was totally into fatherhood. The man doted on his baby girl.

All seemed good until one day when his wife's mother walked into their home to find her little girl buried tongue-deep inside another woman's pussy. The shit hit the fan. Jeremy was understanding of the situation, having found himself in a similar unsavory state of affairs years before. He was never the jealous type anyway, but the pastor and his wife hatefully disowned their blasphemous daughter. On the spot.

The coming fall school semester found the young family in Austin, Texas. Jeremy was determined to follow in Aristotle's Greek footsteps as a philosopher. He had applied for and been granted a U.S. student visa and earned a scholarship at the University of Texas.

After another year, he and his wife had finally come to grips with the fact that there were no longer feelings between them. They had separated amicably to pursue their own paths. Baby Elle had split time with them.

Then came the fateful day a few years into single parent-hood in the bookshop when the little girl knocked me off my ladder and her daddy swept me off my feet. Our fates were sealed.

Much of the latter story, as added by Jeremy, was new to Ambergai Gee, and he hungrily absorbed filling gaps of his own. One of the few persons to accept our ladder meeting at face value. We ended the evening with both dogs up on the sectional, five bodies warmed by a flickering fireplace and prevailing mutual affection. Dozing together as the storm swelled outside.

* * *

The cloven-footed man—if one could call him that— towered over me as I wakened foggily in a bed of pine needles. My eyes opened to the goat-like hooves and worked their way upward, taking in the furry legs, the animal skin waist wrap, the hairy stomach, then the likewise hirsute pectorals and arms. The man's head was covered by thick, bristly growth which framed the saturnine face. His ears were long-tipped at the tops, like a horse, and two curling horns exiting his temples completed the fearsome vision.

I raised up on one arm, holding up the other in front of me to ward off an anticipated blow. The chimera sneered down on my prostrate form and spat, "What in Hades do you think you be doin' here?" Having no clue, I looked around for anything familiar.

It was a mountain setting, to be sure. But, the flora evoked a tropical climate rather than a Rocky Mountain setting. Equatorial conifers, plantains, paw-paw plants, frangipanis…coffee plants. And, I smelled goats. Unsure whether the presence before me was the source, I wondered if this place was, possibly, Blue Mountain.

Feeding my sense of fantasy as well as that of confusion, there arose a distant, wavering warble distinctly mento-calypso in its melodic style. I realized that I was completely naked. And my dick was rigid. The form above me had apparently noticed this already. His goat-foot reached out, nudging my member and it jumped at the touch. His deep, unfriendly chortle at its response disturbed me by the excitement it caused.

While we continued sizing one another up, a stray raindrop hit my face. Then another. Within a few seconds, we were being deluged by a summer-like squall, drenching us. It did nothing to improve the funky smell wafting through my nose.

To compound the bizarre scenario, as we were soaked by the rain, four or five Jamaica goats ran into the small clearing. Their nervous bleating and frenzied pacing bothered me. The Faun-like man drew a lute of some kind from a leather bag over his shoulder. Putting it to his lips, he sounded several staccato notes. That stopped the goats in their tracks. The group stood still, hypnotized. This 'man' was undoubtedly the boss.

At the same moment, a very youthful Satyriskoi boy rushed forward out of the surrounding dense underbrush in chase of the wandering goats, bumping into one of them. The dark boy was totally nude, and boasted a completely aroused uncut dick. A very pretty one, I noted.

The goat-man broke with a lewdly lecherous, lip-smacking acknowledgement of the stumbling youth, which left no doubt whatever as to his new aim. I was weirded out by the entire situation, but also glad to no longer be under the intense scrutiny felt up to now.

Indeed, the tall woodland man-creature forgot me, turning in a twirl that flapped open the loincloth covering his groin. I glimpsed a huge priapic appendage resembling that of a stallion. Huge overhanging prepuce of foreskin, its girth was larger than Ambergai's erect thickness…but this one was floppily un-aroused. Scary. The bucket of balls underhanging the thing were covered in enough hair to weave a basket.

I lost concentration in the fraction of a second of its appearance, finding myself staring at a coarse-haired horsetail arching out and over a very prominent donut-sized anus. The backside of this individual was in my face and overpowering, cascading ponytail whisking ardently back and forth. My mind channeled a mountain lion ready to spring, tail switching in expectancy.

The satyriskoi youth froze as he realized upon whom—or what— he had inadvertently stumbled. His smoky grey eyes widened in surprise, and I believed, fear, as he focused on the mature satyr planting his hooves directly facing the boy's absolutely Adonis-like little embodiment.

If his eyes had opened wide at the first sighting of the being, as I watched now, they grew powers larger. The youth and I saw an absolutely humongous stallion dick steadily rising, directly toward the diminutive sprite. From a rear angle to me, I saw it boing steadily upward in exact mimicry of the thoroughbred stallions I had seen on Animal Planet during the "Mating Season" presentation last spring. Those horse dicks didn't waste time. When they spotted their objective, those bamboozlers were stiff within seconds. This one did that.

The final arch upwards had to be a good twenty inches. It swelled to bigger around than my forearm. The foreskin was so long, I think my foot might have fit into it. For size perspective, only, of course. From the opening, there drooled a long string of ropy precum. An elephant would have been proud.

Through these few moments, I noticed the youth sported deer-like feet, himself, and a furry lower half, from upper thighs downward. Above that, he was hairless. Except for the mop of unruly curls very similar to my own, crowning his head. More ringlets than curls in the steady downpour, the well-hung, markedly adorable androgynous creature stomped his hooves, splattering mud.

I must've mistaken the fearful look earlier, for the sylvan youth provoked the goat-man's erectile behavior by flipping his own turgid curve with a stubby finger. It seemed to hone in on the bigger one like a radar. In relation to the body size of the owner, the boner was outsized in its own right. The accompanying fat, snug balls sucked in tightly underneath.

The Satyr-stud, proudly displaying himself, issued a sharp arm motion toward the smaller being. Submissively, little Pan-boy turned obediently around, proffering a delectable little set of globular cheeks upwards toward the behemoth. He looked over his shoulder at it, pulling the globes apart enticingly with his hands. The larger hooves took three long strides across the clearing, butting the baseball bat right up to the little winking rosebud.

As I spectated, now more curious than worried, I saw what, in human terms, amounted to a veritable fist-fucking play out before me. That was just how large the penis was.

I had heard tell of women strapping themselves to the underside of horse stallions in Mexico and collecting ticket money from goggle-eyed American frat boys visiting the border towns for the weekend. The fuck episode I saw now reminded me of what my mind pictured that would be like.

Except, in this case, the big fucker grasped the small one by his hips with those hairy hands, lifted him off the ground and proceeded to impale, then pummel, the round little ass deep and long. The youth neighed and whinnied like a mare in heat. And begged for more. The goats and I remained stock still.

My dick amazed me by the fact that it was turned on by this action. It throbbed its reaction exuberantly. Just as I felt certain that the big priapus was destined to poke up through the satyriskoi's mouth, so deeply was it embedded, the duo turned in tandem and faced directly toward me.

The twenty-incher pulled out from that tiny ass as it reached climax and both of the two woodland creatures' cocks showered me with more cum than a whale. At least, that was all I could compare it to. A crack of thunder struck in the midst of the milky shower and I found myself rapidly submerging in the copiously gooey fluid. It felt surreally like I was drowning. The stallion dick leaned in toward me and set to slapping me across the face, sloppy thing smearing my lips and nostrils.

So, I thought, this was it. I was butt-naked, paralyzed, drowning in a flood of cum from a mythical couple of satyristic beings in the Blue Mountains during a thunder and lightning storm with Jamaican goats in captive audience. On a coffee plantation. And the horsedick was going to slap me to kingdom come...

...“Luke,” I caught the wisp of a detached, familiar voice, raising my hopefulness that at least someone would know what had happened... the mento beat faded, overwhelmed by the Neil Young melody ‘After the Goldrush’, now rising and fanning across my subconscious. The strangest feeling of otherworldliness overtook me and I arose from the depths... “Luke...Luke...my man, wake up, honey...”

And, then, squinting an eye open a tiny slit, to avoid the shower of spewing sperm, I found both my men staring worriedly down at me from my spot on the big leather divan. Gone were the goats and the pine needles. My own fireplace crackled and popped in front of me as the receding thunderbolt rumbled away across the valley outside, beyond the safety of our Telluride Mountain home.

“Where you been, Luke...you were deep-dreamin’ something mighty big by the way you’ve been workin’ it. You OK, baby?”

I winced back and forth at the two, explaining, “I was down in Jamaica, JK, on Blue Mountain...and it was raining and there were goats and a coffee plantation and a big storm and... you were there...at least, your young self was... and so were you, Gai. And it was beautiful and scary, but I wanted to come home and I couldn’t.

Whoa, it crossed my mind, who was I...Dorothy? I looked around for Auntie Em and Toto.

“You need to get up, now, honey. Gai has been cooking and we’re servin’ up some Caribbean Chicken Delight—it’s a curried chicken mountain dish I grew up with. You’re gonna love it. Luke, my man, wake your cute ass up, now,” Jeremy kept on gently jiggling me, slapping my cheek.

Been there, done that already, I grumbled groggily… metaphysical similes and metaphors teemed.

Damn, where were those ruby slippers when you really needed 'em? Poof…

Chapter 16
Three Dog Night

Jeremiah was a most venerable bullfrog. A wily and es-teemed Catesbian greenback. The jagged white scar stretching diagonally down his back confirmed the over large specimen for who he was. Voy backed the gig away and after a moment of silent reverence, turned in search of other sources to satisfy Winnie. The shallow marshy bywater had proven a particu-larly fertile venue for which to hunt the current object of his very pregnant wife's gastronomic desires. Other Rana legs would have to grace the skillet, Voy decided, because he and the old frog had an understanding.

Two years before, the bullfrog had serendipitously leapt a path of intersection between Voy's bare leg and a pissed off copperhead. The angry snake launched a strike which would have likely caused irreparable, if not fatal, damage had the venomous fangs connected.

By sheer dumb luck, Jeremiah had somehow absorbed the bite and the venom instead. Voy managed to wield his machete and decapitate the writhing serpent but the huge frog had dropped and lain limp, quivering in certain death throes. The compassionate fisherman and river dweller had scooped the

stricken amphibian up and placed him on a flat rock in a protected corner on the off chance that he didn't die. He had
heard the lore about river frogs' resistance to poisonous excre-
tions so dangerous to warm-blooded animals and thought to
offer the critter a chance.

Months later, on a pre-dusk trout line run, the man happened upon the most humongous emerald bullfrog he had ever
seen basking in the last tippling sunbeams of an Indian summer day on the exact rock he had left him that fortuitous
morning. Though grown significantly larger, a jagged scar
adorned his dorsum, proving to Voy that Nature did, indeed,
work mysterious wonders. Human and bullfrog had communed together for a while over the shared incident from that
time before. They exchanged formal introductions under the
new, less volatile circumstances, and the name 'Jeremiah' had
lived on. Subsequent crossed paths had validated their eccentric oddity and now the two carried on in their private
understanding.

Jeremiah's legs would remain intact for the bullfrog's continued jumping pleasure...and needs. Who could say when
serendipity might strike again?

Voy's knee-high heavy rubber boots, a hunting accou-
trement since meeting the big frog, picked their way through
the bog in the hunt for the complementary half of the salt-wa-
ter taffy duo now preferred by his pretty young wife in the
gestational journey to delivery of the couple's third child. His
cut-off jeans rode up on slim hips and crotch as he stalked,
putting inadvertent pressure on the baby delivery device that
was a presently under-serviced organ.

The thick piece responded of its own volition and Voy accepted the pleasurable feeling of his phattening cohort without
either much choice, or effort, at quelling the effect. The gooey
pre-cum escaping and dribbling down his bare leg evidenced
the man's unslaked need for attention. Advanced stages of
pregnancy did little to spawn amorous exploits, as Voy well
knew. He was also aware that the big body part would receive

some proper relief in the coming hours after he finished the present labor-of-love in the quest to satisfy his baby-mama's needs. Winnie's, as it were…

Torchy Lane, his sancha-in-chief, was returning to Rome today after an extended absence on a quest of her own at the international transgender talent competition in Berlin, Germany. She came victoriously back wearing the crown of first runner-up in the overall competition to show for her own efforts. Voy would be picking up the beauty queen at the Atlanta airport in a welcome home that would service multiple purposes. Not the least of which would be the highly anticipated multi-orgasmic emancipation in that newly crowned, un-impregnable bitch's Hershey Highway. The savoring of the thought served as succor to his and his nine-inch buddy's hormonal state of fervor…

A half dozen plump pairs of frog legs later found Voy traipsing the riverbank path toward the home he and Winnie had made almost eight years before. Come to think of it, he reflected, the same year that his big brother, Cal, had first brought Dr. Jake home with him. The two had arrived as a new couple, open and vulnerable, for he and Winifred's wedding. A ceremony officially denied the two soulmates. The fact that matching sets of external plumbing rooted the reasoning baffled the hunky man.

Voy pondered the irony as he entered the solid old brick house. The hunter now cleaned the catch and cranked on the slow-cooker already prepared with the stew-makings for his adored baby-mama's discriminating taste buds. Kissing the sleepy wife and children nesting together in the big poster bed, the tall man showered to shed the smelly grime in preparation for a short drive to Hartsfield International.

The boys had magnanimously celebrated the well-planned nuptials, he remembered, carried out in the First AME Church of Rome sanctuary. With nothing but joy in their hearts for Cal's little brother, the two had avoided asserting the elephant in the room which was their quite unignorable jungle fever gay relationship bursting the seams of small town America's volatile societal psyche… right there for the whole of Rome, Georgia, to see. And judge.

While the esteemed Broadhearst family had doubled down on their joy at recognizing two additions rather than one into their family, the social fabric of the community had openly wrestled with the divisive scenario. The boys had not purposely embroiled the community in a heated public debate then bubbling the nation's conscience, yet the arrival of the unusual up-and-coming couple for a marriage celebration denied to themselves had set off a cannon-shot of controversy still lingering to the present time. The patriarchal professor and his wife had opened their arms wide to both new couples; acceptance and consternation bookended their stance in demonstrable fashion.

Voy and Winnie had tied the proverbial knot and jumped the broom just as generations of young lovers had done before them. The Limerence-smitten gay couple had hailed the union in time-honored custom without any inkling of jealousy or chagrin, not wishing to diminish the beauty of the youngest Broadhearst son's Big Day. Winnie and Voy both got this. Nevertheless, the fact remained of this real-time personification begging the existential question under tumultuous debate throughout the social order. And being argued before judicial America. The ranges of response in Rome crisscrossed the local spectrum in parallel portrayal of the broader nation.

As he reminisced on the shock of the boys' wedding gift, Voy smiled at the memory of incredulous attendees' wide-eyed looks when the brand new Lincoln Navigator had pulled to the curb outside the church as the newlyweds exited the chapel. Bedecked in the silver and lavender wedding colors, tailgate open, the sound-system rang out Beyonce's 'Put a Ring on it' while Siri broadcast the South Beach Fontainebleau Hotel wedding suite as its initial destination. The plane tickets to Barbados and secluded wedding bungalow with all the trimmings, added by the doting parents, had fulfilled a dream honeymoon which Winnie still founded her conception of the perfect wedding model upon.

Still, the naysayers had created reasons to denigrate Cal and Jake as blights on proper society. Voy wondered at the sick bitterness abiding in those hearts as he drove toward the planned rendezvous. His mindset could not wrap around the cynical notion hallowed by such people. The very ones who professed and proclaimed their Christian devotion, yet stubbornly clung to a perceived right of denying sanctuary to those not adhering with their own narrow version of a much-translated holy book. The irony of the issue playing out in the world's citadel of secular freedom, so astutely devised by the Founders, did not elude the country man.

Thinking of his own situation, Voy thanked his lucky stars to have married such a worldly and loving woman as Winnie. A woman who not only accepted Torchy Lane but actually welcomed the benefits of her existence, even blessing the transgendered woman regarding her husband's libidinous needs. The girls realized they provided and derived different advantages in the relaxed arrangement. And, TL had been instrumental in attending to Winnie's necessities during this pregnancy in her capacity as a medical professional. The fact of no worries for extramarital side pregnancies merely added to the gravid woman's ease of mind. Yes, Voy counted himself as doubly blessed for such rare indulgence. As did his middle-leg cohort.

Reaching the international arrival gate, Voy lifted his mouth in a broad smile upon viewing the hubbub surrounding the deplaning corridor doorway. A sexily adorned Atlanta Falcon cheerleader was presently wowing passers-by and flight-greeters by her arrival... The dark-haired beauty waved red and gold pom-poms in time to the musical accompaniment broadcasting from the girl's speaker-app phone device. Her dance routine brought his dick to attention--- as intended, no doubt. Finishing with a back-flip flourish to a full leg split on the concourse, similarly affected male travelers applauded the foxy vixen, little suspecting that the woman working the crowd was his own Torchy Lane.

Ahhh, yes, ironies abounded, the black stud reflected, as he pulled the woman into his arms. Most present thought he was a Falcon team member by his size and athletic physique, so the scenario satisfied many persons' fantasies without a single qualm. The levity grasped solely by the reuniting lovers was a private hoot.

Just as they came up for a breath, a hand on Voy's shoulder pulled him around to the beaming visage of his big brother, Cal. Jake flashed a grin from a few feet away and the four greeted like long-lost war pals in the coincidental encounter. Cal and Jake had come to meet their best friends, Luke and Jeremy, in from the high country of Colorado for a week. The four bosom buddies, best men in each other's recent SSM highland ceremonies several months past, were consummating a pre-planned get together.

The friends of Cal's stood to the side, marveling at the impromptu dance show just experienced. After the six introduced to each other, all made their way to baggage claim for collection of the travelers' things. The small entourage created a kerfuffle amongst many on the way through the airport complex, deeming the three hunky men-of-color to be professional athletes whose names they couldn't quite assign.

Convoying to Rome, the three couples stopped for afternoon dinner at La Scala Bistro. Jeremy and Luke had enjoyed the unexpected spontaneous welcome, Voy and Torchy providing a big city vibe to the small municipality by their bohemian style. The stories of the Berlin beauty contest supplied side-splitting anecdotal fodder. Multitudes of transgendered beauty contestants from around the world made for an hilarious range of entanglements. On top of a Telluride Hallowe'en Bash story mixed together with the Austin antics of the four men, the restaurant flavor became imbued by ribaldry uncommon for the regular clientele. The atmosphere loosened into a Chaucerian merriment and table-to-table communications opened up. The typically quiet bistro filled with the tourist-laden post-holiday crowds strolling outside as the atmosphere infected the streets. The establishment's wine stocks were stretched.

Following the fifth shared bottle of vintage pinot noir, Torchy Lane was practically performing on the tables for the eatery patrons and by the time Jeremy was divulging the raucous ending to an Austin Juneteenth celebration, the entire restaurant populace, from management to staff to patrons, were leaning in for the next re-enactment of the comical stories like an E.F. Hutton commercial…

One elder gentleman fell out of his seat trying to hear Luke tell one episode from Telluride involving an English Lady and her chauffer, while a young long-tressed woman leaned a smidgeon too far over her table's candle, inciting a minor disturbance while squelching the hair-on-fire consequence.

Two hours later, the manager approached them as the six were settling with their wait staff. He informed Cal, the host of the dinner, that there would be no charge for their dinner party. It seemed that the owner had been eating a couple of tables over and seen the camaraderie plus the boosted business brought by the enlivening group. Upon his instruction, the manager let the six know that the eatery couldn't have hired better entertainment or PR so the early evening was on the house if Cal's guests were OK with that... Torchy's streak continued.

"Well, Jake, you do remember that the third week in February is the annual 'Telluride Gay Ski Week Festival', right?" Luke was remonstrating with his friend about joining him and Jeremy soon on the mountain. "And you two need to meet Ambergai and Bryce," he continued. Luke's friends Gai as well as Adolpho and Bryce were holding down the log home during JK's and his visit downland. Luke was excited to introduce them all. The Ski Week Festival would be perfect, if Cal and he could pull away.

"Cal is inaugurating a new location in Seattle around then," Jake replied, "so if you and I can extend our sabbaticals, then it may be golden." He could talk just about anyone into anything, so I knew Cal and the Brack Admin office would be pushovers.

We were lounging on the veranda sharing a joint after saying 'so long' to TL and Voy a bit earlier. Jeremy was picking Cal's brain on something business-oriented upstairs and the cute kids, Viv and Boy, had departed with Sophie back to their riverside home to spend the night in a slumber party with their mom, Winnie. I planned on getting a feel for country living from my homeboys' perspective for the week here in Georgia and so far we had been pleasantly surprised. Who would've thought that Rome, Georgia, home-based someone the likes of the transgendered lady, I thought.

The evening was misty but mild, a tropical system pushing warmth from the gulf over us in contrast to the major winter weather hitting the northeast. We had discarded coats and heavy clothes upon unpacking. Jeremy and I were happy to get comfortable in next to nothing here the middle of January. Following Cal and Jake's example, basic baggie shorts were the norm by our observations. What a difference from the constant heavy clothing we wore outside in the upland reaches.

As we traded tokes, I heard a screen door slam close by and noted Jake turn toward the neighboring farmhouse a hundred yards to the east. As I followed his gaze, there appeared an ebony Chippendale-of-a-man from around the corner. He was easily assessed for the well-built feature as the man wore only cross-trainers. His huge uncut dick was lolling back and forth with each step and he had slung a piece of clothing over one shoulder. He grinned upon spotting us and headed over.

"That is Doy Al, one of Cal's little brothers," informed Jake, "and he looks like he's just been talkin' with old Farmer Brown." Curious observation, I thought.

Six foot and at least five inches in height, the term 'little' was not an adjective first in my mind for describing the approaching nudist, especially in light of the piece wobbling in front of him. The thing looked 'just-used' and seemed to be still saying so by the pearl presently budding from the tip. I was now beginning to put ideas to pictures as Jake's descriptions of the Broadhearst brotherhood came a 'little' more into focus. Voy had proven every bit as drop-dead gorgeous as Cal, and I felt a familiar warming in my groin in passing the blunt over while assessing this member.

"Doy can be kind of aloof when you first meet him, but he and I got past that pretty well after a bit. You'll like him, Luke." Jake's descriptive terms were befuddling. Aloof? The ripped Doy reached us and inadvertently--- I think--- flicked his handsome dick upon stopping within a foot of our seated faces. At that, the goo dribbled from the partially cowled tip and I almost lurched forward to tongue it in mid-air. The thought seemed to be read by the young man.

"Jake dude, I see you done multiplied, now, white boy," he eyed me while voicing the idea so regularly noted when we were together. While the Broadhearst brood were cloned in their looks, Jake and I were similarly brown haired with ringlet curls, mine darker than his auburn ones. The two of us both sported leanly tanned frames, kept in shape by regular exercise.

Our hungness was recognized readily amongst other Anglo males, but in the company of our black husbands we were smaller by inches in both length and girth. 'Hung for a white boy' was the typical adage we heard from them... and definitely OK by us both. Tan lines were kept intact most of the year, so tight white buns provided the easy targets known to turn our mens' eyes. We played the fact to the fullest. Doy went on, "So's, wassup, Doc?" As he motioned for the blunt.

Bending a few inches closer to reach for it, the boy stood back up straight and sucked in a toke as he made sure the thickness sidled close enough for a Tallulah Bankhead inspection. "Doy, this is my best friend, Luke Cevennes; Luke, meet Doy Broadhearst," Jake grinned knowingly at the proximity-baiting by the horndog brother, "He and his husband are in town from Colorado for some Georgia hospitality this week."

It was all I could do to keep from kneeing the deck and swallowing the thing whole. "It's nice to meet you, Doy. Anyone tell you that you're the spittin' image of your big Bro?" I smiled in attempted distraction by wit.

Doy smirked through the in-taken breath and reached up to the wet piece of clothing over his shoulder. It looked to be an undershirt and it crossed my mind to wonder where might be the plainly missing shorts surely going with it...or the drawers. He used the cloth to deliberately wipe over the now thickening piece within inches of my face and Jake wise-cracked, "Luke, this is the shy brother, so don't worry if he seems that way at first."

To which Doy grinned over at him, dropping the cloth to the ground. He exhaled the toke directly into my face and handed Jake the roach. The dick waggled and rose some more. Pointing at me. "Don't seems like I be the shy one right at the moment, Dr. J, not with this here big'un trying--- real hard--- to say 'hello', and yo' boy just ignorin' him like this." With that, the boy rotated his slim black hips and the schlong smacked my cheek.

That was plenty enough of a hint, so I overcame my wariness by forced reaction. Opening my lips, I glanced at Jake and mouthed the turgid beast so visibly attempting familiarization. Jake rose, now, and passed the young stud a power hit. Purposely sucking face very slowly in the passing, he used his fingers to check out Doy's and my connection. He fondled the filling shaft as it slid in and out of my mouth and Doy reached down to free my own straining dick. Within just a moment, we were all comfortably as nude as Doy, only shoes obscuring any anatomy. For now, I wasn't worrying about feet.

My hands came up and cupped the hardness of the round sable cakes backing the crotch I was nuzzling and I fed off the suckling sounds from above me as I acquainted with Jake's bro-in-law. The two seemed already at ease with each other, their hands wandering freely. I concentrated on the blooming cobra, comparing it favorably with my Jeremy's package. It was more upwardly curved, I noted. The thing strained mightily all of a sudden, letting loose a fast creamy load right down my ready throat as Jake tried catching the overflow. He no doubt was aware of the prolific nature of Broadhearst men and also knew how sharing I could be.

Sure enough, the excess was split between Jake and Doy's lip connection and his asshole, so I pretty much guessed what might be coming next. The moment of speculation didn't last long. Doy turned Jake around and bent him over the deck chair. He spat on the proffered hole for added slipperiness, then glanced my way as he was plugging the chute and let me know what he thought of my introduction.

"Boy--- Luke, is it?--- you done right good for a starter-off. I'm a gonna hafta get into a little bit o' my brolaw's asspussy now, should you wanna get that roach lit up again. Bet you and me might have something to talk over while I's busy."

So, we switched gears and I sucked face between hits while Jake enjoyed some fatness hardening right inside of him. Doy told me about how much a whore Jake had proven himself over the last three months. "We can NOT seem t'be able to keep this bitch happy 'nuf, dude. Ever time one of us turn around, he be backin' up on one o'us just like this here." Slapping the pretty white globes, he set a rhythm, and sank his muscly tongue all into my mouth to make plain I needn't reply…just think on it.

His hand kept busy sizing up my hard piece and his mumbles into my mouth confused me as to whether he was complimenting Jake's ass or my 'big-for-a-whiteboy' cock. Either way, within minutes, the trio of endowments produced more loads of sperm to slime the deck and the boinked orifice. Jake stroked himself in time to the top boy dicking, spewing stuff all over my leg, too. The two of us knew each other that well, so it was all good.

Temporarily sated, we stayed still for a few moments. Doy promised us both of the coming feast the other brothers were going to be having on the twosome of white asses now populating the homestead. "Luke, boi, you gonna be a damn good rival ho' for Jake Man." I was reminded by Jake of the double set of twins in the family and actually took compliment by the 'ho' comparison.

While we pulled it together, Cal called from an upper window, "Damn, you boys done goin' for broke already—we'll be right down. Bitches." Two upstairs Cheshire cat grins bounded down the stairway.

* * *

"Don't the amenities in our city parks just keep improving with each passing year, now, young man?" The slim white-haired elderly woman oozed cougar sultriness as she approached the delectably clothed buns so handsomely depicted through the walking shorts attempting to disguise the hard roundness Luke awakened beside each and every morning of his adult life. The errant fly ball had tagged him in the ass just moments before as he tied a bouquet of Happy Birthday helium balloons to the picnic table. Surprising the Austinite, Jeremy had jumped and twirled in surprise at the goosing, landing like a lynx, on the balls of his feet, facing the direction of the intrusion.

Luke watched, amused, as the interaction played out across the outdoor pavilion, aware of the effect his husband engendered in so many of the people he encountered. The muscle shirt covering the torso above the hard butt complemented the figure by its form-fitting style. Cat-like agility inherent to his kinesics frosted the cake in a way that fed the fancy of any person remotely in touch with their sensual side. Indeed, the unpretentious acrobatics displayed in this meeting presented JKell's erogeneity to its fullest.

The elegant older woman did not miss the litheness and obviously wasn't shy in expressing her round-about regard for it. "Why, thank you, young Sir, for saving this damsel-in-distress in her hour of need," she flirted. Sounds of excited chagrin erupted behind her on the softball field from where she had come. Frenzied appeals hounded the woman who had slowed down from the chase-mode to ogle the studly features. Her retrieval of the long fly ball off the bat of the rapidly advancing hitter now rounding first base was thwarting the ballgame's continuity. The crowd of retiree players and spectators contrastingly encouraged and discouraged the sidetracked left fielder. 'What game?' seemed to be her dreamy perspective by Jeremy's unintended involvement.

My man jogged the ball to the woman, junk noticeably bouncing underneath the drawerless shorts he sported. The focus of the woman further deviated from the ballgame. He underhanded the errant missile to her when he was within a few feet but the lady allowed the toss to hit and drop from her glove in further mock distress, obviously hoping for more athleticism by the beguiling beefcake. Not disappointing her, he leaned down and retrieved it once again. Raising up with a knowing grin, he placed the ball into the awkwardly extended glove.

"It appears your game has been saved by my backstop, ma'am," Jeremy jested, referring to the interference afforded by his hard butt, "I hope the deflection isn't graded a natural hazard by the ump, or else you may just be allowing an inside-the-park homer over there." He pointed toward the fast advancing base-runner. The crowd was vociferous in its divided insistence for action.

Seeing the woman's hesitation, Jeremy abruptly grabbed the ball back from the glove and in a roundhouse wind-up, he hoisted it toward home plate. As everyone followed its course, the heave line-drived in a perfectly targeted strike, smacking into the waiting catcher's mitt just as the runner entered a slide into the final base. A pause in the noise expressed the crowd's disbelief in the precise throw, then, a collective cry arose as the ump signaled, "He's OUT!"

"Why, you truly are just the very embodiment of chivalry, young Sir," the lady emphasized the second syllable of the four-course word as she scrutinized the man-of-color in more detail. She exuded flawless southern charm by her inflection and deportment. Jeremy, always impressed by good manners, fairly bowed to the woman. Toward the distant applauding crowd, he evinced just the right mix of charisma and hand-tipping cockiness to maintain his reputation.

As he did this, another sock to the derriere impacted him. An unseen projectile launched from the approaching form that was Calumet. The taller and slightly darker stud had seen enough of the previous encounter to conclude the need for some neutralizing of his closest friend's bravado. The basketball piñata had been readily available. It was as precise as the home plate strike. Jeremy jumped once again and turned to address yet another butt striker.

Acknowledging his best man with a smirk brought the two into the aristocratic woman's view together. She double-took at the doppelganger appearing out of nowhere. "My, my, this must be a Doublemint commercial." Back and forth went her eyes in absorbing the two men. She was clearly a discriminating woman in her taste for tall, dark and handsome, by her expression.

Luke snickered again as he drew closer. "Honey, you have just got to stop interrupting people like this. Just look at how the game and the party are being derailed by your big ole' self?" Approaching the fascinated woman, he extended a hand, "Good afternoon, ma'am, I am Luke, and this is my better half, Jeremy. And, over there is our best friend, Cal."

She remastered her patrician wits and accepted the proffered hand, "Very nice to meet you, Luke. I must say, you certainly have exquisite taste in men." She shook both of their hands. "I am Evelyn and seem to be in the middle of mixing up several different circumstances all at once." She looked over her shoulder at the deserted game, finally apprehending her need to get back. "I would love to stay and chat but really must get over to my game before I am ejected, or whatever penalty one accrues under such instances." She retracted her hand gracefully, smiled all around and begged to redeem herself after the game ended, if we would allow her the chance.

With that, she turned and trotted away. Cal ribbed Jeremy about his recurring theme of drawing attention as we continued our preparations for the birthday celebration in the hours ahead. Several trips of delivered goods and decorations sat haphazardly around the open pavilion, evidencing the progress unfolding for the eighth birthday party of Cal's mercurial nephew, Boy. Others were pulling in to the adjacent parking area as we laughed at the antics just witnessed and several more of the Broadhearst family contingent added to the cacophony of efforts for the upcoming fun.

Sophie arrived, trunk and backseat filled with freshly prepared hors d'oeuvres, hot dishes, iced sides, more balloons and accessories. Additional brothers drove up, all carrying something for the shindig. Over the ensuing hour the pavilion transformed into a spectacle of birthday revelry with forty or so family members and friends aiding in the groundworks. The plan was for Winnie and Voy to arrive with Viv, and the Birthday Boy, once all was readied, in a ploy to surprise the youngster at the park where the kids commonly played throughout the year.

Situated along the Etowah River, not too distant from the Broadhearst home, Etowah Park provided playgrounds, hiking trails, sports fields and greenspaces, besides outdoor cooking and activities facilities perfect for such events. He would little suspect what was unfolding as mom, dad and sis brought him to an outing recurrent for them. The big get-together allowed not only an opportunity for the birthday, but also for the family to gather, and a welcoming venue for Luke and Jeremy to their hometown. The sunny January afternoon promised to augment the festivities.

Festooning crepe streamers, gobs of bunched helium balloons, a big draping banner proclaiming the eighth birthday, a horseshoe pit and volleyball net readied, as well as several other game set-ups with musical accoutrements in the background finally found everyone prepped and in wait for the little guest of honor. Sure enough, the minivan showed up in response to Sophie's text and the party was on.

Viv led her big brother out of the car, basketball under his arm. Wide eyes demonstrated success at catching the youngster unawares. The exuberant kid raced from one spot and group to the next in excitement as he deduced his center-of-attention status. Ending up viewing all from the height of Uncle Cal's shoulders, the celebration was officially kicked off by Loy and Roy's appearance with a colorful three layer, candle-blazing cake and totally off-key rendition of the generations-old salute recently freed from copyright constraint, 'Happy Birthday to him'. The Boy basked.

Three hours later, Boyden Alfrederic sat at a picnic table stuffing his bare little belly with a third piece of cake. Gifts, games and indulgence had swamped him during that time. The boy quietly contemplated some new expectations now facing him by attainment of the eight-year mark in Life, as described by his daddy, Voy. Uncommon thoughtful behavior arose from the man-to-man talk of the previous evening. He had been counseled of the need to look out for his little sis, Vivian. By the new baby's appearance, more responsibility would necessarily fall upon him, the older brother. Importance of a new mission had been driven home by comparison of his position to favorite uncle Cal's at the same age. Overnight, Boy's imagination had dreamt of chivalric daring-do in fending off imagined threats and dangers. Momentarily left alone at the big party, the little big man now conjured some very mature notions.

Just then, a cold gust of air blustered through the tree-studded park. His tiny nipples stood up at the stimulus and he shivered. Winnie came up behind him, thrusting a warm sweatshirt over his torso. The bemusement was interrupted. "Boyden," intoning his formal name and pulling sleeves into place, "the cold spell is settin' in and we need to batten down everything—can you look around for me and gather up things that might blow away, honey child?" The tyke swallowed the last bite of scrumptious sweetness and responded by doing just that. His first assignment. As everyone scurried about, Boy scanned to the edge of the pavilion for carrying out the grownup task.

As the little guy busied himself, focus was disturbed when he heard, then saw, the first of a procession of trucks curving through the distant entranceway. A pole protruding up from the lead truck's bed boasted a huge red flag crossed by a large blue 'X' emblazoned with small white stars. The boy was perplexed and registered a bad feeling about it.

A man and woman stood in the bed with hands on the pole; the man zeroed in and pointed toward the pavilion crowd. Behind the vanguard vehicle came a couple dozen more similarly swathed ones. The line entered, announcing themselves with a dissonance of horn-blaring. One specially-equipped vehicle played a tinny rendition of "Way down South in Dixie". The many people enjoying the park looked up to visualize the noisy entourage. In the distant reaches, from the sports parks and trails, alarm bells were registering this uglier edge of the 21st century. A rejuvenated throw-back mentality had arisen over the American South as the political climate skirted further away from the robust middle America known over the previous progressive decades.

The Broadhearst family quickly grasped the potential danger. They began a virtual wagon-circling effort, as did other groups using the park. Cold northerly winds heralded the change in aura. Roiling thunderheads appeared from nowhere, harsh new sounds replacing the previous friendly atmosphere. A chill enveloped the area and people bundled on warmer clothing, staring toward the parade of acrimonious honkers. Others battened down multiple different levels of 'hatches' deemed suddenly prudent. All six Broadhearst brothers, other cousins, several of the women and Jeremy plus Luke and Jake, all protectively cordoned the on-comers from the partiers.

Little Boyden Alfrederic was overlooked in the clamor. On the fringe and around a corner from the party area, the boy was closest to the raucous truckers. He stood openmouthed as the troupe drew up to his position. "Hey, boys, look here at the little monkey," the front man of the group hearkened back at his cronies. "Looks like he be stragglin' through our park here and needin' some discipline for bein' where he ain't wanted, huh?" His piercing voice cut through the wind now whisking debris all around. A collective grumble arose as the following trucks pulled up to the curb where Boy stood, hypnotized by the ascendant hate-filled tone.

A bare-chested Calumet broke from his shock at the bluster, recognizing the youngster's vulnerable position. He galloped to the spot in a flash, scooped up the nephew and backed away toward the pavilion as more rancorous rhetoric cut through him.

"Well, now, lookee here, a big ole' man-monkey done swooped in to save the french-fry, ain't it so?" The man chortled in condescension as he sized up his perceived advantage in the encounter. Several other discordant voices cackled adjuncts to their leader's insults and the horns all blew again, in unison, as the multiple Dixie flags whipped spitefully in the blitzing wind. "Ain't he just a sight, naked and showing ever-thin' to anyone who's fool 'nuf to be a-lookin' at his big ape self?" Cal was taken aback by the deluge of vituperation. He and Boy retreated wordlessly backward, confounded in the face of such unexpected hatefulness.

The line of brothers and others hastened forward now. To a man, still in shorts and shirtless from the volleyball game. The women-folk, to a person, all thinly fit and toned, wore fashionable sports gear. They projected a collective glow of good health, and were unafraid to show it. This sight set the flag wavers into a further tizzy. An epithet-ridden maelstrom cold-cocked the family and friends in a bewildering verbal assault.

Calumet was, again, the first to regain his senses. Putting the boy into his pregnant mother's arms, he then turned to address the 'murder of crows'. "Etowah is a public park, sir, and this is a private, peaceful family gathering. I am unsure as to what we might all owe such insulting behavior, but we would appreciate it greatly if you would exhibit your antagonism elsewhere. We want no problems here." The eldest son of the late Professor Broadhearst projected an articulate intellectualism toward the group that couldn't be missed. His self-control held the family in check.

"So's, we Sons-of-Liberty just gonna hafta pack up an' leave cuz' you bunch o' pic-a-ninnies tellin' us to?" The reply was backed up by continued catcalling. Jeremy and Luke noted the ominous appearance of several uncovered long guns and pistols. The ante was raised in the confrontation. "All's we's doin' is an exhibition of our first--- and second--- amendment rights rightchere in a public venue, now, mandingo-man, and I don' reckon we gonna be kowtowed by the likes o' you and your kind, ya' thinkin?" The level of baseness was as callous as the display. The entire party group drew closer in a protective ring at the sight of the firearm effrontery. One jackass hoisted a shotgun up and under his arm, pointing it loosely in the family's direction. Hackles arose throughout the alarmed group. Insinuations and invectives were now quickly ratcheting up to physical threat level. They recognized that all bets were off in the face of such an escalation.

Shoulder-to-broad-shoulder now, the bravery of the harassed group was plain. The scraggly bleach-blond woman in the first truck now shrieked her own thoughts at the tall protective wall of ripped brothers. "So, you bunch a' naked heathens and sharia-law lovers think you's bein' all high an' mighty, protectin' all the offsprings an' wenches from the God-fearin' folk o' Rome, do ya?" Her shrillness sent further chills through the crowd. More park-goers were now gathering up to the rear of the surrounded family. Unsure now whether they were being assailed from multiple flanks, an entire ring of adults joined arms around the children and older members. The skies darkened.

"Looks like ya'll hooters are jus' about to be taught a overdue lesson by the good folk of this here community," growled the front man in the truck. He smugly surmised that a race-based clash was shaping up, per palpable intent, and was going to maximize his perceived supremacy. Several more of the truckers now raised their own weapons toward the unarmed park-goers.

Suddenly, a white-haired woman of aristocratic bearing slipped around the edge of the Broadhearst brothers, patting Cal's arm as she passed. "Well, I never thought I would see the day when the likes of you, Odell Rush, or you, Theresa Buckner, would exhibit the absolute idiocy to incite a riot right here in your own hometown, but it is apparent that this woman couldn't be more mistaken, now, could I?" She hiked up her resolute shoulders, cocked her lightning-bolting eyes at the ragged ruffians in Dixie outfits and planted her feet in a stance evincing immense gravitas. "You two miscreants need to turn your cowardly tails right around and head back under the rocks from which you have sprung."

The lady was enraged, but her mannered delivery cut quietly though the listeners over even the shrieks of the wind. When the several pointing gun-toters didn't lower their weapons post-haste, multiple more elderly white ball-players and exercise addicts emerged to amass in front of the beleaguered family-of-color. "Odell, you and Theresa and you, back there, Hiram Belchnor, all of your crowd need to be thinking of what this imbecilic commotion may be provoking here and now. There are police officers and a SWAT team alerted and approaching Etowah Park as I speak. Your options are already slim, young man, and all of you are readily identifiable to law enforcement. Are you actually considering the scenario you seem to be doing? Menacing unarmed, upstanding, innocent citizenry, of all hues and ethnicities, in some misguided Klan-like foray sure to end badly for all of you?"

She wasn't yet peaked in her anger. The ex-lady mayor of Rome, Evelyn Leigh, was ready to smack the smugness from the faces of the vile rabble threatening all before them. Stepping back to stand beside Sophie Broadhearst and Cal, she wedged between the two and locked arms with them. One by one, the elders from the softball game and the crowd of spectators all moved in synchrony. Within seconds, a united front of the strong-willed persons represented an awakened and infuriated portion of Rome, Georgia.

Though a bit nonplussed, Odell Rush still unashamedly waved his arm in an arc behind him, egging the truckers to double-down on their antics. "Ma'am, we ain't but exercisin' our God-given rights by organizin' agin' all the corruption and anti-American activities goin' on at this here public park. We ain't gonna be reduced to second-class citizens by the underminin' o' our history an' legacy which we fully intend ta' uphold to the fullest. We ain't breakin' laws but these here darkies sho'nuf be pullin' our great country apart at the seams. So, none o' your nasty insults are gonna be makin' this group of patriots do anything but continue in our mission to save God and America." The guns raised a bit higher after having temporarily wilted under her honor's tongue-lashing.

As the stand-off continued, unarmed people stood solid in the face of armed and unruly, nasty-mouthed malcontents. Ms.

Leigh once again demanded the hooligans disperse. Only upon the sound of approaching sirens did any disintegration occur. One by one, the guns sank, shoulders drooped and against the nasal railing by both Odell and the woman with him to stand their ground, the group fractured and turned tails, slinking away before the law contingent arrived. Even Mr. Rush finally left the scene, maliciously promising the episode hadn't seen its end yet.

Multiple videos taken during the ordeal spelled out the methods employed in the bullying assault. Police and SWAT team members promised to examine all evidence. Proper action would be forthcoming, they vowed.

With everyone milling around after the brouhaha, the former mayor apologized publicly to the Broadhearst brotherhood and family in her earnest attempt to impress the party of the goodwill throughout the city for every resident and guest. The conviviality, however, had been broken. In the light of the weather change, all decided it best to pack up, clean the sites and head to home.

Voy reassured the trepidated birthday boy of the overall good nature of people. The worthy father counseled his son not to take away the negative from the scene, rather to focus on the way so many came together in their defense and for the common good. The man was privately incensed by the insults heaped upon his little boy and family. Three generations of Broadhearsts had established deep roots of respectable members.

His heart was hurt by the sordid spectacle.

* * *

"Well, Doc Jake, you shoulda seen the door," TL's voice had raised to an octave above its norm. My questioning look seemed likely to push it higher still.

"What does that mean...the door?" I queried, now truly confused. "You just said that the windshield was cracked and the glass hit your eyebrow. Now, excuse my density, TL, but which was it…the door window or the windshield that shattered?" My perplexed bearing was nothing really new when it came to the orderly, what with the serpentine life the young man lived. Or young woman. Depending on the time and day.

"No, the door window wasn't broken. It was rolled down. At least I think it was---the gross-outs yelled at us when we hit, so, yeah, it had to have been down. Had to have been the windshield shard that hit me," he seemed certain of the fact, lying back on the exam table as he was.

"Let me get this straight, TL," as I took another stitch in the freshly debrided and curettaged gash following the exact curve of the previously perfect brow line. It wouldn't be from here on, but if it healed well the scarring should be minimal, I anticipated, "the windshield shattered after you crashed into this truck on Mockingbird and Vine at 3 AM, Sunday morning--- a few hours ago--- and the driver was so drunk he didn't know what happened? And then you and Samuel drove away?" This all sounded dangerous and unlawful and I wasn't at all certain I wanted the details. But I did.

"Not exactly," he winced as I placed another suture, "The drunk was the one who hit us, Doc, and it was on Third and Main. And, it was 2:45 AM, right after leaving 'Jugs'. We only got a block when the idioto came outta nowhere and bashed in the driver's door. But it hit so hard that it dragged the door all the way off. It stuck on his truck and he took off without stopping…the thing was caught on his grill and he left with it."

This was getting interesting. I kept my mouth shut. He wouldn't be able to hold it in anyway and I would get the whole story quicker. The man was a true talker…and I could easily claim 'doctor confidentiality privilege'.

Sure enough, he went on, "We were scared the cops would stop us, no door and all. Samuel was drunk, too; we traded places, me driving. I kept to the side streets but we wanted the door back. I knew if the cops stopped him, especially with that door on his grill, we would all be in trouble. So I drove in circles, Doc, gradually bigger, thinking if the coot was that bad off we might come across him and could get it. We figured out he was still downtown, by the river, when we passed him going down Vine Street--- the wrong way. I waved when they passed and he saw us. The dopes made a circle around a block and came at us again. This time they were tryin' to ram us and when he came around the last corner, he was goin' so fast that he missed and we got sideswiped and the damn door flew off and hit our windshield. That's how I got cut," he smirked smugly in the middle of another wince as the next suture pulled through.

"So what happened to the drunk idiot?" I couldn't help asking.

Hell, the last we saw, the two of 'em went over the riverfront embankment and were sinking in the water with the motor racin'. Shit, I thought it was gonna blow up or somethin'. Both of 'em were hollerin' out the windows. We had our door wedged through our car windshield by then, so I called 911 on my burner phone and told 'em. I'm guessin' they got pulled out…at least we heard the sirens. I kept away. Took Samuel home and stayed there until an hour ago when I came here," matter-of-factly, like it happened all the time.

"You put on the steri-strips?" was my next obvious question; the response anything but.

"After I cleaned and flushed the cut, they fit just fine and held the gap closed. I keep some in my clutch. They hold my prick out o' the way while I'm performing and work better than a truss… I hate those damn trusses, anyway. Y'know how binding those things are, Doc."

"So, you used an inverted Lembert suture on an unsedated eyebrow, Jake?" Luke was interested in more than just the looney tale about TL's escapade a few hours before. He had dropped in at the Rome Clinic to see where I pro-bono'd sometimes and we were discussing cases. Cal and Jeremy were over to the police department filing depositions on Saturday's fiasco which ended the birthday party. Luke had given his already and walked to the clinic since it was only a few blocks. We sat in the break room, laughing over the transgender woman's story.

"Luke, I was afraid to infiltrate that oculomotor branch of the trigeminal nerve any more than I had. You know how persnickety that thing can react sometimes. It could have effected paresis. When I told her that, she said go ahead with just a partial block. She is stoic, now, gotta admit." I was respectful of TL's decision. The rest of the story…well, not so much. Luke agreed.

"That story is crazy, Jake. Do you think it'll come back on her and Mr. Hodge?" he was genuinely concerned for the fall-out after hearing of the harrowing tale and was fairly astounded, yet again, by the volatile political dynamic being encountered in Smalltown, USA, down here in the lowlands. Then, he reminded himself of the Rasta murders up on the mountain and mentally reassessed: crazy happened everywhere these days, he thought.

Jake was worried, as well, but the latest mess involving the park clash held pre-eminence as the foremost concern. The latest 'Torchy story' was more comic relief than serious, he figured. The police chief was a good guy and would listen to Torchy's side if it came down to that. "I think it will probably all work out OK, Luke. But I am wondering how Samuel is going to get his doorless truck through town to the body shop. Torchy will probably need to stage a decoy drag parade somewhere to distract attention, or something." I snickered at the mental picture.

Their men walked in the door at that moment and the white-boy doctors smiled together at the two. For a small community, a good portion of Rome had reacted in admirably cosmopolitan fashion toward the duos. The general acceptance of the unusual jungle fever marriages, while jolting to a certain segment, was not causing as much concern as had been feared. With exceptions such as the weekend Dixie flag truck rally, notwithstanding. Crazy did, indeed, happen everywhere. Big cities were experiencing some right wing backlash, as well.

Cal seemed more upbeat, now, as he walked in. The two had been allowed through the nursing station checkpoint by the nursing staff. What with Jeremy's accompaniment, the nurses were abuzz by the Magic Mike element and we could hear tittering outside the door from the feminine staff members.

"Jake, you are not going to believe the news we just got at the PD just now," the tall man gushed. "There apparently was a mess of an auto accident early this morning and guess who was fished out of the River at O-dark-thirty today?" His grin expressed a lot, but the mention of river and fishing brought Luke and Jake to attention.

"Seems that less-than-respectable Citizen Rush and his buddy, Citizen Belchnor, of late great low-rent park notoriety, were booked on DUI's and resisting arrest for involvement in multiple hit-and-run accidents after leaving a well-known drag bar... our plot thickens," he was ebullient at the weird events indirectly related to Jeremy and him, overheard as they had finished up depositions.

The doctors exchanged knowing glances, which Jeremy picked up on. "OK, you two, what's up, now?" he demanded, well aware of our conspiratorial penchants. "I've seen that look before. Spill it." He wasn't fooled a bit by the pair.

Checking out the door for eavesdroppers, the two hesitantly related the cliffnotes version of medical treatment for a certain transgender person just vacating the premises. Her summary of the preceding events, which the husbands now knew from this different perspective, provided fodder for conversation best saved for other environs. The Starbucks down the street found the four comparing more details a half hour later.

"At this point, we know that charges have been filed against the reprobates. Odell is apparently in not-so-good shape by the descriptions from Detective Lusk a little while ago. He suffered a few cracked ribs and a dislocated shoulder in the wrecks. Along with that, he was so drunkenly incoherent in front of the night magistrate that he was taken under guard to County General for treatment and observation, instead of lock-up. Hiram Belchnor is screaming civil-rights violations out his ass for police maltreatment and false arrest, even though he wasn't scratched.... He has lawyered up and is filing charges. Isn't that rich?" Cal went on, adding that Hiram's ridiculous actions had prompted him to file his own charges over the Etowah Park incident. So with the ongoing saga, separate cases were presently pending. We debated how to proceed in light of the fleshed-out information.

Finally deciding discretion was the best tack for the time being, we headed toward the house to check on the rest of the family. Curving around a bend a few miles from the home-stead, we came upon a truck on the opposite shoulder of the road, listing on three wheels, a fourth clearly flat and non-functional. As we approached, Jeremy slowed the Benz.

The woman leaning on the fender raised expectantly, thumb up, in request for assistance. Cal and Jake put face to name when she came into eye view: Theresa Buckner, the split-end bleach blond wizened shrew from the park episode. A tail-tucked yellow dog shivered off to her side, tethered on a stake in the ground, looking for all the world like a wayward waif. A badly emaciated animal, its sad eyes focused on us dully, evincing a lost look of resignation.

"Cal, we have to stop, baby, if nothing more than to help the dog," Jake was a soft touch for animals and the two white boys ganged up on their men to pull over. The Buckner woman looked hopeful until we pulled close enough for her to delineate two black men in the front seat. That was enough to change her expression from hopeful to derisive. Nevertheless, Jake emerged onto the opposite shoulder across from the banged-up, broken down vehicle.

Not a word was spoken at first. Jake took in the scene, siz-ing up the problems. The skinny dog immediately recognized a friend by the man's aura and whined a greeting, pawing the air from the tethered spot in the wet and muddy roadside. The scrawny, wrinkled woman turned and cursed at the animal. When the whining persisted, she chunked a palm-sized rock at it. The sharp projectile struck the poor thing in the prominent ribs. A yip of pain erupted from a gravelly throat. With her crusty eyes and nose, horribly matted coat and visible skin lesions, it all proved too much for Jake. He approached the beaten beast and crouched before it, holding out a palm. After cowering in expectation of another blow that didn't materialize, the long nose sniffed the new person in half-hopefulness. A tiny, hesitant tail wag acknowledged the possibly benevolent figure and the dog nosed the hand.

"Get away from ma' dog, you trash," the woman issued the ugly, hoarse command at Jake. She snorted like a hyena, clearing a congested throat, "I said, get away from ma' dog. That there is ma' property an' it'll bite your ass soon as lick it. Damn well, I ain't gonna pay for nuttin' if'n the old bitch lights into your ass--- get away!" she ranted.

Jake patted the friendly head of the forlorn beast, then raised up and turned toward the woman. Without a word, he went over to the stake, uprooted it in one motion, returned to the matted dog and removed the constricted collar. He looked purposely at the spiteful hag, then hurled the entire chain contraption into the muddy adjoining field. Still wordless, the young doctor herded the responsive dog toward the Benz, opened the back door and issued a hand signal for the dog to enter. She jumped right up into the plush leather interior, landing on a surprised Luke. The mud-encrusted mutt liked the aura from this potential friend, too. She was still apprehensive but extended a friendly paw again, in a hopeful hello.

"What the fuck---?" squawked the grizzled, badly aging woman. She was slow in arising from the fender she leaned against, reflexes clearly sluggish from alcohol or drugs. Or both. Jake next motioned for Cal to help him. Exiting the driver's seat, the big man-of-color joined in a short pow-wow by the Benz' back bumper. The woman strode halfway across the blacktopped road, rambling in both her steps and her speech. Potentially dangerous in her mentally compromised state, the two men kept a peripheral eye on the hag as they removed jack and crowbar from their trunk, then together approached the flat tire on the rear axle of the truck.

The ugly woman continued a nasty tirade at the biracial couple. The men persisted in ignoring the epithet-laced tirade. The two Austinites, still in the car, worriedly watched the scenario but settled the cur on a blanket from the trunk, offered by Jake in passing.

Working efficiently, the boys quickly blocked the other wheels for stability, jacked up the truck's frame and proceeded to change the bad tire for the spare they found lying in the bed of the truck. Bald though it was, the spare was mostly inflated. After tightening lug bolts, the pair dismantled the jack, removed the rock tire-blocks and replaced the assemblage to the Benz' trunk space.

The crude-spoken Theresa never diminished in her abusive barrage throughout the effort, still focusing on the now ecstatic dog lost to the sanctity and safety of Luke's care. Not one of the men ever said a word to the person excoriating their manhood, their persons, their sensibilities or their efforts. As the trunk shut on the upscale auto, Cal and Jake faced the ungrateful Ms. Buckner. She flinched under the severity of the couples' silent stare like she expected a violent outburst. Surprise flickered across her face when Cal flipped five twenty dollar bills on the ground before the woman, tipped his hand-to-brow, and took leave of the roadside. Back into the quiet of the car.

They left the erstwhile female in their rearview mirror, now profanely flipping off the helpful men, rescuers that they be. The dog had clearly increased in worth to the woman's thoughts by the fact of the men's interest and liberation actions. The quad of friends knew they had probably not heard the end of the matter. Like that made any difference.

Trekking a circuitous route in hopes that the nasty malcontent might not figure out their destination, Cal finally pulled into the venerable old estate. Reminiscent of an antebellum plantation with big carved front pillars, it posed a strange irony in light of recent events. Sophie and Winnie exited the front entrance with the two kids, hugging their family and immediately welcoming the happily freed ragamuffin of a dog.

A gentle soapy bath in the mud room sink cleansed the scruffy and pitted body. Big fluffy towels appeared and eight hands proceeded to embrace the cleaner pooch. Now a much more attractive female mixed breed, she followed into the warm kitchen for an inaugural meal of cereal, meat scraps, cottage cheese and a dessert of pre-adolescent love. Shining eyes evoked a totally changed bearing in the canine and, though still a rib-showing waif, the dog now looked and acted like a different animal. A wide canine grin effused her new demeanor.

She knew she had hit the jackpot this day as the kids and she cuddled together on the cushioned, blanketed nest in the corner. Winnie and Sophie watched the bonding among the three and their hearts melted at the sight of the maltreated dog blossoming in her gratification, moist nose now nestling into the childrens' arms.

"Should we have left more money for the dog?" Jake had taken to second-guessing. Cleaned up and settled before the fireplace with his three closest confidants, the four boys discussed the state of things.

"You two fixed the ingrate's tire and left her mobile, with money, for gosh sakes, Jake. The dog was obviously held against its will under horrible conditions and that woman was battering the poor thing--- No!" was Luke's vehement reply.

Tacitly agreeing, Cal and Jeremy lounged comfortably entwined with their husbands while half-dozing before the warmth of the crackling flames. The girls had spoiled them with a platter of cold cut sandwiches, fruit and freshly steamed asparagus shoots. Analyzing altruistic actions over the past hours had pretty much ceased upon the filling of bellies. The men knew that they had done the right things on several levels. The remnants of concern now centered around the future rather than the past.

All of the Broadhearst family had revved up their protective activities in the knowledge that some form of response was more than likely to be expected in light of the past 36 hours' events. The six brothers and their sisters, several cousins, aunts and uncles, as well as Jeremy and Luke with Jake, too, had agreed upon security measures now in effect. Various family venues were now under guard by discreet armed members, both inside and outside the homes.

Road, river and countryside approaches were being monitored for any antagonistic provocations. It felt like battle modus but in conjunction with local law enforcement, the entire extended family and friend system felt more at ease, albeit on lookout, as a result. The law agencies had liaised with the family, understanding the unilateral nature of the menace presently threatening them and the greater community.

Cal had insisted on Voy's family joining with them at the family home on the Coosa River. The two children were now safely ensconced with the rescue mutt; the women were chatting amiably together. They anticipated Voy's return with Torchy from the remote riverside house to the confines of the central site, too. No one even questioned the need for her protection, for though a supremely capable loner, the transgender woman was no doubt a prime target for the coalescing 'posse comitatus' entity now organizing. Next door, Farmer and Missus Brown had the temporary addition of Doy to their household. The younger twins, Loy and Roy, were shacking up in their old bedroom of the big home, so along with Coy, all of the brothers were close and accounted for.

Local news teams had picked up the story about the Etowah Park fiasco and set up communication points around Rome for relevant news stories and alerts. One group was camped out at the county road entrance to the family compound. So much re-connaissance and goings-on pretty much precluded any clandestine activities. Cal was content for the time being.

* * *

The four runners padded lightly over the packed dirt trail in the cold pre-dawn hour. Sweatpants and sweatshirts covered them from neck to ankles, with knit head covers topping the cold weather outfits necessary since the onset of the wintery mix now burying the area. With running shoes reinforced by double sweat socks, the boys were well-equipped for the sleet now pitting lightly against the heavy material. Colder precipitation had followed the cold air brought by the onslaught three afternoons previous.

Jake and Luke had sprayed the outfits with water-proofing the night before so the cold was mitigated somewhat now as the group followed the 10K river loop Jake had mapped out months before upon arrival in Rome. Of the four, he was the most acquainted with the twists, turns, dips, ruts and such, but Cal was equally adept at the trail, having accompanied his husband multiple times on the familiar route. All had agreed that solo runs were off the table for the present time.

Hal, the great horned owl, had answered Jake's call upon reaching the river trail portion of the run. Having been taught a succinct lesson of razor-sharp talons scraping his head on the one morning he had failed to do so, he made sure both he and Luke hailed the big bird with a greeting. The four listened as the majestic nocturnal hunter had winged by above them, much to Luke's delight.

Luke had a rapport with his own resident owl in the high country and felt gladdened by the sounds of the big bird, missing his morning routine on the mountain. The two men's calls were returned in inquisitive fashion, what with the added hoots from the new guest. Hal was curious, yet apparently mollified, by the heads up to the new running partners. No claw attacks ensued. The boys even felt undefinably reassured by the bird's presence.

The troupe found the riverbank stretch somewhat treacherous for their footing by the frozen precipitation coating it. The pace dropped off to a six-minute-mile pace through the leg of the loop. At one point, after two of them had slipped dangerously, just barely avoiding a fall, they decided to slow to a walk for a quarter mile stretch. Breaking the pace was not desired but when they turned a curve toward a more raised and graveled surface, resumption of the brisk pace to which they were all more accustomed was achieved. They could see the porchlight from Torchy's cabin in the woods across the river off in the distance, the red glow surreal through the sleety mist.

Jeremy was the first to notice the faint blippings of light around the perimeter of the cottage. "Are those electric eels or swamp ghosts?" Half-jesting, he pointed the direction of his sighting. Sure enough, the next moments attested the presence of very blurry, intermittent flickering. It lit the edges of the house in an eerie outline. On guard already, the four slowed again and detoured from the path for a closer view of the spectral effect.

Carefully approaching the far riverbank and visualizing the ongoing shimmery flashes, low conversant tones of furtive speech became discernable. Separated by the river from closing the distance any more, the four hunkered down and spied on the scene as vague forms began to take shape. In the coming minutes, several persons were detected around the boundaries of the unoccupied home. They knew intuitively that someone was up to no good.

Luke, always ready with his iphone in a plastic baggie tucked in a sock, squatted behind a huge cypress tree trunk and pulled it out. He called the detective's number in charge of the ongoing park case. When it went to voicemail he let Cal leave a message for the man about the suspicious happenings.

Afterwards, he left the audio recorder on in his pocket as a safeguard. Fortuitously, as it happened.

Wanting a better look, they located a fallen cypress tree trunk transecting a good portion of the river width and climbed across it. Negotiating the roughened but slippery bark, they drew close enough to make out four people now conversing in exasperated tones over an apparent plan being hatched.

"Donnie, damn it, just tie 'er down best as you can and let's get-er-done, now, asshole. It don't hafta be perfect," came the first determinable words over the water rippling beneath the trunk.

"If'n I don' fasten the damn tie good, it gonna teeter an' fall over, numbnuts," came the hissed reply from Donnie.

"Well, once she's lit, it don' matter none too much, now do it? Who's gonna be a'seein' it much from out here, anyway?" The instructor wasn't brooking any discussion on the matter and was mightily pissed at the argument. "Now, just get 'er done! Ya' pissant."

"Yessa' Massa," came the sarcastic answer.

In the gloom we were able to make out the shape of a close to eight-foot cross. Probably wooden… By the odor wafting toward us, it would seem to be saturated in gasoline or the like. These things did not bode well, and the situation worsened by the realization that the two silent partners were presently dousing the house itself in something similar. The glint of gun metal off the intermittent flares of light alerted that the men were armed. The effect of this knowledge chilled the watchers.

Jake stood up, whispering the need to call the volunteer fire department and re-call the detective, but as he did so he lost his footing on the slippery surface, partially sliding into the running water beneath. Though he was able to stifle himself from exclaiming, the resultant splash and grunts were picked up by the trespassers. Cal saw one of them, presumably the leader, reach over and grasp the barrel of a shotgun leaning against a tree. His hackles rose, skin prickling in sudden fear for Jake and the rest of them.

"Who da' Hell be out there?" came a gruff demand through the darkness. Cal grasped his lover's arm and pulled him back onto the horizontal trunk. None of the four spoke a word, but this did little to allay the alerted interloper's nervousness. "I done heared ya, ya' rascal, and if'n yer don't be answerin' me here an' now, I's gonna be a-riddlin' that there water with enough buckshot to down a damn bear, damn it all!"

The indistinct figure could be seen pointing the muzzle of the gun in the runners' direction and Jake was forced to speak up. "Hey, mister, we're trying to check our trout lines here and I just fell in the water. No need to get yourself in an uproar," he attempted placation.

A sudden stream of harsh light cut through the darkness. All four of the morning exercisers were caught in various positions of vulnerability from atop the wide tree trunk. Nowhere to hide, they slowly raised up off their haunches and shielded their eyes in facing the unknown individuals.

"Well, ain't this just a sweet surprise," it was the nasally leader, now staring the boys down at the muzzle of his double-barrel shotgun. "Done catched me some coons and a couple dandy-boys, now, looks like," his tone was dripping evil and Cal feared suddenly for their lives. The men were carrying out a sneak attack by destructive force towards which the local authorities would take a dim view should the perpetrators be caught. Cal was rightly apprehensive of the choice to be made by these persons since it was coming down to a case of 'us vs them'. He felt they would have little compunction for saving their own sorry skin at the cost of those they deemed inferior, let alone capable of testifying against them. The awareness that dumping dead bodies, especially those of dark-skinned persuasion, was an age-old pastime in the deep South, did not escape him.

Strange Fruit. Cal flashed on the morbid poem from the tree on which they were presently busted...too much mawkish irony.

"Go on ahead an' git yo' shifty black ass selves on down from that tree and let's see's just what we got." The invitation came across anything but welcoming. Under the circumstances there appeared little choice. Clambering down, the runners felt foolish for the mistakes leading to this state of affairs. They began wondering if they would end up maimed, or worse, at the hands of the rough talker corralling them.

The scoundrels gathered the couples together at the barrels of their long guns. One produced a roll of heavy twine with which they were tied up against the gasoline drenched cabin. It was reckoned that when the coming conflagration burned out, so would be the bindings, thereby leaving no evidence. In the arsonists simple minds, the group would be held responsible as guilty parties, caught by happenstance at their own malfeasance...

"Can you reach down to my sock, baby?" Luke hadn't had his iphone discovered. If it could be retrieved, then there was hope to get help. Time now of true essence, the reprobate band had almost finished with their preparations. They knew the match-flicking set-off would soon occur. Tied so tightly as to be unable to get to the possible saving device, the boys tried feverishly to loosen the binding knots. To no avail.

"Gee, boys, it's a right shame you fairies gonna be up in smoke in 'bout a minute...sayin' those prayers a'fore ya' meet yo' Maker?" The leer and nasty reasoning said everything about the character holding himself above his prisoners. Never once seeing the contradiction of his evil actions. The man's offensive reference affirmed they had been recognized, also. Not good.

Things looked more and more grim with each passing moment. Desperation was creeping into the four bound psyches now caught in a proverbial Chinese finger trap: the harder they strained, the tighter their ties pulled. Too proud to beg, the boys deduced that any words would prove moot anyway. The arsonists were noticeably chagrined by the exhibition of stoicism.

Well-placed kicks and punches sought to assuage desires to draw a response. The added cruelty clearly satisfied some deep-held conviction that their group was remedying an imagined slight by the biracial couples' existence. No reasoning would break down the overriding hatred they exploited in justification for their actions. Jake slumped at a brutal gun butt to the side of his head, shivering uncontrollably in his wet clothes. The other three wore various bloody noses, ears and wounds. Cal's silent tears were for the sight of his loved ones being treated so inhumanely. Unrepentant and consumed by despising contempt, the cruel torture continued unabated. Only exhaustion brought cessation to the viciousness.

A long extendo-lighter was ultimately produced and the coming heat was already sensed. But then, just as the leader of the pack flicked to light it, several things occurred.

From the corner of the boys' eyes, a yellow streak bolted through the clearing, bowling into them in the awkward attempt to stop. The stray dog was on a mission. Somehow, she had sensed the danger to her saviors from the house miles away. Whining, scratching the door until let out, the dog had streaked away into the darkness, yowling as she ran. Following her instincts to the house by the river, the yellow cur rushed to the restrained boys and went straight for the tight twine bindings cutting off the blood flow to deadened hands. The miscreant, Donnie, saw the dog and exclaimed about her appearance. She was rabid in attacking the knots with her teeth, ignoring the outcry amongst the four villains. "That old mangy bitch be bitin' those boys' cuffs, Billy, we gotta shoot her 'fore they get loose!" he screamed.

Two rifles raised to stop her but as they rose, two additional streaks broke the periphery of the glade. Black and brown snarling balls of fur launched simultaneously at the aiming guns, like a copperhead at an exposed leg. Before they could even reach their triggers, the gunmen were hit by the airborne canine missiles and both were attacked by teeth full of savage need. Retribution was, indeed, in the air. The yellow dog's similarly abused escaped siblings had answered her yowling calls. The two tore into the malefactors harming their sister's patrons. Screams of surprise and pain ricocheted through the sleet-suffused surrounds and blood pumped from savage bite wounds.

Billy and the other reprobate watched in disbelief, then went for their own rifles. A sudden shriek arose from Billy's accomplice as the man backed toward the edge of the dell near the marshy bog side. Without warning he shot skyward, grabbing a butt cheek in abject agony as Jeremy saw a copperhead pit viper attach itself by airborne strike. It sank its fangs and latched on, embedding deeply into the flabby buttocks. Jeremy next beheld a writhing in the bog grass surrounding the bitten man. With horror, the bound runner watched literally dozens of other snakes strike, threatened by the unwitting arsonist.

Copperheads: the most aggressive of all vipers in the Western Hemisphere and also the most social. They commune together in clans. This den had been prodded into attack when the gunman stepped one foot too close. Within seconds, a horde of the serpents overwhelmed the man. He sank under the onslaught. His cries awakened fauna within a mile radius by his squeals of dread at the mindboggling assault. It would prove fatal by the toxic venom delivered en masse.

Billy, stunned by the vehemence of the violent barrage, pulled himself together. Levelling his shotgun at the boys and the gnawing dog helping them, he curled his finger around the trigger. Before he could pull it, a whooshing flurry of wings and talons struck his eye and trigger hand. One set hit each. The razor-edged talons of the great horned owl sank in just ahead of the weapon's discharge, wresting it away from its intended target.

Hand and eye were both punctured to bone in fractions of a second. Silent screams howled in his brain, yet no word passed his lips. Only copious, viscous drool. The bursting vessels of his hand spewed blood over the gun while the gelatinous goop filling his ruined eyeball gushed over his face. The forgotten lighter and shotgun clattered to the gravel ground cover. The now piteous man followed their descent, all three hitting the ground together.

Yellow Dog chomped through the final cords, thus allowing the prisoners to loosen hobbling ankle restraints. Three of them rose as one, lifting Jake with them who was woozy from the cold and beating. Free now, but dazed by the manifold levels of catastrophe just aimed at the cruel offenders.

No matter the just comeuppance so efficiently dealt as if in their behalf, the spared runners cringed at the ferocity leading to the gruesome scene. The soft pitting by tiny points of ice both swarmed and muffled the atmosphere like a macabre snow globe.

Distant whines of undulating sirens roused them. The four burst into reflexive attempts at triage for the badly injured scalawags. The two men neutralized by the dogs lay moaning in pools of blood and terribly ripped flesh. The snake-bitten man was motionless, copperhead fangs still embedded in the dead, steaming flesh. Billy lay over his shotgun, quietly sobbing from a single eye, shredded hand balled in permanent disfigurement.

It was an incredibly ugly scene. Hopefully not entirely unbelievable, it crossed the two men-of-colors' minds. The scene would no doubt demand multiple EMS units. The plausibility element would also soon play out. Cal prayed for common sense to prevail when the first responders arrived.

Jake thankfully regained significant lucidity after being stripped, rubbed and dressed in Cal's sweats at Luke's insistence. Remaining on alert for concussive symptoms, Luke and he texted the Rome EMT corps who were at dawn shift change, stressing the need for both the oncoming and out-going team members. He and Luke purposely down-played the bloodbath with only perfunctory detail to substantiate the requirements, aware that media members were surely listening in to the police radio channels.

Police cruisers arrived and two police officers, both veterans, pulled to the side to vomit their coffee and donuts. The detective set up a perimeter for security, cautiously skirting the boggy side of the clearing at the boys' snake warnings. The old veteran stared at the scene for long minutes, absorbing the details and the wounded as the young doctors worked feverishly to stabilize the three survivors with zero equipment, supplies or medications. Their husbands lent hands with what could be done by untrained persons. Luke handed over the cellphone audio of the entire scenario to the detective, thanking the gods that be for his foresight to leave the device in record mode. It proved integrally important.

The two siblings of Yellow Dog now sat placidly at the edge of the clearing, grooming one another, while the rescue herself hung close to the men receiving her returned favor. At the opposite corner, two remaining copperhead pit vipers lay limp, morbidly attached to their victim…dead after expending their totality defending the den. Multiple other oozing fang wounds bore out the collective offensive.

Looking up from tending Billie's ruined eye and hand to see the detective's deeply disconcerted countenance probing him, Luke gestured upwards into the canopy of overhanging cypress branches. A magnificent specimen of great horned owl preened its sleek feathers, aloof to the carnage below. The wise law officer absorbed more and more with the passing minutes. The trained eyes missed nothing.

EMT units descended on the site, taking control of the multiple medical emergencies. The wounded were further stabilized, gurneyed and strapped, then loaded for transport. Amazed EMT's looked gratefully to Jake and Luke, along with their husbands, for saving surely terminal shock patients by their astute work. One woman EMT neuro-tested Jake for concussive effects. Satisfied of no serious damage, she extracted a promise for a full work-up within the hour.

After their departure, Detective Lusk thoughtfully approached the young doctors. He stared at the two with their men as the four commiserated together on a large flat boulder. "If I hadn't seen this with my own eyes, there would be no way I would have believed it," he began. "I have been appalled at the tactics and manners these people have employed in their misguided path." Sweeping his hand backward around the open glade setting Torchy's woodland home, he added, "Not only here but over the past days.

"Your family," and here, he nodded at the blanket-wrapped Cal, "has exhibited the integrity and character bred by the America in which I have always believed." The detective held up Luke's iphone and went on, "I have listened to the audio recording Dr. Cevennes so shrewdly thought to capture. The responses in the face of what just went down here, at the Etowah Park incident, and over subsequent times up to now have secured my respect for you two couples, men."

"A lot of people have seen the powerful example set by your family through attacks that couldn't or wouldn't have been weathered by most. Yet not a crack or fissure has surfaced in your principled forthrightness. You men reacted remarkably this morning. I watched as you administered aid, and even tenderness, to people bent on killing all of you out of blind hatred. Standing here now, my hat is off to you four, along with all of your family. It would be my honor to escort you gentlemen home safely. We will sort this mess out together and put things right."

As he finished, a contingent of firefighters arrived, augmenting the police presence. The crew entered with portable hosing and equipment in preparation for siphoning river water to dilute and flush the effect of the flammable coating still jeopardizing the house and forest. The adrenalin-driven duos now experienced a consuming exhaustion after the morning's events and succumbed to the detective's offer. They piled into the detective's Crown Vic.

Driving slowly past the large flat boulder just shared by the two couples during Detective Lusk's touching homily, nobody noticed the smaller boulder to the side of it. Had anyone looked, they would have espied an extremely large, emerald green Catesbian bullfrog there, in seeming repose. His large silver dorsal scar tingled in the sleet. Huge eyes soundlessly winked as he sagely pondered the setting for such serendipitous events short moments before on the waning three dog night.

Chapter 17
Of Odin

The low moan escaped my lips before I could stifle it. As I lay cuddled up into Cal's armpit, relishing his scent, my fetal position and the exposure of my naked ass allowed for an intrepid gatecrasher's invasive access into what had been vacated only a scant hour before. Following Cal's copious eruption.

This wee hour of our first February night in Telluride found us snugly holed up in the rustic log home of Jeremy and Luke. The Kell-Cevennes branch of our family. More specifically, in a shared and coveted spot amidst our closest friends: their king-sized cypress-hewn bed. Nestled between my husband and our friends' semi-permanent guest and new acquaintance, the dreadlocked Jamaican. He had been introduced to us as one Ambergai Gee of reggae music renown earlier in the evening.

The unfamiliar intimate had been quite comfortable in his nudity around the fireplace-warmed home for the entire evening of our arrival. While forewarned, we hadn't been too well fore-armed for the actuality of the package the man carried around. The eleven-inch plus piece had both startled and enthralled we two newly-landed houseguests.

Luke had described the behemoth more than once, but like Helen of Troy's historic beauty, this man's beast was only fully appreciated upon the picture supplanting words. The mind's eye picture now provoked a certain wariness as the thing enquiringly prodded my rounded buttglobes, protruding beyond Cal's protective cover. Cal's continued even breaths confirmed his slumberous state. The giant dick was unfurling gradually upward and inward, determined to know my insides in addition to my external self.

While I very much desired the dick to get it, the increasingly firm girth presented formidable challenge to plugging in. Discreet elbow grease application helped: where the man got it was a puzzle. He must have been a reggae boy scout, I surmised. The involuntary moan as the huge head squeezed through my sphincter was only rudimentarily acknowledged amongst our other bedmates, none of whom awakened to it. Only reflexive rearrangement of the other three bodies registered the discrete shift in the status quo.

Ambergai Gee pushed the big thing forward in its quest, having visually and audibly indicated intent prior to this night foray. My untested white booty had been sized-up on several occasions over the previous hours. Once, even testing the cakes by the old finger-squeeze-and-thump method. The action had brought me up short, halting midstride as the older man's long fingers wrapped around my husband's mainsqueeze butt--- mine, that is--- in inquisitive delving. No one else had been within sight upon descending the staircase from unpacking suitcases. I looked over my shoulder at the touch, not needing to gaze too far downward to view the humongous dick that was, by extension, thumping the 'fruit'.

Apparently, mine proved ripe enough, for he had then commented, "Mi a'gonna be a-getting' a bit o'dat booty, now, ma'new friend Dr. Jake-mon, an' in only a li'l while, so don' be a-keepin' 'dis here Mon a'waitin overlong for de' tastetestin', a'ight boi?" The implication was not subtle, I had inferred.

We had arrived at the house only an hour before that squeezing, being introduced simultaneously to Ambergai Gee and the adorable other half of the handsome Adolpho, whom Cal and I had been knowing for a year or more during previous visits. The 'straight' young sommelier. His new lover, a blond ski bum named Bryce Canyon, had surprised us. We had accepted and presumed Adopho's straight-world predilection because of the Italian boy's own insistence. Until Luke had told us of the news downland in Rome, Georgia... hmmm. Welcome to our world... and family.

Having just departed the lowland environs of the Broadhearst brotherhood, I was well prepared for the blitzkrieg technique commonly employed by men-of-color when they choose to take their pleasures. Both Luke and I reveled in the proximity of desirous men and their proclivities at common junctures, yet the materialization of this homunculus was not something for which I could ever have been quite prepared.

At least an additional one-plus inches longer and 'girthier' than my own ten-inch Calumet, the beast now entering my asshole defied credence. I had thought that the size of this dick existed only in fantasies dreamt up by fiction writers. But here it was. Back-door knocking. Yes, strictly speaking, I had been forewarned. But, I was adding another meaning to the concept of fore-armed, what with the arm-sized cock now familiarizing itself with my colon. Like other residents of this house had already been. First hand.

So, I just inhaled my man's muskiness from the inside of his deep pit and luxuriated, between winces, as I was stretched wider than I had been. Oh, wait, with the exception of Mr. Jumbo. At the Atlanta pleasure house to where Cal had escorted me months before. That one rivaled this. I stood corrected.

Musk aroma filled in for poppers nicely as the menacing anaconda slid slippery up into my warm chute. After a seeming eternity and two miles of depth perception, I felt the hot sizzle of the tall man's ballsack against my perineum. Older men had such patience.

Sighing in both relief and ecstasy, the exaggerated breath finally roused my unsuspecting husband. He sleepily extended his rangy arm down my back in an arc that reached my ravaged hole. At the recognizance of an enormous presence where his own cock had just recently spent itself, Cal awakened more so, fingering the connection. My man loved that particular action, commonly doing it when he and I joined together. He prized the fingering feel of dick-in-ass. The streaming three-dimensionality of it turned him hugely on.

My hand reached down to his fast-arising tens, certain what I would find. Tumescence along with the soft, seductive whisper into my ear augmented already enormous delight, "Ooooh, my baby mandingo-pleasin' boi. You been getting' plugged like you know I like feelin', right here inside of my daddy-shield, haven't you, now? How's that big dick fillin' your sweet pussy, J-Man…you likin' that thing I've been watching you drool at all this evenin'? The big'un ain't been real shy, boi." I turned my head up to stare into his searching bedroom eyes, transferring my enjoyment through to him by locking on them.

His lips found mine as we tongued in unison. The being pushing the still-swelling elevens behind me noticed. "Dese two lover-men jus' joinin' dis home bein' right up de' alley along wi' de rest o'us, now. We all glad t'welcome ya' both, men. Mi been tol' ya' matchin' up ta de rest a'our ways, so all's a'gonna go vera nice, now, I am a'tellin'," the Jamaican dialected us up a notch in eroticism through that accent.

Cal's tongue went into higher gear during the sensuous talk and his fingers wrapped around the piece taking what he had just been stuffing. I got the best of it all but nobody felt slighted. I slowly stroked my man's uncut dick the way it liked. Matching the rhythm Ambergai Gee set showed us three that we would mesh well in the coming times together. The man's animalism scorched us.

Luke and Jeremy lay entwined in subliminal concupiscence, casually caressing Cal on the other side away from we threes' conjoinment. While not apparently conscious of the ardor unfolding so close by, the communality of their bodies against Cal's gave connection to us all even without their active involvement. We knew each other that well, having shared beds many times over years… shared lives for even longer.

Ambergai had pinpointed our connection with Luke and Jeremy in his intuitive manner, continuing to steadily stroke my ass, "Mi be a'knowin' now tha' ma boi-pussies over a'next to you's new mens gonna be a'likin' da facts o'de matters, mi just be a'sayin'." And with the saying, the giant dreadlocked elder man erupted voluminously, flooding a baby-rich load all inside his newly staked claim.

Though he instinctively knew of the preclusion from dominating Cal's ass in the way he did other inhabitants of the high mountain lodge, by using my ass, Gai extended his dominion over the younger generation. Cal got it, endorsing the act without a single misgiving, deriving pleasure instead. He respected elders like no other man I had ever known. The willing precept of this giving-over did not diminish anything he and I had, it only expanded the field. The family grew, then and there.

The high country home absorbed the fact in tacit acceptance as Cal climaxed, tongue-locked as he was with me. Feeling the link between us and the elder musician, my own peak reached massive, fulfilling release. Welcome us, again, to Mountain Village.

* * *

"Boy, I slept like a baby, guys," Luke was refreshed the first morning of Telluride Gay Ski Week. "It is so good to have you two back." It had been since the boys' marriage last July that Cal and Jake had stayed with them and the new situation was starkly different. Ambergai Gee was out before dawn doing nobody-knew-what, per the man's wont. The Island man was a profound presence in the mountaintop home. Bryce and Adolpho came bursting from their bedroom off the great room at just that moment, pummeling each other in the heedless carousing of twenty-somethings. Uninhibitedly toweled and wet-haired from a post-coital shower, the two infused the house with youthful enthusiasm. Yes, the circumstances were accented by change.

Coffees were prepped for each and the five sat around the long marble island in the kitchen discussing the upcoming frivolity which marked this week's annual festival. Already, the village below and Telluride overhill were filling with a plethora of eccentric personalities coming for the fun and great skiing. Over four feet of powder and packed powder presently covered almost the whole 2000 acres of ski terrain. Fully 80% of trails now open and all lifts running full bent. Bookings for the week were overflowing and ski lift passes were in extreme demand.

The group watched as early prep teams groomed the higher trails down below the house, the upper ski lifts reaching to within a hundred yards of the Kell-Cevennes' property lines. The pond was thickly frozen for their own private skating pleasure when anybody was ready. Resident elk were bedded down away to the far rock overhang where Luke had replenished their warm hay cushion two days before, so all knew the bear population was safely asleep for the winter. The elk were always good bellwethers and bear-alert guardians. With their gathering where they were, the boys could bet on good new powderfall within the next two days. The weather forecasters were all in for a long snowy, El Nino-induced winter. With the coming ski festival, spirits were high.

Jeremy came blustering in from jetting up and stoking the heaters for the cedar hot tub, an amenity everyone adored for outdoor enjoyment through the winter season. This was Bryce and Adolpho's, as well as Gai's, inaugural winter season in the log home and their anticipation was torqued with the added family. Over five feet of hard dickmeat graced the log home now and the tub would be fully filled by seven soakers. Lucky they all liked each other… The bundled black man stamped feet and disrobed in the adjacent mud room, appearing in a few moments, winter spandex body suit the sole remaining body cover besides thick, wicking socks. His sexy array of hunk-factor was almost impossible to hide, now proving no exception.

"It should be 104 F within the hour, and jets are on standby mode whenever anyone wants it. What's for breakfast, my cookin' wench?" He grinned at Luke, figuring the jibe would provoke a response. Everybody knew that Jeremy was the chef of the household. A withering smile greeted him as Luke gestured at the full breakfast underway on the counters and cooktop. The bacon aroma pretty much rendered the sarcasm moot and Cal swatted Jeremy in his passing.

"JK, don't be insulting the sous chef. This be a class establishment, and we will just have to bend your ass over my knee for a full spankin' if you don't quit, homes." Everyone feasted on that hypothetical. "So… did you sleep as sound as your 'slept-like-a-baby' man, too?" Cal was fishing.

"Well, duh, yeah, dude," Jeremy sniggered, "at least until I got my booty call at dawn. The standing order. Did you by chance miss it--- ya'll were kinda sacked out when we 'got up'." He smirked, fishing as well, "Late night?" He had actually awakened to the cum-rumbles in the dark hour, sensing his best friends' demonstrative eruptions. With his free hand grazing Cal's butt, he had hardened in vicarious enjoyment but remained stock still due to his husband's continued deep sleep through the whole thing, not wanting to disturb him. He liked watching Luke dream. The morning 'booty call' inside Luke had satisfied a belated rejoinder to the wee-hour hot action so silently perceived. He hoped he had returned the relayed third-party favor.

Jake picked up on the allusion but was curious, "Was the Jamaica-Mon there at dawn when you woke up? He was with us one minute and the next thing we knew, he was gone." The newcomers had experienced what Jeremy and Luke had noticed for months. The man was a wraith. The two wondered at the disappearing act following on the heels of the hot session shared with the older gent. Informed that it was pretty common, the couple was pacified.

Bryce came and sat next to Jake at the barstool beside him, interested in the presence of yet another white boy doctor and the one of whom he had been hearing so much. Luke was so effusive in praise of his bff, Bryce figured the handsome curly-haired man couldn't be all that. The two bent together like old buds, comparing and contrasting notes. Bryce couldn't even fathom Cal's five brothers and their clone-like qualities. As much as the boy loved the mountain, the lowland population and in particular that of Rome, Georgia, sounded pretty damned inviting. Jake equated some stories that failed to dispel the fantasy. All the while, the blonde's eyes kept creeping over toward the tall stud known as Jake's husband.

The hot breakfast hour was filled with more acquainting, catching up on each other's past month and discussing the festival unfolding down from their home. The appearance of screaming gay men and drag queens cavorting over the trails this February week had been enlivening the mountainside for several years, to date. From the boys' high vantage point, the view promised to be exceptional. Only Jeremy and Luke had first-hand familiarity with the perspective.

After cleaning up the kitchen, everyone regrouped. Adolpho announced he needed to spend at least the morning hours in the bodega, bookwork calling the young man's attention away from the gaiety. He knew that in light of the coming week's wine consumption his triple-stock inventory maneuver in the previous months should provide a monetary bonanza with which to start off the year…something he planned to ensure. The books wouldn't wait what with the orders pouring in from hotels, restaurants and bars in the community. Luke loved the young man's work ethic, his own mindset similar. Not many twenty-somethings would stick to the set plan as the huge party overtook the village and township. Besides, he thought, doing the work now would pay off later in the week when the Italian boy could sit back and watch the profits roll in.

Bryce aimed to shadow his soulmate and upon making it known, Adolpho shot him down almost immediately. "Baby, I would do nothing but fuck you all day long if you came along…no, you gotta be in your element now. Go play with the mountain boys out on your ski slopes. I'll catch up to you. Besides, who's gonna be watching all these horndogs out in public? We know they are like to all be in trouble before the first day is out. I saw Luke takin' inventory on the magic drawer yesterday so you just know what's about to happen. Go play, boi." And with that, he kissed him, clutched the succulent buns, slipped out the front door and disappeared downhill.

The young Italiano wasn't far from wrong, as it turned out. Luke and Jake were conspiring in the bedroom by the magic drawer after a shower with their men, giggling over the different modes of 'high-mindedness' available for the extravaganza on snow. Not surprisingly, the green-cross inventories in the township were dwindling. Shortages were being discussed already. It was said there were emergency runs into Denver happening for re-stocking purposes. Everyone always underestimated gay men and in particular, drag queens' partying penchants. The collective exemplary work ethic was balanced by an equally hard-partying reputation.

The variety normally so widely-ranging on the apothecary shelves in Tride town had the entrepreneurial class concerned for the medical mj patients, finding their managers had held precious little back for filling prescriptions. Jeremy chuckled that the elderly neighbor nonagenarian 'love-children', the Chastains, were likely to be caught short.

"Ha, that'll be the day, JK. Those two stockpile more weed and magic goodies through the year than the stores do. They are usually vapin' with the kids back and forth on the gondola--- don't worry too much on their account, honey. We'll be beggin' from their stash if a shortage comes down. What a laugh." Luke was well aware of the lovable older couple's ways, having seen their antics and habits over the years. "Hell, Pearl, they told me once that if a nuclear holocaust hits, they'll be hunkered down high." Missing his own oxymoron, he and Jake lit up a cannon-sized doobie as they continued their count.

Cal came out from the multi-person shower, drying off, mouthwateringly nude. Now wearing the second largest organ in the household, he was as at ease in his skin as Jeremy and the Jamaican. Rubbing his head, the big thing wobbled to the brisk toweling. Bryce, just walking in, was captivated by it. While used to Gai's hugeness, seeing the sleeping tens this similarly tall, slim, muscled man was packing set the small blonde's mind to considering.

He sat down next to Luke, accepting the blunt in quiet reflection. Still glancing in Cal's direction, the boy posed the soft query to his guru, "Are all giant black daddies hung that way, Luke?" he sucked on the roach as he contemplated the black residents in the house and mentally extrapolated to the stories of the Rome brotherhood...all were well over six feet tall and every one of them packed at least nine inches.

Cal guffawed, overhearing the question, 'No, boi, we are not all hung the same. In point of fact, the white race claims some of the biggest endowments. There are plenty of lines of genetically diminutive black men, just like there are over-sized other races. It's just a myth perpetrated by black females to fend off white girls from stealing 'their mens'. Big dicks scare women." His poker-faced demeanor left the surprised kid flummoxed. By firstly being overheard, and secondly over the novel idea. He didn't know Cal well enough yet to apprize the man's sense of humor. The poker face threw him.

A sudden big grin dispelled the nerves edging into Bryce's face and he sniggled in high-pitched relief. "Actually, Bryce," Jake cut in, expelling a cloud of sweet smoke, "the Bourbon Kings of Charlemagne's lineage were purported to average fourteen-inch dicks. For several centuries, the men of that genetic line petrified the women throughout the kingdom. It's thought by quite a few historians to be the reason so many Christian women wore wimples and veils: to avoid attention from the king. The one man who could take anyone, man or woman, whenever he desired. Can you imagine a worse reason to get religion and 'frock up'? In that time, absolute rule and the 'Divine Right of Kings' were paramount and French kings were notoriously lecherous. More than one succumbed to syphilis by their wandering eyes, a slow death sentence back then. Check out King Francis I. The man fucked sheep and turtles, for God's sake."

Cal looked curiously at his husband as he quantified this. "Jake, you're telling me that those French dudes were out-sizing the Hottentots, too? Those 'Tot pygmies are supposed to be sportin' the hugest pieces in the world, now, at least that's what I've read… fourteen inches was an average, you say?"

"Well, I'm just quoting from medical diaries of the times," Jake added, "Centuries and changing social mores can fog things--- look at the Bible, claiming that Methuselah lived to 969 years and all of his line lived to at least 800 years of age." The doctor made a good argument and the group took in the information.

"The Hottentots gotta have twenty-inch dicks just to get within strikin' range of those women of theirs. Ever seen those butts? They cover the front as well as the backsides. Unbelievable. But, evolution provided. Those ladies didn't starve or die of thirst in the droughts of Africa where they lived…and still do live. They store all the fat and fluid and energy right around there, like damn camel humps, and still stay fertile." This came from Jeremy, who had just listened to that Methuselah point. He slapped his own hard glutes to accent the point. "Remember the National Geographic spreads on the tribes back in the sixties and seventies? Those booties could kill someone. It physically took twenty inches to get into the females for consummation. Google it. There are accounts from the Enlightenment and Age of Exploration when Europe imperialized the world. The drawings that came back to Western Kingdoms then were disbelieved by everyone. No one could comprehend booty that size." Jeremy, the doctor of Philosophy in the family, had studied anthropological and ethnological characteristics more than anyone, and all believed him. He addressed the blonde, "You just don't want to be droppin' the soap around those shortys. The three-legged myth started because of those little dudes. Nature can be oddly disproportionate, now." He took the roach and joined in the morning inhale before the slopes were to be negotiated.

Luke, the original addressee of Bryce's question had been silent up to that moment. "Well, boys, all I have to say is I don't want to meet up with any horny blue whales. Those big boys pack dicks longer than we are tall…and they're made of bone. My med school anatomy prof used one for a pointer." Everyone stared at him. "Just sayin'."

* * *

Luke, Cal and Jake shlooshed to a halt at the base lift together on their skis. Hoisting goggles up on heads, they surveyed the run just navigated. The three had been separated from Jeremy and Bryce where Peek-a-boo Run had swept away from the Humboldt Draft turn-off halfway down the mountain. Jeremy's decision to join the young ski bum Adonis on a snowboarding morning left the two careening down the committed path ahead of them. The trio had employed their superior edges in slicing crisply to the side trail. The mogul challenge of the Draft run had called and they now reveled in the accomplishment.

The blonde had enticed Jeremy by joshing him of his over-the-hill status which had whetted the competitive ebony stud's appetite to meet the whippersnapper's challenge. Snowboarders, the trick skiers on snow, required a different skill set than classic downhill skiing and the novelty of the method drew the younger generation like moths to a candle. Jeremy had reached the middle-age crazy plateau of 44 years absent the slightest physical evidence of the fact. Yet by the simple truth of chronological climb, he felt the pressure somewhere in his athletic being to 'hold court'. The distinct duo had missed the turn off and were now probably contesting one another, break-neck style, in a competition of generational pride. Luke smiled at the mental picture.

The exhilarating run down Humboldt Draft had left Luke's vital signs racing. The altitude accentuated the stoned state they were experiencing from the shared joint at the summit, suffusion expanding during the descent. "Wow, Luke, Tride is easily the equal of Ajax trails, boi," Cal gushed, "those moguls were gnarly!" Jake and Cal were accomplished skiiers, having spent countless hours not only on the downhill slopes there, but regularly trekking cross-country trails for cardio fitness. The results of the exertions were evident in the extremely fit couple, thought Luke. He and his man kept pace what with their own fitness regimens and both had sailed easily into their forties with the retained vigor of mid-twenties compatriots. As evidenced by Bryce and Jeremy's present sortie. In general, mountain people tended toward physical activity more than lowlanders. Statistical evidence bore it out. Perpetuation of active lifestyles well into the nineties was not an uncommon feat. Coloradans were well aware of the facts. Besides, keep moving and keep warm: the adage was true.

Turning toward the base gondola and Mountain Village piazza, the friends stuck their equipment into storage lockers and meandered toward a favorite new lunch spot, The Village Table. Opened by a Swiss family a few years before, the place radiated charm. The pre-planned meeting site put the boys at the bar with hot sandwiches, soup and the most deliciously crispy steak fries on earth in the following quarter hour. Raspberry lemonade washed it all down. The trio chatted amiably, still in catch-up mode. Feet propped toward the open fire pit outside afterwards, they sipped hot cocoa. There was still no sighting of the black-white duo of snowboarders. They must have gone back up for big-dickery boasting rights, the three concluded.

As a young lesbian couple waltzed by, Cal overheard a snippet of their conversation. The girls were excited to have sighted Oprah at the gondola station as they finished their run, "Can you believe that woman? She looked so damn delicious. And, helping the trauma crew load up that cute black man with the blonde boyfriend is just so…Oprah. The woman is always involved with regular people. It is so cool here, with all these celebs wandering around in the middle of the gay community—Wren, I am blown away that you brought me," the pretty woman pushed open the restaurant door for her friend and they disappeared inside.

Cal jolted at the allusion and was up in a flash, hustling the white boys into their jackets, "Did you hear them? They mentioned loading up a cute black man by trauma responders and a blonde boyfriend…you don't think…?"

It served to push them into a headlong rush across the piazza. Upon reaching the gondola station, Luke ran to the nearby info window and asked about any incident or injury episodes in the past minutes. "Well, yes, sweetie, as a matter-of-fact, there was an injury load-up about twenty minutes ago. A young man with a broken neck was braced up and taken over to County Hospital. His little boyfriend was beside himself. They should be unloading on the townside station right now. We can sure tell it is ski season, all right. The injuries are piling up. It's the third emergency lift just this morning. Two last evening, too." The helpful lady was still talking, but only to empty space, as the boys jumped on the next rotating car.

Forty minutes later found the three rushing through the doors of San Miguel County Hospital. Heading directly to the Emergency Room, the experienced young Texas ER doctors grilled the surprised reception staff. Reaching past their heads, they punched the emergency door-open button on the inner wall behind them and entered the treatment bays. Luke was familiar with the clinicians on the small high country hospital staff. One looked up from the medical records area, recognized Luke and wordlessly pointed toward the fourth bay. It was a separate room from the rest. He nearly busted down the door in his haste, Jake and Cal on his heels.

The scene nearly melted them. There lay Jeremy with his head swathed. Neck secured in an orthopedic brace, his shoulder hugely bandaged. Bryce was talking quietly into his ear, affection and concern waxing his features. The main conclusions drawn, however, were that the patient was conscious and cogent.

Upon sighting his husband along with both friends, Jeremy fairly beamed at them. "Word travels fast on this darn mountain, doesn't it?" He was clearly not in pain and seemed to be almost enjoying sitting center of attention. Luke's tears changed the man's demeanor just like that. "Oh, baby man, I'm good. Don't worry, I'm just fine." He saw the immense consternation mixed with relief and started blubbering himself. Luke closed the small gap and sized up the man of his life in seconds, concluding no death knell emergency.

"Jeremy Kell. What happened?" Luke demanded as he gently examined the shoulder and checked the fit of the neck brace.

An authoritative voice from the doorway answered, "Dr. Cevennes, we've been expecting you." The articulate voice came from Stan Stevens, the attending clinician on the floor and head of the ER here in the hospital. "Your better half is, as you can already see, stable, aware and pretty much pain free. Reduced subluxated shoulders are rather predictable that way. No fractures, no CNS involvement, good neurological signs.

We plan to observe a couple more hours for concussive signs but no overt fears at this time. The man is hard-headed enough to weather a triple somersault into an embankment, I do believe," he smiled. "Though, next time, I would recommend awaiting the passage of fellow skiers: it might make the landing a bit more predictable.

That synopsis along with two sheepish grins from Bryce and Jeremy were sufficiently telling. Luke settled on to the bed next to him, taking the hand resting there. Bryce moved back a bit, leaning over into Jake and Cal, obviously full of unspoken words but saying none. Just knowing all was well negated any need for the moment. Dr. Stevens approached closer, flashing a penlight back and forth across alert eyes and rested his hand on Luke's shoulder. "You know, Luke, if this young man hadn't been in the stellar shape that he is, I fear things could have turned out quite differently. The conditioning made the difference."

The patient savored the praise and at this, Bryce piped up, "Dr. Cevennes, he was amazing! The hot-dogger came out of nowhere while he was in midair and he still changed his trajectory somehow, landing in the snowdrift instead of smashing that tree. That woulda been…real…bad…" his voice trailed off as he saw Luke's look, realizing he may have offered too much, too quick.

Both Dr. Stevens and Luke zeroed in on the blonde. "Tree?" they expressed, simultaneously. The boy reddened and shrank behind Cal.

Jeremy chimed in at this point, "Settle down, men. Nothin' happened. Just like you said, Doc, my amazing conditioning prevented anything worse from resulting. Looks like that conditioning provided for avoidance of that tree, right? No harm, no foul, isn't that the maxim?" His logic couldn't be questioned; the truth bore it out. Luke and Doc Stevens backed off. Argumentation was the patient's forte, after all, Luke reflected.

Nevertheless, Luke cringed inwardly at the thought of the alternative possibility. He grasped the hand harder. Jeremy reassured his soulmate, drawing his face upwards with his good hand, "Honey, you're stuck with this man, come Hell or high water, so just hold on tight. We got a long road ahead of us. Channel a little Bobby McFerrin, now, how 'bout?" He hummed the tune to 'Don't worry—Be Happy' at his husband. His tender reassurance settled the atmosphere. "Besides, baby, you are always lookin' for excuses to get your damn hands all over this," pointing at himself, "so just look at the upside. I'ma needin' plenty of massagin', now…to keep my 'conditionin' up."

The hangdog grin won the debate.

"I'm sorry I scared you so bad in there, Luke. It's just that I was so happy to hear he's OK, I didn't think. That's what always happens when I'm nervous and excited. My mouth loses my brain," Bryce was walking with me to the restroom a few minutes later. Cal and Jake had been allowed by the ER staff to sit with Jeremy a little while.

"It's OK, Bryce, I get it. He is good and that's all I really care about," my relief truly was there, even though the call had been close. The antics my crazy, athletic man put me through made my psyche lose its grip on occasion. The thought of life without the man left me cold. But, all good and no bad was a prescription for mundanity, so, by rationalization of a lifelong principle, I actually recognized the need for accepting good fortune and leaving the chaff behind. Jeremy and my agreement early on. Time to practice the preaching, I figured.

"So, tell me, what in the world was he thinking--- a triple somersault? On a snowboard? Isn't that a banned move in the Olympics because of the danger level? You know: Broken necks. Permanent disfigurement. Quadriplegia. Brain death. Or even a serious condition. What were you guys thinking?" My exasperation level rose just by the voicing, sarcasm unavoidable.

"That's just the thing, Luke, we weren't doing anything like that. Just jumping moguls on the way down. When we rounded the last curve, we saw where the snow combers had banked the extra on the sides and a halfpipe had been built up. We both went right at it. Jeremy hit it calling out 'Cab 720 Stalefish'! And, he nailed it, Luke. He nailed it! That's an Olympic move, dude." The boy was again all worked up by the feat. "I've never seen anybody try one except at the Games and no one did it that clean even there. That man is a stud, Luke."

"Don't I know. But what was Dr. Stevens talking about? He's the one that said somersault."

"A Cab 720 isn't a somersault. It's a move dreamt up by Steve Caballero and is mostly a two-full-circle twirl move, Luke. I think the doctor musta been kidding, 'cause nothing like that happened. He had already finished the 720 and was turning the landing when that idiot came outta nowhere. Jeremy was just jumping a spread eagle 'cause he had stuck the motha'. He was in the air doin' that when the guy nearly t-boned him." Bryce was making sense of the whole thing for me now. It helped. I should have known. And trusted my man better. Although I was still curious to know when he had picked up that move--- I had never seen him attempt it. Things that make you go 'hmmmm'.

Coming out of the bathroom, we turned down the hallway toward the ER when we were hailed by a velvety feminine voice from behind us, "Luke, is that you?" Annalise Chastain was standing in the doorway halfway down the cross hallway corridor, in-patient section of the hospital. She was dressed in her typical flowing hippie attire with multiple layers and colors, looking very little like an elderly woman. Her evanescent smile beckoned us and we altered toward her.

The first thing in my head was whether old Mr. Chastain had been admitted for some reason, but she dispelled the thought, leaning back into the room, "Bart, dear, come see who is here, too." The old-world gent appeared almost immediately, beaming from ear-to-ear as he beheld the two of us.

"Well, Annie, maybe our favorite young doctor can shed a little light on things, what say you, my love?" He was still so head-over-heals besmitten by his lady that I always induced his every conscious thought began with the woman. He stepped forward as we drew near to wrap me in a manly hug, acknowledging Bryce as he did so.

"We came over again today to be with old Elmer. You remember, don't you, Luke, the aged man who lives up on the divide? You and Jeremy were over to dinner when he was with us awhile back, if memory serves." I was in awe of the couples' lucidity and genteel manners but mildly amused by the reference to their decades-long confidant, Mr. Edgewater. The man was younger than the couple by their own previous admission.

Nobody was entirely certain how old either of the couple were, timeless in their existence and portraying the essence of human entwinement. I was relieved for their personal well-being. "Oh, of course, I remember him well. Has he developed a problem?" Their looks bespoke concern and we turned into the room.

"We hadn't been able to raise him these past days, Luke, and finally made our way to his eyrie there, only to find he had taken a fall several days before. A compound tibio-fibular fracture. He hadn't been able to get to the telephone. We were compelled to call in the high country corps. They evacuated the poor thing, broken leg and all, down here to the hospital." Passing the corner into the room, we beheld the elderly man, meta-splinted leg elevated and face miserable in a troubled sleep. "I am afraid he may not judge our decision as proper as we thought it to be, but so far up the mountain we knew there could be no way aid might be obtained. So there it is." Bart was noticeably torn by the decision, fully knowing that were the positions reversed, it could have been he or Annalise bearing the challenge from a prone and hospitalized position. But, of course, they had each other.

Mr. Elmer Bruce Edgewater, former hockey star, World War II veteran and presently distressed patient, exuded forlornness through a sedated slumber. An ingrained expression of angst bathed the man's deeply lined countenance. He was a known recluse with an irascible persona, yet all who knew the man recognized a sometimes endearing facet. The person was mercurial. One minute amiable, the next unapproachable. One could never tell which incarnation was in charge. Annalise had once enlightened Luke about a troubled past love affair which, to the present day, saturated the highlander's personality with deep contradictions.

Over coffee one summer morning at the Chastain's home, Elvee and Suture napping beneath the table, the lady had imparted the sad sojourn of a young Elmer. His fate had been met and set by falling hopelessly in love with an Austrian alpine ski champion during the 1948 Winter Olympics at St. Moritz, Switzerland.

The first Olympiad held in the post-World War II era, it was called the 'V Winter Olympic Games'. Elmer had been a member of the amateur hockey squad, sent to the Games by the U.S. Olympic Committee. The squad was made up of American AAU, or Amateur Athletic Union, members. A second squad had been sent to represent the USA by the AHA, Amateur Hockey Association. It was a misnomer, as the members were professional players named by a rival group from the International Ice Hockey League.

The Ligue Internationale de Hockey sur Glace---LIHG--- had challenged the newly re-emerging IOC in the first games since 1936, when Hitler had notoriously attempted hijacking the Berlin Olympics for propagandist reasons before WWII. The same ones a certain black American Phenom named Jesse Owens had singlehandedly crashed. The international league had usurped IOC power during post-war confusion and charged itself with naming the national teams to the Olympiad, intentionally at odds with the IOC's and USOC's prime loyalty to the goal of amateurism.

The AHA sent the team of professionals under the aegis of the rival organization and nearly derailed the entire Olympic effort. While the IOC-sanctioned team was finally allowed to participate by the Swiss, as host country, they were not permitted to compete for a medal. Elmer, as part of the true amateur team, found himself with extra free time. His wanderings through the Olympic Village had crossed fateful paths with a beautiful young Austrian skier.

Trude Beiser, from Vorarlberg, Austria, double medal alpine champion in both the combined and giant slalom events, fell hard for the young American athlete during the international sports symposium. In the course of winning both downhill events, the young Austrian had pursued a torrid affair with a supremely handsome Omaha Beach first-waver from the momentous pre-dawn Allied Invasion of June 6, 1944, at Normandy, France. D-Day.

On the heels of the calamitous WWII, a loosening of traditional morals pervaded world society. A teenage Elmer had affected world history by surviving the stormy D-Day invasion, acting in heroic fashion to take out a cliff-sniper nest full of Nazis. Risking his life while hand-delivering a grenade into the enemy post, the shy youthful hero then followed it up by marching through Normandy, assaulting and taking Cherbourg on the way to liberating Paris. He and his platoon had sloshed their way to wet victory while being compelled into early manhood, wooing receptive French girls by the dozen during the effort. As veterans of both war and love by the 1948 Games, Elmer and the young beauty had acted out in ribald fashion, leaving little doubt as to their extreme attraction for one another.

Unfortunately for Private Edgewater, Trude's attraction had been purely physical, whereas his had been rooted far deeper. After St. Moritz, he had desired to bring the glamorous vixen home for a stateside life. The girl celebrated in her newly won acclaim, opting for the alluring course now open to her. She had behaved the 'bon vivant' then returned to the 1952 Olympics, winning further approbation and Olympic medals on her way to marriage and then a shopkeeper's quiet life with a husband from her home country. She and the young veteran had not spoken again.

The American soldier never understood, returning home to Denver in deep depression. Acquiring a parcel of land high up in the remoteness of the San Juan Mountains had been his solution. He constructed a lodge for himself far up the lonely heights of a then-undeveloped Telluride Mountain and wallowed in discreet, and discrete, rejection.

Decades passed before the Chastains and he intersected during the Love Revolution in the 1970's. A close friendship had been unexpectedly forged and the three bonded in beatnik fashion, shacking up together in a free-wheeling ménage-a-trois. The arrangement somehow worked for the better part of a decade when a sudden schism had developed. The loner ascended once again to the divide. Reverting another time to a hermit's existence, he had passed the intervening years in solitude to the present day. The epitome of a brokenhearted loner. And now, a disabled nonagenarian with very few options.

Annalise had persisted in the erstwhile relationship with Elmer Edgewater by her intuitive abilities for reading the poor man's psychological imbalance as no other person had been able. Bartholomew Chastain rose to the challenge by his unconditional love for the woman of his life, overlooking the side-effects left from the faltered entanglement. He even shaped a lasting, if tumultuous, relationship with the difficult old soldier.

Now, standing bedside to her grumpy ex-lover, the worldly woman viewed him with a mixture of emotions plainly apparent in her classic visage. "I just don't know how he will respond to this turn of affairs, Luke," she softly evoked. "He is not capable of dependence on anyone and with this badly broken leg and hospitalization, I am not at all certain how he can adjust." A tear trickled down her smooth cheek as she mulled over the scenario now unfolding. Old Bart wrapped his arm around his soulmate's still trim waist and drew her into him, affording her succor by simple strength of will.

"We will just move him into our place, Annie. It is ready for just such a predicament, dear. We have planned on such events for ourselves and are able to afford him the necessary aid. Don't you worry, my love, we will make it work." Bart attempted rationalizing the situation, in full knowledge of the battles sure to result by trying to help the old curmudgeon before them. Pride did, indeed, come before a fall. And persisted afterwards, as well.

Bryce turned to Luke, tearing up himself, sensitive youth that he was, "Luke, we have you and Jake, both, and with Adolpho and Ambergai, we can all pitch in to help out, right? We are gonna be nursing Jeremy anyway, so why can't all of us just add Mr. Edgewater to our help list?"

"I agree with your compassion, Bryce, but it may not be that simple an answer. You have to understand; Elmer is a very private person who doesn't accept much of anything from anybody. The decision resides with him." I was trying to stay pragmatically detached, especially in light of the Chastain's own independently prideful ways. But, the fact remained that an effort had to be made. I had always maintained that the gay community's existential manifest lay in the way our kind were present in the world for the function of filling needs. For the orphans, the disabled, the destitute, the elderly of society. And such. It appeared our birthright and tenor may be soon tested.

Annalise broke in on us, "Boys, you are so dear to us. We treasure your friendship and familial ties. But this is Bart's and my cross to bear. We must meet it head-on. Elmer isn't going to allow for intervention by what he imagines to be 'strangers' and anyone except myself and Bart, here, classify as that in his mind." She was right. My previous words along with hers rang true. We all stood, contemplating the endless 'Circle of Life' now rounding another boundless corner in its continuum.

* * *

"Honey, I am not the invalid you make me out to be. Stop hovering. And, the itch is two inches higher and three to the right..." Jeremy smirked as he teased my efforts at nursing him. While he dearly loved attention, he had been bordering on defensive since we had gotten him home and propped before a roaring fire in the great room. Pride. He now lounged comfortably on the sheepskin cover over the recliner, big, sexy, two-toned feet propped on the raised portion of the rock hearth. He was delectably naked and the sheepskin lay partially draped over the half-hard shaft of the man's ever-ready endowment. My hands were massaging their way up his muscled left thigh. Notably, three inches to the left of his smooth scrotum. And two inches below.

Cal strolled in with a mug of hot-buttered rum in each fist. Hearing the patient's instructions, he pulled up short, laughing at us. His own package was stretching the pouched front of the baggie boxers barely covering his own crotch. Jake was following with two additional libations and he bumped square into his man's bare back. Froth and warm liquid spilled on the hunk's ebony dorsum and he jumped at the contact. Putting the drinks down on the rock surface, he turned, took the drinks from Jake, set them down too, and then spanked the spandexed buttocks escorting the spilling hands. Jake's peals of laughter filled the room.

God, how I loved these men. The four of us meshed so well that it seemed we had shared a womb. Able to read each other's moods, the four of us weathered good and bad in ways that most friends only wished to do. It crossed my mind at that moment to wonder at the Chastains and Elmer Edgewater's relationship. The three had lived together happily for close to ten years before their falling out. Even so, they had kept one another covered through thick or thin ever since. I hoped they could weather the present difficulties and conjectured, in tandem, whether these three men of my heart would complement me throughout my life in like manner. Excepting any fall-out, it occurred to me. I never intended our bond to wane. Jeremy was my rudder. That would not change. The other two people here were way too integrally important to my existence for separation of any sort. At least I willed such. Luckily, I knew these personalities enough to realize nothing could ever come between us and thanked whatever powers-that-be for the cognizance.

The sun was setting as we gathered for the hot drinks, weak sunbeams wafting through the big picture windows. Gai was asleep upstairs in the master suite after a long night out. He had arrived cold and bleary-eyed an hour before but hadn't shared with us where he had been. Hearing of Jeremy's mishap and assuring himself all was good now, the dread-locked man ascended to a hot bath and warm bed. Adolpho had returned home to worry awhile over JK, too, but as he realized all was OK, he departed with his boy, Bryce, for dinner down the mountain. The boys had a date after being apart most of the day. The dog-boys, Suture and Elvee, were sacked out on their own sheepskin rug, soaking up the fireside warmth, tuckered from traipsing the property for several hours.

The four of us had changed plans due to the hospital run, choosing to hunker down for the evening while the festivities proceeded without us down-mountain. We knew we would not be missed. I was concerned for the Chastains and their friend, Elmer, so was content to lounge with my confidants in case their need came up. Actually, what with the trauma of Jeremy's scare and the vicarious psychological ordeal of Mr. Edgewater's situation, I was secretly very glad to not be out partying. It would seem my three boys were of the same mind. We spent the evening conversing many subjects, coming back several times to the fickleness of Life, with its twists, turns and unexpected cliffs. Home and snug was just what the doctor ordered… Before the eve was old, we were joined upstairs with our Jamaican, safe amidst the bond we all shared…

…I started awake to the clash of my surroundings. Having retired with my husband and best men to the downiness of our communal bed, it was discombobulating to wake up amidst a silvery scene of fluttering gossamer window curtains, puffing inward on a warm, moist night breeze. The distant echoing of thunder filtered in with the wind and struck me as aberrant in light of the lower edge of a full moon outlining the room in moonshafts by Artemis. A sterile smell of Ivory bath soap and pine sol cleaning solution returned me to an earlier time: one reminiscent of college days in Austin, Texas. Faint night sounds came to my ears and I fixed on the discernable dreamscape. It must be. My sensate being seemed intact, though on edge, while my musculoskeletal frame felt groggy and unresponsive. I had to be in a dream. The coldness of the room's atmosphere belied the warm moistness I could smell and feel. After a minute, I identified the chill as aloneness.

Rather than pinch myself, however, I answered curiosity and took further stock of these surroundings. The large open room had six windows. It was nicely appointed and there appeared to be an open bathroom door leading to where the smells arose. The place was sterile and without hominess or charm. A staging company from the home and garden TV channel could have been responsible for it. Not a single knick-knack or personal photo graced the setting. It left me even colder.

After this perusal, I sensed my hand wrapping the arching hardness of the throbbing boner there and slowly caressed myself, enjoying the tactile stimulation. Heavy balls were pendulous between my runner's legs and metaphysical inner self called to me. I was horny as shit. Noticing a pair of familiar ragged jeans hanging over a bedside chair, I rubbed bleary eyes to clear them along with my mind. Arising and donning the pair that I recognized as a favorite grunge fashion set which I had treasured throughout college, I took stock of my younger lithe form in the silvery mirror. I looked hot.

In another recollection, my mind kept playing the med school cadence familiar to all medical school students: On Old Olympus' Towering Tops, A Finn And German Viewed Some Hops…the mnemonic method for remembering the cranial nerves. Olfactory, Optic, Oculomotor, Trochlear, Trigeminal, Abducens… the strange discordance added to my separation from coherence yet provided a cadence for pressuring my piece. I deftly buttoned the old 501 Levi's, slipped on my Tigers, tied on a headband lying next to them and headed down the moonlit staircase.

It took me into, of all places, my Spartan med school apartment. All of the windows were open here as well, and the visible full moon lured me toward the door. I felt an odd mental angst for the neuro exam I knew to be scheduled in the coming day, but in this dream I recognized my opt-out clause through pinch-ability and went with my hormones. Something unheard of, had I actually been in real time. My school-era blinders had been solidly secure, keeping me on the straight and narrow then. Excepting sporadic sexual experiences, the mindset pushed any form of social life to the perimeters, in my desire to succeed. Inhabiting this dream scenario, I determined to virtually explore what I might have missed by the obsessiveness from that time. My conscience was temporarily null and void. Hmmmm.

Intuitively aware, somehow, what would be outside the front door, there was no surprise at finding the darkly close, after-midnight scene. Dim street lights cast a dreamlike glow, only intermittently reaching me due to the craggily spreading oak tree branches lining the familiar street. I knew that down a block and to the west four and a half more, there would be a clandestine aperture through the hedges by which to gain entry to the community park with Shoal Creek running through it. Over on the far side of that, there would be the tributary Hondondo Creek feeding into Shoal with the elliptical trail way marking it. The entire area was hilly and densely wooded.

A notorious late night pick-up spot known by common gossip, I intended to see what went on there in the virtually realistic setting I now traversed. Floods of defunct memories rattled about my brain, invoking a long-ago world as if still extant. An alter-ego version of myself held ascendance over my actual persona. I was ready to explore the illusion. And break rules.

The warm summer midnight breeze wafted over my bare torso caressing my erect nipples as I sauntered through the darkened and seemingly deserted community park nestled beside the bend of Hondondo Creek. The favored well-worn and ragged 501's hugged my slim hips, rasping against my body in just enough of a sensual manner to augment my hormonally heightened state.

Nothing more than the tattered denims, running shoes and headband adorned my taut body and I experienced a sexual strike of oncoming erogenous expectation as the clinging crotch of my jeans nuzzled my prodigious and anticipatory endowment. Oh, I had at some point slipped on an oversized metal cockring to enhance my proud, party-sized phallus and egg-sized smooth balls before leaving the bungalow, so there was that, too. Nasty as I wanted to be.

The comforting cylinder of the Rush bottle in my front pocket rolled erotically up and down my thigh, reminding me of the hoped for coming rapture. A quasi-dangerous effect of the unknown only amplified my tumescent state as I circled the old oak be-studded park, prowling for other similar-minded denizens of the dark this late vernal eve.

I reached up and grasped the inexplicable rolled joint balanced behind my left ear and retrieved the bic lighter from my back pocket, flicking a flame to enlighten my mood by the complementary effect of Bob Marley's iconic legacy. As the aroma emerged from the lit doobie I rounded a corner inhaling the cloying smoke and envisioned a vaguely silhouetted picnic table off to the side of the lane adjacent to the brook.

The babbling of water over river rocks provided a susurrus of background sound. It almost obscured a throaty moaning as the nocturnal wind currents eddied around the wooded setting. My senses peaked as I centered on the primal source of the rhythmic plaints arising from the barely discernible glade by peripheral night vision. Honing in on the table, I gradually fixated on a locus of intense eroticism rendering an outline of two bodies melded in the ancient exercise of hedonic coupling.

One body was bent over the smooth cement surface of the table. Small, round buttcakes arched upward to meet a sizeable glistening protuberance protruding from the second body positioned behind the bowed form of the greedy recipient. Both bodies blended with the shadows. As I silently approached the scene while inhaling another pleasurable toke from the joint, the beautiful swarthiness of the duo's forms came into a bit more focus.

The smaller, hooked participant bore the compactness of a bulldog. Velvety dark skin enwrapping a sexy torso and extremities punctuated muscular brevity. The black male was limned in sweat as he inhaled from a lidless bottle of poppers presently raised to a flared nostril. Short-cropped black hair under a skewed baseball cap crowned his head. Eyeglasses reflected in the intermittent moonlight as puffy night clouds wafted past just above and beyond the rutting pair.

The second figure was the incarnation of Mr. Marley himself, long dreadlocks cascading from his head down his muscular ebony chest and backside. The locks rocked in synchrony with his body movements. Athletic buttocks and legs moved in an undulating fashion thereby enabling a truly stunning ten-inch, blood-engorged member entry into the proffered ass before it.

One hand slowly massaged a pliant buttcheek. The other hand scissored a large blunt to his lips as he inhaled its rich scent. Holding it in his lungs, the satyr methodically slow-fucked the bubblebutt partner of the moment. A lazy cloud cleared the moon at that moment, revealing this wanton act in all of its animalistic glory. I gazed, mesmerized by the carnal scene. Just then, the sturdy topman cocked his head to notice my infatuation with his perfectly cowled manhood as it retracted momentarily from the well-greased and welcoming asshole.

A lascivious grin relayed his sanction of the watchful presence. Never missing stride, only the fleeting delay in re-entry to the pleasure hole proclaimed the black man's pride at my envisioning the pair's salaciously conjoined state.

He slowly exhaled as he pressed back into the begging cavity. The lucky boy receiving the donga dick succumbed to yet another penetrating stroke into his popper-relaxed butthole, noisily expelling a breath full of the high-inducing concoction. With the incoming push, the slut's head turned away from me. His enjoyment continued, wholly ignorant to the voyeurism.

Not so, the Rastafarian. The stud beckoned me forward through the leering grin, angling his amazingly proportioned body to that which maximized my view. Every nuanced gesture flaunted the piercing in-and-out intrusion of the high, round, globular masses servicing him. His perception of my interest obviously magnified the intensity with which he hit that bare hole.

My own dick had long since rejoined the scenario, snaking down the leg of my jeans provocatively. He noticed it, also, and reached out to familiarize with the contours. Quickly tiring of the denim obstruction he popped the buttons open and adroitly exposed my throbbing 8+ inches, sporting a big, perfectly cut mushroom head. Well aware I was hung, for a white boy, he tacitly acknowledged the fact, pushing my pants down below my ass and gathering my hairless balls in his palm, all the while stroking the unsuspecting sybarite bent before him with that greased pole.

The young man writhed pleasurably on the picnic table, loose sockless cross-trainers bumping off the ground with each impalement. The small man suddenly began vocally accessorizing the expanding episode, begging for the huge dick to fuck him, fuck him good, like a bitch. Give him that big load… Dredds Man abruptly spit onto his appendage as it again entered to its total 10-inch length, then positioned the fat blunt inwards in his mouth and leaned toward me, offering a power hit as inducement for my further involvement with the two.

I accepted by meeting his lips and sucking slowly on the barely protruding tip, inhaling deeply from the extra-potent delivery of his own tasty creeper weed. We separated after the sensuous lip-lock, holding the hit as deep in our lungs as possible.

Again exhaling slowly, he curtly complimented my fully engorged manhood through smoke-suffused breath then bounced it with his fingers as he moved back to squeeze my own round buttcheek. Excitement overflowed as he did so and my cock erupted in an unexpectedly volcanic release of cum directly on to his ripped hairless belly, dripping down as he amusedly snickered his surprise.

The boy-toy was finally made aware of my presence by the ricochet of baby-laden cream over his derriere. He turned toward me and stiffened in recognition. It was a current infrequent sex-partner interest! A home healthcare nurse of unquestionably libidinous appetites with whom I shared a steamy, if detached, quasi-relationship. We had spoken earlier that day in an attempt to hook up.

A liaison had been aborted, purportedly due to his claim of a night-long working gig at a geriatric patient's residence. Reality indicated he was getting pummeled before my eyes by the truly sexual being fondling me... the little liar reflexively pulled loose from all 10 inches per one fell swoop in astonished consternation. A tantalizing slurping sound ended with a distinctive "splop" upon extracting himself.

In timely happenstance, Dredds Man ejaculated long, ropey dollops of pearlescent cum both into and all over the abruptly vacated cheeks. A concomitant masculine grunt evinced the black demi-god's exhilarative release for all of us to see and hear--- and feel, in the little nurse's case.

Mildly guilt-tinged, irony-laced contentment ensued for two of us. A thoroughly rattled boy-bitch mutely faced away, squatting on the edge of the picnic bench to grasp and raise his ankle-bound shorts while attempting a modicum of decorum in the current questionable circumstance.

Both Dredds Man and I sardonically observed his discomfiture as we spied large globs of the fuckee's own jism beneath where his sizeable piece had so recently hovered. This gave reason for his vexation... he cast himself, after all, as a consummate "topman". Caught in the fucking act. Busted, ignominiously.

Grasping the tarnish to his masculinity by the passive role in the orgasmic deed, he quickly vacated the debasing scene. Mortification mixed with fatuous hope for later denial summed up his departing expression. Fat chance, I thought, filing the mental video away for future cogitation. As he disappeared into the safety of the darkness, Dredds and I bemusedly contemplated the present state of things, languorous in post-coital repletion. Guilt be damned. That was good...hell, that was too good. And I hadn't even been actively involved.

Not bothering to clean up the sperm-drenched evidence too much, we simply wiped sticky fingers across exposed skin. Reclining on the picnic bench to gather abandoned wits, the partaking of the fucker's residual blunt allowed discussion of the erogenous happenings in the previous half hour.

Unable to ignore the persistent semi-dilation of his humongous endowment, I reached out tentatively and hefted it in my palm. Removing my headband to clean off the exudative remnants from it, he acquiesced without withdrawal. Seeing the thing swell and bloom slightly, I stood and dropped my already lowered pants to the ground in front of him, pulling them off over my running shoes. This left me butt-naked, my own piece now rising for the significant stud relaxing in front of me.

Relighting the remaining roach from my stroll before our encounter, I offered him a reciprocate power hit to which he readily acceded. We both held the syrupy smoke for a time then breathed out in tandem. His dick was now standing at handsome attention between his muscled thighs, foreskin sensuously rolling over half of the pretty head. The big, smooth ball sack nestled beneath in a picture of sensuality. As I watched, he slowly spread those long sinuous 'tennis-player' legs, inviting further attention.

I didn't need more prompting. Spreading my jeans on the ground in front of him, I knelt down on them to minister to his obviously un-slaked need. Remembering my poppers, I retrieved them, inspiring a deep hit and then handing them up to him.

Engrossed attention was then bent toward familiarizing myself with this stud's full-staffed boner. Slathering the head in spit, then working my way gradually down the phatness until lipping the flared base. I worked my tongue slowly around the entire circumference of the thing, taking pleasure in its pungent firmness as I wallowed in ecstasy. The act whetted his appetite for a long, slow, deep blowjob.

Coming back up to the spongy head, I engulfed the whole of it abruptly in one long dive, allowing entry to my esophagus, tongue still swirling around the shaft. My lips and teeth carefully bit down on the root of that beautiful dick with pulsating repetition, holding it and my breath as I massaged the beast contentedly via slow rotating action.

Pulsing the light teeth-clamping technique while enjoying his groans of pleasure, I actionably informed him this represented a future repeatable offense. I backed off the shaft slowly and teethed on the sensitive head right up to the moment an approaching climax forced him to slap my head to cease the action. The short reprieve delayed a premature second cumming.

My own nice whiteboy dick patiently treaded time in a state of fixation between my own well-muscled legs. I remained ensconced before the magnificent piece eyeing me when I took the time to release it from my mouth for visual perusal. I loved the way it throbbed at my face as it anticipated my lips, lightly bouncing off my nose and cheeks.

Not desiring interruption of my preoccupation, Dredds Man took to feeding me hits of poppers in between his own partakings thereby perpetuating both our pleasures. I was enjoying sucking this huge dick as much and more than he was enjoying the reception. The man definitely liked good head... we neither one noticed as two or three other people happened upon our picnic table hotspot, keeping their distance but nevertheless surveilling our uninhibited show.

Beginning a slow, deep rhythmic stroking after a triple popper hit, I set to satisfying the both of our appetites with abandon. Going up-and-down from root to tip, my tongue massaged the tubal protuberance beneath the shaft until both of us nearly came before we desired the episode be over.

Abruptly ceasing all motion on that elastic shaft, both our dicks throbbed their pleasure in unison. I willed the eruptions back down to a controllable level. Then, began the motion all over again. This action went on for a good twenty minutes. I finally couldn't deny either of our crescendos any longer so kept the luxurious rhythm going past the point of retreat. He ejaculated first, scorching cum juice all into my expectant mouth and throat. My own dick reached the pleasure peak, releasing of its own accord, dumping my second load all over those worn jeans I loved to wear when horny.

Holding that dick inside my mouth, I swallowed. His guttural expletives and climactic pelvic thrusts slowly subsided while my own dick suspended in an ethereal cocoon of tingling sensation. During this recovery time, still impaled on the beautiful dick, Dredds Man suddenly muttered through his euphoria-induced haze, "Dude, we are so busted". Assuming reference to the busted nuts, I continued massaging the beast. Unmoving, he continued the post-eruption quivering but I sensed a new tenseness not present until now.

Finally coming up for a breath of fresh air after a seeming eternity in dick-filled oral nirvana, I took quick stock of our surroundings, noticing for the first time the company that had surrounded us. Two shirtless younger guys with dicks-in-hand and pants at knee level were on the periphery of our moonlit creekside clearing. While startling enough, it was not cause for consternation, so looking up at the Dredds Man I glanced in the direction of his stare and quickly surmised the source of his concern.

There, just out of sight of our two voyeurs, stood a cop. Legs planted, hands on hips, handcuffs on his belt alongside a holstered Taser...hard eyes silently surveyed our situation. We existed there, hedonistically unclothed, pot-smoke infusing the air, popper aroma redolent, quavering dick next to mouth with connecting streams of cum-evoking innuendo. Only explicable one way-- all probably soon to be described in front of a judge, no doubt.

My dick still arched proudly over my flat stomach as I leaned backwards in bent-knee pose, chin sperm-smeared. The sated centaur before me sat in thrall to the linger of tingling just savored. I totally lent credence to a mythic satyriskoi caught in the act. All that was lacking was a streaming video. Hopefully. Lacking.

Both of the obsessed jack-baiters followed our looks. Grasping the gravity of the odious offense, the two raced off into the gloom of trees away from us. We two were stunned enough to find neither the wherewithal nor justification for moving, viewing our predicament as a dead end.

The nightshift officer had left his cruiser a fair way away. The ostensible objective: surprising nightime lawbreakers. The ploy had met with success, at least by his take. Slowly, deliberately straightening, the officer set a measured gait in approach to our 'lair'. A smirk of derision bathed his countenance as he closed upon us, one hand over the cuffs.

His words began as a remonstration for the magnitude of our misdeeds. Through our once sought-after state of buzz, we reckoned with the scene he was beholding. Multiple offenses long-listing the path to amends. Not to mention besmirched records and various legal consequences. As Dredds Man had said, "dude, are we sooo busted".

Removing his deputy's cowboy-style hat, he sidled up to us and took transparent note of the ardors and odors of the sexualized 'eau de euphoria' enveloping the site. He spoke out loud enough to make himself heard over a distance, admonishing the vacating voyeurs to make good their exit or face a fate of legal purgatory.

While he enunciated it, I registered his physicality. Slimly tall with caramel skin, clean-shaven visage and head, hairless forearms of well-muscled proportions. Minimally, a size 12 shoe. I couldn't believe this was what I was focusing on under the dire circumstances. But it was difficult to avoid noticing the rugged virility, even through my mental fogginess.

Then is when I noted the distinctly prominent bulge in the crotch of his well-creased trousers. He addressed Dredds Man first, making note of the state of arousal persistent in the stud's nether regions. And on full display for whoever happened to be gawking. In this case: The Law. The still-dripping string of sperm from the partially cowled head staged everything for what it certainly was.

In my spinning head, I thought I heard him order me to the floor...the floor? It was outdoors, well past midnight and my grunge jeans lay stretched out beneath my bent knees. My bare-assed position was within close proximity to one of the prettiest cocks I had ever had the privilege to make come. What a way to end it, I thought.

Bizarrely, I sensed that Dredds Man had again lounged back against the picnic table, still spread-legged on the bench where he had delivered cum into my ready mouth just scant minutes before. Did I detect a stoic resignation to our dual fates of jail-time with hard labor? If so, I prayed we would be cellmates. He reached into his sweatpants laying still bunched where he had tossed them for the earlier bitch-boy action. I was amazed when he withdrew a sequestered cannon of an unsmoked joint from a pocket.

The deputy repeated his comment. What the Rastafarian had correctly heard actually transmuted to "We're goin' for four"... my ears had deceived me. Servicing this officer was to pave our way toward redemption. The deputy's astute evidence-gathering vigilance of my meticulous ministrations over that big ole' black dick might yet provide extrication.

Proof of my abilities had not been lost on the aroused law-man. With all the visible symptoms, the man was now wanting some of his own. A huge hand rose to the bulge tenting that uniformed crotch. Slowly unzipping the fly, he managed to loosen the briefs underneath enough to allow for the escape of another beautiful black dick this late night. The pendulous thing waggled its way over to us, balls bumping. I felt a familiar tugging in my groin.

My fleshy piece again presaged the anatomical machinations of yet an additional event in this eventful night. In less than an hour and a half, I had happened upon a professed top man fuck bud of mine taking bare dick all up in his ass until it lewdly miscarried him a load, next expanded my felonious fantasy by Snoopdogg-toking with an ultra-hot dreadlocked stallion, then slow-sucked his monster dick until he came while three people watched me do it. Unbeknownst, yet un-abashedly.

Now it seemed I would get to suck yet another over-sized cock under the purview of a law enforcement badge...freedom and liberty on the line. Un-fucking-believable.

Throbbing abounded. Dredds Man stood up, watching the deputy shed first his trousers and then his briefs, folding the former carefully on the back side bench of the table next to those size 12's and Dredd's sweatpants. He moved aside for the deputy to sit his fine, bare, tightly round caramel butt on the spot the Rastafarian himself had been settled. The man spread his smooth, fleshed-out legs in an explicitly plain summons for what he expected.

The big, cut, helmet-headed penis curved 9 haughty inches into the late night air only inches in front of my hungry mouth. Salivating at the boner now confronting me, I felt a weight on my shoulder and glanced to find Dredd Man's 10 inches once again proud and full, buoyantly bouncing on my bare skin while he looked inquisitively at the athletic deputy. In response, the lawman unbuttoned his pressed khaki shirt and threw his tie back over his shoulder, exposing a stunningly sculpted chest and stomach, which boasted no less than an eight-pack.

This proved to be all Dredds Man needed to light up the fat joint and offer me another power-hit, to which I gladly, if a bit nervously, succumbed. The deputy simply held the shirttail up to his nose to avoid inhaling any of the noxious weed as we blew it out.

My mouth and mind then set to the avoidance of handcuffs, repeating my oral technique for this upward-curving, fat-headed cyclops. Expertly swallowing the nice curve in one plunge down to hairless pubes and nosing the appealing crotch, I clamped on it with painstaking care, munching just to the limits of titillation.

Deputy Dawg was not shy, readily informing me of his boundaries. My fingers explored the silky stomach ripples and nipple-tipped pectoral perfections while my tonsils tickled the sensitive, spongy crown. I rotated roundly on it. Noisy declarations of incredulity punctuated by sexy gurglings punctuated my mission. The venality and Dredd Man's sweetly tangy dick jouncing on my shoulder kept my own thick piece rigidly happy.

As the bigger black dick had done, this piece took delight in being led to the peak without cresting. Tapping of my temple signaled me when to stop short of eruption. By careful attention to his gestures I not only luxuriated in the turgid mass quaking inside my immobile mouth but we prolonged the shared gratification. Until I felt a finger probe my asshole.

Ahhh... the Dredds Man was ready for another trip up into a tight hole after toking the big blunt he had shared with me 5 minutes before. Well, what can be said? My round buttcheeks levitated by instinct. As I arced upwards the deputy locked his hands over my head to keep my throat fully attentive, anticipating the distraction of the Dredd's uncut monster dick sliding into my ripe ass.

I felt dreadlocks brush my back as a big hand reached under my flat stomach, encouraging further arching elevation of my butt for better exposure. After sharing a popper jolt, which Deputy Dawg surprisingly accepted too, we became a triad of trembling slipperiness. The cum-soaked corona of that great phallus slid steadily up and into my spitted sphincter.

The much smaller hole being invaded fought in vain against the thickness that was Dredd's priapic breadth. The thing tightly wended a pathway up into my guts in one deep stroke, implanting with hegemonic dominance.

I shuddered silently as it pressed inward. The deputy pressed his pretty piece simultaneously all the way past my tonsils. A forever bookmark of the moment will endure as the two tantalizing ebony hunks consummated the bi-ended plugging...to the hilt.

The studs compared vocal notes regarding the sensations of their respective endowments and Dredds Man accorded my ultimate fantasy by encircling deputy dawg's hard-on with his fingers at my lip level.

We all three entered a state of harmonious rapture, rolling in unison amidst our shared tasks. My duties were succinctly outlined by both of them as we pumped and swallowed and surged in the euphoric verve immortalizing that brief eternity.

Shamelessly audible lip-smacking above me evidenced an additional shared erotic connection by the black dominators. My own impossibly rigid dick rhythmically slapped my stomach while Dredds Man matched the deputy man's gymnastics. I ascended into an out-of-body Elysium while both forbidden acts roiled my sensibilities.

After a good quarter hour of proving prowess, the possessive Mandingos surrendered to communal epiphany. Gargantuan gushers and glottal groans heralded the two studs' fire-hot jismic explosions down my throat and deep in my ass.

Only after a seeming infinity of involuntary thrusting did they slow to a steady rhythmic cadence. The pulsing forced my prostate to swell and dick to unload on its own in total submissive release. All motion subsided to a gradual halt as we spasmed in the post-orgasmic glow of avaricious, orgiastic indulgence.

No one moved a muscle. Then, I felt a tiny lessening of pressure in my rectum as the Dredds Man slowly raised himself off my back. He deliberately rolled his cum-slimed fingers across my cheek from their position next to my mouth.

Both of their still-engorged dicks regrettably tremored slowly from their respective orifices, causing me paroxysms of bliss. The three of us sagged in a tangle of sweaty contentment. Totally spent, we shared bodily proximity by mellow, exploratory kneadings which left the scenario without any other possible desirous moves. Soft thrills of mirth from nearby alerted us to the fact of our not-so-private, brazenly pornographic frenzy. While the jack-baiters may have returned, it could also have been woodland nymphs or the trees themselves, for all we knew.

Backing away in more conventional masculine interactions, we pulled ourselves together physically and mentally. The deputy man reverted to less responsive self-consciousness. He collected himself awkwardly, not addressing any wrong-doings yet making plain that nothing was to ever be rejoined again. Denial would hold sway once away from the in-situ setting. All would necessarily be relegated to a fantasy plane only replayable in somnolent ambivalence.

Departing the glen alone, I penetrated the woods. The humid breeze cocooned me and I basked in near nakedness. Unbuttoned and barely clinging denim teetered wantonly down my buttcrack, admitting soft poofings as the drafts caressed my anatomy. Crotch hairs corkscrewed as wafts of air tickled them. Post-coital sensations of the skin surrounding my groin perpetuated a diminishing rapture state. I juddered with after-flashes of sexual overload. Feeling oddly impervious to external dependency, exultance imbued my being in a perceived sovereignty. A keenness like that of a hunting animal catching the fresh scent of prey was in me. Nothing could assail the effect: I was legion in self-contained subsistence. It felt utterly empowering.

As my feet floated above the solid pathway beneath, unimpeded by dips or ruts, there came to my ears softly strange ethereal twittering. Exhilaration enabled the detection and I cocked my head in search of the ululative resonances. Perhaps nymphs of the night were attending my way back toward the deserted bungalow, I thought.

The trail rose before me and turned sharply upward, away from the creek. At the top of the rise, I found myself faced into a giant, gnarled century oak entrenched beside a supple, stately old-growth linden tree. The arborous couple was statuesque and regal in their paired state, exuding a profound connection bound by entwined roots. It made mockery of my nascent notions of self-sustained immortality. Awareness formed in me confirming the trees as the source of the strange twittering. Intuiting a surreal exchange amid Ents of yore, I perked my ears toward the fascinating emanations and realized the ability to absorb patterings of an arboreal jargon previously beyond my apprehension.

The natives of this woodland seemed to be addressing my passing. I perceived the two gargantuans gently admonish me. "Embrace your fortune, Luke…fate may be fickle…grasp the sureness of your humanity, young mandrake…roots must be deeply set and should shriek denial be they unearthed."

Prickling of my skin made me certain of an Odinistic presence.

A cold, lonely blast of wind brought my exultation to an abrupt end. Silver moonbeams transformed abruptly to a roiling sky, ushering in a freeze-framed, strobe-like change. I held back a gasp as I watched time-lapsed enshrouding of the previously warm, welcoming, starry heavens by billowing, shape-shifting thunderheads.

Warned, my feet hit the ground running. Sprinting through the now biting gusts, piercing raindrops and recriminating branches, I made my way out of the park and through the wide spot in the demarcating hedge.

Now intent, I rushed through deserted blocks of darkened houses and burst through the familiar front door. The coldness of the empty, open-windowed apartment gave way to the stairway and I flew up the steps. Slamming the windows and halting the flapping translucent curtains, I reached the sanctity of the cold bed. Pulling the bedcovers completely over my head, I lay there shivering in the solitude of the well-appointed room, so silent and sterile. The previous impression of unassailable autonomy made my isolation all the more stark. There was no relief in shutting out the descending maelstrom.

Overwhelmed by yearning for warmth of human proximity made me forget to pinch myself as back-up for escape. Lost and imprisoned by aloneness, I felt tears well up, spilling over as I cried my way into a fretful torpor.

Chapter 18
Of Ovid

It seemed an eternity but consciousness did return, allowing me succor in Jeremy's voice, "Luke, baby, it's OK. It's only a dream, wake up for me." And with that, the tempest receded and the chill of 'alone' departed. I opened my eyes. The warmth of his arms around me flooded back. My head burrowed into his chest, his nose and mouth buried amongst my curls. Four eyes blurred by tears. No longer sad ones, though, as I surfaced from what I had known all along was only dreamscape.

The allure of the erogenous events had acted the Siren and held my spirit prisoner somewhere for a lesson in humility. Of that, I was certain, as I opened up to the exquisite reality holding me. The effervescent smile first beheld upon falling from a ladder into his arms years ago now greeted me once more. Jeremy tugged me closer to free me from the anxiety.

"Gosh, Luke, I was watching you sleep--- you were trippin', somewhere way off, baby." He reached and grasped my hard-on to make the point, "I saw this grow in the middle of it. You came in my hand. It musta' been good…but then you started jerking and quaking and all those tears started up. You scared me, Luke. I couldn't get to you. What was going on in there?" He tapped my head with a greatly curious expression.

It was still the deep of night, before cock's crow as the Old Ones once called it. Everything was muffled here under our quilt. I began divulging the strangeness that had been willingly enjoined. As I reached the weird encounter in the woods, we recognized a very long-fingered hand curl over Jeremy's shoulder and into our midst. Ambergai Gee was noting the nuances of my telling. Not speaking a word, we knew he would add counsel when requested. So I continued. The big hand clasped mine and held it. I proceeded to tell of the encounter at the trees with the surreal surrounds; it brought chills to me in the recounting. By relating my emotions, plus the interpretation with which I came away, I was granted some catharsis.

I was positive some level of power had absconded with my conscious self to convey something of import. The three-dimensional world in which we exist can only be but a miniscule sliver of the universe. The other fathomable and unfathomable realms amidst which we all swirl elude all but the most adroit minds of humankind. Our instincts are so dulled by technology and day-to-day interactive stimuli that we have become inured to knowledge of those spheres. Some amongst us must be able to perceive such concepts, I felt sure. It was up to the rest of us to appreciate those who may be trusted to equate the truth of it all by their comprehension.

"Vera good, ma' distinctly divinin' young Mon, Luke," Gai broke my bemusement following the rehashing. His sotto voice and island twang gave some understanding to my experience. The wise and 'in-tune' elder almost never offered his deeper thoughts without prodding. Because of this, we were rapt in our attention. "Ya' be a'best served, ma' Mon, by a'writin' dem words in ya' head down on de' paper, as 'dey were well a'spoken and a'thought o', now."

Rarely verbose, the man went on, "Mi been a'tinkin' 'bout some tin's dese past days, as da' winds dey' be a'blowin' in some changin' aroun' of da' ways of da' world right now. Mi done seein' a few o'dem and dey's gonna be a'needin' some unnerstannin', if ya' be a'seein' da' point, ma' Mons. Mi bein' glad for da' seein' you been doin', now, Luke Mon. It bein' some deep sights ya' been havin', to be sure. Keep 'dem inna' fronta' ya' mind for a time, mi be sayin'. An, be a'memmerin' o' da balances in 'da world, mi just be a'addin'." With that, he hushed and embraced the both of us long and deeply, wrapping those lengthy arms around us, pulling into his body. For once, there existed no sexual innuendo. We were frankly taken aback.

Beyond my backside, I felt movement. The boys had apparently awakened to our muted exchange. First one white hand then an ebony one inched over my back, joining in our 'early service'. Yup, I was one very lucky man, no doubt. Family made it so. Though I could still feel the small core of a cold knot in the pit of my belly, the togetherness made me whole. We would handle anything that came along.

* * *

"She was there with her fireman husband. And that really old guy that sings with her sometimes." Bryce always rose to the sight and smell of celebrities. This week, his inaugural Telluride Gay Ski Festival, was sending him overboard. Celebs were rife in their presence. Sightings had the boy fairly salivating in the rounding of corners all over town. Ironically, he hadn't said a single word about Oprah's involvement with Jeremy's episode two days before. We were convinced he was simply respecting his hero, Jeremy, by the lack of comment. Adolpho and Bryce had been down in the village the previous night, and townside the night before, for dinner plus dancing amongst the congregation of alternative lifestylers. The magnetic effect of celebs toward edgy, hard-partying LGBT citizens was well known. Though commonly a basis for jokes, gay people did grasp the world of revelry.

"Do you mean Tony Bennett?" Luke couldn't let this one go without comment, "Arguably the most renowned singer and entertainer of his era?" He wasn't buying that Bryce might actually be unaware. This was gay suicide.

"Oh, is he the one Gaga let do a duet CD with her a few years ago?" The boy couldn't be more incorrigible by his ignorance and the great room fairly erupted in faux disbelief at the possibility.

"Let him… do an album… with Her Highness? The lady who fashion-states raw tenderloin?" Jake opened up on the matter, also agog about the dearth of knowledge. "She is sooo lucky to have him as a mentor. Now she might actually learn to sing instead of just marketing herself. And she knows it, cuteness. You do know about his trademark, 'I left my Heart in San Francisco', right, Bryce?" That should put the matter to rest, he rationalized.

The blank look left no doubt, and we all ganged up on the boy. Even Adolpho looked somewhat mystified, "You are seriously saying you don't, baby boi? That is an insult to both the great American icon and the great American city. The man is a first-gen Italiano, like me, and his family comes from the south of Italy. Reggio Calabria. Bryce, we have to educate you. For your own good, baby." He was chortling throughout this 'tirade', making his boy know all was in fun. Mostly.

Cal interjected, "Ever hear of 'The Way You Look Tonight'? Or 'Stranger in Paradise'? Head shakes made it funnier. "Maybe, 'The Best Is Yet to Come'?" Still nothing. We were all amazed. Some of the younger generations seemed so self-absorbed. The world was literally passing them by. Laughter was the best response, yes, but better yet was to begin the education. Cal went to the extensive music library Jeremy and Luke had collected over the years.

While Cal searched the racks, Luke expanded the conversation, "Mr. Canyon, are you aware that Gaga's husband isn't a real fireman? He is an actor on a fireman TV series." When Bryce expressed surprise at the information, sans any inkling of embarrassment, all recognized that the coming 'battle' would be an uphill one.

As everyone thought about this, the strains of 'Santa Claus is Coming to Town' filled the room. Bryce's beaming grin said it all. Paydirt. "Why didn't you play that first, dudes? Everyone knows that guy. You know--- Frosty the Snowman." The collective groan drowned out the wrong-season song. We kept the banter good-natured. Bryce didn't feel put upon and Adolpho determined to begin a mentoring role to bring the young ski bum and computer programming student into 'the know'.

The landline trilled from the far side of the room and Luke went to get it. The rest went on to planning for the day's activities. Jeremy was symptomless and back to normal. With skiing off his list for a week or more, substitutes were being planned. But the man was on vigil himself, over Luke, since the nightmare scenario. He became animated as he observed his lover's body language from the telephone alcove. The young doctor had gone into professional demeanor and Jeremy saw it.

As Luke hung up the phone, Jeremy sidled over unobtrusively and received a look of both consternation and misgiving. "Honey, that was Annalise Chastain. She's at the hospital and just told me that Elmer Edgewater is agitating for leaving. Against doctor's advice, broken leg and all. She says his girlfriend just arrived an hour ago and the two are 'going home'. What in Hell can that mean…?" His angst was evident. "Bart and Annalise are still trying to reason with him, but she even admitted to understanding his logic. I think the whole thing is about to blow up, or worse. Do you think we should go over and see if we can help?"

"Luke, y'know I'm behind you 100%, whatever you need to do. That said, baby, what do you think the old guy is going to do different because you or we show up? The man is a maverick and a hermit. And we've both seen what his nature is. When he sets his mind, it's 'Katie bar the door', now. You know that is true. I gotta admit, though, I am awfully curious about the girlfriend thing," he said with flavor.

In the end, the decision was to wait. Even should the old fellow decide to truly go home, he must first travel by way of the Chastains' home. That was only a quarter mile over from ours. The two decided they might provide more an ace up the sleeve by being available there than in sterile and universally disliked hospital environs.

As the group left the lodge awhile later, Luke injected an omitted tidbit, "Oh, I forgot to mention. Annalise said that she and Bart were hoping they may get some added back-up. They had a call right before she contacted me and said that the girlfriend's escort may possibly sway Mr. Edgewater. The escort is Oprah."

"It is too Shemar Moore. He cut off his mustache and goatee to go DL. And that has to be his brother--- Shemar isn't married." The loud whisper reverberated through the glass cab.

Luke and I snickered together. It was a common mistake. Jeremy did carry a resemblance to the CSI actor, even though Luke's husband was several shades darker. And Cal was regularly linked with JK due to their shaved heads and ripped physiques.

Luke elbowed me, pointing. The mustached drag queen passed the joint he was sucking on over to Adolpho in highland camaraderie. The Italian boy took it and whispered back at the queen conspiratorially, "Girl, that man has five inches more between his legs than Shemar could ever hope to. Give it up, girlfriend." He winked, grinning at the heavily rouged and lip-glossed character in the chartreuse ski outfit. A long toke later, Adolpho offered it back, but the queen signaled to keep it going, so he passed it to Bryce instead.

Mustache lady's travel companion was a leggy bleach-blond with candy-cane striped pink body suit. She wasn't certain either way, but continued undressing the black hunks regardless. 'Honey child, I thought that was a prop pokin' through it was so big, but if that's real, he can put me down with it anytime he wants." A curved pink fingernail pointed at the bulge resting between my bro-in-law's sprawled legs and we laughed again. The Pink Lady licked lips in the saying and looked at me. "Boy, you picked your seat right, sittin' next to that. Do me a favor and squeeze the snake for me, I wanna see if it is da' truth."

Just stoned enough for the challenge, I doubled-down on the queen's dare. Turning to JK, I interrupted his and Cal's chitchat and when he turned toward me, I reached up and pulled his neck down to my level, lipping and tonguing him lasciviously. My free hand went for the crotch and I fondled the banana as requested. Jeremy, surprised at the act, nevertheless responded in kind. I plainly shocked JK as much as the two queens. He was such a good sport, I thought. When the ripe swelling grew larger almost immediately, Pink Lady nearly fainted, fanning her face in mock shock, "It IS real Marty… my God, it's alive."

The quip broke up the entire cabin. Cal reached down to rub on the changing outline, as well, beaming a grin at the two girls, "Ladies, this junk has graced the thirteenth ass in line to the Throne of England, now, so beware…be very aware…"

JFK good-naturedly carried on the charade, spreading his legs even further. Taking the proffered blunt now making its way to him, he grinned toward the drag queens, "Cal, my man, don't let them know that I am the short stuff between you and me. And that you always cum at least five times per lay-down. That's the dope, now, big man, but they couldn't handle the truth." He replied to Cal's caressing by a like maneuver, diverting the queens' attention to the previously un-noticed silhouette. They were now officially dazzled. If all this weren't enough, the two ebony studs next shared a power hit, sending the cabin into overexertion.

They didn't back off for a good minute and as the cab was peaking at the summit station, the station lady caught the action. Captivated, the older lady remarked to her co-worker. She recognized Jeremy from a couple of days earlier as the injured black skier being expressed over the mountain, gurneyed and in a neck brace. The two pointed repeatedly, catching others up in the spectacle. The sensually expressive duo caused a contagion of response through the gondola summit in moments. "Dear, if that is any indication of how the young man operates with a broken neck, I am flat fearful for his partner when he is healthy."

An hour later, down townside, seated in our favorite sidewalk bistro on Pacific Street, the six of us bantered happily amidst the afternoon bustle of out-of-town clientele. Awaiting the call from the hospital had been impossibly fraught, so the trip over-mountain to enjoy afternoon dinner together proved therapeutic. The gondola trip had loosened us all up and the relaxed atmosphere in the bistro aided the measure. We split a pitcher of 24K margaritas in anticipation of the meal-for-six of grilled tilapia filets served Spanish family style.

Jake cut into the conversation after finishing off his second salted glass, "Luke, don't look now but here comes that cutie from The Late Show--- you know, the Stay Human Band leader...I can't pull out the name..." he said, looking bewildered.

Sure enough, I turned around and caught sight of the sexy man he had noticed, "Jake, that's not Jon Batiste, boyfriend, it's that hottie that I told you about, Ezra Pound. He chefs here. Jeremy and Gai have met him a couple times--- here, and at the lodge. Remember, baby?" Jeremy was grinning at the man as he pulled up to our table with a huge tray of food.

"Yo, Pound Cake, how's it draggin' flyboy?" he greeted the bistro chef.

Recognizing us, Ezra had decided to make a rare delivery himself. Distributing steaming hot platters of Spanish tilapia over wild rice and picoso broccoli crowns with artichoke hearts around our table, the sexy man stood back and scanned our group.

Looking at me, he commented, "Doctor, you are a-workin' it, boi. Dat set o' bookends be growin' by the looks of it. 'Cept you be missin' a couple. Where he be, now?" He fist-bumped JK and continued his scrutiny of the others.

I smiled that he referred to Ambergai Gee as 'a couple'. Gai was that well-hung. "You know, Ezra, he is off on errands and we aren't exactly sure what those are. He'll find us when he's ready. Boi, this all looks delicious. Are you going to join us?"

We introduced the lanky man with huge feet to Jake and Cal, then watched as the chef left no doubt about his likely aim should the chance arise for plugging my boy, Doctor Marshall. His weakness for educated white men had been made plain on several occasions. Firstly, down a deserted alleyway, upon introducing himself to me a few months before. Jake would be enjoying further familiarization. Cal appeared amused. Adolpho and Bryce filled him in on the details.

The busy bistro negated any possibility for Ezra joining us then but his interest in the whiteboy-loaded table assured a visit to our side of the mountain in the near future. He backed away toward the kitchen, kneading his crotch in insinuation. More than one white ass in our group tingled at the move. Bryce, particularly, took reminiscent note, which produced a knowing glance between Jeremy and Adolpho. The young ski bum was insatiable. It was certainly an advantage for him that he had alighted in our world, settling with Adolpho, what with our laissez-faire attitudes toward sex.

Over the scrumptious feast, we all speculated on the tack to be taken regarding the older trio over at the county hospital. Jake felt that Mr. Edgewater's wishes must be respected at all costs, while the younger men felt intervention on the elderly man's behalf was important. I found it enlightening to see how the younger generations missed the value of autonomy and independence in latter stages of life. Deducing the difference must arise from inability to fathom elderly priorities, and having experienced little more than the bubble of adolescence, I remembered my similar rationale from that stage in life.

My pocket buzzed an incoming call and I retrieved the device. "Luke?" It was Bartholomew Chastain. "We are wheeling Elmer out to the limousine for heading around to our home. The entourage is a tad disconcerting and Annalise felt I should call to request your and Jeremy's meeting us there. To assess and discuss his plans. Might there be any chance for you to do so, young man?" He was always traditionally proper in his manners, yet the aloofness I now perceived made me concerned for that which was not being said. I nodded to my husband and his intuition kicked in right away. Assuring the genteel soul of our willingness, I ended the call and all of us finished, then settled up, making our way back toward the gondola station.

The trip over soon put the six of us at the Chastain's front door. I had assumed the 'limousine' Bart had alluded to had been a shuttle van. The stretch limo in the round-about put that premise to rest. Sleek and black, it took up a full half of the curved driveway. Nobody was inside, as far as we could tell. The darkened windows rebuffed perusal, but no reaction to window-tapping had next sent us up the front steps. A minute following our knock, a liveried gentleman-of-color, looking every bit a chauffeur, opened the door. Apparently expecting us, he pulled the door wide. We heard a hoarse, blustery voice exclaiming something unintelligible from inside.

Ushered in and depositing coats in the foyer, we made our way into the cozily sunken family room. A big rock fireplace boasting a yew log crackled its welcome. The vision of a wheel-chaired Elmer Edgewater attempting to arise on old-fashioned wooden crutches while lambasting the group surrounding him evidenced that our welcome was not universal.

Beside the older man was a stately woman of regal bearing in ski apparel. Her long blond tresses hung almost to her waist but the two braided plaits made them more like hanging ropes.

Next to her, we were surprised to see Ambergai Gee and Sheila E with her partner, Cat.

The Chastains were apart from the patient, over close to the fireplace, conversing with a small, compact, shapely woman in flowing black. Jeremy nudged me, "Honey. I cannot believe my eyes, but if that isn't Chaka, then I'm going nuts. I swear, that is her!" He sounded absolutely certain. The rest of us honed in on the dark red-haired beauty, curls blossoming in a controlled disarray of wildness, falling in abundance about her radiant smiling face.

From behind us, the liveried man announced our presence, "Madam, the doctors have arrived."

"I ain't needing no more goddam doctors," came another eruption from Mr. Edgewater. He sank back into the wheelchair, unsuccessful in arising. The braided woman cushioned his descent. Annalise turned our way, plainly relieved at our appearance.

"Luke, Jeremy, please… come in. We are so very pleased you could come," her elegant, long-fingered hands matched her voice and she gestured to join them. Clouds of displeasure smoldered around the irascible Elmer but he held his tongue. A small degree of respect at recognizing who we were muted him. At least, for the moment.

Ambergai and the girls met us with hugs, "Mi tinks it be a'good timin' for ya' a'comin', now, ma' Mons," including all six of us with the broad sweep of his hand, "der' be da' need o' da' addin' o' da' calmness a'ready in da' room. Mi do believe ya' be a'knowin' da' ladies, here, an' ma' old friend, Miss Khan, now, mi bein' correct?"

Totally blown down, we shook hands with the diva, her warmth and openness apparent. "I am happy to know you, boys. Mr. Gee and my girls, Sheila and Cat, speak highly of you." She fixed on Jeremy, "Dr. Kell, I understand through Annalise and Bartholomew that you have been challenged recently, yourself. I trust that an athlete of your stature is mending well, especially under the guiding eyes of two doctors… following their orders well, I am certain?" The luminary smiled widely as she spoke, having surely been apprised of a few details. Her astute gaze roamed up and down my man in open recognition of his masculine good looks.

Like everyone, she was immediately taken by his winsome aura and toothy smile. "I am surprised nobody informed me of the magnitude of your handsomeness. And, much more, that your entourage here rivals your own sexiness…" this, as she took in Calumet and Jake, along with the youths accompanying us.

"Ma' lady, da' Khan, ya' be a'knowin' da better, now, an' admit it all. Mi, did, in fact o' da' matters, be a'tellin' ya o' ma' Mons' fetchin' selves, be ya' a'tellin all o' da truth. Mi jus' be a'sayin'," Gai dwarfed Chaka as he enwrapped her shoulder with his huge hand.

A distinct cough from old Bart broke the thread and we all focused toward the wheelchair. Annalise took my hand and led me to the stately blonde, "Dr. Cevennes, I would very much like to introduce you to Elmer's friend, here. She has traveled far afield on very short notice to be here at this time. May I introduce Mrs. Trude Jochum-Beiser of Lech am Arlberg, of the Vorarlberg in Austria."

I was again stunned, unable to even stutter. The tall woman extended her hand, like a queen to a vassal, aristocratic bearing weighty in its gravitas. I took the proffered hand, almost kissing it. My man came to the rescue, stepping in and ably welcoming the Olympic icon. He in turn introduced the rest of our family. She spoke gracefully, but without any sign of self-absorption, deflecting attention to Mr. Edgewater instead.

"It is my good fortune, and luck, to have been tracked down by Miss Winfrey and Miss Khan, along with these girls and the dear spirit, Mr. Gee, in my hamlet these recent days past. Being informed of the misfortune overtaking my dear old flame here in Telluride, I was glad to hasten here to be of whatever small service I could." With that, she placed her hands on Elmer's shoulders, endearingly embracing the old codger.

Disarmed by her touch, the old fellow peered upward, almost smiling. A different persona entirely from just moments before. No rancor or animosity were evident now as the man fairly melted in surrender to the fond display.

"I ain't saying that I need any undue attention, now, Trude, but I will admit you are a sight for sore eyes." A slight edge sounded in his next words but his manners held. "I am surprised your husband allowed you to come, for sure. I remember Alfred as quite the jealous husband, at least from the news reports." The quizzical look bespoke much.

"Well, El, since Alfred has been gone these past three years, I must say that he did not raise much protest at my abrupt departure. And, you must admit, he had quite a reason for envy, in light of your and my slightly checkered history, you old dear," she again squeezed his shoulders and leaned down to peck his shock of white hair.

Ambergai sensed the mood and nimbly herded all of us toward the kitchen. A dozen pairs of feet shuffled through the door to allow the couple some privacy. We compared notes and discovered our Jamaican friend's idea to find Trude. Employing the far reach of Oprah and Chaka for the leg work. The two had worked together with Sheila E and her lady, bringing the plan to fruition in what seemed to be the nick of time. What might actually result remained the looming question. Nonetheless, Mr. Edgewater was about the only person with any answers.

Cal broached the elephant in the room, "Now that the two are in there together, what are their options? It would seem a given they both need some help. Is she thinking of spending time here with Elmer, and where would they be doing it, if so? Even a strong woman like Trude, at close to ninety years of age, herself, must be daunted by thinking of caring for him in the present condition. Won't the two need home health care, physical therapy and skilled nursing, just for starters? And, again, where will everything happen?" All were poignant issues.

Old Bart again insisted that the gent could stay in their home during convalescence. Annalise was in agreement, but had reservations. Especially now that Trude had arrived, they couldn't know whether the two even desired help. Needed or not. The pride factor was a strong instinct, as she well knew.

Chaka intoned the idea which was probably most relevant, "You know, this whole conversation may be unnecessary, as none of us truly have any say in the matter. It looks to be a decision for the two in the next room. Maybe our plans should await their input before we get smacked right down by those very strong personalities…" She pointed at the door separating us from them. Ambergai added his agreement. None of us could gainsay the premise. So for the time being, we poured a couple bottles of wine around the Chastain's table and ruminated.

Before we had finished settling other world issues, the door bumped open to the push of Trude rolling Elmer into the room. "We have pretty much made our decision how to go forward," she said. "Elmer Bruce and I are going up to his home and settle in. Now." The resolute faces told us they were not brooking any dissent. "Both of us deeply appreciate all that has been done in our behalf. Now, we mean to travel the path which we have decided is in our best mutual interest." Elmer soaked up the presence of the one person for whom he had spent most of his life waiting. The look in his eyes was one which even Annalise had never encountered.

With our collective, if hesitant, blessing, the couple began their plans for the ascent. Travel up the steepness to Elmer's eyrie was, in itself, an obstacle, due to the challenge of the patient's ambulatory capacity. We all pitched in to help in what manner we were able. Over the next hours, provisions were packed and bundled, the limo was loaded and two snowmobiles were acquired from the village. In the present weather, transportation would prove a huge challenge, we knew. Luckily, Elmer had prepared his home in the recent years for contingencies like this should something occur. Having discussed this together, Trude and he felt they could manage. Our consternation aside, a cavalcade soon materialized and the trek began.

Before sunset, sixteen people, including the reunited paramours, arrived and settled the two in the very rustic environs where Elmer had spent most of his life. Solidly snug, Trude was enthralled with the place, feeling as if she had been transported back to her childhood in Austria.

The views were splendid. Craggy San Juan peaks surrounded Telluride Mountain in snowy majesty. Elmer had used his talents constructing the abode for fullest effect. We all huddled in the large, low-beamed room facing outward to the rugged snow globe diorama. No other homes or buildings were in sight; this was the highest edifice on the mountain. In the short time allotted for helping establish them, a wary level of comfort that maybe the duo could succeed in their professed aims had taken hold.

They acceded to our insistence of daily check-ins, nursing visits, and even with my and Jake's promise for regular home doctor visits with an ease which surprised us. Pantry and pharmacy, plus provisions, had been stocked in excess.

We all tempered our misgivings and left the doting Trude cuddling with a semi-comfortable Elmer on the downy bed overlooking one of the grandest views the world could afford anyone. Elmer had planned well.

Descending the heights back to the Chastain's home found us heaving sighs of hope and semi-relief that we had delivered and left the old-world chatelaine and her long lost lover to their private devices…nothing more could be done. At least, by any of us.

Unwinding to more good red wine and green-cross pharmaceuticals for the early evening hours, everyone ensconced before the roaring fireplace. We toasted the two, in absentia, with well-wishes for lives still being well-lived.

Chaka and Gai finally ushered in the end to a bittersweet day by announcing their resolve to depart. It broke the reverie. All of us gradually made our ways in divergent directions toward the village, Telluride town or respective homes.

I invoked physician's privilege by escorting my reticent husband to our lodge. Cal and Jake decided to accompany the boys down-mountain for a bit of relief-by-merrymaking. Our old Black Forest cuckoo clock finally counted midnight with Jeremy and I laying snuggled together alone in our own private eyrie, whispering conspiratorially.

Listening to my man's breathing even out to the deep breaths signaling his submission to Morpheus, my ears picked up the high country reverberations of wolves howling somewhere in the far, high peaks above us. My own eyes fluttered shut to the comforting hoots from the owl resident outside in the tall spruce guarding our balcony.

The world was where it should be.

* * *

"Riddle me this: Cauliflower must admit: it is really broccoli just trying to get an Oscar." Adolpho was perplexed by the idea. He and I were the only ones up in the house the following morning. We were sharing coffee before the fireplace, watching fat snowflakes flutter past the windows in the early morning light.

The young sommelier was filling me in on the carousing he and Bryce had reveled in with Cal, Jake, Sheila E and Cat G late into the night. By his portrayal, the whole of Mountain Village must be painted in deep shades of crimson now. Cal and Bryce had apparently answered the call of the wild to entertain the packed ballroom in the Hotel Madeline.

From Adolpho's telling, he and Jake, with Sheila and Cat rooting them on, had watched as Cal had enticed the shy

Bryce, in youthful throes of stoned ebullience, to perform a cabaret-style impromptu strip-tease on the stage. Or a bar. I hadn't quite determined that part yet. The two must have brought the house down, I surmised, knowing the sex-appeal of both the men. I envisioned them together charming the crowd. Cal was notoriously exhibitionist in his party-mode and the pent-up anxieties from the previous day had evidently psyched him well for an over-due release.

Adolpho related how another celebrity presence in the area for the festival, the star of the Broadway musical, 'Kinky Boots', Wayne Brady, had been talked into joining the drag revue unfolding about the time my boys had arrived. Thirty minutes into Brady's donning of the drag queen MC's thigh-high, red-sequined boots, Cal had been spotted near the back of the room. Towering over everyone, he had been power-hitting Jake.

It hadn't taken much to coerce the tall hunk into joining Wayne on stage where an extra pair of boots had been produced. Cal had played the crowd, slithering up on the bar, extending his legs skyward while his pants were removed and the boots were pulled on him. All right there in front of the looney crowd. The mental snapshot of my brother-in-law up on the stage in speedo and thigh boots was an arousing one.

He had then literally collared and yanked the naïve blond bombshell, Bryce, up beside him. The two had camped the place, along with the Broadway icon, erogenously re-enacting Wayne's opening scene and disrobing in strobe.

Ersatz kitsch and bombast had abounded, per Adolpho's entertaining depiction. As it happened, by the end of the scene up on the adjacent long mahogany bar, Cal's tens had somehow been coaxed awake. The enormous boner had apparently peeked past Cal's speedo confines, which had rocked those queens' world... I could just picture it all. Not the least of which was the image of my best man, Jake, hanging back on the wall, calmly taking it in. Content in indulging his alpha-man husband and no doubt happy in his own anonymity.

At least I now understood the mystery of all four boys bouncing into our bed at 2:30 AM, covered in some kind of oil and very little clothing. The ensuing orgy had pulled Jeremy and myself in and gooey loads later, we had all collapsed together. The sheets were going to need bleaching, I smirked to myself.

Presently, Adolpho and I were the only bedmates capable of rising and taking nourishment. Fleecy white bathrobes draped us following our wakeup shower and we mulled things over. The dogs lounged contentedly beneath us after a snowy romp.

I responded to the initial enquiry about the MC's allusion to cauliflower. "Dolph, I think she must have been talking about the oversight by the Academy in nominating any minorities for Awards this year." It seemed allegorically feasible, I thought, and a fitting joke given the alternative venue laced by celebs, as the place had been. We snickered over the clever witticism.

"You know, I think that Wayne Brady must be at least bi-curious," Adolpho opined. "He was salivating over Cal the whole time. And come to think, it was him that singled out Cal from the stage to begin with. Jake and I thought it was just ramping up audience participation, but Mr. Brady sure kept 'accidentally' bumping and grinding Cal up there. It's pretty obvious why Cal sprang a boner. That horn dog." I wondered to whom the Italiano was referring.

Though Cal was extremely carnal, Wayne Brady was infamous for his gay innuendos in public forums. Many guessed his proclivity, even though he wasn't 'out'. That in itself was a stirring thought. The 'new Monty Hall' was a hottie in his own right. It was a wonder that the Kinky Boots star hadn't shown up here with the boys last night.

Third cups of Blue Mountain coffee later found Dolph helping me crank up the hot tub heaters and jets. I figured everyone would enjoy the morning snowfall amidst the nursing of certain hangovers, and my husband needed heat application with massage for his aching neck and shoulder. The idea sounded great on both scores. There were already several snow rabbits, a doe and a couple of black squirrels hunting and grazing close by as the snow flurries thickened. The ambience was perfect.

Racing back inside, barefoot and freezing in only our robes, we found my man and Jake pouring mugs of fresh coffee. They were also sporting just robes and acted surprised when we burst through the door in the same. "You guys must be nuts--- or nutless, one of the two--- being out there like that," Jake scolded, "Here, lemme check out those scrotums, boys." He was still revved from partying, and we jested about the vaudeville performers shirking the morning upstairs. He playfully cupped us both in passing, sure enough palming shriveled, retracted ball-less sacks.

"Baby man, it sure sounds like we missed some performance last night. Did you hear what went on downhill at the Madeline?" Jeremy fucked me silly before we had fallen asleep and I knew he wasn't complaining. I swatted him as I sat on him in the fireside recliner.

"What, the accommodations weren't to your liking, JK? Is that what I'm hearing?" It was always fun ragging Jeremy, as the man took everything out of my mouth as gospel, even after two decades. The fact warmed my heart. His puppy-dog look appeared and the sore-shouldered patient surfaced. I rubbed everything except my man's sore spots in making my tease points. He loosened up. The lack of cynicism was so endearing.

"No, my man, you are not. I ain't ever gonna be gettin' ee-nuf' o' MY bootilicious stuff," as he slanged and squeezed my cakes. I nipped his lip, informing him about our plan for soaking outside. Basking in my luck…and his swelling lap.

Homemade granola with fruit and yogurt later, and after dragging the straggler dick-dancers downstairs, all six of us traipsed to the hot tub. Sharing a couple of joints, we played happily together in rejoining the Oreo Review, as Jake was dubbing it.

My best boy's take lent even more nuance to the already lurid tale. It would seem that Bryce had pulled Adolpho into the bathroom afterwards and the two had been caught red-handed there. Bryce went to begging his man's forgiveness for acting out like he had, seeking atonement by blowjob. Not even necessary, Adolpho wasn't turning down the attention. The two had been blitzed enough that they hadn't bothered to break it off when accosted. iPhones had tallied an additional tale, and probable uploads to free video websites, for ski week adventurers to re-hash upon their return to the real world. Dolph had abashedly omitted the juicy tidbit and we all razzed the two mercilessly between tokes.

Pulling on heavy lined boots over waterproof outer wear in our en suite closet, Jake and I discussed whether to call for an update on the couple up at the summit before hiking down to dinner on the piazza. We were looking for more immersion with the festival mood what with the snowy onslaught but our need for the knowledge of well-being was bothering our consciences. "You know that the visiting nurses will let us know the status, and it's still early yet, Luke. Besides, with the whiteout, they may be having trouble getting up the trail. We should just go ahead with the boys. We have our phones, y'know."

Returning to the Madeline for lunch, on purpose, made for an exceedingly gratifying reception by the hotel occupants and staff. Jeremy and I had missed the entire thing. I suppose we were looking for vicarious fulfillment. Bryce and Cal were rock stars in the staff's eyes, the streamed show having spread like wildfire overnight. We ate lunch amid adulative recognition, loving the attentive drag ski and party participants. Fettuccini, Colorado Bass filets and coq au vin went down deliciously with Oolong tea. Cal was fending off over-the-top men of all stripes and relishing every second. The man was in his element.

Bryce, not so much. He wasn't seasoned at the art of deflection, unused to being center of attention. The previous night, he had been swept up in the party without much forethought. But now, he was obviously uncomfortable. Adolpho went into protective mode for his new other half but we watched the basically shy Italian get swamped by the attempt.

We more seasoned partiers coalesced around the two in big brother fashion, putting the young couple in our center and insulating them. They caught their collective breath and gradually deduced our strategy. Our 'baby bro' was hit by the strong, solid wall of caring he had gained in our family. The 'coming out' talk at Hallowe'en amongst us four flooded back to him, now permanently impacting his spirit. Faith was instilled. We had his back and he finally believed it.

Before we finished dessert, Bryce was already accepting he wasn't alone and the pressure melted before our eyes. He seized on the overzealous crowd, maturing a little right there before our eyes. Cal and Jake caught on to his reaction and Jeremy grasped me tight in tacit acknowledgement. And Adolpho…well, he drooled on him. His boi was growing up.

The Art and Psychology of leaning on one another. The basic concept of Family. The gay community was coming of age through the allowance of equal rights. The harvest was ready for the reaping. Let it be understood.

While Cal signed an autograph, hat-size increasing as he scribbled, we strolled across the piazza toward home. As we walked, I felt the vibrating iPhone in my pocket. Answering it, I was astonished to hear Ambergai's voice. The man rarely ever spoke telephonically. But it was his words which really threw me. In assent to his assertive instructions, I quickly hung up. "We are needed up at Elmer Edgewater's place. Right away."

Not aware of any specifics, I was unable to enlighten the rest. We took off for the house and grabbed both double snow mobiles from our shed. Three bodies on each slowed our progress but we made it up the mountain in twenty more minutes, finding two four-wheel drive vehicles with snow chains parked in the snow by the door.

Double stepping the stairs, we were greeted before we knocked by a tear-streaked Annalise, linen handkerchief to her nose. Bart was on her heels, wet eyed, too. We saw Gai, Susan, the home health nurse, and Miss Winfrey standing at the large bay window anchoring the front view in the house. All were statuesquely quiet; reverentially so. The aura of calamity hung in the air. And the house was freezing cold.

Hugging the old couple, we entered. From up the staircase there emanated the sound of Glen Miller's Band playing 'Moonlight Serenade'. No one said a word. We listened as the big band hit played on. Its haunting melody filled the old lodge.

Ambergai pulled away from Oprah after a few moments and approached us, unusually reserved. "Mi Mons, 'der be a big change in da' stars—dey been done realigned over da' night. If ya be a'followin', now, let's us go up to da big room 'der. Da couple done bein' havin' 'der own private ideas for da' future…"

At the ominous words, we followed as Gai took Oprah's arm. The powerful woman smiled sadly at us and we trailed the two up the stairway. The music grew louder as we reached the landing. Topping the last step and turning into the roomy bedroom, our eyes beheld both Elmer and Trude. They were in the bed. Frozen in final embrace.

The scene shocked us but the serenity on their faces said everything. The two were cheek to cheek, but more, they were unclothed and holding one another close, in full body mode.

The couple appeared to have locked together in the act of consummation, now evincing unearthly beauty in expiry. Discernible ending moments in mutual rhapsody resided in their death masks. Arms wrapping tightly around one another, her long tresses had been unwound and brushed through, now caressing both of them in a golden mantle.

In amazement, we saw Elmer's splinted left leg covering Trude's right one: or the part remaining, anyway. Amputated at the knee, his disabled one protected her lost one. We found the Olympic athlete's prosthetic propped next to the bed out of sight. No one had known of the Olympic skier's obviously recent amputation. Metastatic disease was agonizingly consumptive.

The lovebirds had opened all of the windows throughout the house and shared their passion before the now smoldering fireplace. Two partly-filled wine glasses rested on the side table by the bed. Elmer's empty opiate pain medication bottle lay next to those and an opened push-tab wrapper labeled, 'Tadalafil/20 mg', close by that. Burned-down bee's wax candles were positioned in profusion around the room. A smoked roach lay cold in the small ash tray. Fresh snow powdered the sills and floors.

Jeremy leaned into my ear, "Honey, there has never been a more moving sight…look at them." He nuzzled my face and I felt his tears collide with my own. Each of us were totally stunned. Nothing would ever alter that etched memory for the rest of our lives.

Glen Miller finished the song. After a few seconds of static from the old Motorola turntable, set to endless repeat mode, there came another. 'In the Mood' soothed the room. An unmatchable sense of sangfroid and karma swathed us. I felt like an intruder, suddenly, as did we all.

Jake made motion to cover the couple but Cal stopped his husband, gently pulling his hands to his own, "My Jake, they left with their spirits together. Far be it for us to decide they would want to be covered now. Leave them in peace, baby." We knew how right-on he was. Departing the love nest, we descended in deferential silence. Meeting the Chastains and Susan at the base of the stairs, we sought seats in the windswept living room, shivering on more than one level.

It was Oprah who noticed the envelope on the mantel. Fallen flat in a gust of wind it had gone unnoticed. She read the addressee and handed it to Annalise. The elegant woman carefully opened the seal. Pulling out the single sheet of paper, the elderly couple read together, more tears streaming.

The music ended again and Annalise looked up at us. Snowflakes settled on her head through the open window, carried in on the soft sigh of an alpine draught. She gracefully read to us as a new melody began. It was Glen Miller's recording of 'Elmer's Tune'.

"Dear ones.

We regret the shock to your senses, but did, indeed, decide our course. Know that it is the right one for us and be happy. We are supremely so. Here in the heights, we are both certain our spirits will have a very short trek to our eternal spot.

Let it be said that we left on top of the world. Cry: it is cleansing. We miss you all already. But don't be sorry for us. We will only be making up for lost time in a dimension where there is no sense of it.

Notice the bequest we leave for our woodland friends. A haven to be shared. Seek us just twenty yards to the southwest of this front door. Come and commune whenever you like.

Please grant us this one favor. Let this bed and this home serve as our bodies' final resting site. And our pyre.

Forever at Peace, Elmer and Trude.

The fitting melody progressed into the lyrical reprise and as she finished, the words wafted over us:

'Why are the stars always a'winking and blinking above?'
'What makes a fellow start thinking of falling in love?'

'It's not the season, the reason is plain as the moon.'
                    'It's just Elmer's tune.'
'What makes a lady of eighty go out on the loose?'
'Why does a gander meander in search of a goose?'
'What puts a kick in the chicken, the magic in June?'
                    'It's just Elmer's tune.'
'Listen, listen, there's a lot you're li'ble to be missin'.'
'Sing it, swing, any old way and any old time.'
'The hurdy gurdies, the birdies, the cop on the beat.'
'The candy maker, the baker, the man on the street.'
'The City charmer, the farmer, the Man in the Moon.'
                    'All sing Elmer's Tune…'

* * *

Jeremy sat on the Adirondack chair at the edge of the ice. He watched contentedly as I pirouetted and twirled on the ice skates in a private show for him. My scarf trailed behind me as I carved designs on the pond outside our home. With a final turn, I skated across to him, slowing as I drew close. I ungracefully ended by collapsing in his lap and he applauded my efforts.

"Boi, you are making Apolo Ono jealous as shit right now. I should be streaming this somewhere to show you off, my man." Never mind that I had been figure skating rather than speed skating.

More like Brian Boitano, I hrmmphed to myself. He and I had practiced on the pond over the preceding winters, strengthening our ankles in the doing. Since I wouldn't yet permit my patient to risk himself falling on the ice, JK good-naturedly put up with my protectiveness with graceful aplomb. He pulled me down for a slow kiss and we snuggled in the last vestiges of the epic snowstorm.

Only fluttering snowflakes fell at this point, as Nature finally exhausted itself. An inexplicable weather system had sprung a surprise on the region's meteorology experts, fostering an event which grew into a snowstorm of epic proportions, raging over Telluride mountain for three days' duration. Paralyzing the mountain during that period, the Ski Festival had been forced indoors, as ski lifts and even the ever-running gondola system had been shut down.

Barely making it down from the divide following our impromptu wake at Elmer's lodge, blizzard conditions had set in. The night of the couple's deaths, as authorities pieced things together afterwards, it seemed a combustive event had been triggered by a closed flue capping the big rock fireplace. Whether a tragic accident or a forethought stratagem, the ancient heartwood oak and spruce log home had caught fire and blazed through most of the night.

Without ability to get fire equipment up the steep incline during the blizzard, no relief had been possible. By three mornings later, the foundation and two fireplaces were all that remained. Officials had identified dental remains and announced that the elderly Olympians had succumbed to the vagaries and caprices of Mother Nature at her worst. Or finest. Tragedy had taken them and all had been deemed unpreventable by Man.

That night, the seven of us had hunkered down in our cozy abode as intermittent glimmers of an ongoing conflagration up on the divide flared through the maelstrom. Trude and Elmer had been safely sent on their way to eternity and there would be no interruption in their plans. It would seem that they had been bequeathed their last wish.

The truth of the matter, which would follow all of us to our graves, was this. The group celebrating Trude and Elmer's 'lives well-lived' had closed the ground floor windows after listening to the swan song letter penned by Trude and built up a roaring fire to heal the coldness. Breaking out the pantry provisions and wine cellar stocks, we had paid tribute to the duo upstairs by holding a memorial wake as the two had requested and would have wished. The Glen Miller Band had serenaded throughout. In the middle of the fete, we had all trekked the twenty yards to the southwest as Trude's letter had directed and come upon an exquisitely poetic discovery.

A secluded alpine glade had been carefully cultivated there. Snowdrifts insulated a sylvan setting where Elmer had long ago dug a fire pit, ringed it with large smooth pink granite stones and set a heavy, heartwood-oak bench to one side. The comfortable seat had been lovingly hewn from a single mammoth trunk. Large enough to seat four people comfortably, it had most probably come from the hoard of hand-cut logs used to construct the log home following the Olympic Games in the 1940's. The old recluse had no doubt spent countless hours in reverie at the site over the years. Situated behind the fire pit, the bench faced outward, commanding a magnificent view of the valley for miles around.

To the side stood two mature trees which a young Elmer Edgewater had nurtured until they were self-sufficient. Both were imported as saplings. Not native to the area, it had taken years to be confidant of their survival. Now, intertwined not only in their branches, but in their roots as well, the gnarled old Chinkapin Oak and the elegantly straight and tall, heart-shaped leaved Linden tree served as sentinels over the entire vicinity.

Newly carved into the bark of each, we encountered one half of a heart. In the oak, the initials E.B.E. were carved. In the Linden, the initials T.B. had been traced. Each set of initials were based by five interlocking rings. Olympic rings. An entire heart had been wholly etched in a nearby granite boulder, both sets of initials together there. The lovers had spent some of their final moments at this site, making their mark. A contagion of goosebumps proliferated amongst us during our visit to Elmer and Trude's eternal dwelling. Their spirits were probably unpacking as we explored. Or making love. But surely laughing at us…

We had then made our way back to the lodge and closed everything up. Tight. But only downstairs. After sharing a commemorative doobie in the couple's honor at Bart and Annalise's insistence, the final act had been to stoke the fire and toss the healthy blunt on the flames before heading out the door. Nobody seemed to notice the first wisps of smoky backdrafts invading the common room. The tight downstairs closure had included the fateful clamping of the main flue. It would bode serious risk for the old lodge's integrity, one that was fraught with danger of a fiery accident.

Or a funeral pyre.

* * *

"Gramps, do you think William knows I'm back?" Little Elle had proven adamant about the subject since her and her mama's arrival to our eyrie a few days before. On every previous visit, the young ram had faithfully shown up to welcome the little tyke on whom he had an interspecies crush. Now, the pig-tailed girl was demanding information from her grandfather, the All-Knowing, and was not going to be put off any longer.

"Baby girl, William isn't used to you and your mama coming this time of year. He's up on the mountain looking for girlfriends the way most rams do right now. I think he'll be around soon…your tree trunk is all warmed up and that boy can feel it, I am pretty sure. So, be patient, sweetheart." Jeremy was asking the impossible of a six-and-a-half-year-old but the new nickname was still flummoxing the man so it was the best he could come up with at the moment.

'Gramps' was a shock to his system, I could tell, and even though the little sprite meant the world to the big teddy bear, as Big Elle continued to do, the timber of his voice betrayed JFK's trepidation at the word. Walking away from our spot in the hottub, the little girl gazed forlornly at the spruce tree across the way.

"Well, Gramps" --- she emphasized the word--- "he better get his butt down that mountain soon, 'cause he's missin' me."

I couldn't hold in the smothered snicker and Jeremy elbowed me at the reaction. I was tickled by the sprite's usage of the forbidden word, 'butt', however her grandpa was still focusing on the second intonation of the now officially detestable reference to his status, inferring my amusement as due to…that word.

I splashed him and pushed his head under the surface of the roiling hot tub bubbles. He responded by gripping my piece around its base from his submerged position. Though my trunks kept him from a good grip, his mouth followed the hand, and teeth next portrayed faux vexation by engulfing me through the material. I was surprised by his contact and almost shrieked in delight.

Not missing a thing, Elle Jr piped up, "Grandpa Luke, is he getting on your junk again?" I was shocked by her precociousness and gulped water in my sputtering.

"Well, Luke, is he?" This from big Elle's mouth. Jeremy's grown up daughter had exited the back door, carrying a tray of lemonade and a fresh bowl of hot popcorn. The two females were ganging up on us boys.

"Hey, Elle, I didn't hear you," as I tried extricating myself from the submerged piranha still teething. Not thinking his granddaughter could see, let alone know what he was attempting, he sure wasn't aware that his daughter was now querying the same subject. I yanked my man away and pulled him topside to face the music.

Shaking his handsome head, Jeremy rubbed his eyes to clear them and visualized his girls. 'Oh, hi, Ellie… hey that looks good." He reached out for a tall glass and was playfully rebuffed by the dark beauty bearing the tray. Mock anger crossed her face as she berated her daddy, "Can't I even leave you two alone one minute without you getting nasty in front of this innocent, boys?"

I nudged him again and he grasped the undercurrent of the unheard questions by looking from one to the other. In feigned state of embarrassment, he turned to me and planted a lip lock kiss over my mouth. Both girl's 'yucked' in their dismay at his lack of humility. Finally backing off, he turned to them again.

"My girls. You two may as well pull yourselves out of the Stone Age and come to grips with the fact that this here is my…husband… and we love each other. He can't keep his hands off of me.

A huge splash erupted from his submerged hand-swipe upward and hot water soaked them both. Their peals of laughter halted the allied onslaught. The two attempted fakery in the form of peeved insult. The front lasted all of five seconds before big Elle put down the drinks and now-soggy popcorn. Both of our 'baby girls' tumbled into the hot tub with us. In true collusion style, all three of us collectively dunked the big stud. Gramps succumbed in tickled defeat.

Toweling off in our shower room, Jeremy rolled his and popped my ass, "Boi, you are in deep trouble. Siding with that pair of harpies against me? I believe you are in line for a spankin', now. So, I'll be benevolent. Either get over this knee--- right this minute--- or get on this." He pointed down at his swelling dick. Seeing my glance at the door, he added, "You saw me lock that door, you bad boi, so make up your mind."

I chose both. It had been two days since we had shared pleasure, an unheard of period of chastity between us. Our collective desire was uncontrollable. Lifting me over his shoulder, my man hefted me out the en suite door. I was deposited unceremoniously onto our bed. He set to slaking his ardor in a series of moves which succeeded in satisfying our combined needs over the next hour. Laying exhausted after multiple climaxes, we were interrupted by loud knocking at the bedroom door.

Little Elle had been ignored long enough. "Are you two about finished in there? We have things to do and places to go out here, y'know. You old guys need to put it away and get back to me and mama." We were dazed, again, at the little imp's audacious display and smothered one another under pillows to stifle our mirthful disbelief.

The next sounds outside the door were hushed admonitions by Ellie, pulling the little big mouth back down the stairs. We did shriek from under the same pillow then, "My God, what is going on with that imp? She is Ellie on steroids!" We both remembered back to big Elle's precocious ways at the same age. While she had been just as astutely observant, the young mama Elle had exhibited much more reserve in her delivery. Or were we misremembering? Could that be? Apparently coming to similar conclusions, we lay awhile longer in commiseration before rising and dressing.

Arriving in the kitchen a bit later, Jeremy took the reins of preparation for dinner while I set to laying a fire, picking up around the house, then getting Elvee and Suture situated with a romp around the property. Little Elle accompanied us. I was re-familiarizing with everything after being absent these past four months and reconnoitered with them.

Following the tumultuous February festival with all of the revelry and activity, punctuated by the trauma of loss, a period of quietude had descended on all seven of us in the household. For a good couple of weeks, we had recuperated. We sequestered ourselves away from the hubbub for refortification. The time had been salutary.

The Chastains had reconciled their consciences over the loss of their close cohort. The celebrity factor had vacated town along with the gay influence. Ambergai had finally felt comfortable that we 'boys' had healed enough psychologically and taken his leave back to Blue Mountain on the island for attention to some necessary issues.

Adolpho's very successful wine business had needed inventory re-stocking and he had cajoled Bryce into switching his computer programming and coding courses to online status, enabling the duo to visit Tuscany and Florence again for several months. Our best men, Cal and Jake, had stuck with us until we four had decided the downlander world must be rejoined. For the past four months, Jake and I had shifted back to medical rounds at Brack, in Austin, and Jeremy had resumed his spring semester courses at UT. Cal left to tour all seven of his regional corporate offices for long overdue hands-on supervisory and organizational tasks.

The high country had pulled on us like sailors to the sea throughout the time. Finally, as May rolled into June again, Jeremy and I had answered the call. We had set a sojourn into sync with our girls and were now returned for the next months. The Elles were with us for two whole weeks and we were loving every minute. They both changed way too much and too quickly when apart, for our tastes. Though we knew Ellie was supremely happy in her life and wouldn't try swaying her to change it, the interludes at the highland lodge were just too brief.

Well, I pondered, as I watched little Elle race with the boys on the far side of the pond, it was what it was and no matter preferences, some things simply couldn't be different than meant to be. The profundity made me think of the glen up on the divide. Jeremy and I must visit there soon. And it would be good if we took the Chastains with us. Annalise had told me the two of them had not returned since the day of the fire that took away their friends' reality. A visit would have proved too emotionally wrought, she had said. I would see if Jeremy and I could arrange the four of us going together. A good thing for us all, I figured.

The trio of exuberance suddenly surrounded me, snapping me to the everyday, and we made our way to the house for dinner.

* * *

"Jeremy, look there--- is that a Bighorn?" I pointed through the windshield up at a high peak as we rounded the hairpin curve. Having left our girls at the Montrose airport an hour before, we had been introspective on the return trip home. I had been perusing the landscape in silence and just spotted the curled horns on a cliff above.

Squinting upward through the windshield, "Yup, I think it is, Luke. Wonder if it could be W.C. That old goat…" My husband was still miffed that the big ram hadn't ever shown himself while we had the girls in residence, 'after all we had done for him', as he had unfairly accused. Like the mature orphan owed it to us onetime fosterers. I smiled to myself. It had been a bit disheartening to see Little Elle's disappointment at missing her friend, but she had experienced a dose of reality. The letdown would end up being a positive someday in the future. I chose to believe that.

My hope was that the magnificent beast was OK. We had heard a lot of clashing horns up in the heights since our homecoming. There were never any assurances when it came to maintenance of the status quo in Nature, and we realized our ram might have been successfully challenged in his supremacy. It was a sobering possibility.

The sighting once again reminded my intention for visiting Elmer's glen. "Honey, can we plan to go see 'The Trees' now that we're by ourselves? I really have had it on my mind that we should. Even if Annalise and Bart aren't ready yet." The innate tugging had increased over the past two days and I surmised that on some level there was a reason for it. Being but an ignorant human with diminished instincts, I tried to pay attention to my inner self. Lately, Sir Id had been much more insistent in his statements. I felt a need for action.

So we agreed.

The ruins of the place were mind numbing. As we stood before the skeletal remains of two lonely obelisks formerly known as fireplaces, the previous February's wounds opened anew. Contrasting the picture of the former log home in its glory to this rubble stole my breath. Jeremy wrapped my waist with his arm, drawing me to him. "Luke, I didn't think the sight would bother me this much. No wonder the Chastains haven't come up yet. They understood."

A powdery residue of ash still covered everything. Sporadic puffs of a faint breeze stirred little whirlwinds of the stuff, accentuating the mood of wistfulness. We climbed up what remained of the rock steps. Turning to take in the grand view from the former front porch, we became pensive.

The venerable old hand-hewn lodge had stood on land cut out of a nature preserve decades before. Elmer had somehow cajoled the state land office and the federal authorities to allow him the one-time privilege of procuring acreage under a defunct set of rules since changed. That was why the man had been able to erect the only edifice on the divide. The veteran's G.I. bill and some other enigmatic justification had afforded him leverage, as cryptically notated on the Federal Bureau of Land Management application dated June, 1949. The exception for his construction, listed as 'by executive mandate', proved to be the only one ever certified. It was a true puzzle we were likely never to decipher. The idea occurred to wonder what Elmer might feel should he see what remained of his physical life here. Would he be bereft? Or satisfied?

As we descended again, a metallic glint caught my eye. Reaching under the edge of one of the foundation stones, I touched a small sharp object fastened in some way underneath the base layer. I had to dig a bit to loosen the thing. Upon doing so, I found that the sharpness comprised but a fraction of the object half-buried there. The two of us worked for several minutes undermining the gravelly base beneath but finally succeeded in freeing a small metal box. It had apparently been there some time. During the fire, settling of the foundation must have occurred, exposing it. The edges were rusted together as were the hinges. We sat on the step and examined the compact case.

"Do you think Elmer maybe put this here?" I was thinking out loud, and JK responded.

"Well, I think we should open it. If it was put here by him then someone should remember what he was about, don't you think?" It made sense. The edges were mortared shut. Jeremy pulled out his Swiss Army knife--- I had long since ceased joshing him for carrying the useful tool--- and over five minutes, he whittled away at the crusts. The box made a clicking sound when he worked at the hinges and the lid moved a tiny bit.

Carefully breaching it, we finally visualized a lining of aged cobalt-blue silk. Set in the middle lay a medal. It was a gold five pointed star, each point tipped with trefoils. A green laurel wreath surrounded it. Suspended from a gold bar inscribed 'VALOR', the whole was surmounted by an eagle. In the center, a woman's head was encircled by 'United States of America'. When we examined the reverse side, it read: 'The Congress to Elmer Bruce Edgewater, Private First Class. June 6, 1944'.

Prickles arose on my skin as we examined it, "Jeremy, I think this is a Medal of Honor. I haven't ever seen one for real but from what I have read, this could be. The picture of the woman must be Minerva. She was the Roman goddess of wisdom and war. Her Greek counterpart was Athena. If this is, how amazing! Why do you think he would have put this right here? And if he did, it must have been done when he laid these rocks, all the way back in the 1940's. That would mean he never preserved it, but buried it soon after it was awarded to him. Look here, below the silk lining. It reads: 'Presented by President Franklin Delano Roosevelt, U.S.A. In honor of bravery, your country thanks you'. We have to give this to Annalise. She should have it...or she will know what to do with it."

Pocketing the box after carefully sealing it as best we could, we headed down the trail to the glade. 'The Trees' was the moniker I used for the place. A nerve had been struck in me regarding the two trees there. The same kind had populated my dream back in February during the ski festival. I remembered being touched, scared, awed and impassioned, among other emotions, when I had related it to Jeremy. The scare had arisen from the sense of aloneness. Ambergai had heard and advised me to write it down. I hadn't done so, but it had remained in my memory more vividly than any other dream ever experienced. Strangely, having been aware it was a dream during its unfolding, I had chosen to follow it. Inherently, I had known it held relevance. For a long time, I figured it was a lesson in humility, because of the 'hedonics-gone-awry' involved. The characters in it had all mimicked my real life in some manner, though in a parallel universe. As if giving me a view of what things might have been. But after reflecting, I had deduced that the latter stages of it provided more import. The part where I had come upon the Oak and Linden trees and reckoned they were 'speaking' to me.

When we had been directed to the glen by Trude and Elmer's letter, all took on new meaning. The guardians of this place were, in truth, the same as those in my dream. They were not indigenous to the area. Elmer had brought the two here, nurturing them. My inner self told me these were why I was frequently pulled this direction. There was a connection. I felt it. As we came near, Jeremy felt it too. He clasped my hand when we entered the small encircled glade.

There was the well-used fire pit with the round pink granite stones. And the painstakingly carved oak bench. And, of course, the august old trees. Nurtured for decades. The two soared toward the sky, tall and stately. They were now, in the summer, surrounded by volunteer purple and green oxalis. And a plethora of mountain flowers. Alpine Columbine flowers, with their elegant blue and white bells, wrapped the flares of each behemoth. The very flower chosen for our wedding ceremony the previous summer.

We were again engulfed in goosebumps. This place was one of the loveliest settings either of us had ever beheld. With the spectacular vista stretching out and downward, any Greek God in the vicinity must mistake it for Mount Olympus. My memory was prompted to Ovid's fable about the ancient Phrygian couple, Baucis and Philemon, who had been transformed into an Oak and a Linden tree by favor of Zeus, so as to ensure the couple's eternal togetherness.

Absorbing the panoply, there came to our ears a subtle bleating sound, arising from the leafy periphery. We were astonished to pick out the long white beard and curling horns of a mountain ram peering from amidst the riot of flowers behind the thick oak trunk. Lying sternally, feet enfolded beneath him, was William Canadensis Ovis, our no-show foster sheep. He gazed calmly at us, thoughtfully chewing his cud, seemingly unsurprised by our appearance. His coat appeared sleek, without any sign of damage or wounds, easing my initial fear. Upon stepping towards him, he rose, standing at an angle to us. His ears twisted forward in curiosity and greeting. His muzzle wiggled back and forth as if acknowledging reason for our presence. Those deep eyes never once left us. He didn't move toward or away, simply holding his position, as if signaling us to get on with it.

'Well, I'll be," Jeremy was bemused. "He has been here for a while, honey, waiting for us. Look at the indentation in the undergrowth where he was laying. No wonder we haven't had a visit from him." Relieved incredulity permeated both of us. Freshly aware he was meant to be here, like us, we didn't approach closer, but acceded his presence and turned away. He seemed to condone the action, continuing the methodical cud-chewing.

Sitting on the bench, we mused together. Leaning into my husband, Dr. Jeremy Fallsworth Kell, I reveled in his strong, bracing arm. Surely, the two Olympians, Elmer and Trude, were the denizens of this place. Their spirits flourished in the trees. In our shared reverie, a gentle highland zephyr caressed our skin. Through the shimmering rustle of the leaves, I thought I heard the poetic jargon from my dream once again. Softly, they spoke, "Young Mandrakes. Live your Lives and thrive together. Plant your legacies and root them strongly. Experience the World. We shall await you."

I shivered involuntarily as the ethereal lyrics washed over me, but neither from fear nor aloneness.

Beside me, Jeremy turned my chin to his face,

"Did you hear that, too, My Man?"

The End.

Thank you for reading my book. If you enjoyed it, won't you please take a moment to leave me a review at your favorite retailer?

Or contact me directly:

Follow me on Twitter: http://twitter.com/@ZackJack69

Friend me on Facebook: http://facebook.com/ZachariahJack

Subscribe to my blog: http://zachariahjack.com

Website: http://zachariahjack.com

Favorite me at Smashwords: http://www.smashwords.com/profile/view/zackjack

Discover other titles by Zachariah Jack

The River's Bluff
And coming soon: *The Mandrake Legacies*

Biography

I am a professional with a history in veterinary medicine, zoology and marine biology, but a fledgling in the realm of talespinning, just now launching a new stage of life. The existence of a contentedly settled home life with my man, our dogs and cat makes me whole. I finally took to heart the sage advice from the esteemed author and activist, Sir Armistead Maupin, who advised his audience over two decades ago to 'Proclaim Yourself!'. As a member of that audience, it was never forgotten. The remonstrance was belatedly acted upon in a mountain wedding two months following the SCOTUS concession of yet one more of our 'certainly reserved rights'. In accordance with the much overlooked ninth and tenth amendments to the United States Constitution. See for yourself. Think on it.

Check my publications out at your favorite retailer. And, please, review my work. Thanks, ZJ.